MEDICAL
Pulse-racing passion

One Month To Tame The Surgeon
Carol Marinelli

An American Doctor In Ireland
Karin Baine

MILLS & BOON

ONE MONTH TO TAME THE SURGEON
© 2024 by Carol Marinelli
Philippine Copyright 2024
Australian Copyright 2024
New Zealand Copyright 2024

First Published 2024
First Australian Paperback Edition 2024
ISBN 978 1 038 90258 0

AN AMERICAN DOCTOR IN IRELAND
© 2024 by Karin Baine
Philippine Copyright 2024
Australian Copyright 2024
New Zealand Copyright 2024

First Published 2024
First Australian Paperback Edition 2024
ISBN 978 1 038 90258 0

MIX
Paper | Supporting
responsible forestry
FSC® C001695
www.fsc.org

Published by
Harlequin Mills & Boon
An imprint of Harlequin Enterprises (Australia) Pty Limited
(ABN 47 001 180 918), a subsidiary of HarperCollins
Publishers Australia Pty Limited
(ABN 36 009 913 517)
Level 19, 201 Elizabeth Street
SYDNEY NSW 2000 AUSTRALIA

Cover art used by arrangement with Harlequin Books S.A.. All rights reserved.

Printed and bound in Australia by McPherson's Printing Group

One Month To Tame The Surgeon
Carol Marinelli

MILLS & BOON

Carol Marinelli recently filled in a form asking for her job title. Thrilled to be able to put down her answer, she put "writer." Then it asked what Carol did for relaxation and she put down the truth— "writing." The third question asked for her hobbies. Well, not wanting to look obsessed, she crossed her fingers and answered "swimming"—but, given that the chlorine in the pool does terrible things to her highlights, I'm sure you can guess the real answer!

Visit the Author Profile page
at millsandboon.com.au for more titles.

Dear Reader,

I have loved revisiting The Primary Hospital in London and finding out that major upgrades are underway and a new pediatric wing is near completion. It was fun meeting the current staff and patients. Pippa is a pediatric nurse and struggles to show her emotions. Luke is a visiting doctor and only back in London for a month…

At the start, it really is Pippa's story, given that Luke can't even remember when and where they first met—he just knows that he vaguely recognizes her. Gosh, that would sting!

Still, in fairness to Luke, he has very good reasons to prefer not to revisit that long ago day…

It really reminded me that we never know the effect we might have on others and that when people are going through difficult times, even the smallest kind gesture can have such an impact.

Luke might not remember, but he was incredibly kind at a time when Pippa needed that the most.

I hope you love them as much as I do.

Happy reading,

Carol xxxx

DEDICATION

For Rosie,
Thank you for being a wonderful friend
Cxxxx

PROLOGUE

PIPPA WESTFORD HAD learnt to make the school library her haven.

Here she could catch up on her homework or do some uninterrupted study.

She didn't make friends easily.

Well, as a little girl she had, but her family had relocated so many times that by the age of sixteen Pippa was used to being the new girl—and always the outsider.

She had vague memories of nursery and infant school in the small village in Wales where she'd been born. Then they had moved to Cardiff, to be closer to a major hospital. As her older sister Julia's condition had deteriorated, they had moved again, to make the endless appointments in London more manageable. Then, when Julia had been placed on the transplant list, they had moved again, to ensure the tight four-hour window to get her to the hospital should a heart and lungs become available could be met.

Now, with Julia's transplanted heart failing, the library felt like her only refuge.

The chairs were heavy and comfortable, and there were lots of little nooks in which to hide. It was May—not that you could tell. The library had small, high windows that let in little light, and dark mahogany furnishings. Though the table had lamps, it felt as if it could just as well have been midwinter rather than approaching summer.

Pippa sat in a small recess, coiling her dark curls around her fingers as she read the sparse notes she'd made with the careers counsellor.

Hearing the thump of a bag, and someone taking the seat opposite her own, she took a calming breath and didn't look up. The peace she'd come here to find had been broken.

What *did* she want to do with the rest of her life?

Removing her fingers from her unruly hair, she picked up a pen, determined to tackle the blank form that had plagued her for weeks. She filled in her first name in full—Philippa—and then sighed—at only sixteen years of age she felt more than a little overwhelmed at the prospect of choosing the A level subjects that would shape her future.

The careers counsellor and her teachers had all said that the decisions she made, though important, could be changed, depending on the results of her GCSEs.

Pippa was rather certain that the results were not going to be the ones she hoped for.

She turned to the front page of her school diary and looked at the study schedule she'd meticulously mapped out when she'd started the new school year at her latest school.

Her hand tightened on the pen she was holding and she was tempted to scribble angrily all over it, or simply tear the pages out, because she'd barely managed to meet a quarter of the hours she'd allocated.

There was always something…

'Pippa, can you stop at the shops…?'

'If you can meet us at the hospital and bring in Julia's dressing gown…'

'Go and talk to your sister, Pippa. She's been home alone all day…'

Somehow she'd managed to work around all that, and then the news they'd been waiting for had come.

'There's a donor!'

Was she the worst sister in the world, because she'd sat in the waiting room with her parents as the hours had passed, wishing she'd brought her homework?

Mrs Blane would understand if her homework was late. Pippa knew that. She wouldn't be in trouble. Just permanently behind….

And now, as hope faded for her sister, Pippa felt as if her own heart was in decline. Far from being jealous of Julia, she loved her more than anyone in the world.

She wasn't just losing her sister; Pippa was losing her best friend.

'Having trouble deciding?'

Pippa looked up and blinked when she saw that it was Luke Harris sitting opposite her and, what was more, he was asking her a question.

She tried to think of something suitably witty but only said, 'A bit.'

It was hardly a dazzling response, but it was all her sixteen-year-old voice knew how to say when she was under the gaze of his brown eyes.

Everyone had a crush on Luke.

A slight exaggeration, perhaps, but certainly amongst Pippa's peers he was the most popular boy in school. Two years older than Pippa, Luke Harris was the one they all cheered on at school sports day or whispered about in assembly if he gave a speech or some such.

He was good-looking, with straight hair that was a softer shade of brown than his eyes, and he was good at everything. He had the Midas touch and, really, he was just…gorgeous.

'How did *you* decide?' she asked, both curious and wanting to prolong this small conversation.

She expected to be fobbed off, or given some vague answer, but Luke really seemed to consider her question before responding.

'I think it was decided for me, before I was born,' he said with an edge to his tone.

'You're going to be a doctor?' she asked, because she had watched the senior school's Speech Night online with Julia, and his father had presented some awards.

'A surgeon,' he corrected.

She finally looked up and saw his red eyes in the lamplight. For a stupid moment she thought that Luke—effortless Luke—had been crying, but then she realised he'd probably just come from the pool. Naturally he was good at swimming too.

Then, embarrassed to be staring, she dragged her eyes from his and saw a little graze on his strong jaw. It made her smile just a little that perfect Luke must have cut himself shaving.

He returned her smile, though his was a curious one, as if wondering what might have amused her. 'I'm Luke,' he introduced. 'Luke Harris.'

'I know,' Pippa said, smiling. 'I do pay attention in assembly. Well, sometimes…'

His smile widened and her heart seemed to do a small somersault, almost escaping the confines of her chest.

He looked at the upside-down form she had started to fill out. 'Philippa?'

'Yes, but—' She'd been about to tell him she usually went by Pippa, but then found she didn't want to get into names.

Especially if it led to surnames.

Westford wasn't a particularly unusual name, but there was just one other at their school.

Julia.

And in that moment Pippa didn't want to be recognised as Julia's sister.

They looked nothing alike—Julia was petite and blonde, with huge blue eyes, whereas Pippa was all wild, dark curls and more sturdily framed. As for her eyes… Well, last week's art homework had been to find the closest hue to your eyes on the colour chart. Try as she might to match something wonderful, like jade or malachite, Pippa's had discovered that her eyes were plain old army-green.

And even more awkward than comparing their looks, whenever anyone found out who she was there was always an uncomfortable pause, a flicker of sympathy, a particular weighty hush or an enquiry as to how Julia was doing.

Always.

Luke was in the same form as Julia, and even if she had been too unwell to attend much school this year, he'd know her.

He would also know, as everyone did, that Julia had cystic fibrosis and that her heart and lung transplant hadn't been the success everybody had hoped for, and he would naturally enquire how she was…

Pippa knew she was the lucky one.

Sometimes, though, all she felt was invisible.

The one who could take care of herself. The one whose problems really didn't matter.

What was a pair of broken glasses when your sister had been admitted to hospital that very day? What was getting your first period when your sister had just been given the news that she'd been placed on the transplant list? And why on earth would you cry over a few spots, even a face full of them, when your sister was dying?

Pippa had felt guilty, rubbing in the cream she'd bought to try and get rid of the spots. She'd clearly used far too much cream, because the peroxide had turned the long strings of brown curls on her forehead into an odd shade of orange.

Though she didn't want to admit to being Julia's little sister, Pippa loved her very much, and was terrified at the thought of a world without her. But Pippa had no one to go to with her fears, because her parents were consumed by enough fears for all of them.

It was nice, for a moment, to sit in the quiet library and talk about herself.

'The careers guidance wasn't much help,' Pippa admitted.

She had tried to discuss it with Julia, who had been happy to do so, but her mother had ushered her away and then scolded her in the kitchen.

'Have some tact, Pippa,' she'd told her, reminding her that Julia didn't have the luxury of planning a future.

And so another topic had been added to the forbidden conversation list. She certainly hadn't felt able to ask her parents about subject selection, and the fifteen-minute interview with the careers counsellor had been confusing rather than enlightening.

'What GCSEs are you taking?' Luke asked, and Pippa told him.

'I like French,' she said. 'But I don't think I could make a career out of it.'

'So you're not looking to be a translator?'

'Gosh, no. I think I'll just save it for holidays.' Pippa smiled. 'It's the same with art,' she admitted. 'I like sketching and ceramics—' she chewed on her pen for a moment '—actually, I love art. Well, I did until last week…' She suddenly smiled.

'What's so funny?'

'Nothing. Just…'

'Just what?'

He persisted, and it felt new and unfamiliar to have someone persist, to have someone other than her sister truly wanting to know her thoughts, or wanting to know the reason a smile had flickered across her face.

It was so pleasing that Pippa readily told him about the homework assignment, and the rather disappointing conclusion that the colour of her eyes was army-green.

'It's not very exciting.'

'Better than brown,' he said. 'You clearly enjoy art.'

'I do, but…' She shrugged tightly in a manner that usually would have closed a conversation, and yet he waited…waited for her to elaborate. 'It's the same as French, though: I can't see myself making a career out of it…'

'You could always combine the two and be a pavement artist in Paris…'

Pippa laughed at the very notion. 'I think I'd feel ripped off if I was in Paris getting my portrait done and I got me as the artist.' She realised that probably didn't make sense, and began to explain better, but he just smiled.

'Anything?' he asked. 'If you could be anything?'

She turned the question to him, 'What would you be?'

His head moved to one side, as if he'd never actually considered it.

'Anything?' she insisted.

'Rock star,' he grinned.

'Guitar?'

'Oh, no.' He shook his head. 'Drums.'

'Drummers are the wild ones,' Pippa mused. 'Can you play the drums?'

'I've never tried,' he admitted, and Pippa started to laugh.

'Shh!' they were told by the librarian.

Luke came around the table and sat beside her. She could feel him next to her, reading through the notes she'd made during the career counsellor's session.

'The police?'

'Detective.' Pippa pointed to the clarification. 'That was her suggestion,' Pippa said. 'I stay calm in a crisis and I'm big on trust.' She shook her head. 'I don't think it's me, though…'

He looked at her for a long moment. 'No,' he agreed.

'You have to be in uniform first, and I can't run.'

'You can't run?'

Pippa shook her head.

'Can't or won't?' he asked.

'Both,' Pippa admitted, and then watched as he went back to the odd little notes she'd written.

'Cake?' He frowned at the single word. 'Are you into baking?'

'No.' Pippa shook her head. 'It was just… I was explaining to the careers counsellor that I'd thought about nursing.'

'But what does that have to do with cake?'

'I just…' Her voice trailed off.

Pippa knew she couldn't tell him without sounding a little selfish. She hadn't considered nursing for altruistic reasons; it was actually because of something nice that had happened. On the day she had been turning seven she had woken up excited, yet when she'd gone downstairs it had been a neighbour in the kitchen who had explained that Julia had been taken ill in the early hours.

That evening Pippa had been taken to see her sister, who by then had thankfully stabilised. Pippa had hugged her, just wanting to climb in bed beside her, but it had been all masks and gowns for adults, and she'd been told to stay well back.

Pippa had felt guilty for her own disappointment that nobody had even wished her a happy birthday, but then a nurse had come into the side ward, carrying a cake. Everybody had sung 'Happy Birthday' and for a short while she had felt remembered.

'Why does nursing appeal?' Luke persisted, dragging her back to the present.

Pippa realised then that it wasn't just his dark good looks that made him popular—he listened, and he engaged with people—with *her*—fully.

'I just think it's something…' Pippa didn't really know how to elaborate—and not just because she didn't want to mention Julia. That nurse had made such a difference. Had made her feel like an important part of the family, even if just for a little while. 'Something I might like…'

'So what do you need for that?'

'Two or three A levels, one in science. I know I want to do biology and English…' Pippa spoke in a low whisper and thought how nice it was to actually talk it through with someone. 'I really want to do art, but…' She shrugged.

'But…?'

'I don't think I'm *that* good.'

'My mother paints. She's dreadful at it…' His voice faded, as if he was lost in thought for a moment, but then he quickly regrouped, and his gorgeous brown eyes were back on Pippa. 'You really enjoy it?'

'Very much,' she admitted. She'd been taught to hold in her emotions, or to handle them herself, but in art class she felt she could let them slip out. 'I find it peaceful. Ceramics especially…'

'Then do it.'

Their heads moved closer together and she expected to smell chlorine, given that he'd just been at the pool. Or rather, given that his red eyes had made her assume he'd been swimming.

She looked up and in the lamplight saw again his reddened, slightly swollen eyes. She swallowed.

He had been crying.

Was it possible that Luke Harris was also hiding from the world in the library?

Just as she didn't want to reveal her surname, Pippa knew he wouldn't want her to probe.

Still, she did enquire a little with her eyes.

There was just a moment when each stared at the

other, and Pippa forgot about the tape on her glasses and that her fringe was streaked with orange.

It was as if both knew that behind the smiles and easy chatter there was hurt.

'Don't give up art if you enjoy it,' he said, still staring at her.

'It might be a waste. Maybe I should just focus on two…'

'But it's your favourite subject.'

'Yes.' She nodded. 'It's really relaxing. It's not like being in a class.'

'Then don't let it go.'

Pippa knew he was right—knew he was confirming what she'd wanted to hear, that she should do a subject she enjoyed—and so she nodded. 'I think I will do it.'

'Good.'

But now her dilemma was a little more solved, Pippa found that she didn't want to leave the path of his gaze. His eyes were more than chocolate-brown. She wanted to go back to her colour charts and try to identify it. Yet, despite their beauty, she could not ignore the redness of the whites and the slight puffiness of his heavy lids.

'Are you okay?' she asked.

He didn't answer straight away. Nor did he query why she might ask such a thing.

People were packing up, the end of lunch bell was ringing, and activity was all around. Yet for a moment they remained there, her question still hanging in the air between them.

'I will be,' he finally said, and then gave her a sort of downturned smile.

'Can I help?' Pippa asked, and then blushed. Because as if she could offer Luke Harris advice on anything! 'I just—'

'I'll be fine.' He stood up. 'Better get back. What have you got now?'

'Double art,' Pippa said, and his smile turned a little upwards. 'You?' she asked as they walked out of the library together.

'Double sport.'

Her art class flew by, as it always did, and as well as glazing a pot she'd made Pippa worked on a little ceramic heart to go into the kiln.

'Is that for Julia?' the art teacher asked, because she often made little ornaments for her sister.

Pippa didn't answer.

She walked home, stopping to pick up the new pair of glasses she had ordered, and also to get some groceries her mother had asked her to fetch. And then she went on to the chemist to pick up the special lotion Julia needed for her skin, now that she was spending most of her time in bed.

All the while, though, Pippa was replaying her time in the library with Luke, and then, as she turned into her street, she found herself in a daydream. One where the bell hadn't gone and she and Luke had been locked in the library for hours, days… A convenient siege situation or a blackout or something. And, given it was *her* daydream, she'd been a year or two older, and not wearing taped-up glasses with flares of orange in her hair. But what about the loo…? There were none in the library!

That tripped up her fantasy, but she decided to ignore that issue for the moment. She returned to her daydream.

When she got home, Pippa thought, Julia could give her the inside gossip on him. Perhaps she could work Luke into the conversation and find out more about him? Or even tell Julia that the totally normal crush she'd had on Luke had been massively upgraded to full-blown infatuation…

She took a breath before she turned the key in the front door. It was something she'd only recently become aware of: a certain nervousness as to what she might come home to.

'Hi?' she called out, and then saw her mum coming out of the kitchen. 'I got the shopping.'

'How was school?'

'Good. We had to think about A-level subject selection—'

'That's nice.'

'I'm thinking about—'

'Julia's got something exciting to tell you,' her mother interrupted, without waiting to hear any more about Pippa's day. 'It's good news!' She prompted an appropriate response as Pippa put down the groceries. 'But I'll let her tell you herself.'

'Sure,' Pippa said, and then headed up the stairs.

'Hey…' Pippa knocked on the open bedroom door and smiled at her sister, who was sitting propped up in bed and just finishing a nebuliser. Pippa took the mask, and was hanging it up when Julia's breathy voice came.

'Guess what?'

'What?' Pippa asked, and sat on her sister's bed.

'Luke called. He's *finally* asked me out.' Julia smiled. 'Luke Harris!'

It was selfish, Pippa was sure, to have such a painful sinking feeling…to be jealous of her sister's happiness when she had so little in her life.

'We're going to the school dance,' Julia elaborated and lay back on the pillow, her cornflower-blue eyes shining and a smile on her dusky lips.

'He just called,' their mum said, coming into the bedroom, all smiles. 'Said that he'd missed seeing Julia at school.'

'Oh.'

For a few seconds it was all Pippa could manage. She'd known, deep down, that he'd just been being nice this lunchtime and had *never* been going to ask her out. But it was such a painfully abrupt end to her daydream, to her little escape.

She forced out a more suitable response. 'That's brilliant.'

Luke came to the house a couple of times, although Pippa stayed in her room. But at school Luke looked straight through her the one time she passed him in the hall. She consoled herself with the likelihood that he was either going in or coming out of an exam.

On the night of the school dance she helped Julia with her make-up, and thought her big sister looked gorgeous in her pale silver dress.

'You look beautiful,' Pippa said as she added a little more blusher. 'Are you excited?'

'Nervous,' Julia admitted. 'But excited too!'

It had taken weeks to get Julia well enough to attend the dance. Her medications had had to be tailored for this one precious night, and there was oxygen set up in a private room at the hall should she need it. But for now she looked simply perfect.

'He's here!' Their mum came in. 'Dad will carry you down the stairs,' she asserted, 'so you can save your breath for dancing.'

'I don't want Luke to see me being carried,' Julia warned.

It was Julia's night, so Pippa stayed upstairs as her sister was carried down. She knelt on the bed, fiddling with the little ceramic heart she'd made on that special day, now on the window ledge. Since then it had been fired, and she'd painted it the closest shade she could find to match Luke's eyes. The next week she'd glazed it and it had been fired again.

Now she watched Luke walk Julia to the waiting car and felt guilty for wishing that she was the girl on his arm.

For the first time ever, she wished that she was Julia.

CHAPTER ONE

'Wow!'

On a cold November morning, when she should be dashing to get to hand-over, Pippa stood at the hospital entrance, take-away coffee in hand and mouth agape...

'It looks like a space ship.'

May, the emergency department's nurse manager, had been walking ahead of Pippa, but she too had stopped to take in the new paediatric wing at London's Primary Hospital.

For the past couple of years the east wing of the post-war concrete building had been undergoing a facelift and extension, and now the scaffolding had been removed, revealing gleaming white arches and an awful lot of glass.

'I'm getting dizzy just looking at it,' May said in her strong Irish brogue. 'I can't imagine walking along those corridors.'

'I can,' Pippa said with a smile. As a paediatric nurse at The Primary, she was thrilled at the long overdue upgrade. 'Where's Paediatric Emergency?' Pippa asked, and May let out a hmmph.

'It's the same old Emergency,' May said, rolling her eyes, 'just a fancy new entrance and a few more bays. Basically, we'll be filling up that whole place with barely any extra staff...'

'Surely not?' Pippa said, laughing.

'Well, a few extra,' May conceded. 'What's happening with your ward?'

'We'll be moving to the first floor of the new building, taking acute admissions only…'

'It won't be the same.' May voiced Pippa's thoughts. 'Anything half interesting will be admitted to its own specialised unit.'

May was right.

At the moment, the paediatric ward took everyone from babies right up till fifteen- or sixteen-year-olds, and there was an eclectic mix of patients, from planned admissions to emergencies and anything in between.

Once the new wing opened they'd be more of a short-stay ward, or a holding area before the patient was moved to a more specialised unit.

'Look at the time,' May said, flustered. 'We're both going to be late…'

Perhaps so, but before she entered the old building Pippa took one more look. She had pored over the plans that had been posted, and read all the notes about the new units, and there was one that had captured Pippa's interest.

She hadn't told a soul, but next week Pippa had an interview.

Times were changing…

And so was Pippa.

'Sorry!'

The apology wasn't aimed at him.

As Luke Harris stepped out of a side ward, a

blur of dark curls and a grey coat was dashing past, trailing a scarf, apologising to the staff waiting to hand over.

She brought the chilly autumn air in with her, but there was the scent of summer too. Perhaps it was her perfume—or was there just something about her that drew the eye?

'I'll just get changed!' she called to the gathered nursing team, and he turned his head and watched as she ducked into what was presumably the changing room.

Yes, there was something about her that drew his eye—something familiar.

Given that he'd spent the last two years in Philadelphia, Luke was more used to unfamiliar faces. Of course on his travels he'd crossed paths with the occasional former colleague, and even the occasional ex… Now that he was temporarily back in London, he expected a lot more of the same.

He couldn't quite place her, though.

There was something about the loosely coiled dark curls that made him lose the thread of his conversation with Nola, the ward's unit manager, as she took him and his junior doctor for a brief ward round, while also showing him the layout of the paediatric unit.

'As well as the cots and isolation rooms, we've twelve general beds and eight high-dependency beds, both medical and surgical.' Nola gestured to the two glass-framed four-bedded wards that were closest to the nurses' station. 'The new wing opens soon, but for now your paediatric surgical patients—'

Then she laughed.

Not Nola.

Nor Fiona, the rather eager junior doctor who had been a third-year med student at St Bede's when he'd last seen her—and an annoying one at that.

No, the sound of laughter came from the nurses' station, and Luke knew—simply knew—that it came from *her*.

Her?

Luke glanced over. Despite his rather wild reputation with women, he did at least remember all his exes, and she was not one of them. Her dark hair fell in long coils, which she was tying up as she chatted and laughed. She had taken off her coat and scarf and she stood there, solidly built, yet curvy, in pale blue scrubs. Luke was absolutely certain that he knew her.

Perhaps she'd worked at his old hospital? He'd known most of the staff there.

Indeed, that had been part of the problem. In the end, he'd felt he had no choice but to leave.

It must be from there that he knew her, Luke decided.

And if that was the case, he certainly wouldn't be acknowledging the connection.

Luke let his mental search go as they made their way down the ward and he met the patients and parents.

'Chloe James, seven years old,' Nola informed

him. 'Fell five metres from playground apparatus on Friday and suffered a lac liver. No surgery…'

Luke listened as he read through the notes and then introduced himself to the anxious mother.

'A locum?' Mrs James frowned. 'So you're just standing in? How long have you worked here for?'

'I'm just starting today—' Luke began to explain, but his attempts to reassure the anxious mother were hastily interrupted by Nola.

'Mr Harris was a surgical consultant at St Bede's, so we're very lucky to have him at The Primary.'

Luke felt his lips tighten a touch—not just at the interruption, but because the Unit Manager clearly knew his work history.

Then he glanced over to the junior doctor, and as he met her eyes he saw her go a little pink.

Ah, so Fiona must have told Nola where he'd worked. He wondered what else Fiona might have revealed…

'Mrs James.' Luke addressed the concerned mother. 'I'm sure you've seen more medical staff than you can keep track of, but I'm currently standing in for Mr Eames while he's on extended leave. I'm a general surgeon, with a specialist interest in trauma, and I'll be overseeing Chloe's care from here on.'

'So you're not just here for today?'

'No, I'm here for a month—and, judging by the look of things, Chloe will be long since home by then. How has she been?'

'Better,' Mrs James said. 'Well, she's starting to

say she's hungry, and she's asking to play games on my phone.'

'I see that,' Luke said. 'Can I take a look at you, Chloe?'

'Am I allowed to have breakfast?' Chloe asked, lifting her blonde head from the game she was playing.

'I think it's a little too soon for that,' Luke admitted, 'but I'll know more when I've had a look at your abdomen—your tummy,' he corrected himself.

'I do know what an abdomen is,' Chloe said, putting down the phone and lying back. She gave him a smile that displayed a lot of missing teeth.

'Well, I'm sorry for talking down to you,' Luke said as he lifted her gown. 'I take care of adults too,' he told her as he felt her abdomen. 'Some of them say stomach…some say belly—'

'Or guts!' Chloe said with relish.

'Chloe!' her mother warned.

And Luke laughed at the clever, cheeky young girl, very pleased that her abdomen remained soft as she too laughed at her chosen word.

'Can you sit up for me?' he asked, giving Mrs James a little shake of his head as she went to assist. He was pleased when Chloe moved well and required only the slight support of his hand to sit up.

'She couldn't do that before,' Mrs James observed.

'I'm sure.'

Chole, having terrified everyone, was clearly a

lot better than she had been when she'd arrived in the emergency department on Friday afternoon.

'They bounce back a lot quicker than us,' he said, with raised brows. 'Emotionally too.'

'Yes.' Mrs James gave a half-laugh and held out a trembling hand. 'I'm still shaking while she's begging to have breakfast. Can she have something to eat?'

'Clear fluids only for today,' Luke said. 'We don't want to rush things. I'd like to organise another ultrasound.'

'But I'm hungry,' Chloe whined, looking up at him with a glum expression.

'So am I,' Luke responded.

The little girl smiled. 'Didn't you have breakfast?'

'I didn't.' He shook his head. 'We'll get some more pictures of your abdomen and then see how you are.'

And then *she* came in.

The mystery nurse.

'Hey, Chloe…' Her voice faded when she saw that the doctors were with them.

'Oh, sorry to interrupt,' she said quickly. 'I'll come back.'

'No problem,' Nola responded. 'We're finished here.'

He knew that voice, Luke thought as he left Chloe's room and saw the nurse replacing the IV fluids.

A memory stirred…a name, a moment in time demanding to be placed.

Still, as they left the side ward, it was the patient that was discussed.

'I'd like to be paged when she goes down to imaging. If I'm not available, David?' He glanced at his registrar, who was looking at his pager.

'I need to go down to the ED,' David said.

'Sure.'

With David out of the way, Luke addressed Nola. While the polite thing to do might have been to excuse Fiona from the conversation, there was a very good reason he did not.

'I can reassure the patients and their carers as to my qualifications myself,' he said, rather curtly.

'I just thought—' Nola swallowed and glanced at Fiona, who was positively scarlet. 'Well, Mrs James was clearly worried that it was your first day and…'

'As I said, any concerns as to my professional abilities I'll deal with myself. Please don't speak on my behalf when I'm standing right there!'

Luke knew he was being blunt, but it was essential he made his position clear on this point from the start. The cloud of scandal hanging over him when he'd left St Bede's, more than two years ago, clearly hadn't dispersed completely and he didn't want it to poison his new role here.

They took the elevator up to the adult surgical units, and he walked in silence with his junior. He silently berated himself for the way he had handled the situation, because he was in no doubt that Fiona would soon be sharing far more of his past with her colleagues than just his résumé!

Gossip spread in a hospital more rapidly than any virus.

He considered trying to address it here and now, but how?

Should he *order* Fiona not to repeat what she had seen and heard a couple of years ago? Or *ask* her, maybe?

But wouldn't that just add fuel to a fire that he had fervently hoped, after two years, had gone out?

Who was he kidding?

It wasn't just Fiona.

As they made their way to Surgical Unit One he nodded to *another* familiar face—a theatre tech he'd worked alongside at St Bede's.

'Jimmy!'

'Luke!'

Pleasantries were exchanged, and they had a brief catch-up in the highly polished corridor that ran between Theatres and Surgical Unit One, but he could see the flare of interest in his colleague's eyes.

'Back in London?' Jimmy asked.

'Yes.' Luke nodded, though he could almost hear the question that wasn't voiced—*Avoiding St Bede's?*

'I went out the other week with the old mob,' Jimmy told him. 'Well, a few have moved on, but we keep in touch. Ross is a cardiac technician now.'

'Good for him.'

'And Shona moved to the ICU.'

Just for a moment Luke felt relieved at Jimmy's casual mention of her name. Maybe the world really had moved on. But then Jimmy cleared his throat and mumbled something about needing to get on, and Fiona started checking her pager, which hadn't even gone off, and Luke could feel the sudden awkwardness caused by the mention of Shona's name.

'Good to see you,' Luke said, and knew then, for sure, that he was in for a month of hell.

His...*active* sex life and his refusal to commit had been popular topics for gossip at St Bede's. Luke had always carried his reputation well—this leopard was happy with his spots and his care factor was zero when it came to gossip. For the most part his short relationships ended amicably, because he chose his partners wisely and always spelt out from the start that things would not be progressing further than a casual liaison. He would *never* settle down—and he made sure they knew that.

A couple of years ago, though, his reputation had caught up with him. Assumptions had been made about him and Shona, a married theatre nurse at St Bede's. Rumours had started to spread—as they undoubtedly would here at The Primary.

They had, however, been completely unfounded.

But Luke, for reasons he would never reveal, had been in no position to correct them.

And it was for those same reasons that he was only in London for a month or so. He was here to sell his apartment—or at least get the ball rolling on the sale of it—and then get the hell out.

This time for good.

Pippa didn't notice the surgeons leave.

She collected the charts the junior doctor had updated and then spoke at length with Mrs James, who was upset that Chloe couldn't eat.

'Why don't you go and have some breakfast away from Chloe? When I've finished doing the drugs I'll come and have a chat with her,' Pippa suggested. 'She's a clever little thing; she needs to know why she's not allowed to eat.'

'But I don't want to scare her,' Mrs James fretted. 'I need to go home for a few hours and get some milk expressed. I can't relax enough here, and—'

'And you need to see your baby.'

'Yes, but if Chloe gets upset I won't be able to leave her.'

'I'm not going to upset her. Go home and have a shower and some breakfast,' Pippa suggested again. 'Like I said, she's a bright girl. Chloe knows you need to go home this morning.'

The little girl just didn't like the fact!

As Mrs James went to collect her wash things Jenny, one of the RNs, rolled her eyes. 'She needs to learn to say no to her. Honestly… It's "Chloe this…", "Chloe that—"'

'Chloe's got a new baby brother and she's had a nasty accident,' Pippa interrupted. 'It's no wonder she's a bit clingy and her mother's anxious. Gosh,

I pretended to break my arm when I was seven just to get my mum's attention—at least Chloe's reasons are real.'

Pippa left a grumpy Jenny and made her way to the drug room, where she started preparing the morning medications for her patients.

'There you are,' Nola said as she came in.

'Just in time,' Pippa replied with a smile. 'Can you check these with me?'

'Of course,' Nola said, but rather than get on with checking the drugs she took a moment to discuss something else. 'Pippa, you know that applications close today…?'

Pippa frowned.

'For my maternity leave position,' she prompted, patting her bump affectionately. 'You often fill in for me, yet you haven't applied…'

'No.' Pippa felt a little flustered. She'd been hoping not to say anything just yet, but now Nola had specifically commented on the fact that she hadn't applied for the role she knew now was the time to tell Nola everything. 'I've put in an expression of interest for a unit manager role when the new paediatric wing opens.'

'You didn't say.'

'Because I wasn't sure if I even stood a chance. It's a big leap. I've only been a fill-in here. It's for the PAC Unit.' There were so many new specialities coming to The Primary that she wasn't surprised when she saw Nola frown at the terminology. 'Paediatric Acute with Comorbidities.'

'So, looking after chronically ill children?'

'Yes, with an acute illness or undergoing routine procedures. It sounds like a really interesting role but, like I said, I didn't know if I had a hope when I applied. I've been invited for a preliminary interview. I was going ask if you'd mind being a referee for my application?'

'Of course,' Nola said. 'But Pippa…' She pressed her lips together for a moment in slight exasperation.

'What?'

'Why didn't you say anything before?'

'I told you. I wasn't sure if I'd even get to the interview stage.'

'We've been talking about the new paediatric wing for months. All of us have been working out what positions we want…' She looked at Pippa and gave a slight shake of her head. 'Not you, though.'

'Is that a problem?'

'Reference wise, no,' Nola said, and didn't elaborate as she was called to the phone.

Pippa was left standing, and knew she'd been told off—just a little.

She was friendly enough at work, and got on with her colleagues for the most part. She'd held several nursing positions over the years and, apart from her training, her time here at The Primary was the longest she'd spent anywhere. But because she didn't bring her private life to the break room, or the hand-over desk, she was considered a little aloof and standoffish.

It wasn't just her private life where she held back, though, Pippa acknowledged. She *hadn't* joined in with discussions about careers and promotions either. She simply wasn't used to discussing her decisions with others or debating her options. She had grown up dealing with her emotions on her own, or keeping them in check so as not to upset anyone.

Nola was right—all the staff had been excitedly discussing the options and opportunities that the new paediatric wing had created for weeks. And while Pippa had been present during a lot of those chats, she hadn't told anyone about her interest in the PAC Unit.

When Nola returned, Pippa could tell she was still a bit offended, and decided an apology was in order. 'Nola, I'm sorry I didn't say anything earlier.'

'It's fine.'

'No, I should have told you. To be honest, I'm not a hundred percent sure it's the right role for me.'

'Isn't that what colleagues are for, Pippa? And managers?' Nola sounded a bit exasperated. 'We could have spoken about it.'

That was the issue in a nutshell. Pippa wasn't sure she could explain her reasons for wanting to work with chronically ill children without getting upset and teary.

She hadn't told her colleagues about Julia.

By the time she'd finished her training, attached to another hospital, Pippa had worked out that she couldn't speak about Julia without tears coming into her eyes. Her emotions when it came to her sister had been silently forbidden as a child and as a teenager. Now, as an adult, breaking down was the one thing Pippa dreaded the most, so she avoided the topic entirely.

It was one of the reasons she was nervous at the prospect of an interview.

'You're really good with the chronic patients, Pippa. I don't doubt you'd be brilliant.' Nola gave a tight smile. 'And, had you asked, I'd have told you that.'

'Thank you.'

'Do you want to run through some interview questions with me? We can do a mock-up, if you'd like.'

'I think I'm as prepared as I'm going to be,' Pippa said. 'But thanks.'

'Well, if you change your mind…' Nola offered. 'Anyway, your lac liver is going for an ultrasound sometime today.'

'I'll put it on the board,' Pippa said, and also made a mental note.

'You can tell he came from St Bede's,' Nola added. 'He's so arrogant!'

'Who?' Pippa asked.

'The locum consultant. All I did was try to reassure a patient and he snapped at me!'

'Snapped?' Pippa checked, tapping out the bubbles from a syringe.

'Oh, yes,' Nola said, and put on a haughty tone. *"I don't appreciate you speaking for me."* I was just trying to tell Mrs James that he wasn't some guy we'd dragged off the street taking care of her daughter and that he'd once been a consultant at St Bede's.'

There wasn't any rivalry, but St Benedict's—or St Bede's as it was affectionally known— was a renowned and highly esteemed teaching hospital.

'Can you update the board when you get a minute?'

'Sure.'

'Mr Harris,' Nola told her, clarifying the new locum's name. 'Luke Harris. We've got him for a month.'

Very deliberately, Pippa didn't react. With the drugs checked, Nola signed her name and then left Pippa, and she stood alone for a moment in the small annexe.

It couldn't be the same Luke Harris, surely?

Well, of course it very well could be.

She'd known that Luke hoped to be a surgeon, and had long ago gleaned that his father was a professor of surgery at St Bede's.

But if it had been Luke on the ward then she'd have recognised him, wouldn't she? After all, there was still a picture of him on her parents' mantelpiece, standing beside Julia on the night of the school dance.

Pippa cast her mind back twenty minutes or so. She'd recognised Fiona—she'd been here for a couple of months—and David, of course, but as for the dark-haired doctor in scrubs, all she'd seen was his tall and rather broad back.

Luke Harris had been her first crush—she cast her mind back—wow, almost fourteen years ago now.

Her very guilty first crush.

Her memory didn't just take her back to the warm glow of the library…instead it shot her straight back to the pain of the past.

To a time when she'd had a sister.

And then to a time when she no longer did.

Pippa closed her eyes for a moment.

Instead of being curious, or even excited at the prosect of seeing Luke again, she felt a surge of annoyance at this intrusion in her life. The jumble of emotions from the that time had long ago been sorted and put away.

Well, not exactly *sorted*.

Luke still occasionally flitted into her mind, and she blushed at the thought…

Not that anyone needed to know that!

As far back as she could remember, Pippa had learnt to keep her feelings in check for fear of further upsetting her parents—particularly her mother. And when Julia had died, Pippa had felt as if there was no one she could share her feelings with.

She'd been to see the school counsellor but, too used to holding things inside, had been unable to open up to a stranger. Julia had been the sole person she'd been able to talk to, the one person who had understood her. And, ironically, she was the only one who would have been able to comfort her in her grief.

The very person she'd needed the most had no longer been there.

At first Pippa had buried herself in art. Later, through university and beyond, instead of working through her confusing emotions she had bundled them up and shoved them into a box labelled *Too Hard to Deal With*, and Pippa did *not* want them brought back out.

And she did not want Luke Harris here, churning up and muddying waters that had taken years to settle.

Heading to Chloe's room, Pippa couldn't help but smile when she saw the little girl, purple ear muffs on and fine blonde hair sticking up, her face pouty as she lay on the bed, looking completely fed-up.

'Hey,' Pippa said, and gestured for her to take off the ear muffs—which, with a dramatic sigh, Chloe did.

'Those babies are so noisy!' she moaned, though Pippa rather thought it might be more to do with the breakfasts being given out. 'Why can't I eat?'

'Because we don't want to do anything that might upset your tummy.'

'It's upset now because it's hungry!'

'I can hear that it is.' Pippa smiled, because it was gurgling loudly as she sat down by the little girl's bed. 'It sounds very cross.'

'Have you had breakfast?' Chloe asked, and Pippa gave a less than honest shake of her head.

'No.' Pippa chose to fib, deciding her almond

croissant on the way to work was something Chloe didn't need to know about! 'I was in a rush.'

'That doctor hasn't had breakfast either. He said I might be able to sit out of bed later, but I just want something to eat...'

She started to cry, and Pippa comforted her. Really, apart from letting her organs rest and recover, one of the reasons that Chloe was being kept on clear fluids only was in case she suddenly started bleeding and had to be rushed to Theatre. There was no need to scare the little girl with too much information but, almond croissants aside, Pippa had learnt early on in life from her sister, and then later at work, to be as honest with children as she could be.

'Do you remember on Friday how they thought you might have to have an operation?' Pippa checked, and Chloe nodded. 'Do you remember being asked when you'd last eaten?'

'No,' Chloe said, but then, as Pippa gave her some tissues, she gave a little nod and wiped her tears. 'I think so.'

'The reason they asked was because if you have to have an operation then it's better if you haven't eaten. You wouldn't want to be sick while you're asleep, would you?'

'No—but I'm getting better.'

'You are.'

'I don't need an operation now.'

'It doesn't seem so. You've been resting so well, and the drip is allowing your tummy to rest too.

We're going to get some more pictures of it today, and if you keep improving it won't be long until you're able to eat.'

Mrs James came in then, and gave Pippa a tentative smile. 'Is she still asking for food?'

'I think she understands why we can't let her eat just yet.'

'In case I'm sick,' Chloe said, a touch happier now things had been explained, and willing to negotiate with her mother. 'Can I play on your phone?'

'I've got a game you can play,' Pippa said, when she saw Mrs James' tense expression. 'Mummy needs to go home for a little while.'

'No!'

'Yes,' Pippa said in a very calm voice. 'And Mummy needs to have her phone with her so I can call her if necessary.'

'You mean, call her about me?'

'About you,' Pippa agreed.

'I don't want to be here on my own.'

'Chloe,' Mrs James said, 'George has hardly seen me since Friday.'

'He's just a baby,' Chloe dismissed. 'He doesn't know.'

'He does know,' Pippa said. 'And as well as that, Mummy needs to feed him. If she has a nice quiet morning then she can make extra milk.'

'And then come back?'

'Of course I'm coming back,' Mrs James said.

'But what if I have to get my X-rays while you're not here?'

'Then I'll come with you,' Pippa said, and looked at Mrs James' torn expression. 'Chloe, nobody's going to forget you.'

Chloe looked anxiously over to her mum. 'Promise?'

'Of course I'm not going to forget you, silly,' Mrs James said as she kissed and hugged her daughter.

There was plenty to do before Pippa got around to updating the board—erasing *Locum* and writing *Mr Harris*, while explaining to her nursing student that doctors who had completed their fellowship for the Royal College of Surgeons were to be called Mr.

'What if they're a woman?'

'Still Mr,' Pippa said, and then, seeing the student frown, she smiled. 'I was joking—they're called Miss.'

'What if they're married?' the student asked.

'Still Miss,' Pippa said, answering the questions easily and not letting anyone glimpse how unsettled she felt—a skill she had honed to perfection.

Luke Harris had been the beat of her heart for months.

No, make that years!

Even before that conversation in the library she'd had a crush on him, just as most of her friends had, but after the day in the library…after he'd arrived to take Julia to the dance… When things had got hard at home, she'd used to picture herself in a silver dress, being led to a waiting car.

She could still, with absolute clarity, remember the thrill of him speaking to her that long-ago lunchtime. Taking the time to really listen to her.

She recalled it now.

Not so much the conversation they'd shared, but how she'd felt listened to—how it had felt to be in the spotlight of another's attention, rather than constantly on the periphery…

Luke Harris had made her feel as if her thoughts, her opinions, really mattered. And even if she hadn't told him she was Julia's sister, he'd made her brave enough to share other little parts of herself.

The memory of the library made her want to cry, for some reason, and crying was something Pippa simply did not do.

Certainly not at work.

Nor with family—heaven forbid!

Not with anyone.

Not even herself.

Her last relationship had ended with a dash of bitterness.

'The thing is, Pippa, I don't know you any better than I did the first night we met.'

Another relationship fail.

Another round of being told that, despite her friendly demeanour, there was nothing behind that wall.

Because she never let anyone in.

Oh, sex was okay—ish. Though she took for ever to be seduced into bed, and then very quickly decided she ought to go home, or wished that he would…

No pillow-talk for her!

She wasn't a superficial person—in fact, her emotions ran deeper than most people's. Pippa just preferred her relationships to be that way: on the surface. She didn't know how to share her feelings, let alone her private thoughts. Just as she didn't know how to drop Julia into the conversation, and neither did she know how to tell someone she was dating that she was a carrier for CF.

At the age of twenty she'd made the decision to get tested, to find out if she was a carrier, and the counsellor at the clinic had asked if she had support...

'I do,' Pippa had replied. *'I just want to know.'*

She had the same support she'd relied on since she was a little girl: herself.

'And you understand that even if you are a carrier, it doesn't mean your child will have CF. The father would have to be a carrier too, and even then...'

She hadn't told her parents the result.

They'd never asked, but then they so rarely asked anything when it came to her.

Instead, even though she hadn't been dating anyone at the time, Pippa had gone on the Pill, and was always careful to make sure her lovers used condoms.

There had never been an accident.

Sex had never been exciting enough for breakages!

CHAPTER TWO

IT WAS A typical busy day on the paediatric ward, yet an extremely untypical one for Pippa.

She felt as if she was on heightened alert and kept glancing at the corridor, or towards the nurses' station, where doctors often gathered. It was a relief when the day neared its end—especially when Mrs James called to say she was half an hour away.

'I'm just about to take Chloe down to Imaging,' Pippa informed her. 'I'll let her know that you'll be waiting for her when she gets back to the ward.'

'The porter's here,' called Kim, the sister on late duty. 'If Mrs James isn't back in time then I'll send someone down to relieve you,' she assured her.

Escorting Chloe, Pippa was simply pleased to have made it through the day without seeing Luke. She wanted to get her head together before facing him.

Still, even if she was aching to get home and somehow process the fact that Luke was actually working here at The Primary, she kept her smile on for her patient.

'Do you remember being in here on Friday?' Pippa asked Chloe as she and the porter wheeled her to Imaging.

'Not very much,' Chloe said. 'They gave me an injection. It made me sleepy.'

Chloe had had a CT on Friday, with contrast, but today it was an ultrasound.

Just as the procedure was about to get underway, the radiologist looked up and smiled. 'Hey, Luke.'

'Mike! I didn't know you worked here.'

Pippa felt her throat go tight. Even before she glanced up, just hearing his voice confirmed her worst... Was it fears? Her worst fears? Or actually her deepest wish?

She wasn't sure. All she was sure of was that it was most definitely him.

Luke.

She glanced over and found she couldn't tear her eyes away.

Age had *not* wearied him.

Gosh, he'd been a stunning teenager, but as a thirty-something man he was far beyond stunning. That straight hair was superbly cut now, and he looked incredible in his dark navy scrubs, but she couldn't comment on his dark brown eyes because Pippa found that she dared not meet them.

He was big—or rather tall—his shoulders were broad, as if all those years of swimming had paid off, and the slender youth was now a very solid man.

'Hey.' He gave her a brief smile. 'You're from the ward?'

'Yes.' She nodded, but then abruptly looked away, as if it were her heart on the monitor, about to be examined and exposed. 'Chloe was a bit upset about coming down to Imaging without her mum.'

'You'll be fine,' Luke said to the little girl. 'It's

not going to hurt at all. It may be a little bit uncomfortable, but we just want to take a good look.'

'How was America?' Mike asked as he washed his hands.

'Incredible,' Luke said.

'You've been to America?' Chloe asked, and Pippa was very grateful for a nosy seven-year-old who could ask any question she chose to when her little tummy was about to be examined. 'Did you go to Disneyland?'

'I didn't,' Luke replied.

'Why not?' she asked, clearly appalled that he'd go all that way and not go to Disneyland.

'I was in Philadelphia. That's a long way from the theme parks.'

'But you could have gone on the way,' Chloe insisted. 'My friend Sophie went to New York, but they stopped at Los Angeles on the way.'

'Why didn't anyone tell me I could do that?' Luke said, smiling at her idea of geography.

'We're going to Disneyland Paris. Mum promised me on Friday.'

'Oh, I'll bet she did,' Luke said with a grin. 'What else did you wangle?'

Pippa found that she was smiling too, because he'd clearly worked with children before and knew their ways.

'I'm getting a new lampshade for my bedroom, and Daddy bought me these earmuffs—' she held up her bright purple fluffy present '—so I don't hear George crying all the time when I'm at home.'

'Sounds like you're being very spoilt,' Luke said, distracting Chloe as the radiologist probed her abdomen. Yet while he chatted easily his eyes were hawkish as he stared at the screen and Chloe's liver was examined, the laceration measured, and her abdomen was checked for any free fluid. He seemed pleased with the findings, and soon the sheet was back over Chloe's stomach.

'Thanks, Mike.'

He glanced over to Pippa and gave her a very brief smile—the same bland smile he had given to the radiologist—and it was clear to Pippa that he didn't remember her at all.

She had to wait thirty minutes for porter to arrive and take Chloe back up to the ward.

'Oh, sorry.' Kim glanced up when Pippa returned to the ward. 'I forgot about you. Mrs James is here.'

'It's fine,' Pippa said.

'Can you settle Chloe back into bed?' Kim asked. 'Laura's taking care of her tonight, but she's in with Cot Two. His drain is blocked again.'

'Sure.'

It was actually Mrs James who needed settling. 'Surely someone can tell me how the ultrasound went?' she said.

'The staff are a little tied up, but I'll remind them to come and talk to you.'

Pippa knew that the evening meals would soon start to be given out, and mealtimes were particularly difficult for her patient right now. She could see the very active little girl was starting to feel better and her mother was going to have her work cut out to keep her quiet and resting. 'Chloe… Do you like jigsaws?'

'No.'

'We've got some Disney ones.'

Her face lit up, and by the time Pippa had found a couple of jigsaws to keep the little girl amused she was almost an hour past the end of her shift.

Not that she minded, because when her phone buzzed, and she saw that it was her mother, she actually breathed out a sigh of relief that she was still at work.

She often dropped in on a Monday, if her shifts allowed, but today Pippa really wanted a night to herself.

'I'll come over at the weekend,' Pippa told her.

'Well, I'll try.'

'You haven't been to the cemetery for a while.'

Pippa could hear the slight accusatory tone of her mother's voice and ducked into a treatment room to continue the call.

'No,' she said. 'Work's been busy.'

She could hear her own excuses, her own lies. Her mother went to visit Julia's grave most days, but the truth was that Pippa drew no comfort from going.

'We're flat out…' she started to say, but then paused as the overhead chimes went off. They weren't for Pippa's ward, but she was thankful for them all the same.

Once she'd called her mother from home, pretending to be at work. A neighbour had knocked at the door and Pippa had felt caught in the lie. Another time, she'd been in the Tube station on her way home and an announcement had given her away. She felt guilty for not going to see her parents, but relieved at the same time—and wishing it didn't have to be this way.

This evening Pippa knew she couldn't face them. She really just needed to be on her own.

She glanced up and felt a blush spread across her cheeks as Luke came into the treatment room and started going through the drawers.

'We're really short-staffed,' Pippa said to her mother once the emergency chimes had gone quiet. 'So I'm staying back. I really do have to go. Love you…'

She let out a tense breath and then pocketed her phone, relieved that was over—at least for now. But then she looked up and saw Luke turning on the light over the treatment bed. Her sharp intake of breath was just as tight when he spoke.

'Would you be able to give me a hand?' he asked. 'I need to reposition a drain and I'm going to bring him in here.'

'Cot Two?' Pippa checked. 'I think Laura's taking care of him. I'm actually finished for the day.'

'Oh! I thought I just heard you say you were staying back…'

She gave a small laugh, albeit through gritted teeth. Weren't private conversations that you were forced to have in a place where you could be over-heard supposed to be politely ignored?

Not only that, but Luke persisted. 'Tut-tut,' he said as he located the alcohol swabs and tape.

'Sorry?' Pippa did a double-take, a little unsure as to what he was referring to.

'Pretending to be stuck at work… I find honesty a much better policy.'

'Not when it comes to my parents.'

'Oh!' He smiled. 'My mistake.' He took a hand-ful of saline flushes and added them to the dish he was filling and then looked right at her. 'In that case, I totally get it.'

It was an odd conversation, being pulled up for a white lie and at the same time meeting his eyes properly.

They were still the same beautiful kaleidoscope of shades of brown. He still had the same thick, dark lashes that barely blinked as he held her gaze. She stood in silence, trying to decipher if the flare of interest that had ignited between them was rec-ognition or attraction.

Pippa knew that in her case it was both.

As for Luke, she wasn't sure.

'I'll let Laura know you need a hand.'

'No need.' He gave her a small smile that perhaps meant he wasn't really in need of a hand after all.

He stared right at her and Pippa felt flustered. For once, she was worried that she might actually be showing it, because she could feel heat spread-ing up her face.

'I'd better go,' Pippa said, although her feet refused to obey and she stood there, still facing him, trying to think of something to say. 'Oh, and Mrs James wants to know what's happening after the ultrasound.'

'Yes,' he said, his eyes never leaving her face.

It would seem that Luke Harris was either trying to place where he knew her from or blatantly flirting.

Or both!

'Do I know you?'

Pippa didn't answer. She didn't want to be evasive, but his words hurt—like a boot stomping in those muddied waters she'd fought all her life to clear, and she wasn't quite sure of the strength of her voice even if she were able to find the right words.

His eyes narrowed a little, as he obviously kept trying to place her, yet Pippa found she was looking at the dark shadow of his jaw, and the loosened tie around his neck. His jacket was off, sleeves rolled up, and his citrussy scent was somehow morning-fresh, because it cut through the antiseptic smell of the treatment room.

It was hell to know she was attracted to him all over again.

He seemed to take her silence as a game. 'I'll work it out,' he said, and then turned away and carried his tray of items over to the treatment bed, to prepare for his patient's arrival.

She felt as rattled and jolted as the Tube that took

her the couple of stops to her home, and the feeling refused to leave her as she went up the stairs to her tiny and very cold flat.

Pippa turned on the electric throw, which she carried with her between the living room and bedroom, before stripping off.

It was so nice to have a shower and pull on her dressing gown, and then, for the first time in…well, in a long time, she went to take a certain photo album from the shelf.

Pippa's mother had had every single photo of Julia printed for her, as well as other family shots and ones that the school had given them.

Her parents had an almost identical album, but unlike Pippa they went through it most days—at least most of the days that Pippa was there. It sat on the coffee table, or in the kitchen.

Pippa's album was tucked away on a low shelf, not at eye-level. Present, but not immediately visible. And even though her hand went to it straight away, as she took it from the shelf she paused, and her fingers closed over the little ceramic heart she'd made in art that long ago day.

Gosh, she'd been crazy about Luke Harris then.

Now, sitting on the sofa, with her warm blanket wrapped around her, Pippa went slowly through the album.

Julia's first, second and third birthdays. She'd looked so chunky and healthy then, but already she'd been sick.

Pippa knew that Julia had been in hospital even on the day Pippa was born.

Her mother had once proudly stated how that night she'd been wheeled from Maternity down to the children's ward, to stay with her fretful toddler. Newborn Pippa had been left alone with the other babies on the ward.

She turned the page and there was a photo of the two of them on a beach. Julia, ever the big sister, was holding Pippa's hand. Then there was the first day at infants school, junior school, new houses, another new school...

God, she missed Julia so much.

She felt so very cheated on her behalf for the life her sister had never got to live.

More than a few times her mother had shamed Pippa by accusing her of being jealous of the attention given to Julia.

Had she been?

Pippa sat quietly, finally asking herself a question she'd buried deep down inside her.

Maybe? she ventured. *Sometimes*, she admitted. Especially when she'd been a little girl.

Yet for the most part, especially as Julia's condition had deteriorated, *jealous* wasn't quite the right term to use.

Their parents had done all they could to cram so much into Julia's too-short life—trips to theme parks, swimming with dolphins and grand days out—almost willing her to live on for a few more months. And for eighteen years Julia had obliged.

Living, but slowly growing almost translucent.

After the dance, Luke had faded away too. Pippa's mum had said that Julia didn't want him to see her so weak.

So weak…but in other ways so incredibly determined and strong.

One night Pippa had padded out of bed and climbed into Julia's…

'Clever you!' Pippa had said, because Julia had found out that day that she had been accepted into the University of St Andrew in Scotland.

The prestigious university had been Julia's first choice, and despite a failing heart and lung transplant, and endless stays in hospital, as well as multiple procedures and appointments, Julia had made schoolwork her priority.

Pippa had always been in awe of her sister, and never more so than that day.

Julia must have known for some time that she hadn't a hope of going to Scotland and St Andrew's, yet she'd studied incredibly hard and had got the most amazing grades.

Pippa had known that if it had been her she'd have given up long ago, or decided there was no point, yet Julia had pushed herself, living as if she wasn't dying, grabbing on to life and making the most of every precious moment, even if it led nowhere.

'How does it feel to get in?' she'd asked her.

'I made it…' Julia had breathed.

'You did.'

'Go and see it for me.'

'You'll go yourself.'

'Stop,' Julia had said huskily. *'I do the happy-clappy routine for Mum and Dad, but I don't want to put on an act with you.'*

'You don't have to.'

It was true. Though their mother had done her level best to police their conversations, they'd always found time to talk—really talk—as only siblings could.

'Will you go and see it for me?' Julia had asked.

'I don't know...'

She'd lain beside her sister, and Julia had stroked her hair. Her wonderful sister had comforted her as Pippa had let a sliver of her fears out.

'I think it would be too much. I mean, I can't imagine going anywhere without you.'

'I'm so tired, Pip.' Julia was the only one who had called her that.

'I know.'

'Tired of fighting...just to breathe. I'm ready.'

'I don't want to let you go,' Pippa had whispered.

She'd paused and taken a deep breath, because she'd known her mother would forbid this conversation if she knew.

'Are you scared?'

'No,' Julia had said, but then she'd hesitated. *'Pip, everybody gets scared at times. I just tell myself I'll let myself be scared tomorrow.'*

Pippa hadn't known what she meant, but then Julia had asked, *'Are you scared?'*

Pippa hadn't wanted to upset her sister, but her answer had been honest. Almost. *'Sometimes.'* The truth was that she'd been petrified. *'I don't want to be on my own.'*

'You've had a lot of time on your own,' Julia had said, wise beyond her years. *'Really, you've always been on your own.'*

'I've had you,' Pippa had stated, though she'd known Julia was referring to the disparity in the way their parents treated them. It was the first time it had properly and openly been acknowledged between the girls.

That truth had opened the door for Julia to reveal her real fear. *'I'm worried about them. How they'll be when I'm gone...'*

Pippa had wanted to reassure her sister, to tell her that things would be okay, to say she'd be there for their parents, but Pippa had been worried about that too, and had known in her heart that she wouldn't be enough to fill the gap.

She could never come close.

'They'll keep on loving you, the way they always have,' Pippa had said.

And absolutely her parents had.

At home, even now, it was almost as if Julia had never left. Her bedroom lay untouched; her clothes still hung in the wardrobe. Pippa's old bedroom, on the other hand, was now her mother's sewing room.

Fourteen years on, Pippa looked at the picture of her sister in her silver dress and ran a finger over her pretty face.

Translucent. That really was the word for Julia, because even in the photo it looked as if she was fading.

But not Luke. He stood bold and confident, wearing a suit as if he'd been doing so for a lifetime.

Even if he didn't know it, Luke had helped Pippa a lot, emboldening her to make choices she might not have otherwise. She would never regret taking art.

Returning to school after Julia had died had felt so odd. People had avoided asking her about Julia, or simply avoided her altogether. And there had been no Luke Harris to daydream about bumping into. He'd been off on his gap year. Her one solace had been the chalky, papery smell of the art room. It had become a haven from the despair of life at home.

Back then Luke Harris had still popped into her thoughts, into her daydreams and dreams. But now Luke was back in real life.

In real time.

Grown-up time.

He'd asked where he knew her from and she'd hesitated to answer. He'd taken it as a tease, but she'd actually been completely tongue-tied.

Was it ridiculous to be hurt that he couldn't place her or recall the precious hour they'd shared?

He'd forgotten.

And forgotten was how Pippa had felt all her life.

His question '*Do I know you*?' had catapulted her straight back to the agonising times of her youth.

I loved you! she'd wanted to shout.

Yet that would have been her teenage self responding to him.

Teenagers knew nothing about love.

Now she turned over the little heart she had painted that day in art class. Kobicha-brown, copper and russet—all the shades of his eyes as she'd gleaned in that precious hour alone with him.

Pippa managed a little laugh at the intensity of her own teenage emotions, then tried to rationalise their long-ago conversation.

He'd simply been being nice. Doing his polite Head Boy duty and helping a younger student.

Apart from attending the same school and having one conversation in the library, they didn't share a past.

Julia was really their only connection.

That was all.

CHAPTER THREE

PIPPA WASN'T THE only one to notice Luke.

It wasn't just his effortless charisma and dark good looks that had people talking, nor his clear skill as a surgeon. It wasn't even the slightly detached arrogance that ruffled some of the staff.

Luke Harris had come to The Primary with scandal attached!

Louise on Maternity had once briefly dated him—or so one of the midwives had told Laura when she'd gone to borrow a breast pump. And on her return had gleefully spread the word.

Oh, and one of the domestics had worked in the residences at St Bede's when Luke had been a medical student there.

As for Jimmy, the theatre tech, he seemed delighted to tell tales of a decadent past.

Rumours swirled in abundance.

Now, on the eve of Pippa's interview, as she sat at the nurses' station in a brief lull as they waited for the late staff to arrive, Luke was the topic of conversation. Pippa was trying not to listen, and to focus instead on that morning's patient discharge papers. She was tempted to ask Chloe if she could borrow her earmuffs as the conversation again turned to Luke.

Jenny was feeding little Toby his bottle at the nurses' station, as his parents hadn't come in yet, as well as providing updates on the sexy new consultant. 'He was just made consultant and then suddenly he threw it all in.'

'I'd hardly call studying trauma in Philadelphia throwing things in,' Nola responded. 'With all that experience he'll be scorching hot and snapped up wherever he goes.'

'Yes, but that wasn't why he left. He was sleeping with one of the senior theatre nurses and it all blew up.'

'Who *hasn't* he slept with?' Nola sighed, and then let out a soft laugh. 'Aside from us!'

But that wasn't all the gossip Jenny had. 'She was married; her husband worked on the ortho—'

Jenny halted abruptly and, glancing up, Pippa knew why the conversation had been so rapidly terminated. The man being discussed was making his way down the corridor towards the unit.

'Sorry to interrupt,' Luke said drily, as if he knew he'd been the subject of the conversation. 'Martha wants to discuss a patient with me.'

Martha was the paediatrician.

'She's in the ED,' Nola said.

'Is Fiona here?'

'No,' Jenny said, shaking her head. 'She was a short while ago, but she got paged to go to Surg One. They sound busy.'

'Then I'm hiding here,' Luke said, and took out a wrapped canteen sandwich from his pocket.

'Why aren't you eating in the consultants' lounge?' Nola asked.

'That's a very good question,' he replied, nodding, though Pippa noticed he didn't answer it. He looked at baby Toby and said, 'Somebody's hungry.'

'You are, aren't you?' Jenny cooed to the baby.

Pippa glanced over and couldn't help but smile. Jenny might be a dreadful gossip, and to Pippa's mind somewhat abrupt with the parents, yet the babies and children adored her.

Even Toby, a little 'Failure to Thrive' and known to be a fussy feeder, was taking his bottle and gazing up at Jenny in adoration.

'Toby knows better than to not drink his bottle,' Pippa teased. 'He must know you like your charts to be neatly filled in.'

'Absolutely, I do,' Jenny agreed.

When Nola took herself off to the office, Jenny looked at Luke.

'I was in the army for ten years,' she told him.

'Paediatrics?'

'Mostly.' She nodded. 'A couple of years on Maternity in Germany.' She sat Toby up to burp him. 'You were at St Bede's, weren't you?'

But Jenny's fishing expedition ended as Toby's father arrived, and her rather brusque tone returned as she addressed him.

'I thought you were going to be here to give him lunch, so that I could observe.'

Pippa glanced up and saw Luke's subtle eyebrow-raise as Jenny headed off with the somewhat sheepish father.

'Is she always so approachable with the parents?' he asked.

Pippa didn't reply to his sarcastic question, just turned back to her work. But she could feel her neck turning pink and knew his attention was on her. In the days since their paths had first crossed she had occasionally felt his eyes on her, just as they were now. She felt his gaze rather than met it, and it was the most deliciously unsettling feeling she'd known—a flutter of nerves dancing through her veins as she quietly thrilled at his long assessment.

'I do know you,' Luke said. 'I just can't work out how.'

'Because I'm so unforgettable?' Pippa teased. Or was she flirting? Or just covering up how much his vague remembrance hurt when *she* could repeat their conversation verbatim?

'Pippa, I'm saying that I know you from somewhere—not that I've slept with you. I'd certainly remember if I had.'

She actually laughed.

'So,' he persisted, 'where *do* I know you from?'

She was about to tell him, but for one teeny second she was back there, in the library, being listened to for what had felt like the first time in her life. Feeling important. Not an important person, just important enough for someone to listen to her...

'That's mean,' he said, taking her silence as refusal. 'Come on, Pip...'

'Pippa!' she warned, just as she did with anyone who called her that, because only Julia had ever called her Pip.

'Then it's lucky for me that I don't have a speech impediment.'

Pippa couldn't help her reluctant smile at his unsuitable joke as she filled in her paperwork. 'If you want to be precise, my name's actually Philippa.'

'Oh, I'd love to be precise.'

His words were delivered in a low voice, for her burning ears only. Burning because a roar of heat had moved from her throat to her scalp. It seemed he was taking their little *Where do I know you from?* game up a notch.

She should possibly warn him that he was wasting his time. Pippa was the last person to get involved with someone at work—especially some visiting locum who came with a side dish of scandal.

But this scandalous visiting locum was Luke Harris.

And for Pippa that changed everything.

Still, she was saved from responding as Jenny and Nola returned.

'Still here?' Jenny asked him in her blunt way.

'Yes,' Luke answered easily. 'I'm trying to work out where I know Pippa from.'

'Do you two know each other!' Jenny gaped.

'I'm sure we do.'

'How?'

Pippa chose to put him out of his misery. 'We went to the same school.'

'Did we?' His eyes widened as he took in the news.

'You two were at school together?' Nola was clearly delighted by this snippet of news.

'Hardly together,' Pippa said. 'He was two years above me.'

Should she remember that? Pippa pondered. If she hadn't been so crazy about him, would she recall that detail? But then she came up with a good excuse as to why she might.

'He was Head Boy in his final year.'

'Did you have a crush on him?' Nola teased, from the safety of being six months pregnant and in a happy marriage. 'I know I would have.'

Pippa casually shrugged. 'Everybody did.'

'Get out!' Luke refuted.

'Come off it,' Pippa said with a smile, stapling the discharge papers and standing up to file them. 'It's true and well you know it.'

'Were you on the swimming team?' he asked, clearly still trying to place her.

'No.' She looked over, and with her eyes willed him to remember their one conversation, that lunchtime in the library, when the world had stopped for a slice of time.

He looked at her lanyard, clearly to read her surname. The recognition obviously startled him and he looked up in shock.

'Westford... So you're Julia's sister?'

Of course that was how he would remember her. She swallowed down the hurt and nodded.

'You have a sister?' Nola asked with a hint of surprise and also some confusion. 'Julia?'

'I... Yes,' Pippa managed, unsure how to voice the fact that her sister was dead and uncertain how to handle the fact that she had never mentioned her. 'I *had* a sister,' she added, unable to say outright that Julia had died, watching Nola's smile fade as she heard Pippa place her sister in the past.

'Oh, Pippa...' Nola said as she stood. 'I had no idea.'

'It's fine.' Pippa put up her hand to stop Nola from coming over, but Nola just kept on walking towards her.

'I'm so sorry.'

'Thank you,' Pippa said automatically, feeling her nose pinch and terrified of breaking down. She got up from her seat.

Damn you, Luke, Pippa thought. *Damn you for resurrecting these feelings in me.*

She'd hoped to leave all that pain and confusion in the past. But rather than discuss the agony of loss, it felt easier to voice a different hurt, and so, as Pippa walked off, she threw over her shoulder, 'Luke used to go out with her.'

Luke was about to correct Pippa, and say that he had never gone out with her sister, but then he halted himself. Because this certainly wasn't the place. He could see that her face was on fire and knew that she was upset. It was clear her colleagues hadn't known about Julia and that he'd just revealed something she had carefully kept to herself.

Boy, he'd messed that up, Luke thought, seeing Nola and Jenny exchanging quizzical looks and then turning to him.

'Luke?' Jenny said, clearly hoping for more information.

But Luke would not be enlightening the two nurses further, nor offering any explanation. Instead, he followed Pippa down the corridor.

He had been messing about…just making light conversation, Luke told himself. His stride briefly faltered, because *of course* he'd been flirting. He'd been determined to avoid all that during his brief time here. But then attraction had flared from the moment he'd locked eyes with Pippa. Before that, in fact. For awareness had been there from the moment she'd dashed past him that first morning, her scarf trailing behind her and bringing with her the scent of summer. He'd wanted not just to remember her name and where he knew her from, but to get to know her some more.

No, it hadn't been idle conversation—and he was the one who'd brought the private game they'd been playing right up to the nurses' station…

In fact, he'd been pleased to have an excuse to take a quick break on Paeds. He'd tried to tell himself that Pippa wasn't the only reason he'd taken his lunch there. But he knew he'd been hoping to suggest meeting up away from work. And now their discreet little flirtation had got out of hand.

His eyes briefly shuttered in self-recrimination, because he'd clearly not only hurt her, but in bringing up her sister he'd been indiscreet—and that was most unlike him...

He knew from bitter experience the damage careless words could cause. Loose lips didn't just sink ships—they torpedoed relationships, changed the course of careers, capsized lives...

He thought back to his old hospital, to those last painful weeks at St Bede's and the conversations that had abruptly halted when he'd walked into the break room—people had acted the same way Jenny and Nola would undoubtedly act now, when Pippa returned to the desk...

Only on this occasion it was entirely his fault.

'Pippa,' said Luke, as he caught up with her in the kitchen. 'I'm so sorry about that.'

'About what?' Pippa asked, pouring hot water over a teabag for a drink she didn't even want—it had just been an excuse to get away.

'If I spoke out of turn about Julia.'

'You didn't.' Pippa attempted a nonchalant shrug, but her neck and shoulders were so rigid that all she did was slop her tea. 'It's not as if it's a state secret or anything,' she said, mopping up the little spill on the bench, glad to have something to focus on rather than look at him.

'It's clear they didn't know.'

'Only because it's never really come up,' Pippa responded, picking up her mug and intending to walk off. 'Unlike most people here, I don't bring my personal life to work.'

'Whatever the case, I was indiscreet,' Luke said. 'And for that, I apologise.'

His voice was both serious and sincere, so much so that it stilled her, and instead of brushing past him Pippa turned and met his eyes. They were serious and sincere too, and also concerned. She hadn't expected him to follow her, and certainly not to confront things so directly and apologise.

'It's fine,' Pippa said, but she knew there was a raw edge to her voice as she accepted his apology; there was still hurt there. 'Thank you.'

'I knew I remembered you.'

'Well, mystery solved,' she said, forcing a smile as her heart seemed to crumple.

After all, *that* was exactly what hurt, though she didn't want to draw any more attention to it with Luke standing there.

She was back to being Julia's sister all over again.

That conversation in the library—that precious hour which had meant so much to Pippa—had clearly meant nothing to him. He couldn't even recall it.

'I've got to go and do hand-over.'

'Hold on a moment.' He halted her attempt to leave. 'Do you want to catch up?'

'Catch up?'

'I should be finished by six.'

'Are we going to sing the school song?' She attempted a joke, but her voice came out just a little too bitter, and so she checked herself. 'Catch up about what?' she asked, a little bewildered, because his eyes were still on hers, and she had the ridiculous thought that his hand was going to move to her cheek.

The fantasy of him had not just returned, it had been remastered, and it was in full Technicolor now, as she looked into those eyes whose colour she'd once faithfully attempted to capture. Not just Technicolor, though—this fantasy came with the bonus of a citrussy bergamot scent and the bizarre feeling that he was going to take her mug of tea and place it down, so that he might hold her and better apologise with a kiss.

But his next words popped the bubble of hope in which she was floating.

'I don't think work is the place for a private catch-up...'

His voice trailed off and with a sinking feeling Pippa thumped back down to reality. She guessed he wanted to talk about Julia, and her final days.

He hadn't been at the funeral. Her eyes had briefly sought him. In the depths of her grief, she'd wanted just a glimpse of him, to know he was near. Pippa had later heard that he'd gone off on his gap year almost the minute his final exam was over.

His request for more information about Julia

now took her right back to the days, weeks and months after her sister had died—to the funeral, to the endless albeit well-meaning conversations in which people had asked after her parents and pressed her for details as they attempted to probe the family's grief.

Pippa had soon had it down pat.

'They're getting there.'

'She died at home, as she wanted.'

'It was very peaceful.'

That was what she'd said, because it had always seemed the right thing to say.

She hadn't added that she *hoped* it was peaceful—her parents hadn't thought to pull her out of school to give her a chance to say goodbye.

Pippa had felt ill that entire day.

She'd even been to the sick bay and had been given two headache tablets, wishing she could be sent home.

The day had gone on for ever, and when she'd finally got home she'd turned the key in the door with familiar dread to find her aunt standing there.

'Pippa…' her aunt had said, and then she'd guided her into the kitchen.

There, her aunt had told her that just after nine that morning Julia had died.

It had made no sense. While she'd been doing biology, eating lunch, sitting in the library, followed by an art lesson, Julia had been dead…

'Where is she?'

Pippa had turned to run up the stairs, but her aunt had told her that as she'd been walking home from school, her headache pounding, for once not daydreaming about Luke Harris, Julia's body had been being taken away by the undertakers.

She'd never shared that part…nor how her parents had sat on the couch, holding each other and sobbing.

'She's gone…' her mother had said, barely looking up. 'Julia's gone.'

They hadn't followed her when Pippa had gone into Julia's room. Hadn't checked on her as she'd lain on Julia's bed…

Damn you, Luke Harris, for coming to work here and making me remember everything I've tried to forget.

She looked up and saw he was awaiting her response, and even though going for a drink to talk about Julia's death was the last thing she wanted, she certainly did not want to discuss it here. So she ignored the effect of his gaze and the close proximity of him in the small staff kitchen and managed a casual, 'Sure.'

'How about The Avery?' Luke said, naming a nice pub with a great menu that was close to The Primary.

'Sure.'

The Avery was also close enough that she could go home and change, rather than meet him in the jeans she'd worn into work.

That wasn't just vanity.

Just that he was in a gorgeous dark suit with the palest blue shirt.

Okay, it *was* vanity that later had Pippa leafing through her rather boring wardrobe and taking out the nice grey wrap dress she was intending to wear tomorrow for her interview. She moved to put it back, but then, given it was just a quick drink and this was the nicest outfit she had, she decided to wear it.

The dress was versatile—it could be either dressed up with heels and make-up, as it would be tomorrow, or made last-minute smart-casual with boots.

For this evening she chose the latter.

She was soon back on the Underground, on her way to meet him.

For a catch-up.

Breathe...

She wasn't a gawky sixteen-year-old now, with her first crush.

Instead, Pippa reminded herself, she was about to turn thirty, and, if anything, was a little averse to relationships. Anyway, this wasn't a date. Luke just wanted to find out what had happened to Julia.

As the Tube rattled her towards her destination there was time for another honest appraisal.

She liked this.

Going out.

Whether on a date, or out with friends, Pippa

preferred a nice noisy bar where you couldn't really talk too much. It was deeper conversations she avoided—and not just at work, but in all areas of her life…

Still, even if it was Luke Harris, at least she had the conversation down pat.

Died peacefully…yada-yada…

He stood out.

Even in the crowded bar, Pippa saw him straight away. He really was divine, and it made her confident stride falter. If they'd never met—if she'd had no idea who he was—she'd still have noticed him first.

She pushed out a smile and walked over to where he stood at the bar.

'Just in time,' he said. 'What will you have?'

'A grapefruit juice,' she said, and then added, 'Yes, please,' to the offer of ice.

As their drinks were being poured, she glanced around and saw the pub was pretty full, but that there was a high table free in the middle.

'Shall I go and grab it?' Pippa suggested.

'No need.' He shook his head. 'I've got us a place in the lounge,' he said, gesturing beyond. 'It's quieter.'

Her heart sank.

It was indeed quieter.

There were couches and low polished tables that allowed for more intimate conversation. Thankfully he was making his way to some chairs, and Pippa took off her coat, placing it on a hook before taking a seat beside Luke but far enough away to feel opposite to him.

'So,' Pippa said, attempting the dreaded polite small talk, 'you're here for a month?'

He nodded.

'How are you finding it?'

His response was non-committal. 'I'm really just back in London to tie up loose ends.'

'Loose ends?'

'Yes. I want to sell my flat before I head off.'

'Back to America?'

'I'm not sure,' he admitted. 'I was hoping to have a break and get the flat ready to go on the market while I worked out where to go next, but then this offer of a month's work at The Primary came up. It's a great trauma centre, and I couldn't resist… I've left the flat to the estate agent to pretty up.'

'You mean, remove its soul?'

Luke laughed at her perception. 'You could say that. I now have cushions everywhere, as well as rugs I keep tripping over, and this bottle of wine on the counter with two wine glasses and a corkscrew that I'm not allowed to touch.'

'Did they place a cheeseboard in the kitchen?'

'How did you guess?'

'I love looking at houses for sale,' Pippa told him. 'I had vague ideas of being an interior designer once—' she started to say, but then halted, reminding herself that they were here to talk about her sister.

Might as well get it over and done with.

'You wanted to know about Julia?'

He frowned, and she didn't quite know why.

'It was very peaceful,' Pippa told him, and then she gave a practised, reassuring smile. 'She died at home, as she wanted—'

'Pippa.'

He halted her, perhaps a little too abruptly, and in the silence that followed Luke found he was unusually uncertain as to how to proceed. Julia wasn't the reason he had asked her out tonight, but to tell Pippa he wasn't here for a Julia update might sound cold.

Was it cold?

He didn't really know, but there was something he wanted to make very clear.

'I didn't date your sister.'

Her green eyes almost flashed a warning as they met his. 'Yes, Luke, you did.'

'No,' he said. 'I took her to the school dance. That was all.'

'You came over to the house,' Pippa disputed. 'More than a few times.'

'Because she was too unwell to attend the information nights. But we were never dating. Julia wanted to go to the school dance and I was…'

As Luke's voice trailed off she felt foolish as realisation hit. He'd been Head Boy, after all, and

no doubt there had been certain duties that came
with the role.

'Were you told to ask Julia?'

'It was my pleasure to escort her.'

For someone so arrogant, Pippa thought, he was
supremely polite—and his cautious answers gave
little away. Yet Pippa wanted clarity.

'But you *were* asked?' she persisted, and he gave
a slight nod.

Pippa felt a sudden giddy rush of relief.

They hadn't dated. Luke had just been doing his
duty.

'I thought…' She ran a hand through her thick
curls, unsure herself how to proceed, and torn because she was still loyal to her sister, who'd clearly
had a crush on him too. 'I just assumed the two of
you were dating.'

'Pippa…' he said, leaning forward in his chair.
He was so tall that, despite the distance between
them, their knees and arms brushed. 'I never saw
her after the dance. Or visited her in hospital.'

Pippa could feel that she was blushing as he
spoke—not just at her own misconceptions but because the heady whoosh of relief she'd felt at the
news wasn't abating. If anything, it was heighten-
ing…

'I know my relationships are all short lived,' he
went on, 'and that at times I can be a bit ruth-
less, ending things, but even I wouldn't be bastard
enough to break up with someone who was termi-
nally ill.'

Pippa blinked as he spoke out loud the words that had been forbidden in her home.

'Sorry.' Pippa reclaimed her knee and moved slightly away, then took a sip of her drink to cover her confusion. It was hard to look back on that time in light of his revelation with him here. 'I was sixteen,' she said. 'I guess at sixteen you think everyone's getting it on.' She gave a hollow laugh. 'Except you.' It was she who frowned now. 'I mean except *me*.'

'I know what you meant,' he said with a smile. 'God, who'd be sixteen again?'

I would, Pippa thought, but didn't say.

The year she'd turned sixteen had been glorious—at least the start of it.

Julia had received her new heart and lungs, and Pippa's birthday and the Christmas that had followed were the happiest weeks Pippa had known. She and Julia had gone Christmas shopping and out for lunch, and then looked at make-up, painting the backs of their hands with lipstick rainbows. Then they'd gone on to a fashionable jewellery shop, where they'd tried on rings neither had been able to afford.

Or so Pippa had thought.

She twisted the silver ring Julia had bought her, which she still wore on her little finger, recalling the bliss of that Christmas Day, when no one had seen the dark clouds gathering and no one had known that the following year everything would change.

And so she got back to the real reason he'd asked her here.

'She died that September,' Pippa said.

'I'd gone on my gap year,' Luke said, nodding, 'but I do remember hearing that she'd died.'

'She'd just found out that she'd got into the university she desperately wanted—St Andrew's.'

There was that swell in her chest again…that rise, that wave, that feeling…but it had nowhere to go. She recalled her sister receiving the wonderful news, the smile on Julia's face, and the shine of pride in her fading eyes.

'She was so pleased to have been accepted. It was her first choice.'

'Oh, yes,' he said, 'that's *such* an achievement. I got my second choice. I was actually hoping for a reason not to be a student with placements at the same hospital as my father, and being accepted at Cambridge would have been a very polite way to bow out…'

She gave a half-laugh, but then realised he was serious. 'You don't get on?'

'I admire his surgical skills.'

And there it was again, the diplomatic response that gave nothing away. But for Pippa it was what he didn't say that spoke volumes.

'So why—?' Pippa halted.

She was usually the least nosy person. And her personal conversations usually dripped like a leaky tap. With Luke, though, it was as if the pipes were shuddering to life. Drip, drip, and then a sudden burst.

'Why did you select it if the two of you weren't getting on?'

'We were getting on fine when the applications went in.' He drained the last of his drink, but instead of heading to the bar, or summoning the waitress, he said, 'My grandfather was a surgeon there…and my father…'

Now Pippa understood what he'd meant in the library when he'd told her his future had been decided even before he was born. She felt a little as if she had a cheat sheet on him, and had to keep remembering to discard what she already knew.

'Still, I really wanted Cambridge. I missed out by a point.'

'Ouch.'

'I ballsed up in the chemistry exam. I can still see the question.' He grimaced. 'Fragmentation…'

Pippa dragged her mind back to her biology lessons, but unlike the library, which she could recall with detail, biology lessons were in the dim past. 'Parent plant?'

'No, that's biology. In chemistry…'

He attempted to explain, but completely lost Pippa along the way.

'Mass spectrometry. Fragmentation.'

'I don't even know what that means!' She groaned at the memory of her science lessons, and especially the homework. 'Chemistry was a nightmare.'

'I liked it. Don't you remember that old chat-up line?' he asked, and she shook her head. 'Excuse me, have you lost an electron? Because you are positively attractive.'

'That's dreadful!' Pippa started to laugh. 'We definitely moved in different circles. I couldn't get past the periodic table.'

Luke smiled. 'Well, I still dream about that damn exam—sitting there, knowing I should know it...' But then his smile faded. 'My head was all over the place,' he admitted. 'My mother wasn't well at the time.'

She watched the column of his throat as he swallowed, the bob of his Adam's apple, and she thought of his red eyes in the library. But she didn't know how to address that—how to discuss a conversation he couldn't even remember.

So she settled for safe. 'St Bede's is a great hospital, though?'

Luke said nothing to that. He just picked up his glass, but then, seeing it was empty, set it down. Clearly he didn't want to prolong the night.

Instead, he got back to being polite. 'So, how have you been since you lost your sister?'

'It's been fourteen years,' Pippa said, but then realised she didn't really know the answer to that question. 'I've been fine, I guess.'

'How about your parents?'

'They're...' It would take more than the dregs of her grapefruit juice to tell him about that. 'They're well.'

'So why are you avoiding them?' He wagged a finger. 'Don't forget, I heard you on the phone.'

Pippa gave a wry laugh at both the memory and his perception. 'Okay, fine…they're not doing so well. They've never moved on from it and I doubt they ever will.'

'It must be hard…'

'Of course, losing a child—'

'I meant it must be hard on *you*.'

Oh.

Pippa hadn't been expecting that. Seriously had not been expecting that. Because since Julia's death, most people only asked about her parents.

She didn't know how to respond, but her silence didn't stop Luke.

'So how come you haven't told anyone at work about Julia?'

'It's just…never come up.' Pippa shrugged, but she saw the frown that said he didn't believe her.

He wasn't wrong. She was a nurse on a paediatric ward, and her colleagues were friendly.

'I haven't worked there for long.'

'How long?'

'Two years…'

'I rest my case.'

She actually laughed.

'And then I went and put my foot in it.'

'Not really,' Pippa said. 'I guess it came out naturally. I mean…' She took a tense breath. 'I just don't like talking about it.'

There was a stretch of silence, and she let it hang there to see whether he would fill it.

He chose not to. Fair enough.

Their drinks were empty, the subject of Julia had been covered—well, not really—but just when she expected the evening to end, Luke picked up the menus and handed her one.

'I thought we were only having a drink?'

'Just a drink?' He frowned. 'At six in the evening? I don't know about you, but I'm starving. Anyway, like I said, I didn't think work was the right place for a private catch-up.' He gave a wry smile. 'Not that we've ever properly met...'

Pippa took a breath and told herself to simply let it go. She was annoyed with herself that it still hurt this much. That he couldn't remember their short conversation was a ridiculous reason to take offence, and yet she still felt slighted.

'We have met,'

'Oh?' He put his head slightly to the side. 'So you *were* on the swimming team?'

'No.' Pippa shook her head and laughed ruefully. 'You helped me choose my A-level subjects.'

Watching his eyes narrow as he tried to recall something that had meant everything to her—and clearly *only* to her—hurt so much it felt almost like a physical pain.

'We were in the library...?' she persisted.

He shook his head.

'The day you asked—' She corrected herself. 'The day you were asked to take Julia to the dance?'

* * *

Luke frowned, and not just because he was trying to place her. There was a flicker of a long-ago memory lying just beyond his reach. He hadn't wanted to take Julia to the dance; he hadn't even wanted to go himself. He'd have rather been studying. But for other reasons entirely the school dance had been the last thing on his mind that day.

He'd found out his father was cheating.

A couple of weeks away from important exams, racing home during a study period to grab his forgotten swimming gear, he'd found out that his father wasn't so perfect after all.

'*Get her out*!' he'd screamed at his father.

After the woman had gone, he'd demanded, '*Who is she?*'

'*It doesn't matter.*'

'*It doesn't* matter?' Luke had roared.

'*I mean it's nothing serious.*'

That had only enraged Luke further, and the argument that had followed had almost turned physical.

'*You've got everything!*' Luke had shouted. '*How the hell could you throw it all away?*'

'*I'm not throwing anything away,*' his father, Matthew, had said placatingly. '*Luke, you have no idea...*'

He changed tack then and followed up with, '*Your mother doesn't need to know.*'

'*I am* not *keeping this from her. Either you tell her, or I will,*' Luke had warned him.

And, grabbing his sports bag, he'd raced back to school.

His father hadn't told her, of course.

His delightfully dizzy, always vague mother had been all smiles when he'd stepped through the front door after school.

'Darling you're home...' She'd given him a kiss. *'Luke, you simply must call Julia. I know you've got homework, but no more putting it off.'*

And so he'd called Julia and asked her to the dance, but his temper had been bubbling beneath the surface the whole time. Once he'd ended the call, his disgust had returned in full force—not just at the deceit, but at the fact that his father would bring his lover into the family home.

'Don't sulk, Luke,' his mother had scolded him lightly. *'The poor girl needs something to look forward to.'*

'I'm not sulking,' he'd said, and when she'd headed into the lounge, he'd looked at his father. *'I'm going for a walk. If you haven't told her by the time I get back, then I will.'*

He'd had no idea what he'd return to.

Flashing blue lights in the driveway.

His mother being stretchered away.

Luke hadn't been able to understand how willing his mother had been to throw it all away either. He still didn't.

He'd not only sworn off marriage that day, he'd vowed that, apart from at work, he would never let anyone be that reliant on him.

Luke didn't want to return to his memories of that time—and certainly not on a Monday night in The Avery. So he looked at Pippa, who was insistent that they'd spoken in the library.

'I don't remember,' he admitted, and then got back to his charming self. 'Do you want some wine?'

'Sure,' she said quietly.

'Red, white…? Or champagne, given it's a reunion?'

Pippa was tempted to point out that it wasn't much of a reunion if one person had no memory of meeting the other, but she knew she had to let that go or nurse it in private.

That reminded her… 'I thought you wanted to talk privately…?'

'I do,' Luke agreed. '*You're* the reason I wasn't eating in the consultants' lounge.'

Pippa swallowed and frantically looked at the menu, trying to make sense of his words. Was he saying that he'd come to the ward to see *her*?

'That's why I suggested we come here. I'm sure you'd rather your colleagues don't get wind that there's anything going on between us.'

'There *isn't* anything going on between us,' Pippa said sharply.

Only when she dared to glance up he looked as unconvinced by her statement as she felt.

'Are you sure about that?' Luke checked.

His question was too direct to avoid. 'No…' Pippa admitted.

'Good,' he responded, then gestured to the menu. 'Have you chosen?'

He expected her to choose what to eat after *that*?

'The chicken Provençal.'

He screwed up his gorgeous straight nose. 'I wouldn't have that here.'

'Have you tried it?'

'No,' Luke admitted, 'but if I'm eating French then I want an arrogant French chef preparing it. There's a restaurant near me… You can hear Anton cursing in the background.'

Pippa laughed.

'And the waiters and waitresses all speak only French and pretend not to understand your attempts to communicate. I swear, it's agony…'

'It sounds dreadful.'

'Ah, but so worth it.'

'Well, I'll have the Greek lamb salad, then,' Pippa said, 'and I don't care if it's not authentic.'

Luke had steak with salad, but no chips, and ordered a bottle of red wine, which felt very decadent for a week day.

'Philadelphia was incredible,' he told her as they began to talk about work. 'I think it's the most beautiful city I've ever seen. It has its problems, of course—and that's why I went there, for the experience. I just wasn't expecting to love it so much.'

'I've never been to America,' Pippa said with a sigh. 'It's on my list. I want to go to Colorado.'

'Well, add Philadelphia to that list.'

'So, was it always the plan? To study in the States?'

'Not at all.' He topped up their glasses. 'There's no clear path for a trauma surgeon in the UK.'

'Really?'

'For post-grad qualifications you have to go to the States or South Africa.'

'Why, when there's so much trauma here?'

'Exactly! And when they get around to making a clearly defined role, I'll be ready.'

He shrugged and smiled that slightly arrogant smile that made her knees weak.

'I'm taking a break after The Primary. I'm going to the Outer Hebrides. I want to see a Scottish winter, and certainly no trauma.'

'I wouldn't be so sure. You'll be on air and sea rescue, or something.'

Luke opened his mouth to correct her—to tell Pippa that he wasn't going to Scotland to work. Nor even to avoid the agony of playing Happy Families on Christmas Day with his parents and enduring the endless questions from his mother and sister as to when he'd settle down.

No, he was getting away for a much-needed break.

While he loved his job, Luke was self-aware enough to know that he needed time away. The horror of broken, damaged bodies took its toll— he'd accepted that. But lately the hell of breaking bad news, of watching families fall apart before his eyes, had found him wondering not just about whether his patient would make it, but also, with the uphill battle ahead, would their loved ones survive…?

But he hadn't discussed it with anyone, and he wasn't about to bring the mood down now.

He looked at Pippa's soft dark curls, and though this gentleman generally *did* prefer tall, leggy blondes, he thought Pippa Westford might just be changing his mind. Even when she'd been dressed in unflattering scrubs he'd noticed that she was gorgeous, but he'd underestimated quite how much. Her dress affirmed soft curves, and her pale skin flushed easily and told him more than her guarded green eyes.

She intrigued him. There was an air of independence about her, and when combined with a certain restraint it was a stunning mixture.

Their meals arrived—including chips, instead of the salad Luke had ordered. But he didn't comment, just thanked the waiter.

'Won't you miss London?' asked Pippa.

'No.' He gave a very definite shake of his head. 'That's not to say I'm not enjoying my time here.' He looked right at her then. 'And now.'

He meant them.

This.

Here and now.

She could feel the energy between them.

Now that she knew the truth about him and her sister, she could allow herself to feel it...to look back into his velvety eyes, to enjoy him—enjoy *this*—and to feel those eyes drifting to her lips.

She looked at him. Whatever she felt here and now, he was just passing through—or rather, tying up loose ends so that he could leave.

'Isn't it nice to have a base here, though. Couldn't you rent your apartment out?'

'That's what I've been doing, but it's in a very old building and always needing maintenance. It's too much commitment—and I don't need a base here.'

'But your family—' She halted. 'Sorry, that's none of my business.'

Usually Luke would have taken up her polite offer and shut that line of conversation down. He *never* discussed his family—or at least he kept his responses to questions about them minimal and superficial.

Luke didn't even discuss family with his family...

Not any more.

'How could you, Luke?' his mother had asked two years ago.

As vague and dizzy as she'd appeared at times, she'd known all the theatre staff and all the goings-on at St Bede's, and his sister, Anna, worked there in the ED. When it had all blown up, and Shona's husband had been placed on stress leave, Hannah

Harris had looked up at her son, white with fury, but with tears in her eyes.

'I thought you of all people would know better,' she'd sneered. *'Like father, like son.'*

He'd gone to the States, and now he was back, it seemed that all was forgotten. The dust had settled.

Luke still couldn't forgive his father, though.

'It's fine,' Luke said in response to Pippa's apology. 'After all, I just asked about your family. Like you, I'd prefer not to talk about it.'

He gave her a smile that had her stomach feeling as if it were made of jelly, though not in a jiggly, fat way…more as if her insides were wobbling in response to his smile and the darkness of his eyes.

'Have a chip.' He changed the subject and pushed forward his plate. 'You know you want to.'

Pippa smiled—only it wasn't her usual smile. It was a new smile. And she knew that to be the case because there was an unfamiliar feeling of her top lip stretching, or pressing, or pouting… She honestly wasn't sure what it was doing. It was, she deduced, the smile she wore when she was sitting in The Avery with Luke and flirting.

She wasn't a flirty person.

Usually.

Yet here she was, pushing her half-empty plate forward to allow him to stab an olive. Usually Pippa didn't share her food—didn't share anything, really. Not her deep thoughts, not her emotions, and certainly not what was on her plate…

Things felt different with him.

They chatted so easily. She even told him about her tiny flat a couple of stops on the Tube from where they were.

'Is it a flat-share?'

'Gosh, no.' Pippa shook her head. 'I'm way past that.'

'How old are you?'

'Twenty-nine,' Pippa told him. 'But I gave up sharing the day I finished university. I like my own space too much. What about yours?' Pippa asked. 'Is it on the market?'

'As of today, it is. I'm hoping it will be snapped up; I really don't want to be here too long...'

'I thought people ran away *to* London?'

'Who said anything about running away?'

'No one. I...um... I...'

For the first time the conversation faltered, and she stammered over her words, but she was rescued by someone coming to clear their plates.

Luke must have noticed, because as he topped up their wine he addressed her awkwardness. 'You've heard the gossip?'

'I try not to listen, but...' Pippa flushed. 'God knows I hate it when they gossip about me.'

'About you?' His eyes widened. 'Do tell!'

'That's just it; there's nothing to tell. But because I don't drag my personal life into work they assume I'm frigid...or a lesbian...'

'An interesting combination,' he mused. 'I'd love to debunk both assumptions...'

He gave her such a wicked smile that Pippa couldn't help but laugh.

'So what have you heard about me?' he asked.

'Just the usual. I know I shouldn't listen, but it's hard not to at the moment—you're the talk of The Primary.' She pushed out a smile. 'Breaking hearts wherever you go.'

'Incorrect,' he said, shaking his head. 'I don't get overly involved with anyone and, given I make that crystal-clear from the get-go, nobody gets hurt.'

He must have seen her tiny frown, because he went on.

'That rumour you've heard about a married woman is false. For one thing, I would never get in the middle of someone's relationship.'

'And for another?' Pippa was pushing for more information because she had a burning curiosity to know him more.

'I loathe cheats.'

'Fair enough.' She took a sip of her wine.

'Are *you* seeing anyone, Pippa?'

His enquiry was direct. The preamble that had lulled her seemed to have shifted, and like a skilled interrogator he'd caught her unaware with the simplest of questions.

Pippa held her wine in her mouth, knowing her response mattered.

Yes, she wanted to say, even though it would be a complete and utter lie.

But, given what he'd just told her, it would keep the lion in its cage.

Yes, she was tempted to say, *I am seeing someone*.

Because then they would go their separate ways....

Yes, she decided to say as she swallowed her wine.

It was a single word that failed her.

'No,' Pippa responded, and shook her head. 'I'm not seeing anyone.'

'You're sure about that?' Luke checked.

Given her delay in responding, his question was merited.

'Quite sure,' Pippa said, nodding, and then added, 'I'm not brilliant at long-term relationships.'

Their eyes held and she saw the same flare she had seen there on his first day at The Primary— only she knew now that it was desire. It was at that moment when Pippa realised she might have given a false impression and made it sound as if she preferred short-term flings.

What she'd meant was that even though she wasn't good at long-term, she always went into a relationship with hope. Hope that this time things might be different...hope that she might finally be able to open up and truly be herself with another.

It had never worked out, though. Because she always felt a certain sense of threat as things turned more serious. She was coming to accept that she didn't like people getting too close. She didn't even like getting in touch with her own feelings, let alone allowing someone else in.

Last orders were called, and Pippa blinked when she saw the time—the evening had flown by.

'Excuse me a moment.'

It was a relief to escape to the loo. She stood in front of the mirror and took a breath, trying to digest what he'd said about never dating Julia.

She'd been frozen in her teenage mind where Luke and her sister were concerned, and it felt exhilarating to be freed from the misconception that her parents perpetuated even to this day.

Pippa took a shaky breath, almost feeling the years peeling away. Yes, she liked him still. Of course she did. But in a different way. Fourteen years ago her unblemished, innocent heart had believed in silver dresses and being swept away in his arms… That was all she'd dreamt of really…and perhaps a kiss…

Now, her rather bruised heart knew there was more to it.

Luke Harris was here for a month and no more. He'd made it clear so that she understood this was going nowhere. He was a player, not a partner. Pippa understood his terms.

But the trouble wasn't just keeping the lion caged. Rather, it was the lioness inside her, pawing to get out…

Pippa wanted to know true passion, and she wanted to douse the torch she still carried for Luke Harris.

But wasn't she too serious for a casual fling, though? It simply wasn't her…

And yet that heady gush of relief that he hadn't dated Julia *still* hadn't abated.

Pippa caught sight of herself in the mirror. Her hair was tousled and the grey interview dress somehow looked indecent as it clung to her breasts. Those boring army-green eyes were no more. Now they were black with unfamiliar desire...

She thought of her sister and wished she could call her and ask for advice.

But then she realised she already knew Julia's take on life.

Julia had lived her life as if it wasn't ending.

If her sister could study for straight As, knowing there was little prospect of going to university, let alone making use of the grades, then surely she could live the same way...

Julia had grabbed life and taken every opportunity she was offered—smiling and happy, seemingly carefree—squeezing every last drop out of life all the while knowing it would be over too soon.

Julia had lived her entire life without the promise of a future, she realised. Surely she, Pippa, could manage a month.

If Julia could do it...

'Then so can you,' Pippa told her reflection.

Less than a month, she amended, as she made her way back to the table, given he'd been at The Primary a full week now.

The table had been cleared, the bill paid...

'Ready?' he said, and Pippa nodded and put on her coat.

It had rained while they were in the pub. Now, cars and buses swished past, their headlights casting light tails, the beams from streetlamps highlighting the heavy drops that still fell. They stood under cover and faced each other.

'Thanks for dinner,' Pippa said. 'I had a great night.'

'It hasn't finished yet.'

He took her face in his hands and with his velvet-soft lips he kissed her…incredibly slowly.

It was everything she had ever thought it would be.

Actually, it was better—and not just because it was real.

As his tongue slipped in, she could taste the wine they had shared, only it seemed sharper and more potent, and the soft stroking of his tongue evoked a different, unfamiliar type of hunger…

Luke Harris had been her teenage dream, but now he was here, and he was kissing her, and she did not want to let the dream go.

Not just yet…

She thought of her sister—how she'd lived without fear, following her goals and passions.

And that made her brave.

Their kiss ended, but his hands were still cupping her face. She wanted to run her tongue over her lips, if only to taste him again.

'We could have a very nice month, Pippa…'

A month.

Perhaps she should feel offended that he'd named

the end date of their affair as it was only just bursting into life, but instead it sent a shiver of excitement through her.

No promises that could never be kept.

No false hope.

Just a chance to live her dream.

And no recriminations over her refusal to open up her heart.

Luke didn't want that part of her.

Wanton and emboldened, she released the lioness.

'So,' Pippa said, 'are you going to show me this flat of yours?'

CHAPTER FOUR

LONDON LOOKED ALL SHINY, as if wiped clean by the rain.

'Right you are,' said the taxi driver, when Luke gave him their destination. 'That was some storm!'

'We didn't see it,' Luke said, and turned to resume their kiss.

But the driver had other ideas. 'All the traffic lights went out and…'

He carried on talking and didn't seem to require a response.

Pippa felt all shiny too, like the city, and she was laughing at the press of Luke's hand, and the nudge of his knee, because they'd somehow landed the chattiest taxi driver in the world.

They passed St Bede's, the gorgeous old hospital with its beautiful arches, and then turned down a very narrow cobbled street. This was old, old London, Pippa thought, as Luke paid the taxi driver. His apartment building was very close to the hospital. He'd really had a whole life here, and it bemused her that he could so readily leave it all behind.

Why?

It wasn't as if he denied his reputation—indeed, he seemed at ease with it. Why would he run from some rumour he'd said was false? It didn't equate to the confident, self-assured man who now moved up the steps with her to the heavy entrance doors of the building. As he opened them up, she glanced at a row of doorbells and saw *LH* near the top.

'It's quite a climb,' Luke warned, as he led them into the foyer.

Pippa looked up at the gorgeous swirl of a circular stone staircase with polished banisters, and as she gazed higher, to the incredible domed skylight, he caught her unawares and lowered his head to kiss her throat. His mouth found hers and he guided her to the wall, never breaking the kiss for a second.

'Sustenance,' he said as his hand slid inside her coat and pulled her hips against his. 'We could have a *very* nice month,' he said again, lifting her hair and kissing the side of her neck.

'It's only three weeks,' Pippa gasped, as he pulled her so close that she could feel how turned on her was.

'Haven't you enjoyed it so far?' Luke asked, kissing her as she had secretly wanted him to.

'Yes…'

'So, a month,' he said.

But then they heard footsteps and politely parted, Luke nodding and smiling to a woman who passed them with the cutest little dachshund puppy.

'Hi, Luke,' she said as she passed.

'Hey,' he said. As she opened the door and took the little dog outside, Luke rolled his eyes at Pippa. 'Can you believe she called him Sausage?'

'It's cute.'

'She hardly put a lot of thought into—'

'I think,' Pippa suggested, 'we should go up before she gets back.'

'Agreed.'

They almost flew up the stairs in their mutual race to get to the top, but they held hands the whole way, unable to drop contact. It was as though they were tied together in some new version of a three-legged race.

Not once had she felt like this—laughing, practically running up flights of stairs just to get behind closed doors. Never had she felt so at ease at the prospect of sleeping with a man for the first time.

He opened a large dark door and as he kissed her and moved them inside he shrugged off his coat, then slowly removed Pippa's.

He showered her with kisses that made her breathless as they attempted to undress each other. The bedroom was apparently too far away and buttons were too complicated.

She felt the roughness of his unshaven chin and the probing of his tongue, and there was the ever-present thrum of demand as his kiss changed tempo and they sank to the hardwood floor.

Pippa kissed him back hard, more passionately than she'd thought herself capable of, lost for a moment in the bliss of him. His hands were parting her dress, pulling at her opaque tights, and she lifted her hips with the same urgency his hands communicated. It was Pippa who was pulling her tights and knickers down as he slipped a condom on. She attempted to pull off her boots, but they were too desperate for intimate contact to negotiate even that.

'Ow!' he said as her closed knees pressed into his stomach, but neither of them cared.

'Yes...' she moaned as he pulled her hips down onto him and ground into her. 'Oh, my...'

She must have the female equivalent of premature ejaculation, she thought, because she was starting to come. Not that it mattered; Luke was more than ready to reciprocate.

Her hands were flat on his chest, and she was enjoying the delicious sight of Luke coming. One breast was exposed, her tights were wound like a lasso around her thighs, and he was still inside her...

She was panting, stunned at her own body's rapid response. His hand was on her red cheek as she now attempted to gulp in air.

'Bed,' Luke said, in a voice that told her they'd only just started.

CHAPTER FIVE

'Morning,' Luke said lazily as his phone bleeped them awake. At least, it had bleeped him awake. Perhaps used to being summoned immediately, he propelled himself to sit up. 'Do you have to be at work?'

'No…' Pippa, still half dozing, tried to peel her eyes open, then remembered she'd fallen asleep in her contact lenses and promptly closed them. 'I'm not back till tomorrow.'

'So you're off today?' he asked, already up and out of bed.

'Mmm…although I've got—'

She stopped herself from telling him about her interview this morning. Because this interview, even if she was trying to play it down to herself, was the most important of her life.

She wanted this job.

It was everything she wanted in her career.

So it didn't make for good idle conversation with a new lover.

Pippa had thought about telling him about the interview. Simply because he was wise. It was an odd thing, to stare at a self-confessed playboy who was just passing through and think about how wise he was.

But he was the one who had talked about how he didn't like to get involved. Surely that kind of conversation would be the definition of *involved*?

Talking about the interview would also mean mentioning Julia, and she couldn't do that without crying.

Which would not be a good look at six a.m. after their first night together.

'Got what?' Luke persisted, with a yawn.

'Places I need to be.'

Her response was evasive—the perfect casual lover reply. She peeled her itchy eyes open and wished for twenty/twenty vision, because the sight of a naked Luke stretching and yawning was one she'd rather not have missed!

'Were you in the army?' she asked.

'No—why?'

'I've never seen anyone get up so fast.'

'If I hit snooze…' He shook his head. 'It's a dangerous path. Especially as I've got seven a.m. ward rounds,' he added 'Coffee?' he offered.

'Please.' Pippa nodded as he wrapped a towel around his waist before striding into the lounge. 'Two sugars!' she called to his departing and very attractive back. 'White.'

Sitting up, she shivered and pulled at the throw blanket placed over the headboard. She wrapped it around her bare shoulders, then blinked as the world according to Luke came into focus.

She looked at the rumpled bed with its navy sheets and pillows that she hadn't really noticed last night. Then she gazed at the polished hardwood floors, whose beauty was hidden beneath too many scattered rugs, then up to the very high ceiling, with its cornices and intricate central ceiling rose spoilt by a surprisingly modern light. Above the very beautiful and rather neglected fireplace was a very large print of two buses in Oxford Street; it seemed a rather odd choice for a bedroom.

'Awful, isn't it?' Luke said as he came back into the bedroom with two mugs. 'The estate agent's handiwork, to cover some bumps in the walls. Did you see the one he put up in the lounge?'

'I wasn't really paying attention,' Pippa said, laughing. 'You could dress up the fireplace instead of covering up the walls,' she added. She looked at the huge windows, and then up again at the ceiling. 'And a chandelier in here would be nice.'

'In a bedroom?'

'A small one.' Pippa nodded her thanks as he handed her a mug.

'Sorry, I don't have any milk.'

'It's fine,' Pippa said. 'Your flat is even colder than mine.'

'I've put the heating on, though it takes for ever. I'm meant to leave it on all day.'

'Why?'

'Potential buyers,' he said, sighing. 'Not my idea…' He looked at her and smiled. 'That blanket you're wearing is for display purposes only.'

'Oh? And there I was thinking how thoughtful you were,' Pippa teased. Taking a sip of her coffee, she screwed up her nose and placed it on the bedside table, deciding to stop at her favourite coffee shop on the way home. 'I'm going to get going,' she said.

'Have a shower?' he offered. 'I'm going to.'

He gave her a smile that invited her to join him, but all her bravado from last night seemed to have left.

'I'll wait till I'm home.'

'Pity,' he said.

Pippa bit her lip. She wanted to ask when they might see each other again, but didn't want to sound needy.

So, instead of making a complete fool of herself by asking, or following him into the shower as she'd *really* like to, Pippa got dressed, and was just putting in some fresh contact lenses, which she always kept in her purse, just in case, when he came out.

'I don't sleep in them usually,' Pippa told him, trying to ignore his big, damp body as he hastily dried it. 'I'd really better get going.'

'Pippa!' He called her back. 'I'm on call for the next few nights, and I don't know how busy I'm going to be. I might not be the best company for a while.'

'It's fine.'

'Come on, Pip, give me your number.'

He'd called her that again, not noticing the press of her lips as he took out his phone.

She couldn't quite believe she'd slept with someone who didn't even know her phone number.

But she knew that was the game she'd signed up for, Pippa thought as they exchanged contact details, and she shook it off as she closed the door of his flat behind her.

And she knew something else—something she dared not admit…

She'd only ever have dared to play this game with him.

Pippa wished she'd taken Nola up on her offer of a mock interview, because the real one wasn't going very well.

'Philippa?'

She'd been introduced to a panel of three people.

'Pippa Westford,' she had said, shaking hands with the formidable trio.

One, Miss Brett, had been the manager of a hospice Pippa had once worked at, although clearly she didn't recall Pippa, because despite her initial correction she kept calling her Philippa.

Pippa had intended to wear the grey dress, but after last night it needed a trip to the dry cleaner's, so she wore a navy suit and low heels instead. She had straightened her wild hair and put it up and, while she knew she looked smart, she feared she didn't sound it!

The first part had been okay…*ish*. Pippa had been given an imagined scenario: an anorexic thirteen-year-old who had taken an overdose but was too acutely unwell to be admitted to Psych—or rather to the new eating disorder unit that would be opening in the new wing.

It had all gone downhill from there.

She'd been expecting a question about how she dealt with conflict, but instead of asking about conflicts with patients or parents, they'd just asked about conflict between colleagues.

'I generally get on well with my colleagues,' Pippa responded, and then kicked herself, because it was a pretty poor effort. 'I always try to see the other side.'

'But as Unit Manager you won't be able to sit on the fence,' Miss Brett pointed out.

Later, she would blame it on lack of sleep, or the night spent with Luke, but she knew that would just be making excuses.

'What do you think you can bring to the PAC Unit, Philippa?'

'Well, I've worked in a lot of different areas. Not just on general wards—I've worked on Oncology, in a hospice, as well as on a renal unit.'

'Yes…' One of the trust directors looked at her sternly. 'You've moved around quite a bit.'

'I have,' Pippa agreed, hearing the slight barb behind the words.

It was true; she had moved around rather a lot. A year here, eighteen months there, two years now at The Primary…

'I'm very happy at The Primary. I just feel…' Her voice trailed off.

She'd been so logical in making the decision to apply, but logic seemed to have gone out of the window since Luke's return. Old wounds were resurfacing, and an interview wasn't the place to rip off the plaster and express the raw feelings that were churning inside her. 'I think that my experience, though varied, is all appropriate for the PAC Unit.'

'What would you like to achieve?'

This one Pippa *had* prepared for!

'A higher-level management role, eventually, but—'

'I meant for the PAC Unit,' Miss Brett said, and Pippa realised she'd misunderstood the question. 'What goals would you set for the PAC Unit?'

Pippa stumbled through the rest of the interview and knew she'd done dreadfully, though it was all pleasant handshakes and 'Thank you for your time,' when it concluded.

As Pippa made her way down the corridor to head for home, she saw Nola.

'How did it go?'

'Awful.' Pippa rolled her eyes. 'There's a reason I didn't want to tell anyone I was applying. I flunked it.'

'Don't worry,' Nola said kindly. 'I won't breathe a word.'

Pippa didn't believe her for a moment.

The day only went downhill from there.

Luke didn't so much as text.

Rather than waiting for him to call, Pippa kept busy, and even went over to her parents' house— something she'd been putting off.

'I thought you'd be here earlier,' her mother reprimanded as soon as she came in. 'It's been ages since you've been to the cemetery.'

'I might try and go in the week,' Pippa said as she took off her coat. 'Hi, Dad.' She gave him a kiss. 'Or on my birthday.'

'That's weeks away.'

'It's two weeks away. I'm on an early shift,' she ventured, just in case they were planning anything.

Sure, Pippa thought wryly. *As if they would.*

Birthdays were practically a *verboten* subject, and Christmas remained a teary affair.

And even though Pippa was trying not to think about Luke, even at her parents' there was no chance of escape, because there on the mantelpiece was that photo of Julia and Luke, staring back at her.

'You'll never guess who's working at The Primary,' Pippa began.

'Who?' her mother asked.

Yet even as she opened her mouth to respond, she glanced at the picture and knew it would upset them. 'Miss Brett. I worked with her at the hospice.'

Her mother stared at her blankly.

'Briefly,' Pippa amended. 'She was the manager there. She's one of the big bosses at the hospital now. I had an interview today and she was on the panel.'

'That's nice.'

Conversation with her parents felt like hitting the 'Print' button, knowing full well that the printer was switched off, or out of paper, or not within range.

There was no enquiry as to how her interview had gone, let alone any interest in what it might have been for.

Just the usual, 'That's nice.'

Thank goodness she had the excuse of having to leave to get to her art class. She stopped on the way and brought wine, as well as some crackers and cheese, and she felt the familiar relief as she stepped in to the studio.

The same relief she'd felt in the art room at school.

Tonight it was open studio time, and although Pippa had intended to work on her charcoal sketching she found herself mixing oils instead, with the wine and cheese forgotten. She was soon absorbed.

'What are you working on, Pippa?' asked her teacher, Cassie.

'Light beams.' Pippa looked at her effort, thinking back to last night, and how the car lights had reflected on the wet streets, but also how she'd felt as she stepped into the adventure. 'I can't seem to capture them, though...'

The same way she could never capture Luke.

Pippa knew better than to dream, or even try to hold on to him. It would be easier to hold light in her hand.

She didn't regret their night together, even if she wasn't usually that bold or effervescent.

She was, Pippa knew, too serious by far.

A little dreary, even.

Yet last night she'd felt golden and bright and, yes, for the first time, a little radiant, and she wanted more of the same…

As the teacher guided her to blur the lines, to be bolder with her strokes, Pippa watched her work start to come alive.

'Just have fun with it!' Cassie suggested playfully, and moved on to the next student.

Pippa looked at the shimmering lines she'd created, proud of her work, and took a breath, replaying Cassie's words but with Luke in mind…

'Just have fun with it…'

CHAPTER SIX

PIPPA WOKE UP the next morning annoyed that not only was she thinking of Luke, she had even dreamt of him!

And that was *so* not Pippa.

It hadn't been a sexy dream, or anything like that... In truth, as she took the Tube to work, Pippa couldn't really remember what it had been about. She simply wasn't used to having another person so constantly in her thoughts.

And while last night she'd felt emboldened as she'd painted, now she was back to wondering if she had what it took for a casual fling.

It was all very well to 'just have fun with it', but Pippa knew she still needed to guard her heart.

She stopped for her regular coffee and chatted to the barista while it was being made.

'We had a food truck on the river for Diwali last night,' Rohan explained as he made her milky brew. 'You know—the festival of light.'

'One of the mums at work told me about it.' Pippa nodded. 'I should go and have a look.'

'Do,' Rohan agreed, putting the lid on her coffee. 'They're lighting up the London Eye in the colours of the Rangoli tonight.'

'Sounds wonderful. I will go!' Pippa said, collecting her drink and dashing off, because she really didn't want to be late for work.

Very deliberately she didn't pause to look at the

brand-new extension. She was still disappointed at how the interview had gone yesterday. Even though her ward would be moving into the new wing, it was the PAC Unit that she wanted, and she was certain she'd blown it.

Oh, why hadn't she asked Nola for help in preparing?

She was mulling over that, rather than Luke, as she walked down the corridor, overheating in her long scarf, when she heard his voice.

'Excuse me, have you lost an electron?'

Pippa laughed. 'That really is the worst line. And I know I'm not positively attractive this morning.'

'Me neither.'

Pippa chose not to debate the point—he was wearing navy scrubs and had a theatre cap tied on, and he was looking incredibly sexy.

'What did you get up to last night?' he asked.

'I had my art class,' Pippa said. 'Well, *class* might be stretching it a bit. Really it's a weekly "Paint and Sip…"' He frowned, but there wasn't time to elaborate, and anyway she wasn't sure how to play this. 'I'm late…'

'Not too late to stop for coffee,' he pointed out.

'They know my usual order,' she said, and couldn't help adding, 'And they always have milk!'

Instead of responding to her little jibe he said, 'Can I steal it?'

'Not a chance.'

'Seriously… I'm dead on my feet. Just a few

ward rounds and then I'm crashing—hopefully until tomorrow.'

'Busy night?'

'Yes.' He nodded, but didn't elaborate, because his pager went off then—and not just his pager, but the overhead chimes too, asking for the trauma team to come to ED. 'Damn,' Luke said, looking at his pager. 'Multi-trauma on its way.'

It was a horrible time to be called—just before the pagers had been handed over to the day team—but it happened all too often.

'Here,' she said, handing over her precious brew, then rolled her eyes at herself as he took it and sped off.

Honestly, there wasn't anyone else she'd have done that for.

Not that he could ever know that, Pippa told herself, determined to keep things light between them, to be the woman she'd hoped to be—the one who grabbed life...

She walked on to the children's ward, and had barely taken off her scarf before Jenny chimed up. 'So, you've applied for the Unit Manager position on the PAC?'

So much for Nola's discretion. Pippa just rolled her eyes again and headed to the kitchen to make a horrible cup of the hospital's instant coffee, still surprised she'd given her own away—even to Luke.

Thank God Pippa had given him her coffee.

It was warm, sickly sweet, and nothing like the

strong black he preferred, but it was incredibly welcome after a long night that wasn't even about to end soon, judging by the alerts coming in regarding a major RTA—Road Traffic Accident.

Fiona arrived, breathless from her run through the hospital, just as May, the ED Nurse Manager, was giving a briefing, giving the staff the latest update from the scene.

The accident was on the A4, and although there were other hospitals closer, some casualties were being flown in by helicopter or driven with lights and sirens to The Primary, which was a major trauma centre and covered a vast area.

'There are eight casualties in total; we're accepting three.' May held up three fingers to the gathered teams. 'First one's a traumatic chest. Med flight eight minutes. Gino's got him.'

Luke knew there were teams already at the helipad. Gino, one of the senior surgeons from the first on team for the day, would take care of this young man from one of vehicles, though as the patient was wheeled into Resus, Luke could see he didn't look good.

'Go and assist,' Luke told Fiona—and not just because they were short-staffed. Fiona needed the experience, and David, Luke's registrar, had just arrived.

A second patient was rushed past, screaming for her children. She had a displaced hip and, from what Luke could see, a nasty lower leg fracture.

The emergency team took over her care and then

May pointed to Luke as he drained the last of Pippa's coffee. 'Four-year-old male, multi-trauma, unconscious. ETA five minutes. I'll go and meet him.'

As she went to meet the patient Luke began checking drugs as the nursing team set up for a paediatric trauma patient. Remi, the anaesthetist, was selecting various-sized endotracheal tubes, preparing for all possibilities.

When he came, it was clear that the patient was small. It was the first thing Luke noticed as the paramedics wheeled the stretcher in—as well as the fact he'd already been intubated at the scene.

'Darcy!' The paramedic said the child's name very specifically, and soon Luke understood why. 'Identical twin...'

The grim features of the paramedics and trauma team told Luke that what they'd seen had been upsetting. He didn't ask about the other twin, deliberately keeping his focus solely on the patient he had.

'He's four?' Luke checked. The information was important for drug doses and such.

'No, turned five last week,' he was told by the paramedic.

A doctor who'd happened to be on the scene described the life-saving procedures that had been performed. 'Hypovolemic shock, became bradycardic...cardiac massage commenced, then intubated.'

His pyjamas had been cut open, revealing a skinny frame and a distended abdomen which Luke palpated and then percussed, tapping it and eliciting

dull sounds that indicated fluid. When the anaesthetist confirmed the airway inserted on scene was
patent and secured, the boy was carefully rolled
and examined. Luke made the decision to get him
straight to CT, and if that wasn't clear then up to
Theatre.

'Is CT ready for him?' he called out to May, who
came in then. 'Or is the other patient still...?'

'It's clear,' she said, and shook her head.

When Fiona appeared, coming to assist him,
Luke knew the young man must have died.

'They're ready,' May said. 'I've let them know
you're on your way.'

They were indeed waiting, and soon images were
coming through that, mercifully, showed no sign
of serious head injury. But his torso had taken the
blunt force, and he had a ruptured spleen and a lac-
erated kidney; this little boy needed Theatre now.

'Let's get him straight up,' Luke said, and saw
that May had now joined them, carrying paperwork
and a phone. 'Was that the mother in the ED?'

'Yes. They've had to sedate her.' May briefed
him as they walked at pace through the corridors.
'They're reducing her hip in the ED.'

'What about the father?'

'He's coming from Heathrow. They'd just
dropped him off there.' She grimaced.

'Can someone try and get him on the line for
me? If I can get verbal consent...?'

'I've got the father on hold now—Mr Williams,'
May said, but before she handed him the phone she

brought him up to speed, 'Identical twins,' she informed Luke, in case he didn't already know.

'I'm aware.'

'Just check for any identifying features. Best to confirm we've got the right twin. The mother was hysterical on scene. The other little boy's still trapped.' Luke said nothing, just listened as May spoke on. 'The father's first name is Evan; the wife is Amber. Darcy's twin brother is called Hamish.'

Poor man, Luke thought, and took a steadying breath before taking the phone as he walked up to theatre.

'Mr Williams,' he said, introducing himself, but he didn't get any further.

'The police are bringing me there now. We're fifteen minutes away,' the panicked man said. 'Is there any chance I can see Darcy before you operate?'

'I'm sorry, no. I can't wait.' Luke was firm in his decision and he listed the boy's injuries. 'Every moment is vital. Now, Mr Williams, before you give your consent, we need to be as sure as we can that we have the right twin.'

Mr Williams was clearly used to the question, and as Luke put the telephone on speaker he said, 'Darcy has a strawberry birthmark behind his left ear.'

May halted the trolley and did the brief check. 'He does,' Luke said.

But after Mr Williams had given consent he started to break down. Unfortunately there wasn't even time for that.

'The anaesthetist wants to have a brief word.'

He handed the phone to the Remi, whom he'd been working with a lot these past few days. She was an elegant redhead, and she spoke calmly to the man. 'So he has asthma?' she checked and then asked if he'd ever been intubated before.

'I'm going to be with your son,' Remi assured the father. 'I'm not leaving his side.'

She was very, very kind as she told the anguished father she had a daughter the same age.

Then, 'You can tell him that yourself,' Remi said. 'He's intubated, so he can't respond, but I'll put the phone to his ear. Your daddy's on the phone, Darcy...'

Luke was so grateful for Remi. He could not bring any emotion into Theatre, and snapped his focus to the operation ahead. He always felt great responsibility when operating, but especially when it was a child. Knowing the child's father wasn't even here, Luke felt the trust placed in him fall heavy on his shoulders this morning.

Remi feels it too, Luke thought, looking thoughtful as she spoke with the rest of the theatre staff while he raced ahead to scrub in. She remained close to the little boy, stroking his hair and talking to him.

'Where's David?' he asked, when Fiona arrived alone.

'Still in Emergency,' Fiona said, and he could hear the slight trembling in her voice. 'A fourth patient was brought in. They only got notified last-minute.'

'You'll be fine,' Luke said reassuringly.

He was such a small fellow, Luke thought as Darcy was moved over. His ribs were visible. But the thing that twisted Luke was his little knees, one with a bruise and the other covered with a plaster. Though they were quickly covered by green theatre drapes, it was that brief glimpse of a normal little boy who must have recently tripped and fallen that got to Luke. And then there was the thought of a father racing across the city to get to his son...

He couldn't think of that now.

Very deliberately, he hadn't asked for any updates on the other twin. He simply wouldn't allow emotion into the operating room, but he was grateful that his anaesthetist did.

'Daddy's coming,' Remi told the boy, over and over, and, even though he was now under anaesthetic, she was still stroking the little boy's dark hair and reassuring him. 'And Mummy's here at the hospital.'

How he needed his upcoming break, Luke thought. It was getting more difficult with each passing day to push emotion aside and focus on the job.

'Let's start.' He glanced at the scrub nurse. 'Good to see you.'

They'd done a couple of cases together before, and he knew she was excellent, but apart from the brief greeting he said little. Gone were the days when he'd chatted at work, or spoken easily with the other staff.

Well, with one exception... But there was no space in his mind for anyone other than Darcy Williams right now.

'Splenectomy,' he said, as soon as the abdomen was open. What he saw confirmed his decision to remove the spleen, because it looked as if it was beyond saving, and any attempt to do so would take precious time from the other injuries. 'Perforated bowel.'

He surveyed the damage with a practised eye and was so grateful for his time in Philadelphia and the lessons passed on to him there—the main one by Carl, the chief under whom he'd worked: *'Do what you have to, then what you can...'*

Fiona did an incredible job—the whole team did.

David, his registrar, was already with his patient when Luke got to Recovery—the unexpected fourth arrival.

'Motorcyclist,' David explained. 'Looked like minor injuries at the scene but, given the mechanics of the injury, the paramedics brought him in.'

He went through the motorcyclist's injuries and the surgery that had been performed with Luke, and as David went to speak with the man's family, Luke made his way to a separate waiting room.

It was this part that he was finding increasingly difficult.

He gave it his all in Theatre, but lately, when dealing with a family, he tended to adopt a polite, professional distance, telling himself it was his surgical skills they required, not his personal ones.

Luke knocked on the closed door and went in.

Given that his wife and children had just dropped Mr Williams off at the airport, Luke had expected a businessman around his own age, in a suit, but instead an incredibly young-looking man dressed in a high-vis vest was pacing anxiously.

'Mr Williams?'

'Evan,' the man said. 'Is it bad news?'

'Darcy's in Recovery,' Luke told him straight away. 'Shall we sit?' he suggested as the young man almost dropped in relief. 'Soon we'll be moving him to the ICU.'

'Is he awake?'

'The anaesthetist did rouse him briefly at the end of his surgery, but we're going to be keeping him sedated for the next few days. However, he responded appropriately, fighting the tube and moving all his limbs. That's good news,' he added, and then carefully he went through the boy's injuries, both the good and the bad. 'He doesn't appear to have any serious head injuries,' he finished.

'He was unconscious, though. They said his heart stopped!'

'His heart didn't stop. It slowed to a dangerous level because he'd lost a lot of blood,' Luke explained. 'I had to remove his spleen.' He saw the father wince, then bury his face in his hands as Luke mentioned the bruised kidney. 'In Theatre, we found a small perforation to his bowel. It closed nicely. We've avoided a colostomy.'

Mr Williams swallowed air a few times. 'What about his legs?'

'His legs are fine.'

'Someone said…' He pressed his fingers into his eyes. 'No, I'm getting mixed up.'

'Your wife has leg injuries.'

'I know, but…'

Mr Williams was clearly overloaded with information.

'Darcy has a couple of old bruises on his knees. I saw a plaster on one,' Luke said, and watched the father's mouth stretch into a pale smile.

'He loves plasters.'

The bad news hadn't ended yet.

'Darcy's had to have a lot of blood. We're still transfusing him.' He didn't want to overwhelm the father, but the volume of the blood transfused was of great concern. 'While he desperately needs the blood, we need to monitor him very closely in case he runs into complications.' Luke decided that was enough for now. 'You should be able to see him before he's moved to the ICU.' Then he asked the question he'd been avoiding prior to operating. 'Have you heard how your other son is—Hamish?'

'He's in Intensive Care at St Bede's.'

'Okay.' Luke took that in. 'Do you know any more than that?'

'He's awake, but they're talking about sedating

him.' Urgent eyes looked to Luke. 'I don't know where I should be.'

'Would you like me to call St Bede's and find out what I can?'

'Please.' He nodded. 'I was at work…'

Luke found out that Evan was an aircraft cleaner at Heathrow and had been just starting his shift when the news had hit.

'Amber drops me off at six. We have to wake the boys…put them in the car in their pyjamas… You think you're doing the right thing… They'd have been safer in bed.'

Luke had heard similar words many times from loved ones. Had they done the right thing? He'd asked the same question of himself over and over after his mother's emotional collapse. He'd insisted his father tell her about the affair…had been so certain he was right.

It was one of the reasons he found offering personal advice to families difficult. He always second-guessed himself.

'Let me find out what I can,' he said now.

Luke headed back into Recovery and checked in on the little boy, and from there he called St Bede's to find out what he could about his brother.

He was quickly transferred to the ICU.

'Sister Adams.'

'Shona.' Luke was too tired to care who it was on the other end of the line. 'I'm calling about Hamish Williams.'

'You've got his brother, I hear?'

'Correct,' Luke said. 'He's about to be moved to the ICU.' He went through the injuries and prognosis. 'Still too early to say—he's had a lot of blood.'

'DIC?' Shona asked, knowing that there could be serious issues with coagulation.

'I hope not,' Luke said. 'How's Hamish doing?'

'The main injury is a small subdural haematoma,' Shona informed him. That was a small bleed into Hamish's brain. 'He's conscious, but restless. They're talking about sedating him. Horace is with him now. I can get him to speak with you?'

'Don't pull him away,' Luke said, pleased that Hamish was under the care of such a brilliant neurosurgeon. 'I really just want to know what to tell the father. If he's needed more here or there.'

'Give me a moment. I'll see what I can find out.'

'Thanks.'

It was a long moment.

Luke didn't like Shona. In fact, he actively disliked her. But he knew she was good at her job, and very thorough, and would be speaking with Horace now. Professionally speaking, he trusted her.

He could hear the sounds of the ICU at St Bede's, and familiar voices in the background. It felt odd to be miles away...

Shona returned to the phone. 'I've spoken to Horace. He thinks having Dad here might help settle Hamish, and at least he can be there as they sedate him.'

'Thanks,' Luke said. 'I'll let the father know.'

Without further ceremony he ended the call and headed back to Mr Williams.

'Okay.' Luke stayed standing while talking this time. 'I've spoken with St Bede's and I think it would be a great comfort to Hamish for him to have you there.'

'I see.'

It was clear Evan Williams was torn. 'The staff here will call you if there is any change, but for now Darcy's as stable as he can be.'

'So you think I should head there?'

'I do,' Luke said, knowing there was no easy answer. 'See Darcy before you leave, but then head over.'

'What about Amber? If she's awake she'll be frantic.'

'I'll go down there now and talk to her if I can. Or let the ED staff know what's happening so they can inform her when she's awake.' It did sound as if St Bede's really did want the father there. 'You go and be with Hamish.'

As the theatre nurse led Mr Williams in to see his son, Luke made his way to Emergency and updated Mrs Williams, who was awake but said little. Her face was pale with shock and pain, and she was clearly terrified for her sons. 'I need to see them.'

'I know,' Luke said. But she was about to go to theatre to have her lower leg pinned. 'It's simply not possible yet. Evan will soon be with Hamish, and Darcy is sedated.'

He came away from the grim conversation and saw the flushed face of May.

'There's a debriefing for all the personnel involved in the RTA at two.'

'I'll hopefully be asleep by then.'

'There's another one at eight for the night staff.'

'And I'll hopefully *still* be asleep then,' Luke responded.

But May tutted. 'You ought to go.'

'Are you going?'

'I have a deaf husband,' May chuckled. 'He knows when to nod and when to shake his head.'

Luke smiled, and then headed up to deal with the patients he'd been about to see before his pager had gone off, who were no doubt still waiting for him.

Luke's patients were indeed waiting for him, but Pippa knew he would come when he could.

'Where *is* Mr Harris?'

Mrs James was up at the nurses' station and agitated. She'd been hoping to take Chloe home, but there had been no early-morning ward round.

'He's still in Theatre,' Jenny said. 'It might be a while.'

'You said that two hours ago. How much longer is he going to be?'

Jenny shrugged and walked off, and although Mrs James was being prickly, Pippa knew it wasn't without reason. She was exhausted, Pippa could see that, and on top of a sick child she had a new baby at home and other concerns too—such as how she

was going to manage her usually active and demanding daughter, who really needed to have a
very quiet few weeks.

'There were several emergencies brought in this
morning,' Pippa explained.

She knew about the multi-trauma not only from
being with Luke when he was paged, but because it
had been on the news during her break. She didn't
go into any sort of detail with Mrs James, though,
just explained things as best she could.

'The operating theatres are really busy. I know
it's frustrating, but emergencies have to come first.'

'I know they do.' Mrs James closed her eyes.
'They were talking about taking Chloe to Theatre
at one point.'

While Mrs James clearly irked Jenny, she didn't
bother Pippa. In fact, she thought it nice that the
woman was so worried about her daughter and her
little baby, and how to juggle her young family.

Had it been the same for her own mother when
she'd been born?

Pippa had spent a lot of time at her aunt's house…
A lot.

She knew how delays and emergencies upended
so many things in a hospital, and even if it was true
that emergencies had to take priority, it still caused
inconvenience and upset.

'He's not going to recognise me,' Mrs James said
with a sigh.

'George?' Pippa checked, referring to Chloe's
new brother.

'I wanted to breastfeed, but that's starting to fall by the wayside.'

'Whether it's today or in a couple of days' time, you'll soon be home,' Pippa said.

But she knew getting Chloe discharged from hospital wasn't the only problem Mrs James faced.

'How am I going to keep her amused? I know she's a bit spoilt, but we thought we were just having the one child. She's already a bit jealous of the new baby.'

'I'll get the doctor to speak to her, and I'll talk to her too.' Pippa paused when she saw Luke and Fiona arriving. 'Here he is now.'

As Mrs James went to sit with her daughter, Luke and Fiona came to the desk. They both looked pretty grim—understandably so, given they had been on call all night and then operating this morning. With the added emergencies they must be dead on their feet.

'How's the child from this morning?' Pippa asked him.

'On the ICU,' Luke said, but didn't elaborate. Instead, he looked over to Fiona, who looked as white as he looked grey. 'Why don't you go and grab some lunch?' he suggested. 'And could you get me something to eat and a coffee?'

'I was going to go to the…' She paused. 'Sure.'

Fiona walked off, no doubt exhausted, and it was then that Luke pulled a face.

'Damn, she probably wants to go to the debriefing.' He brought his attention back to his patients. 'What do you have for me?'

'Just the one. Chloe James.'

'How's she been?'

'Bored. Mum's worried about her following directions at home.' Pippa smiled at Jenny as she came over with a drug sheet for Luke to sign. 'We're just about to go and see Chloe.'

'Well, remind her mum she's not the only one on the ward,' Jenny said. 'And that it's the NHS. We don't have private chefs!'

Luke didn't know exactly what Jenny meant, but guessed that Chloe wasn't happy with the food. He'd expected, perhaps, for Pippa to roll her eyes, for her to ignore Jenny's statement and simply get on, but instead Pippa turned around and looked straight at her colleague.

'Give her a break,' Pippa told Jenny.

Jenny said nothing, just took the chart, and then they went in to see Chloe.

'Take your earmuffs off, Chloe,' Mrs James said as they walked in to the small side ward.

'Sorry for the delay,' he said.

'Where have you been?' whined Chloe.

'Busy,' Luke said. 'How are you?'

'Better!' Chloe said. 'I want to go home.'

'Then let me take a look at you. You've been eating?'

'I had a takeaway last night.'

Luke turned sharply to Pippa. 'I specifically instructed that she was to be on a low-fat diet.'

'She didn't like the dinner,' Mrs James hurriedly explained.

But Luke shook his head. 'I don't want her eating takeaway. Not until she's been seen in Outpatients.'

'But we're getting pizza tonight,' Chloe protested.

'Do you want to go home?' he asked.

'Yes.'

'Okay, then let's take a look at you.'

Having examined her, he sat on the chair by her bed. Pippa could almost feel his weariness, but he smiled at the little girl and her mother.

'Chloe will need to come in to the clinic in two weeks' time.'

'Can she go to school next week?'

'No school until we see her at the clinic, and then it will be a modified return.'

'What does "modified" mean?' Chloe asked.

'No sport for a while,' Luke said.

Now might not be the right time to tell her she wouldn't be able to go out at playtime for a little while yet, so he qualified his words.

'Or anything like that. We'll talk about it at your Outpatients appointment. I need to have a private word with your mother, but first I want you to listen to me. You are going to have to do everything your mother says for the next few weeks and eat what she gives you. No takeaway, no pizza. Just plain food.'

She pulled a face.

'It's very important, Chloe. If you don't, I'll find

out at the clinic and tell your mum that there's to be no Disney.'

'No!'

'Yes,' he said. 'That injury in your tummy is getting better every day, but I don't want you falling or getting knocked over and having to come back here. This is very important.'

'Okay…'

'You've had a nasty knock and I don't want you climbing or playing roughly with anyone for a while. No jumping up and down on the bed or the sofa. You might be bored, but you can manage that for a couple of weeks, can't you?'

Chloe gave a reluctant nod.

'I'll see you in the clinic, then, unless I hear from your mother before.'

He hoped he was stern, but kind, and knew the clinic appointment in two weeks would take a lot of pressure off Chloe's exhausted mother.

He spoke to Mrs James outside the ward and told her to use his name as a threat as much as she liked. 'If she wants to play, or eat something unsuitable, tell her you're going to call me, or that you already have and that I've said no. Mrs James, this isn't a punishment. This is about her recovery from a serious injury.'

'Yes, I understand.' She closed her eyes. 'Thank you for everything.'

'My pleasure. I'll see both in two weeks. Take very good care.'

They shook hands, but before Pippa could follow Mrs James back into the side ward, he looked over to her.

'Nurse, can I have a quick word?'

'Sure.' She smiled at Mrs James. 'I'll be in with you in a moment.'

Pippa and Luke stood by the linen trolley, which was hardly private, but it would look as if they were just discussing work.

'Thanks for the coffee, earlier,' he said.

'My pleasure,' she said, and smiled begrudgingly. 'Sort of.'

'Well, it was much appreciated.'

'It sounds as if it was pretty grim…'

'Yep. Poor kid. He had this plaster on his knee…'

And even though he halted, Pippa understood exactly what he meant.

'It's the little things,' she ventured. 'They get to you sometimes.'

Luke said nothing, but he gave a small, weary nod.

He looked at her then. 'It seems a long time since that night.'

Pippa gave a soft, slightly ironic laugh. It felt like an *eternity*, and while she knew he'd been impossibly busy, they'd parted without any promises or plans and she hated the uncertainty.

'I think tonight's a write-off,' Luke said. 'I'll see, but…'

He'd see?

Had he not been so obviously dead on his feet,

Pippa would have shot back a smart retort. Thankfully, he was saved from seeing her pursed lips, because Fiona returned, with a paper bag containing food and a large coffee for her boss.

'Thanks.'

'Do you want me to go to Surg One?' Fiona offered. 'Start the paperwork on the discharges?'

'No,' he said, shaking his head. 'I'll do it. You head off to the debriefing,'

'What about you?'

'I don't need a debrief. I didn't work on the fatality.' Luke shrugged. 'I'll see you tomorrow, Fiona. Thanks for your help—especially in Theatre this morning. You did an incredible job. It was touch and go for a while.'

Pippa had watched the exchange, and as Fiona walked off she saw him pull a face as he opened up the bag and pulled out a Scotch egg and a bag of crisps.

'And I tell the patients not to eat junk!'

'Do as say, not as I do.' Pippa smiled, but it wavered. She could see his mind was elsewhere. 'Nola said there were young twins involved,' Pippa ventured. 'Have you heard how the other one is?'

'I've been focussing on the patient I had.' Luke's response was a touch curt, but then he seemed to check himself. 'The other twin has a head injury. His father's in a taxi on his way to him at St Bede's now. I believe the mother's on her way to Theatre.'

'Gosh...'

'Hopefully they're all going to make a full recovery.' He took a bite of Scotch egg. 'Unlike my arteries.'

'You prefer health food?'

'Not really. I just prefer my eggs not to be wrapped in sausage meat and deep-fried!' He shook his head, and then managed a half-wave as he went to walk off. 'Ignore me. It's been a long night…'

Luke couldn't ignore his thoughts of Pippa, though.

He woke late in the evening in a bed that held the subtle scent of summer on a dark wintery evening. He thought about calling her, but knew he wouldn't be great company tonight.

Instead, he returned a call from his father.

'You called?' Luke said curtly, because when his mother wasn't around they were still barely talking.

'Good to hear from you,' Matthew Harris said, in the cheery voice that indicated he was at home. 'Your mother wants to talk about our fortieth anniversary.'

'You're not serious,' Luke replied.

'I know it's a way off,' Matthew carried on cheerfully, as if his son wasn't sending daggers down the phone, 'but we want you to pencil in the date. Hold on a moment…'

Luke lay there, looking at a ceiling that needed painting.

'Your mother wants to know when you're coming over.'

'I'll call her,' Luke said. 'It's pretty full on at The Primary.'

'Well, you insisted on crossing to the other side,' his father quipped. 'I heard you got the brunt of that multi-trauma.'

'Yep.'

'We had a couple admitted…'

Luke said nothing in response. He didn't want updates—especially if the news wasn't good.

His father broke the silence. 'So, what are you up to?'

'I'm about to have something to eat and then go back to sleep. I'm back on tomorrow at seven.'

'Come over,' Matthew suggested.

'And go through the guest list for your party?' Luke asked, with more than an edge to his tone, because he knew his mother would insist on his father's colleagues being invited. Who knew whether his latest mistress would be amongst them? 'I don't think so.'

'I meant,' Matthew said, 'come and have some supper. Your mother's about to go into her studio to paint. We can talk…'

'I thought you didn't want to discuss things.'

'I meant come over and get the hospital out of your head for a bit. You know what they say—all work and no play…'

'Don't,' Luke warned, because he did not need one of his father's little pep talks.

And yet behind the jovial tone he knew that, despite appearances, certain patients did get to his father and he was trying to connect. Luke just didn't want to hear it tonight.

'I'm going back to sleep. Tell Mum I'll call her soon.'

Luke ended the call and tossed the phone onto the mattress. He was still furious with his father—he simply did not get why a man who had everything would risk it all.

No, he didn't get it.

He tried to get back to sleep, but the scent of summer was still on his pillow and in this instance his father was right. All work and no play did make one dull, Luke thought, and came up with his usual solution as he pulled up Pippa's number. He wanted food, and sex, though when he thought of the night they had spent together, possibly not in that order...

'Hey,' he said when she answered. 'I just woke up.' He glanced at the time and saw that it was almost nine. 'I know it's a bit late.'

'It's fine,' Pippa said, though he could barely hear her. 'What do you want?'

'You,' Luke said, because usually it was that easy. 'And food.'

'Then you'd better get dressed.'

Only then did he hear the music in the background. 'Where are you?'

'Thanks, Rohan.' Pippa took two paper plates piled with scented dahl and roti bread and handed one to her late guest.

It was all very well being bright and spontaneous, but Pippa knew boundaries were urgently required if she was to hold on to her heart.

Determined not to be sitting at home if he called, Pippa had made herself go out. As Rohan had said, the Diwali atmosphere was incredible, and whether or not Luke called, Pippa was glad to have come out and seen it.

'You two know each other?' Luke checked as they walked to the river's edge, because he'd seen Pippa had bypassed quite a queue to get their food.

'Rohan works at the coffee shop I use,' she explained. 'That's his father's truck.'

They stood, looking at the London Eye, all lit up in a rainbow of colours that meant good luck and prosperity. They dipped hot roti into fragrant dahl, but all too soon his bread was gone.

Pippa still had a decent bit left, and he eyed it hungrily. 'I'm starving, Pippa…'

'Then line up,' she said, and popped the last piece of roti in her mouth.

They dropped their plates into a bin and then got back to enjoying the music and the lights.

'Any interest in the apartment?' she asked.

'No idea,' Luke said. 'Given that I'd hoped to be in bed, I told them no viewings today. How was your day?'

'It was all right,' Pippa said, even though for the most part it had been difficult. But she was determined not to get into all that.

And this was why, she told herself. Because with his arm around her, watching the lanterns bobbing on the Thames, she was as happy as she knew how to be.

She'd lit one for Julia, before Luke had arrived.

Not that she'd tell him that.

But now she stared at the lights and knew that hers was out there.

'You're freezing,' he said, and turned her to face him.

'I've been here since sunset.' She thought for a moment. 'Luke, I know what you said the other day, but I don't want anyone at work knowing about…' she gave a casual shrug '…this.'

'They won't hear it from me.'

'Good.'

'You don't want them knowing about your wild side?' he asked.

'Something like that,' Pippa said, and then she told him what she'd decided. 'But don't think I'm on call for you, Luke. I won't be waiting by the phone, and nor will I be at your beck and call.'

Luke turned her to face him and looked at her properly. She looked far from wild.

Pippa wore a grey woolly hat, and the curls escaping it were soft from the damp air. Her scarf was double-wrapped, and he ached to unravel it and expose her pale neck. But there would be time for that later.

Right now, it was nice to take in the night and this woman who had dragged him from his bed to civilisation.

The lights from the river and above their heads were reflected in her pale cheeks, and the wind was making her eyes glassy. And, while he would have liked to still those chattering lips with a kiss, instead he took her frozen hands and placed then beneath his coat and pulled her in.

'You're right,' he agreed. 'And I wouldn't expect you to be on call for me,' he said.

He had enjoyed getting out this evening, slightly to his surprise, and it also occurred to him that it felt good to be back in London…

Pippa closed her eyes and held on to his warmth. When she opened them, she saw all the lanterns and smiled. She felt like an imposter in the body of a woman who knew how to let loose and be happy…

She rested her head on his chest, hearing the thump-thump of his heart and blinking back sudden tears as she saw the lanterns floating out of view.

She never cried.

She definitely wasn't about to start now.

Thankfully, he made her smile instead.

'The heating is on at mine,' he said into the shell of her pale, cold ear. 'Come on,' he told her, taking her hand and leading her through the happy crowds.

But Pippa halted him.

'Do you have milk?'

'We can get some on the way.'

He didn't call it home.

Yet.

Ah, but London had her ways…

CHAPTER SEVEN

THEY WERE GOING to be late.

'Go!' Pippa said as she came out of the shower, watching as Luke hastily attempted to make the bed. 'I'll do it. You have to be at work by seven.'

'I do,' he agreed, selecting a tie from his wardrobe and putting up his shirt collar. 'So hurry up and get dressed.'

Pippa shook her head. 'I can take the Tube. I don't have to be there until half-past.'

'Or is it that you don't want to be seen arriving with me.'

'Both,' Pippa openly agreed.

Only her words clearly didn't offend him, because rather than picking up his keys and heading out he crossed the bedroom towards her.

It had been a week since that night at The Avery.

And even without her contacts in Luke in the morning was a very nice sight indeed.

'You haven't shaved,' Pippa said, not because he was close enough for her to see it, but because his farewell kiss was rough and probing and his hand was moving to the knot on her towel.

'When is there time to shave?'

'Go!' Pippa said, even though she'd rather not be the sensible one.

'You're bad for me, Pippa,' he said, reluctantly releasing her.

'I think it's the other way round!' Pippa joked as he walked out through the door.

Or rather, he was by far too good for her, Pippa thought as she heard his footsteps fade on the stairs.

She didn't mean that he was too good for her in a self-deprecating way—more that this week had been the best she'd ever known.

And not just making love—though there had been plenty of that in their busy schedules. As well as the evening they spent at the Diwali celebrations, they'd crammed in a candlelit concert in a gorgeous cathedral, and just last night, though she'd been on a late shift, they'd taken his neighbour's puppy for a walk.

'How did we get roped into this?' Luke had asked as the puppy had sat and refused either to wee or walk. 'It's your fault!'

Pippa had not been able to resist patting Sausage one day in the corridor, and the next thing they knew Luke had been lumbered with feeding it and walking it.

Finally the puppy had weed, and he'd picked it up and carried it home. Then they'd let the puppy back into its owner's apartment.

'"It's just this once",' Pippa had said, mimicking the owner's voice, as they'd given Sausage his necessary treats and then placed him in his crate. 'Mind you,' she'd added as they'd left, 'that's how it starts…'

'And that's how it ends,' Luke had said, posting

the keys through the letterbox, clearly refusing to get embroiled.

He had said he didn't like to get involved, and if she'd needed any further proof then this was it.

Now, instead of making the bed, Pippa sat on it. She kept a strip of contact lenses at his flat now, and she popped a fresh pair in. The room certainly looked clearer, and her eyes landed on a couple of packing boxes neatly stacked in the corner, under the large, ugly painting the estate agent had chosen to draw attention away from the bumpy wall.

The bedroom felt silent without their easy chatter—yes, easy, because they didn't really touch on anything deep. Luke refused to bring his work home with him, and neither of them spoke much about family. Occasionally they touched on the past—a teacher they'd both had, or a person they recalled—but nothing too weighty.

And, given they weren't looking to the future, she didn't tell him of her surprise that she'd been called back for a second interview; nor did he mention his upcoming job in Scotland or whatever lay beyond that.

They were happily suspended in the now.

But in the peace and quiet of the morning there was too much space for the thoughts that Pippa had been trying to ignore.

In a couple of weeks Luke would be gone.

You got through it once before, Pippa reminded herself.

Yet she'd been sixteen then, and hadn't known his kiss, let alone anything else.

Now she knew how it felt to touch him, to have him on her and in her... How behind that rather brusque demeanour he was still the guy she'd met that day in the library...

He still had a piece of her heart, and Pippa was doing all she could not to let it show.

'We're expecting an admission from the ICU,' the night sister informed the day staff. 'Darcy Williams, five years old.'

'From the multi-trauma?' Pippa checked.

She nodded. 'Splenectomy, contusion on left kidney, perforated bowel and concussion. He was extubated forty-eight hours ago. GCS thirteen to fifteen.'

The Glasgow Coma Scale was a score given to measure the severity or worsening of a brain injury, and fifteen was the best score, so Darcy was doing well.

'He's opening his eyes, though mainly to verbal command, but he's barely talking. His mother was admitted here, but she's being discharged today. His identical twin was taken to another trauma centre.'

'What about the father?'

'Running in between hospitals, apparently.'

'When should we expect Darcy?'

'I've told them we won't have a side room until lunchtime.' Laura raised her hands skywards. 'But they want to send him up before that.'

'Just tell them we're not ready,' a grumpy Jenny snapped, but thankfully Nola stepped in.

'Pippa, can you see about moving Room Four up to the main ward? She's due for discharge.'

It became a dance of the beds, because Mrs Williams had a serious leg injury, and Room Four was the smallest, so it would be difficult for her to move around in there alongside her son's bed when she visited. But finally Room Seven was ready and waiting, meds and breakfasts had been given, and Jenny was feeding Toby at the desk because his parents weren't in yet.

'Hi, Luke,' Nola said as he came up to the desk.

'Is my admission here?' he asked.

'Not yet.' Nola called over to Pippa. 'Go and have your break before he gets here.'

'Sure…'

As Luke went to check on his other patients Pippa made a mug of—horrible—coffee and found Fiona sitting in the break room.

'Is Darcy here?' she asked. 'The ICU admission?'

'Not yet.' Pippa shook her head. 'They'll buzz if he arrives—that's why I'm on my break.'

It was actually a relief to be away from the ward while Luke was on it. Pippa still felt a blush creeping up when he was around, and he wasn't quite as discreet as her. He often pulled her aside, more than willing to chat or even discuss their evening plans, when Pippa would have preferred things to stay strictly professional at work and to be kept private between them.

'Have you heard how the other twin is?' Pippa asked.

'He's doing well.' Fiona nodded. 'They're talking about moving him to the neuro ward. I've asked Luke about transferring him here.'

'And?'

'He says it's not my decision,' Fiona responded tartly. 'Easy enough for him to say when he's not the one dealing with the parents.'

Pippa said nothing.

'He's brilliant in Theatre,' Fiona elaborated to her silent audience. 'And I know you have to have a certain ruthlessness to do his job. But still, a little sensitivity outside the operating room wouldn't go amiss.'

Still Pippa said nothing. Okay, Luke wasn't all jokes and small talk—and, yes, he was strict with his orders. But it was always with the patient's best interests in mind.

Still, Fiona hadn't quite finished, and now she was giving a dramatic eyeroll. 'He's always been like that…'

'Like what?'

'Straight on to the next one…' She raised her eyebrows meaningfully. 'And not just with his patients.'

Pippa left Fiona to it and returned from her break early. Darcy still hadn't arrived, and Luke was looking at X-rays, his phone tucked into his neck. He was sounding less than impressed.

'Seriously?' Luke's voice was impatient as he spoke into the phone. 'How am I supposed to manage that when I have ward rounds at seven?' He shook his head impatiently. 'Let me get back to you…'

'Trouble?' Nola asked.

'Apparently so.' He sighed, pocketing his phone, and then, perhaps seeing Pippa appear, he asked Nola, 'Do you make your bed in the morning?'

'Of course,' Nola said.

'Jenny?'

'I was in the army,' Jenny answered. 'So yes.'

'And do you tidy the bathroom? Wipe down the shower?'

She nodded.

Then he glanced over at Pippa, who must surely have gone as red as a beetroot.

'Pippa,' he asked, 'do you make your bed in the morning?'

'Of course,' she croaked, knowing full well what he was referring to. Not only had she not made the bed this morning, she'd dressed in a hurry and left his bathroom in morning chaos.

'*Every* morning?' he checked, and she looked up to see his incredulous smile.

'If I'm on night duty, yes,' Pippa amended. 'If I'm on a late, sometimes…'

'What about if you're on an early?'

'That depends.' Pippa shook her head and refused to flirt, but both of them knew they were discussing this morning.

'Well, I've just been told by my estate agent that if I want people brought round while I'm at work I'm to leave my flat inspection-ready.'

'Obviously,' Jenny said.

'I got the golden package. I thought they'd at least—'

'You thought the estate agent would dash around and do a quick tidy?' Jenny harumphed as she walked off. 'Oh, no...'

Luke waited till Pippa was in the drug room and then wagged a finger as he walked in. 'What happened to "I'll do it"?' he quoted back her own words.

'I lost track of time,' Pippa admitted, but instead of telling him she'd been sitting on the bed, thinking how impossible it would be to say goodbye to him, she came up with something lighter. 'I was looking at your walls.'

'My walls?'

'Yes, they need wallpaper. But if you don't have time for that then, like I said, you should dress up the fireplaces rather than put ugly prints on the wall.'

'Says the would-be interior designer? I'll leave it to the experts, thanks.'

'It's okay, Luke,' Pippa said with a smirk, seeing his slight look of horror, as if his latest squeeze had told him she was thinking of moving in. 'I'm not hoping for a trip to IKEA with you, or to pick out bedspreads. I just love old buildings.'

'Luke,' Jenny called. 'Your ICU transfer's here.'

'Thanks.'

Pippa went too, as she had been assigned to care for little Darcy. His father was with him, and he and Luke were clearly on first-name terms.

'Hi, Evan,' Luke said, and then went over to his little patient. 'Hey, Darcy. You're looking even better than you did this morning,'

Dark, solemn grey eyes looked briefly at Luke and then flicked away.

He was recovering well from his dreadful injuries, Pippa heard from the ICU nurse who gave hand-over.

'Luke has said he can start on sips of water, but so far he's refusing. He's really quiet, which is apparently unusual for him. He's barely spoken, except a couple of times to ask for his mum.'

'She's being discharged this morning?' Pippa checked.

'Yes. You know he has an identical twin?'

'I do.'

'They're arranging transport so Mum can visit Hamish, then she'll come here. Darcy hasn't asked for his brother or anything, which Dad says is also unusual. He's really withdrawn.'

Evan, the twins' father, walked over then, and thanked the ICU nurse for her care. When she'd left he spoke to Pippa.

'My wife and I are going to take it in turns to stay with Darcy, but Amber's got a fractured leg.'

'Yes, we've put Darcy in the biggest side room, so that we can put a recliner in there for her, as well as a bed.' She glanced into the side room and saw the anaesthetist had also arrived to assess Darcy, and there was quite a crowd in there now. 'I'll show you the facilities.'

'Thanks.'

Pippa took Evan round and showed him the parents' room and the small kitchenette, as well as the shower and bathroom. 'How's Hamish doing?' she asked.

'Better than Darcy,' Evan said with a relieved sigh. 'He's off the ventilator and talking. A little bit confused… I'm crossing my fingers that he can be transferred here. I've asked Mr Harris if he can look into it, but I haven't heard yet whether it's possible…'

Darcy was indeed very subdued, his eyes barely tracking as Pippa did his obs late that afternoon, though he did look up when Luke came into the room.

'How are you feeling, Darcy?'

He didn't answer, just turned his head away.

'Who's this?' Pippa asked, tickling the face of the scruffy and clearly much-loved teddy Darcy had tucked under his arm.

'That's Whiskers.' Evan spoke for his silent son.

'Does Hamish have a bear?' Pippa asked as she

checked the various drips. Out of the corner of her eye she saw Darcy stir.

'Coco,' Darcy whispered.

'And is Coco with Hamish now?' Pippa asked.

And even though it was Evan who answered, he was clearly pleased at the one-word response from his son.

'Yes. Amber told me to fetch them the day after the accident. The boys hide them when their friends come to play.'

'You hide them?' Pippa gave Darcy a shocked look, then smiled at the little boy. 'I hide my teddy too. Mind you, I'm a lot older than you...'

But Darcy wasn't engaging any longer. He just closed his eyes and held on to his bear and lay there listlessly as he was examined.

'Try and get him to take some fluids,' Luke told Evan, moving away from the bedside.

'He's not really interested.'

'The drip is keeping him hydrated,' Luke explained, 'but if you can encourage him to drink it will aid his recovery.'

Soon it became a bit of an issue.

Unlike little Chloe, who had been begging to drink and to eat, Darcy continued to show no interest in food or fluids.

'He wants his brother,' Nola said to Luke late the next afternoon. 'Can't you speak to Allocations?'

'It has nothing to do with Allocations,' Luke responded tartly. 'His brother is on a top neuro ward and really wouldn't benefit from an ambulance ride across town.' He glanced over as Jenny called his name. 'Yes?'

'Martha wants to speak with you,' she said, gesturing with her head towards the office.

'Sure.'

But as he stood Evan Williams made his way over to ask again if there was any chance of his other son being transferred.

'It would just make things easier all around,' the harried father said. 'And I know it would cheer Darcy up.'

'I do understand where you're coming from,' Luke said.

Pippa was feeding a baby at the desk, so she was able to listen as he explained the situation a little more gently to the father.

'By all accounts Hamish is doing well, but he's had a serious bleed on the brain and he needs to be closely monitored. I don't think a transfer right now is in his best interests. He's where he needs to be.'

'I know he is…' Evan ran a tired hand over his forehead. 'Darcy wants me to take Hamish his bear. I told Darcy he needs it for now, and that Hamish has Coco with him.'

'Probably wise,' Luke said.

No! Pippa glanced up, wanting to intervene. If Darcy wanted Hamish to have *his* bear, then that was probably the right thing.

But Nola was in on the conversation now, and was agreeing with both Luke and Evan. As well as that, the social worker had arrived and Martha, the paediatrician, was at the desk. It wasn't Pippa's place, especially in front of Mr Williams, to disagree.

As they all moved into the NUM's office to discuss things, Pippa not only wanted the PAC Unit job more than ever, she knew she was right for it. Knew she was ready to have more of a voice.

'Luke?' she said as soon as he stepped out of the meeting.

'What?' He was tense and distracted. 'I'm waiting for a consult from Mr Benson. Can you fetch me the moment he calls?'

'Sure,' Pippa said.

'In the meantime, ask Toby's parents to come through to the NUM's office.'

Pippa nodded, but she was frowning, because Toby wasn't his patient.

Then she saw Jenny, standing by the cot, making small talk with the parents—which was unusual for Jenny. It was clear to Pippa that she wasn't letting the baby out of her sight.

Nola came out then, and briefly brought Pippa up to speed: some rather worrying information had come to light regarding Toby.

The social worker wasn't here about Darcy and Hamish, Pippa realised. The moment to talk about teddies and on whose bed they belonged had passed.

CHAPTER EIGHT

EVEN BEFORE SIX in the morning it was already her happiest birthday ever.

Although Luke didn't know that he'd just made love to a thirty-year-old!

Pippa lay facing the wall, with Luke spooning her, both relishing the aftershocks of early-morning sex. The alarm hadn't even gone off yet.

'Sorry to wake you,' he said.

'You can wake me like that every morning!'

Pippa smiled to herself, but it soon faded as she realised there wouldn't be many more mornings like this.

Still, if this was how it felt to be thirty, Pippa thought, then bring it on!

She hadn't told Luke that today was her birthday, and it wasn't just because they were keeping things light. She never made a big deal out of it.

Nor did her parents.

There would be a card with some cash in it waiting for her the next time she called in. Still, given it was a milestone birthday perhaps she hoped they might call and ask her to come over. Surprise her with cake...

Pippa was aware that birthdays were extremely painful for them. Her own eighteenth and twenty-first had barely been mentioned, and on what would have been Julia's thirtieth, her mother had been in bits.

Pippa closed her eyes, trying not to recall the tears and drama and return to the blissful floaty feeling of being wrapped in Luke's arms, feeling safe and warm on a cold late-November day.

Even the alarm didn't intrude on the pleasure, because Luke uncoiled himself from her and turned it off. Instead of rolling straight out of bed, as was his usual practice, he turned on her electric blanket topper, turned onto his back and pulled her into him.

'There is an advantage to staying at yours…' he said.

'Because we don't have to make the bed and tidy up?'

'Well, there's that,' he agreed. 'I meant it's closer to work. We don't have to rush.'

'True.'

There was even time for tea and toast, topped with ginger marmalade from the night market they'd been to earlier in the week. It was fiery and spicy and the perfect winter breakfast.

They were now both 'two toothbrush households'—something he'd said drily when, having first ended up back at hers, morning had broken and there'd been no time for him to go home and wash and change before work. Thankfully, Pippa had found him a spare toothbrush, and now he brushed his teeth at her place with a neon pink one. At his, Pippa had the spare toothbrush from the goody-bag from his flight home from the States.

They weren't yet 'two deodorant households'. So it was Luke's turn to smell of baby powder for the day. Fair enough, given that for most of this week Pippa's usual scent of summer had been rather drowned out by some kind of twenty-four-hour-lasting concoction for 'active men'.

Luke even had a couple of shirts hanging in her wardrobe, still in their plastic from the dry-cleaning service, and as he ripped open one of the covers, Luke couldn't help but think how he usually used the lack of a fresh shirt or a toothbrush or whatever as a good reason to head off early, or even leave in the middle of the night.

Not now.

When Pippa had said she needed to pick up her dry-cleaning, it had prompted him to throw a few clean shirts into the car.

It just made things easier.

Or rather, it made things a little more complicated than he was used to… But then, he reasoned, their affair would be so short-lived that it wouldn't matter. It was good to spend as much time as they had together rather than shuffling back and forth.

He looked at Pippa, lying in bed watching him and wearing a sleepy smile.

'The blanket's warming up,' she said, with all the temptation of a practised seductress.

'That's not fair,' he said, knowing she was naked and warm beneath the sheets. For the first time ever he was considering being late for rounds. 'Have you got your contacts in?'

'No.' She smiled.

'Pity…'

'I'm not blind!' Pippa laughed, and looked down at how turned on he was, and then back up to his face. 'You know you want to…'

He resisted temptation—but with a proviso. 'I should be able to get off at a reasonable time tonight,' he said. 'Maybe we could—'

'I'm not sure I can tonight,' Pippa interrupted. 'I'll let you know.'

'I'm on call tomorrow night,' he reminded her.

It wasn't like Luke to push, but he was getting to the pointy end of his contract and time was fading fast. He'd also had to put a deposit down for a cottage he'd found…

'I've found a nice place in Scotland… Skye,' he told her. 'A stone cottage, with peat fires in both the bedroom and lounge.'

'Estate-agent-speak for freezing,' Pippa said with authority. 'Does it have hot water?'

'I assume so.'

'Never assume.'

'You can take a look tonight,' Luke said.

And then he halted—not just because she'd said she might have plans, but because in recent days he'd been thinking of asking if she would join him for a couple of weeks in Scotland. He'd never done anything like that with another woman.

'Or whenever,' he amended, pulling on his suit jacket and trying to quash the thought of spoiling things by suggesting they extend their arrangement.

'You can make sure I won't be fetching my water from a well…'

Pippa gave him a thin smile, deciding she definitely would *not* be helping him choose the accommodation that would be enjoyed by his next lover…

When he'd left, she checked her phone, hoping for a birthday message—then reminded herself it wasn't even seven yet. Her parents would barely be awake.

They still hadn't messaged when Pippa checked her phone later that morning, when she was on her break.

She didn't get to go to lunch until late, because Darcy threw up in a major way. Evan had gone with Amber to visit Hamish, and Darcy was teary, so Pippa changed his bedding while Laura went to page Fiona to come and check on him.

'It's okay, Darcy,' Pippa told him, when he was tucked up in a clean bed with his teddy. 'Mummy will be back soon.'

'I'll stay with him,' Laura said, coming back into the room. 'Fiona's going to come when she can.'

Eating her cheese sandwich, Pippa went through her messages, but although a couple of friends had texted, as well as her aunt, there was nothing from her parents.

Pippa was more angry than hurt.

Or was she more hurt than angry?

She honestly didn't know how she felt as she headed back to the ward.

Evan was back from visiting his other son, but Amber was staying with Hamish for now.

Fiona had come to see Darcy.

'How's that tummy?' she asked as she gently probed Darcy's stomach.

But Darcy didn't answer her. Instead, he looked over to the more familiar face of Pippa. 'Where's Hamish?'

'He's being looked after in another hospital,' Pippa told the little boy, as she had many times before. 'Darcy, the doctor wants to know if your tummy's sore.'

Darcy just turned his little head and carried on staring out at the grey afternoon.

'Is he drinking anything?' asked Fiona.

'Just small sips,' Pippa said, 'and only with a lot of encouragement.'

'So just the one vomit?' Fiona checked, and Pippa nodded. 'I might speak to David…'

'Thanks.'

It was Luke who came to check on the patient later in the afternoon, but there were no clinical changes.

'I'm going to call the anaesthetist and ask her to come and do a pain review,' he told Pippa. 'And I'll increase his IV fluids. He's very listless.'

Luke was more than aware that he was the bad guy here. Especially as there was an empty twin-bedded room that had opened up on the paediatric ward.

Darcy wanted his twin!

As he sat at the desk checking labs, Nola pointed it out to him. .

'So I've repeatedly been told,' Luke snapped.

By several of the staff, by the bed allocations team, and by Darcy's father, who had just brought Amber back to be with Darcy and was now peering into the spare two-bed room…

Luke was well aware of the impact on the family, and had even touched on the prospect of a transfer with Horace. For now, though, both had chosen to err on the side of caution and agreed that, for the time being, it was better that each twin stay where he was.

'Delivery for Pippa Westford.'

Luke glanced up at the delivery man and saw a huge potted plant that surely belonged in some retro musical land on the edge of the nurses' station.

'Good grief,' Nola said when she saw it. 'Who's that for?'

'Pippa,' Jenny said. She peered at the little white card and took it off the plastic stick.

'Jenny!' Nola warned.

'It's stuck down with a heart.' Jenny said, and sighed. She went to put it back, though not quite in time, because Pippa emerged from the office. 'This came for you,' Jenny said.

'Do tell me who it's from,' Pippa said rather pointedly as she took the card from Jenny. But instead of opening it, she pocketed it in her scrubs.

'Who sent it?' Jenny asked.

'I'll find out when I get home,' Pippa retorted,

and then looked at the large plant, now taking up a lot of the desk. 'When the two of us get home. Heavens, look at the size of it!'

She stashed it in the office temporarily, and then headed into the drug room.

Luke worried that he was turning into Nosy Jenny, because he was dying to know what was in the envelope.

He was more than used to women and the games they played. A lover had once sent flowers to herself, pretending they were from an ex, in an attempt to make him jealous and nudge him to commit.

It hadn't worked.

This plant, though, must be a triffid. Because even though it had been put away, he could still see its shiny leaves, waving from the office door.

And, given how little time they had left, it niggled him that Pippa had been so vague about her plans tonight.

As her shift was about to end, he caved in and headed to the drug room.

'Your secret lover has terrible taste,' he said, when he found her.

Pippa laughed. 'My aunt sends me a plant every year. I don't know why she doesn't send it to my flat.' She glanced over. 'Don't tell Jenny who it's from.'

'Wait—it's your birthday?' he checked, and did a quick mental calculation, because if she'd been two years below him at school… 'Your thirtieth?'

'Don't remind me.'

'But why didn't you say anything?'

'I just didn't.' Pippa shrugged.

'So what are you up to?'

'I'm catching up with friends at the weekend.'

'But what about tonight?'

'Luke, I really don't make a fuss about birthdays.'

'Maybe *I* want to make a fuss.' He came a little closer than he usually would at work and named the very nice French restaurant just a short walk from his flat.

'I really don't need—' Pippa started, but then she took out her phone and saw that there was *still* no message from her parents. Hell, she wanted to celebrate her birthday—and for once there was actually someone who wanted to celebrate it too. 'I'd like that,' Pippa said.

'What about your plans?' Luke checked.

'They've changed.' Pippa smiled.

'Brilliant. Should I book it for seven?' he asked. 'I should be finished here in an hour or so.' He checked his pager. 'Maybe two. It might be better to meet there…'

'Sounds great.'

It really did.

It was the first birthday she'd dared even hope to celebrate like this, and she was rushing as she pulled off her scrubs and changed into jeans, her head full of what on earth to wear, wondering if she had time to hit the shops…

'Drama, drama!' Jenny said as she came into the changing room. 'Shona just called and asked to speak to Luke.'

'Who?'

'That ICU nurse from St Bede's.'

'You've lost me.'

'Shona—the one he had the affair with.'

'That's just gossip.'

'Oh, no, it's not,' Jenny said, pulling on the vast jumper she'd knitted. 'Fiona told me all about it. She caught them in the break room herself. Shona must have heard he's back in London. You should have seen Luke's face when I told him who was on the phone, asking to speak with him privately.'

Privately?

Pippa felt her heart sink—but then reminded herself how much she loathed gossip. And anyway, Luke had said himself that the rumours were false.

'He asked to take the call in Nola's office,' Jenny elaborated. 'His face was like thunder.'

Sure enough, she could see Luke on the phone in the office. The blinds weren't closed and, even though she tried not to look, Pippa could see the tension in his shoulders as he stood with his back to the ward, his hand raking through his dark hair.

'Told you!' Jenny said, clearly delighted with her gossip. 'Go in and get your plant. You might hear—'

'I've got to dash,' Pippa interrupted, unsure whether she was refusing to engage in gossip, or burying her head in the sand, or just selfish, because she wanted one perfect birthday with this man she had liked for far too long...

She decided she would leave the enormous plant at work overnight, so she could make it to the shops. In the end, she found a lovely lilac dress that was so soft she thought it was wool—but she looked at the label and saw it was silk.

And then she saw the price. Even though it was in the sale, it was still out of her league.

But then she was already playing way out of her league...

Yes, there was a fair chance Luke had looked her in the eye and lied about his past, but Pippa knew she too had been lying all along...pretending she belonged in a world of casual lovers and passion that came with no strings attached.

'Try it on,' the assistant suggested.

Perhaps she should have walked away in The Avery, or should walk away even now, yet she found herself in a cubicle, stripping down to her underwear and pulling the dress on over her head.

It was—unfortunately for her credit card—perfect.

She angled her head in the mirror, hoping she'd look dreadful from behind. But no, it was as if a thousand magical mice had been working on the gown all night.

It wasn't really a gown, but it made her think of Julia, in her silver ballgown, heading out for one fabulous night...

Well, Pippa would have one fabulous birthday!

Back in her flat, Pippa decided she would go all-out tonight and make a real effort.

She put loads of product in her hair, then hung her head upside down and tackled the diffuser. It took for ever, and even then her thick dark hair wasn't completely dry, but she was running out of time.

Pippa put on some make-up, as well as the fabulous underwear that she'd added to her purchase—and even stockings, heels and dangly earrings...

When she checked her reflection she worried that it was too much, and didn't suit her.

Because this night mattered more than any other ever had...

'Madame...' the greeter said, and smiled when she gave her name and then said something in French.

It took a second's delay to work out that he'd asked for her coat. Pippa handed it over and then was shown to a reserved table. A little unsure, she ordered a glass of red wine, but he stared at her blankly, so Pippa dragged out her schoolgirl French.

Her wine came with a little silver dish of nibbles.

The garlicky, herby scent was making her stomach rumble. She looked at the other couples there, and the pair of elderly ladies who were laughing as they went out for a cigarette.

The waiter was back, brandishing the wine bottle.

'No, I'm fine,' Pippa said. *'Non, merci,'* she corrected herself.

And only then did it enter her head that Luke might not be coming.

He wouldn't stand her up on her birthday, would he?

Unless something had come up at the hospital…?

But then surely he could have fired off a quick text?

No, he was a trauma surgeon, Pippa reminded herself. He was hardly going to ask one of the staff to message her; she was the one who had insisted on discretion after all…

There were so many arguments taking place in her head. She wanted to trust him, to believe it was nothing more than work delaying him. But the voice she had been trying to ignore chimed up a little more loudly.

Had the call from his ex derailed his plans for the night?

Finally, there came a text, and it felt as if every pair of eyes in the restaurant were on her as she read it.

Sorry. Talk later.

An apology, but no explanation.

Still, it told Pippa enough, and she signalled for the waiter.

'Could I have the bill, please?' He gave her a non-plussed look. 'You know exactly what I mean,' Pippa snapped, and to the waiter's credit he gave her a little smile, then headed off to fetch a velvet folder.

Pippa paid for the *extremely* expensive glass of red wine, and even added a tip because—well, she was burning with embarrassment.

No, it wasn't embarrassment. It was the disappearance of hope that *one* birthday, just one…

It was a long taxi ride home, with a thankfully quiet driver.

Behind closed doors, she peeled off her shoes and stockings and washed off all her make-up, then donned an over-sized T-shirt. She poured herself a far cheaper glass of wine than she'd had in the restaurant and moved her heated blanket from the bedroom to the sofa and curled up under it.

This was supposed to be fun —and yet it was starting to hurt.

It was close to ten when there was a knock at the door and Pippa knew it was Luke. She was tempted not to open it, but she knew that would be petty.

'Hey,' she said, trying to pretend it didn't really matter.

'I'm so sorry, Pippa, for leaving you stranded on your birthday.'

'Hardly stranded,' Pippa said as she let him in. 'I've been stood up in worse places.'

But then she saw his tense expression and watched as he sat on the couch, picked up her glass and took a drink.

'I got a call from St Bede's.'

'Shona?' Pippa nodded, refusing to skirt the issue. 'Jenny told me.'

'She's working on the ICU now.' He frowned, but then dismissed whatever thought he'd just had. 'Hamish collapsed.'

'Hamish?' Pippa felt a jolt of panic dart through her, but she remained perfectly still. 'You mean Darcy's twin?'

Luke nodded. 'Evan was already on his way to visit, and I had to go and tell Amber that he'd taken a sudden turn for the worse.'

'Oh, my God.'

'Amber was frantic. She didn't know what was happening. And, what with them being identical twins, she wanted me to check on Darcy—bloods, infection…'

Pippa nodded. It had been days since the accident, though, and hopefully the boys hadn't been brewing any infection or unknowingly sharing an undiagnosed condition. Of course it was vital to check, and only right that the doctors would be concerned for the healthier twin.

'Did you find anything?'

'No. Nothing related. It would seem that Hamish's brain bleed had extended.'

Pippa swallowed.

'I heard an hour or so ago that he'd died.'

She watched Luke put his head in his hands and felt goosebumps prickle her arms and even her bare legs as she stood there in nothing but her T-shirt.

She was helpless, waiting for Luke to correct himself, to say it had been a mistake, for the world to go back to a more correct order.

Luke must have noted her complete lack of response because he lifted his head. 'Are you okay?'

'I don't know,' Pippa admitted, a little stunned to see his face streaked with tears.

She took a seat on the couch beside him. She felt shaken up inside, but kept her breathing steady. 'Who's with Darcy?'

'An uncle or a cousin arrived to sit with him just as I left, although Darcy was asleep.'

'He knew,' Pippa said through pale lips. 'Darcy knew something was wrong…'

'Pippa—'

'He did.' Pippa was insistent. 'When Julia took a turn for the worse I felt ill all day at school.' She let out a sliver of her hurt. 'No one thought to call me to come home and say goodbye. I found out when I got back from school.' She looked over. 'It needs to be his parents who tell him—not his uncle.' Pippa's voice was urgent. 'My aunt was the one who told me and—'

'Pippa,' he interrupted. 'I'm sure Amber and Evan will tell him together; they just don't want him to be on his own tonight…' He frowned at her pallid face. 'I'm sorry to bring bad news.'

He took her hand, and although she wanted to cling to it, Pippa was scared by her own devastation and the dreadful memories it was unleashing.

She wasn't used to sharing her grief, and surely Luke, who was already clearly upset, didn't need his short-term lover to crumple emotionally.

'How was Amber?' Pippa asked.

'I told her well away from Darcy; Nola brought her into the office. I've had to give bad news to a lot of parents, but this one's really got to me.' He took a shaky breath and wiped his cheeks. 'Looks as if I'm like my father after all…'

'Meaning?'

'He's come home upset a couple of times. You'd never have guessed if you only knew him at work. I came downstairs once and found him crying. It scared the life out of me.'

'What did you do?'

'Offered to get my mother…' He looked over. 'She paints too…'

It was an odd moment for Luke.

To be sitting with the woman he realised he needed tonight.

And, while Pippa wasn't exactly effusive, she wasn't shut away in her studio like his mother. Instead, she sat beside him, pulling her T-shirt down over her knees…

It wasn't the wildest birthday for her.

Pippa lay on the sofa with her head in his lap, while Luke finished the wine.

Both were locked in their own thoughts.

But they were together.

And tonight, that meant the world.

* * *

Pippa would have hated to hear this news tomorrow, in hand-over. The dread that gripped her was similar to the way she'd felt when she'd been told Julia had died. She'd panicked when Luke had told her about Hamish, yet he didn't seem to mind.

She felt his hand still in her hair, and then heard his voice, which rarely revealed any uncertainty.

'I should have transferred Hamish. At least Darcy would have been with his brother.'

Pippa thought for a moment. 'And witnessed his collapse? Heard the resuscitation attempts? Seen him die?'

She shook her head, and then turned in his lap so she could see him.

'It would have been dreadful for Darcy. Aside from that, St Bede's is one of the best neuro hospitals. You did the right thing, keeping Hamish there. What if he'd died in the back of an ambulance?' She watched as he closed his eyes and finally accepted her words. 'By not bending to everyone's wishes and moving him, you gave him the best chance.'

'Thank you,' he said, 'for saying that.'

'It's the truth,' Pippa said with conviction. She moved up on his lap. 'You did the best you could—life just doesn't always play fair.'

'No,' he agreed. 'It doesn't.'

Luke looked at this woman whom he'd stood up tonight—there'd not been a single text demanding where he was…not one angry call.

'I'm sorry I ruined your birthday.'

'You didn't.' Pippa shrugged. 'I hate birthdays anyway.'

'Hate them?'

Pippa blinked, about to retract or cover up her statement. But yes, on this, her thirtieth birthday, thinking of little Darcy and poor Hamish, it felt safe to say she officially hated them.

'Yes.'

'Why?' Luke pushed. 'Do you mean since you lost—?'

'No.' She shook her head, because it wasn't all about Julia's death, and he'd been honest about how he was feeling, so she felt a little braver. 'I always hated them,' she admitted. 'I used to turn down friends' party invites.'

'How come?' he asked, his hands on her bare thighs.

He looked into green eyes that were finally a little less guarded than they'd been since the day they'd met.

'Julia couldn't go to parties, you see. Mum didn't think it was fair.'

'What about *your* birthdays?'

'Some were nice...' she said. 'My parents forgot my seventh birthday, though.'

'Totally forgot?'

'With good reason.' She told him how sick Julia had been, and about the nurse who had remembered at the eleventh hour. 'Maybe Julia told her,' Pippa mused. 'I don't know where she got that cake.'

Luke mulled this over. For all his father's faults, he'd never missed a birthday. Hell, even though they were still barely talking, he'd called the other night to check on him.

'So they don't bother with your birthday at all now?'

'There'll be a card with some cash next time I go over.'

He thought of her checking her phone in the drug room. 'Do they call?'

'Birthdays upset them,' Pippa said, in her parents' defence. 'No one can know how they feel unless they've lost a child.'

Luke swallowed down a slightly caustic reply, because it would be aimed at Pippa's parents rather than at her. He thought of Amber, about how desperate she had been to get to Hamish, and yet she had never for one second forgotten the son she was leaving behind and had begged Luke to check on him...

'Anyway,' Pippa said, shrugging, 'I don't make a big deal of them.'

He kissed her then, and Pippa kissed him back, chasing away the horrors of the day.

As he undressed, he saw Pippa reach into his jacket for a condom. Knew they were both urgent for escape.

They made love on the sofa, but it was necessary sex, to drown out the noise in their heads. It was passionate, rather than intimate.

But it was in the small hours of the morning that they ran into danger...

CHAPTER NINE

PIPPA WOKE BEFORE DAWN, and although Luke lay still beside her, she could feel he was awake.

'Can't sleep?' she asked.

'No,' Luke said, and then, 'You thought I was with Shona?'

Pippa realised that it wasn't only the sad events of the night keeping him awake.

'Tonight?' Luke persisted. 'You thought I was with her.'

'I didn't know what to think,' Pippa admitted. 'I *don't* know what to think.'

She stared up at the ceiling, asking herself who she was to play judge and jury over his past. But there were things that mattered…that were important to discuss.

'She was *married*, Luke.'

'So was my father…'

Her head turned to face him 'What?'

'It wasn't *me* having the affair.' In the darkness, they rolled over and faced each other. 'It was my father and Shona.'

'So why did *you* leave St Bede's?' Pippa frowned. 'Why did you take the fall?'

'I just knew I didn't want to be there any more. I'd lost all respect for my father. And Shona's husband worked on one of the wards. Nice guy…' He thought for a moment. 'I'd already been looking at studying in America, and that gave me the push I needed.'

He didn't speak for a moment, yet Pippa could feel he was still thinking.

'Truth be told, I was never one hundred percent sure I wanted to work there… That bloody chemistry exam!'

'Fragmentation,' she said, and he laughed and gave her a playful punch.

His hand remained on her arm and she could see his dark eyes shining…knew they were locked with hers. She felt closer to him than she ever had to another. Whispered conversations in the night with Julia didn't count, because this was very different. This was two adults confiding and sharing, being vulnerable, touching and supporting, letting the other in…

'How did you find out? About the affair, I mean?' Pippa said. 'Gossip, or…?'

'No. It would seem they were actually very discreet. That's why people thought it was Shona and me.'

He smiled at her frown.

'It was pure chance,' he explained. 'Just a couple of things. My parents and I didn't live in each other's pockets. When I started my residency, he was setting up a surgical department in a new hospital in the Middle East.'

'Your mother went with him?'

'Yes. They only came back a couple of years before I left St Bede's.'

'Was it odd?' Pippa asked. 'Working with him?'

'We didn't overlap much, though we were certainly operating within each other's orbit. Still, you know how tight-knit Theatre is?'

'I guess…' Pippa started.

But then she thought back to her training and nodded. Theatre, more than anywhere, had been its own separate world. She thought of her shoes squeaking on the sticky mats as she entered, the flap of doors behind her, and how the nursing staff, at least for the most part, even took all their breaks there.

'Yes,' she now agreed. 'Although since my training—apart from handing over a patient or picking them up in Recovery—I've never really been inside a theatre.'

'I'd heard him laughing a bit more vibrantly in Theatre—his "holiday laugh", I always call it, because he's a different guy when he's away from the hospital.'

'Nicer?'

'Mmm,' Luke affirmed. 'He lightens up a bit. But suddenly he started to seem a bit more cheerful at work.' He ran a hand down to her waist. 'Perhaps the same way *you've* been more cheerful at work of late.'

'No!' Pippa said, laughing. 'I'm hopefully more discreet than that.'

'You are. Though I guess they were discreet too…that was how they got away with it. If I hadn't been his son I'd never have known.'

'So how *did* you find out?' Pippa asked, and her interest was not so much in the affair but more in how Luke had worked it out.

Even if there was no future for them, she still wanted to know more about him—ached to know more and therefore get closer to this man who enthralled her.

He always would.

Even that inward admission startled Pippa a touch. All this time she'd been telling herself she could do this—could keep things light and enjoy their time together. Yet here they were, on a night like no other, wrapped in each other's bodies, and she was asking him to confide in her.

'You don't have to tell me…'

'That's just it,' Luke said. 'I've never told anyone. But I want to tell you.'

It was the same way he'd felt the need to come here tonight—not just to apologise for messing up her birthday, but because he'd needed to see her. And that was a very unfamiliar feeling, but one he'd chosen *not* to push aside tonight.

'I always get my parents theatre tickets for Christmas—well, I used to,' Luke explained. 'That year I'd got them tickets for *Hamilton*. Anyway, one morning I heard him humming a song from it in the changing room. I didn't have time to give it much thought. I had a big case that I was rushing to get to.'

'How long after Christmas were the tickets for?'

'March,' he said. 'I'd pretty much forgotten about it till I heard him humming, and I made a sort of note in my head to ask him if he'd enjoyed it. But then I remembered that my mother had been away with friends that weekend. I guess I figured they must have changed the tickets. To be honest, I didn't dwell on it. Shona was scrubbing in for me that morning, and I just asked her how come I hadn't seen her recently. Had she been avoiding me? That kind of thing. It was just a joke, but she went so red...'

Pippa was listening intently, and he was enjoying the closeness they shared as he told her his story.

'Then, a little while into the operation, someone asked her if she'd enjoyed *Hamilton* on Saturday. It all just clicked—his singing, him being in a good mood around Theatre more.'

'What did Shona say?'

'Nothing. She was passing me forceps and her hand froze. I looked up from the patient and saw she'd turned scarlet again.'

'You were certain just from that?'

'Shona couldn't even look at me. I realised that she really had been avoiding me—a guilty conscience, I guess. And I found out I was a really good surgeon that morning, because I just got on with the operation.'

'What about Shona?'

'She said she felt unwell and scrubbed out.'

'What a mess...'

He nodded. 'Once the patient was in Recovery, I went to the break room. She followed me in and started crying, grabbing at me and pleading with me not to say anything. Her husband's a senior nurse on the orthopaedic ward. A great guy. She was saying it would break his heart, and I was telling her she should have thought of that before...' He gave her a mirthless smile. 'You know my junior?'

'Fiona?'

'She was a med student then. She, along with a couple of others, walked in on us arguing. I just left. But, given that Shona was standing there crying, they thought I was breaking up with her, or whatever—that it was the two of *us* having an affair. It was a natural assumption, I guess, given that we're closer in age. My father's in his mid-fifties.'

'Gosh. Why didn't you...?'

Pippa's voice faded. The answer was obvious, perhaps, but to her it seemed so unjust that he'd taken the hit.

'I spoke to my father and told him exactly what I thought of him. My leaving wasn't about taking the blame for him, or anything like that. I just couldn't stand to be working alongside him, and nor did I want to work with Shona and face her husband every day, knowing what I knew, but not being able to say anything.'

'Is it still going on?'

'No idea. I haven't spoken to her since, apart

from professionally, and nor do I want to. That call earlier was about work. She's on the ICU now.'

'Did you tell your mother?'

'No. I'd already tried that once.'

'It wasn't your father's first affair, then?'

'It wasn't.' He was silent for a long moment before answering. 'I stayed out of it this time.'

'I'm sorry I said anything.'

'It's fine.' He shrugged and sighed. 'The rumours are everywhere. I'm no saint, but I told you, Pippa, that I'd never get involved with someone who was already in a relationship.'

'I know you did.'

'Why do you think I never want to settle down? Or get overly involved with anyone? I trust people, but I don't trust couples. I don't want the hurt or the lies that come, or how people pretend things are fine when they're clearly not.' He looked at her. 'I swore off serious relationships and marriage before I'd even made it to medical school—'

He stopped abruptly, as if the memory was something he did not want to revisit.

'Is that why you want to get out of London?' she asked.

Luke was about to nod, but he knew it wasn't really an honest answer, and it seemed they were all about honesty tonight.

'It certainly factors into my decision not to go back to St Bede's,' he said, then hesitated.

His decision to leave London had been set in

stone when he'd returned from the States—sell and get out. Yet now, having told Pippa, he realised that saying everything out loud and having her react so calmly had honestly helped. And, despite the gossip at The Primary, he was enjoying his time there.

London no longer felt like the closed-in, locked-down world from which he'd been so pleased to escape.

Pippa broke his silence. 'You'll be in Scotland soon,' she said. 'Well away from it all…'

'Why don't you come?' He saw her eyes widen. 'I mean, for a visit.'

'Why?' Pippa smiled. 'Because you'll be sex-starved in your little stone cottage?' she teased. And they laughed as they moved in closer to each other. 'Or so you can stand me up in Scotland too?'

'You're not going to let me live that down, are you?' he said, pushing her hair from her face. 'How long did you wait at the restaurant?'

'Half an hour.' She smiled. 'Okay, forty-five minutes, maybe? It was excruciating.'

'Why?' He pulled her closer to him. 'I often eat there alone.'

'In a new dress and dangly earrings at a table set for two?'

'On occasion,' he teased, his hand coming down to her bare arm.

'Did you really buy a new dress?' he asked.

'I did,' Pippa said, because making fun of being stood up in a gorgeous restaurant felt a whole lot better than everything else that had happened. 'And underwear.'

'Damn,' he said, then moved his hand to her smooth naked hips. 'And body lotion…'

'That's not new,' she said. 'I even wore make-up…'

'I'll make it up to you. Your next day off—our next mutual day off—I'll book and we can go again.'

'No way! I am never going back there,' Pippa said, laughing. 'The shame!' She thought of the awful waiter and then she met his eyes. 'It honestly doesn't matter.'

'It honestly does.'

Sometimes his kiss felt like an escape, a fantasy come true, or even a delicious glimpse of paradise—as if their mouths mingling somehow took her to another place. Only, in this pre-dawn morning it didn't feel like that. It felt as if she was exactly there, and so too was Luke. Both together in a place they had somehow made—a place that actually existed.

His kiss was different. Not the rough kiss of earlier, nor the decadent, sexy ones they often shared. This kiss was slower, yet deeper.

She opened her eyes and found that she was staring into his, the contact so probing and direct that she closed her eyes. She felt as if he could see right inside her soul, and if that was true then he might see that there was a place in it reserved only for him.

Yet even as she broke eye contact, still there was nowhere to hide in this bed, where deeper intimacies were being shared.

His hand moved behind her head, with a slight pressure that felt exquisite, and Pippa put her hand on his chest, feeling the soft mat of hair. Then she explored the side of his torso, running her hand down to his waist and relishing her slow perusal of his body as their tongues mingled.

They were soon wrapped around each other, and when she rolled onto her back it was so mutual that Pippa wasn't sure if it was his command or her body's beckoning. His thighs nudged hers apart and she lifted her knees. In her cold bedroom, the warmth they made together felt essential.

Pippa heard her own soft moan as he squeezed inside her. Luke had propped himself up on his elbows, but she could still feel his delicious body pinning her to the bed. He moved, slowly at first, but so deeply that she felt a tightening low in her stomach. Her thighs parted further to allow for more intensity.

'Pip…'

For the first time she didn't object to the shortening of her name. There was no breath left to waste on such irrelevancies anyway.

His pace did not increase, and yet with each measured stroke Pippa felt as if she was falling apart. Even as she tightened beneath him and turned her head from his kiss he would not let her hide, and he moved her head to face him. Pippa put up her hand to bring his head down, but he removed it and pinned her arms behind her head, then looked at her as he moved deep inside.

'Pippa…'

He was up on his forearms, and she knew he was asking her to look at him. She knew that even if she kept her eyes closed she would still be letting him in to that place reserved solely for him.

She was coming undone, starting to cry, sobbing his name, and still he did not relent—he only thrust deeper. His breath was hot on her cheek as he finally increased his speed, suddenly moving too fast for her to think. She was always thinking—but for a second all thought stopped. Her hips rose in an urgent and involuntary motion as she climaxed and felt him still. Then came his breathless moan, and as she ached with the end of her orgasm he took her straight back there again, reviving her intimate pulses as he came deep inside.

She could feel the sheen of sweat on his arms as he collapsed onto her, and the coolness of her own tears on her cheeks. She was silently appalled at her capitulation…at the fact that she'd let go as much as she just had.

And now her mind was back, trying to count how many times they had made love in their short time together. She scanned her memory…

Then she heard the bleep of his phone, and as he rolled off her Pippa knew, with absolute certainty, that she'd just made love for the very first time.

* * *

As his phone alarm demanded they part, Luke hit snooze for the first time since they'd been together.

'Pippa…?' He too sounded as if he had found himself in an alien world.

'What?' Pippa asked, perhaps a little abruptly. But she was trying to catch her breath, and was terrified by what had just happened between them.

He was going to tell her that things had got too intense, she was certain. Had he read in her eyes or felt in her body the love she'd been trying to hide? After she'd sworn not to love him.

'Pippa,' he said again. 'We didn't use anything.'

Oh, was that all?

In the grand scheme of things, it didn't seem as earth-shattering as her most recent realisation, Pippa thought. He was probably panicking in case his bachelor life was over.

'It's fine.' She looked back at him. 'I'm on the Pill.'

'Even so…'

'Luke, you're on call.'

It wasn't like ward round mornings when he could risk being a bit late. The pagers would be handed over, and it wasn't fair to anyone if he wasn't there.

'You need to get ready.'

He nodded and, like the secret soldier she had begun to suspect he was, he rolled out of bed. Thoughtful as ever, he turned on her electric blanket before heading to the shower.

Pippa tried to correct her thoughts. It couldn't be love because that took two, she reasoned. Still, it had been intense, that sudden move from safe sex—both figuratively and emotionally—to soft, slow sex.

She lay there as he used her tiny shower, feeling the tension that had lived in her for ever starting to return.

She was falling deeper into this man, when she'd honestly hoped that this month together might break the spell of him. Always before the gloss had worn off...always she'd backed off because they'd got too close...

This time, though, *she* was the guilty party.

Oh, where is my casual lover mask? Pippa thought as he came out of the shower and started to dress.

'We need to talk, Pippa,' he said as he knotted his tie. 'Look, I'm sorry I didn't take better care this morning. It hasn't happened before—I always wear protection—but I'm happy to go and get checked if it makes you feel any better.'

'Checked?' Pippa frowned and, despite the blanket starting to warm up, she felt the same goosebumps she had last night.

She felt a sudden sense of panic, as she wondered if he was asking if she carried the CF gene, and what his reaction would be if she told him she did.

But that wasn't what Luke was asking.

'If you're worried I've got anything…' He was matter of fact. 'Though I'm sure there's no problem.'

No problem? It wasn't the unprotected sex that was the problem…

She could deny it no more.

Luke Harris was back in her life and again he was taking over her heart.

CHAPTER TEN

SOME DAYS, PAEDIATRIC nursing was the best job in the world.

Others…

Evan was dealing with the awful practicalities that death brought, while Amber was in with the child psychologist, working out the best way to tell Darcy about his twin.

Pippa was just clearing his IVAC when the question came.

'Where's Hamish?'

'Why don't I get Mummy…?' Pippa started, but was saved from having to avoid the issue by fetching his mother because Amber had walked in.

'Darcy was just asking where Hamish was,' Pippa explained.

'Were you, Darcy?' Amber said as she limped over on her booted leg, taking a seat in what must be an extremely painful position on the edge of her son's bed.

'Would you like me to leave you?' Pippa offered, but Amber shook her head.

'Stay,' Amber said, and then took a deep breath and gently told her son the simple truth. 'Hamish has died, darling.'

'So when is he coming back?'

Pippa put her hand on Amber's shoulder to support the poor mother as she tried to do what was best for her remaining child.

She answered his question as simply as she could. 'He won't be coming back.'

'Ever?'

'Ever,' Amber said.

'Like when Yoyo died?'

'Yes,' Amber replied gently, stroking his hair and talking to Pippa. 'Yoyo was the boys' budgie.'

'Will Hamish go in a box in the garden too?'

'No. There's a special garden for people.' Amber's voice was shaking, and yet she was being so tender with her explanations. 'And when you're well enough, we'll go and visit the garden.'

'Is he there now?'

'No, not till next Friday,' Amber told him. 'Mummy and Daddy are going to go and say goodbye, and when you're well enough, and ready, we'll take you too.'

'You're crying, Mummy,' said Darcy, and his little hand went to her cheek.

'Because I'm sad. You'll be sad at times too, but that's okay. We'll look after each other and give each other cuddles... Can I have one now, please?'

As Darcy wrapped his arms around his mum's neck she hugged him back hard and then quietly addressed Pippa.

'Thanks,' she said. 'I think we'll be fine now.'

Very few things made Pippa cry. Actually, until Luke had brought her undone last night, nothing really had. But hearing Amber being so gentle with her son brought a rare flash of tears.

She sniffed them back and went to tell Nola,

along with Luke, who was updating his notes, that Darcy had now been told about his twin.

'Amber was really good with him,' Pippa said, and repeated what Darcy had said and his concept of death. 'He knows that his brother's…' She felt the unfamiliar sting of tears threaten again, and excused herself.

'You okay?' Luke checked, when he found her back in her default position of pouring boiling water on a teabag in the break room.

'I'm fine.'

'It's tough.'

'Yes,' Pippa agreed, unsure why she had used that tone of voice when he was just being nice. 'I'm going to have tea.' She added sugar and pulled out the teabag, and then added too much milk.

'Pippa,' he said, halting her, 'it's fine to be upset.'

'I know.' She nodded but then, desperate to escape his scrutiny, she walked off.

'Pippa!' he called her back. 'Can we talk about last night?'

She felt her back stiffen. It was as if last night she'd revealed a glimpse of her soul, and now she truly wished he hadn't.

'If there are any repercussions…' Luke said. 'I know you said you're on the—'

'Luke!' Her eyes flashed a warning. 'We're at work.'

'No one can hear us.'

To make extra sure, he closed the door.

'Someone might come in!'

'What? And catch us *talking*?'

He walked over to the large kitchen table and took a biscuit from a packet before leaning on it.

'Let's give them something to talk about. *Ooh, Luke Harris was eating a biscuit,*' he mimicked, *'and Pippa Westford was drinking tea.'*

She let out a soft laugh and knew she was being paranoid. And it wasn't her colleagues she was worried about catching them.

She was worried that Luke might see into her heart.

'You were upset when I mentioned getting checked. Did you think I meant for CF?'

He was trying to have a very sensible conversation, she knew. And because he was a doctor, and knew about Julia, he was facing it head-on.

'Is it a concern?' he asked, and she knew he was asking if she was a carrier of the gene.

'Luke, I've told you—there's nothing to worry about. My sister died of a congenital illness. And as if I'd leave contraception up to a guy...' She watched his eyebrow rise as she hit a little below the belt.

'Have you been tested?' he asked.

'I'm not going to have this conversation—and certainly not at work. Why would I open up with someone who won't even be here this time next week?'

'Pippa, I always said I was leaving.'

'You always did,' she agreed.

'It's actually next Saturday that my contract ends. I'm not flying off on the first plane out, but even so, it's best we address this now.'

She simply did not know how to be close to someone—to a man—and certainly not to one who was leaving. They were only ever supposed to be temporary. She took her Pill religiously, because she carried the gene, and the only person whose business that was, was hers.

'There's nothing to address,' she told him.

'Good,' he said, and turned to go.

But as he reached to open the door Luke apparently changed his mind.

'For the record, you haven't opened up at all…'

'Why would I?' she asked. 'You probably wouldn't remember if I did anyway.'

'Am I sensing some resentment here? Because I don't remember a conversation fourteen years ago?'

'Of course not!' she attempted, but she knew she'd raised the subject once too often, and this time Luke didn't let it go.

'Am I being chastised because I didn't fancy you when you were sixteen? That's not very MeToo of you…'

'Stop it!' She actually laughed. How was he able to do that? To make her laugh on what was a very sad day? In a way that made a harsh world a little softer somehow?

For both of them.

* * *

Luke knew she'd been in with Darcy, and that this morning would have been very hard, so he reeled in his own frustrations.

'I'm sorry I don't remember,' he said.

'It's fine. You told me you wanted to be a drummer…'

'I think you're mixing me up with someone else,' he said with a frown. 'I've never even played the drums.'

'It was definitely you. You'd been crying that day. Your eyes were all red.'

'Probably because I'd been swimming.'

'No.' She shook her head. 'You had double sport later that afternoon.'

'What? Do you have a super-memory, or something?'

Only where he was concerned, she thought ruefully.

But rather than admit to that, she shrugged.

'I don't know. Maybe I am mixing you up.'

She forced out a smile and remembered that they'd agreed upon fun times only. She'd told him and herself that she could do this…

She just wished she could convince her heart, but it was still busy furiously objecting.

CHAPTER ELEVEN

THEY TRIED TO get back to being casual lovers, but the genie refused to return to its bottle.

'Here,' Pippa said, as she entered his flat the next night, holding the massive pot plant. 'I've brought you a present.'

'Please, no...'

'Well, it was you who suggested I come straight here after my late shift,' Pippa reminded him. 'Anyway, it would take up half my flat. She does this every year.'

'Your aunt?'

'Yes, and every year I have to rehome a plant.' She deposited it in an alcove by the fireplace in the lounge. 'It looks nice.'

'I'll kill it,' he warned.

When he looked at the vast pot plant his smile faded as he realised why her aunt did this each year— no doubt to prompt her colleagues, or to push the reticent Pippa into revealing that it was her birthday.

It made his heart constrict, and he looked from the plant to her, but Pippa was all smiles.

'You said we had to walk the puppy.'

'So I did.'

It was frosty outside and Pippa said that she thought they might get snow.

'It's too soon for snow,' he said, as the little dog shivered, and pawed at Luke's legs every time he tried to put him down on the pavement.

He sighed as he gave in and picked the puppy up, and they walked around the corner to a small park, where they sat on a bench, hoping Sausage would wee on the grass. But still he scampered to be picked up.

'How was Darcy?' Luke asked.

While usually he tried to leave work at work, he couldn't help but enquire about this patient.

'He's drinking a little bit.'

'Still not eating?'

'No.'

'Is he talking?'

'Not really,' Pippa said. 'I think—' She halted.

'Go on.'

'He's just hurting.'

'Have you spoken to him?'

'Of course.'

'I mean, about losing your sister?'

'I'm hardly going to unburden myself to a five-year—'

'Pippa,' he warned, halting her prickly reply. 'We both know you're not going to *unburden* yourself to Darcy. Have you spoken to him?'

'No.'

He left it there, and watched as Pippa stared into the night.

'Are we okay?' he checked.

'Of course.'

'Did I scare you by asking you to come to Scotland?'

* * *

Gosh, Pippa thought, she really must be playing it
cool if he thought *that* was what was on her mind.

'Nothing like that,' she said. 'It's a nice offer. I
just…'

She flailed about for a reason to explain why she
was stalling. How to explain without fully revealing that saying goodbye next week was going to
be hard enough.

'The off-duty roster isn't up yet.'

'Fair enough.' He nodded at her casual reply.
'Good boy!' Luke cheered as the puppy finally did
a wee, and then added for Pippa's ears only, 'Mind
you, he squats like a girl.'

'I don't think they lift their legs until they're
older.'

'The things you learn…'

And they were back… Back to protected sex and
laughter…back to cramming everything in.

Jenny had had some spare tickets to an interactive theatre production which Pippa had bought
from her.

'I have no idea what it's about,' Pippa told Luke
as they were admitted.

'I'd better not get tickets to this for my parents,'
Luke said jokingly as they walked from room to
room, watching the most torrid scenes.

There was an awful lot of nudity—full-frontal
and everything.

'Good heavens!' Luke exclaimed as they stepped

back into the night. 'Are you trying to corrupt me, Pippa Westford?'

'Blame Jenny,' Pippa said.

They stood facing each other and she put her arms up on his shoulders.

'It was fun,' he admitted. 'Though I'm not quite sure what it was supposed to be.'

'Maybe you *should* get tickets for your parents...'

'Maybe...' He gave a half-smile. 'Did I tell you my father called me? That he wants us to go for a drink?'

'No.' Pippa shook her head. 'Will you go?'

'I don't know.' Luke shrugged.

Try as Pippa might, she still couldn't get the genie back in his bottle. And sometimes she forgot to keep things casual.

'I'd kill for my mum to call me and ask me to go for a drink,' Pippa admitted. 'Luke, he clearly cares about you.'

And sometimes Luke, too, forgot not to go in too deep. because as they stood outside the theatre, instead of kissing her, or hailing a taxi to take them back to his flat, he asked the question that had plagued him for years.

'Then why does he play Russian Roulette with his marriage?'

'It's *his* marriage he's dicing with,' Pippa said. 'You'll always be his son. Talk to him.'

'We'll see...' He looked right at her. 'Have you ever told your parents how you feel?'

'No,' Pippa admitted.
'Isn't that a little hypocritical?'
'True.'
She laughed, and so did Luke.
They were safely back on track…
Bound for nowhere.

CHAPTER TWELVE

KIM WAS GIVING the night hand-over.

'Luke suggested that the parents bring in his favourite takeaway for Darcy.'

Pippa raised her eyebrows, because she'd rather thought she'd gleaned his stance on that a few weeks ago. 'Did he eat it?'

'No.' Kim sighed. 'Well, one little French fry. But he wasn't really interested. The parents have to go and meet with the undertakers this morning. They want to do that together, but they're worried about leaving him.'

Nola looked over to Pippa. 'Can you special him today?' she asked. 'I'll give you Cot Four as well, but she's got her mother with her and is due to be discharged. I won't give you anyone else—well, not if I can help it…'

Darcy had refused breakfast and much to his mother's upset didn't seem remotely fazed when she kissed him goodbye before going to meet her husband.

'I can help Darcy with his lunch,' Pippa said to Amber as she filled a bowl from the sink to wash him. 'If you need a little longer.'

'Thank you,' Amber responded anxiously, and then gave Darcy another kiss before leaving.

Pippa followed her outside. 'I'll call you if he needs you, I promise, so take all the time you need.'

'What time are you on till?'

'Four,' Pippa said. 'I can push it till five, though, if necessary.'

'We have to take in an outfit…' Tears started streaming down Amber's face and Pippa guided her into one of the side rooms. 'I can't bear it, Pippa.'

Pippa put her arms around her as she wept for a moment.

'I don't want Darcy to see me like this.'

'I know,' Pippa said, admiring Amber for being able to cry gently with her son, but not so much that it scared him.

'I feel like I've lost Darcy too,' Amber sobbed. 'He barely speaks…'

'It's early days,' Pippa soothed.

But then she thought of what Luke had said and knew—or rather felt—that it was right for her to step up. As well as that, she had her second interview for the PAC Unit tomorrow, and wanted to test out if she could bring her very private past into work.

'I lost my sister,' Pippa told Amber, and she felt her go still in her arms. 'I was much older than Darcy, and we weren't twins, but there's such a bond…'

'Was it sudden?' Amber gulped—polite responses were forgotten when you were drowning in grief.

'No.' Pippa shook her head. 'But I remember being seven and nearly losing her.' She looked at Amber. 'Do you want me to try talking to Darcy? He might be scared of upsetting you.'

'Please,' she said, shivering. 'But only…'

'I'll be gentle,' Pippa reassured her. 'You go and see Hamish.'

Pippa was washing Darcy from top to toe.

'Your bruises are turning yellow,' Pippa said as she rinsed his little back. 'You look like you've been fighting with paint!'

She turned him onto his back and knew her light-hearted chatter wasn't helping. She tried to remember being five, but it was all a bit of a blur.

She'd loved nursery—that she did remember— and she recalled coming home and finding her mother crying in her bedroom…and her selfish wish that she'd still be able to go to the nativity play that night. That her mother would stop crying and that things would be okay…normal…

Whatever normal was.

It was lunchtime, and Darcy was gagging on a spoonful of mashed potato, when Pippa put down the spoon and spoke to him.

'I'm so sorry you're hurting, Darcy.'

He looked down at the dressings on his tummy.

'I meant here,' Pippa said, and tapped his little chest. 'Your heart's hurting. That's how I felt when my sister died.'

He didn't answer, but his big grey eyes didn't pool with tears, and for the first time they properly met hers.

'You're going to be okay, Darcy,' Pippa said, gently but firmly, in case he was scared that he might be about to suddenly die to.

Then she thought of what she'd used to wish for most in the world—Julia too.

'Mummy and Daddy are going to be okay, too. They're very sad, but they will be okay.'

She knew in her heart that in Darcy's case this was true. His parents were doing everything they could to take care of both their little boys.

'They love you so much.'

And then he said some words that cut through her heart. 'I want Hamish.'

'I know you do.' Pippa nodded. 'I wanted Julia— that was my sister—so badly after she died. She was the only person I could really talk to. She was my best friend.'

Darcy nodded, as if she'd finally said something he understood.

'I was so sad, and I needed her so much, but she wasn't there any more.'

He started to cry, and Pippa cuddled him and let him weep.

'You can always tell Mummy and Daddy when you feel sad.'

'But then *they'll* cry.'

'And that's okay,' Pippa said. 'Mummy has said to you that you can all be sad together, but I promise you will smile and laugh too, even if you can't believe that now.'

Darcy pulled back, and Pippa thought that she

herself was going to cry when he picked up his teddy bear. 'I want Hamish to have Whiskers.'

'What about Coco?' Pippa carefully asked, referring to his brother's bear.

'I want Hamish to have Whiskers *and* Coco.'

She held on to the teddy for a moment and looked at the bear's glassy eyes. She knew this was something for Amber and Evan to negotiate.

Then she looked at Darcy who, now he had cried, was ready to sleep. 'Why don't you cuddle Whiskers for now?'

'And then Hamish can have him?'

'No!' Amber was aghast at the idea.

She'd returned from the undertaker's holding Hamish's bear, Coco. Nola was there, and Luke, who was writing up some notes on another child, just happened to be in the office. He had put down his pen and was listening.

Amber was adamant. 'I've brought Hamish's bear for Darcy to have. They should be together.' Her eyes flashed at Pippa, loaded with accusation. 'What on earth did you say to him?'

Luke watched quietly, wincing inside when Amber reared, but Pippa took it well.

'I told him how I felt when I lost my sister.' Pippa had already reported back on the conversation she'd had with Darcy, and she responded calmly. 'Giving Hamish his own bear was Darcy's idea.'

Evan took his wife's hand. 'Darcy wanted him

to have it even before Hamish...' He couldn't complete the sentence.

'But he might regret it.' Amber looked to Nola, who gave a small nod, and then to Luke, who opened his mouth and then closed it again.

'What if he changes his mind?' Amber demanded. 'What do I tell him then?'

'He wants to do this for Hamish,' Pippa reiterated. 'He's going to be sad and upset, whatever you decide. He's always going to miss his brother.'

'I don't know what to do,' Amber sobbed into Hamish's bear.

'Pippa's right,' Evan said.

'There's no right or wrong in this situation,' Pippa said, and took a breath. 'But I think Darcy wants to do something for his brother. Why don't you go and see him with both bears, and talk to him about it?'

Nola stood. 'I'll take you to him.'

Nola helped Amber stand, and Pippa watched as Evan pulled some tissues from the box on the table and wiped his eyes before putting his arm around his wife as they headed off to see their son.

'Thank goodness you answered,' Luke said, taking up his pen. 'I had no idea what to say.'

'They're so good with him,' Pippa said. 'In all their grief for Hamish, they still think of Darcy every step of the way.'

'They do,' Luke agreed. 'What were your—?'

He halted, knowing this wasn't the time or

place—especially when the ever-indiscreet Jenny came in.

Then again, Luke thought, it was never the time or place when it came to Pippa...

'Nola's crying her eyes out in the loo,' Jenny informed them.

'Yes,' Luke responded gruffly, feeling a bit choked up himself. 'We've just had the Great Teddy Bear Debate, so go easy on Nola.'

'I know,' Jenny said, pulling some tissues from the same box that Evan had used and blowing her nose. 'She told me...'

To Luke's surprise, the formidable Jenny sat on one of the chairs and started to cry.

'I might crochet something,' Jenny suggested. 'For both of them.'

'That's a lovely idea,' Pippa said, and went and sat on the armrest. She shot Luke a quick *yikes* look. 'But I think that's something for the parents to work out.'

She gave Luke a small smile as she put an arm around Jenny, and it hit Luke then that he still didn't get Pippa. Okay, he didn't know Jenny's past, and he understood that Nola might be emotional...but, hell, even the hardened Luke felt moved by the parents' plight. Yet the one member of staff who should be dissolving, wasn't. The person who had lost a sibling, and who had dealt with Darcy's questions, as well as the distraught parents, was sitting on an armrest, comforting Jenny, when surely she must be in agony.

'Go home,' Jenny said to Pippa, while blowing her nose. 'You're supposed to be finished. You're off tomorrow, aren't you?'

'Yes,' Pippa said. 'Then back for nights.'

And Luke was stuck here.

'See you,' she said, and smiled at him just as she would if it were Martha, or Nola, or anyone else sitting in the office.

He nodded, and when Pippa had gone he flashed a smile to a still watery-eyed Jenny. 'I'll give you some privacy…'

Luke caught up with Pippa at the elevators. 'Are you okay?'

'Of course.'

'Amber didn't mean—'

'Luke, I do know what to expect from grieving parents.'

'Of course,' Luke said, but he knew how tough it must have been. Still, clearly Pippa didn't want to talk about. 'I've booked the restaurant for Saturday.'

'What restaurant?'

'The French one.'

'No way!' Pippa shot out a laugh.

'Well, I might have something to celebrate. Your pot plant seems to be working. I've got a couple coming back for a second look on Friday.'

'Fingers crossed,' Pippa said, wishing her lift would hurry up and arrive.

She was still in the land of teddies, and not up to

being flirty and fun—and as well as that she had art class tonight, and was really not in the mood.

'What are you up to tonight?' she asked him.

'I might go for that drink with my father,' he said. 'Can't keep putting it off.'

'Well, I hope it goes well,' Pippa said as her elevator arrived. It didn't feel quite enough. 'He is clearly trying...' she started, but then she reminded herself that what they had was fun, casual, flirty, and most of all temporary. Instead, she only said, 'Good luck.'

'Thanks,' he said. 'Enjoy your class!'

Tonight it was guided art, and they all attempted to follow the teacher and paint a view of Santorini... Only Greek islands and oil paint weren't the best mix for Pippa's dark mood.

The scent of paint and turps reminded her so much of art class back when she was at school, and how she'd mourned not just Julia but also Luke. And the thought of hurt soon to come turned the gorgeous Aegean Sea an ominous grey, and made the little fluffy white cloud over the domed buildings dark...

'Wow,' Cassie said as she came round to inspect her work. 'There's some storm brewing in Santorini!'

There was.

Taking her painting home, she was ridiculously desperate to stop at Luke's. She wanted to make a stupid joke as she handed over her painting...only she couldn't pretend for much longer that she wasn't falling apart on the inside.

She wanted to tell him her fears about the interview tomorrow. And to sob her heart out about Darcy…to be in Luke's arms when she told him how hard it had been to relive the confusion and terror she'd felt as a child.

But he was leaving soon…

And, no, she didn't want a couple of weeks in Skye to visit him and prolong the agony…

He might be trying to get closer to her, but Pippa was certain that if Luke knew the magnitude of her feelings he would break the sound barrier running away.

Pippa loved him.

She didn't feel sixteen all over again, when she'd felt so lost and alone.

Pippa felt thirty and adrift…

And dreadfully, scarily in love with Luke.

CHAPTER THIRTEEN

'PIPPA!' LUKE SMILED in recognition and then, looking at her unusually smooth hair, all neatly tied back, he frowned. 'You look very smart.'

'Thanks.'

'I'm guessing you're not up in Human Resources to sort out your leave or your pay?'

'Sorry…?' She frowned. and then gave a small shake of her head. 'Oh! No, I'm not.' She glanced up at the time. 'I really have to go…'

'Good luck,' he called.

Pippa swung around and frowned.

'For your interview.'

Pippa gave a wry smile. 'Has Nola been gossiping again?'

'I don't think so. At least, she didn't say anything to me.' He put his head on one side in a knowing gesture. 'Just a guess. I know interviews for the new wing are taking place at the moment.'

He looked down at the grey dress she had worn on their first date, now styled more formally with heels and such.

'I'm surprised you didn't say anything.'

'I haven't got the job yet. I messed up the first interview.'

His eyes widened. 'So this is your second?'

'Yes.'

'Yet you never mentioned it?'

Pippa knew it was quite an omission, and she could see he was a touch offended—possibly even hurt.

'We're not a couple,' she pointed out. 'You said at the start—'

'That was at the start, Pippa! Things have changed—or at least I thought they had. We were talking about Scotland…or I was… Hell, I've told you things I've never discussed with anyone—ever. And you've told me…' He looked upwards then, as if scanning back over all their conversations, their moments, their time. 'Nothing.'

'That's not true.'

'It's close,' he said. 'Because if I hadn't already known about Julia you'd never have said anything.' He took a breath. 'Look, I'm not going to get into this discussion now, because you've got an interview. Is it for Nola's job?'

'No.' She raked a hand through her hair. 'It's for the PAC Unit. Paediatric—'

'I know what PAC stands for.' He nodded, and then, because he did know about Julia, he seemed to understand immediately why she might want to work there. 'You can't have done that badly if they've called you back.'

'Believe me, I wasn't expecting them to. The first interview really was a bit of a disaster. I just…'

'What?'

'Clammed up,' Pippa admitted, 'and gave bland answers.'

'Of course you did.' He gave a wry smile.

'What does that mean?'

Her voice was defensive, she knew, but then her shoulders dropped. Because she also knew he was speaking the truth.

'I'm scared of saying the wrong thing,' she admitted, but it was only half an admission. 'I'm dreadful at conflict.'

'Good!' Luke said, and made her blink. 'Do you really think they want to hire someone who thinks they're brilliant at conflict? That's a red flag if ever there was one!'

She gave a reluctant smile. He made a very good point.

'And you are good,' he added. 'You stood up to Jenny when she was being mean about a mum…'

'That's not conflict.'

'It doesn't have to be a boxing gloves situation to be considered conflict.'

He'd made her feel better—at least, he'd stilled her racing heart enough for her to admit her greatest fear.

'I'm worried I might get overly emotional if I…'

'Pippa, I can't even imagine…' He paused, looking around him. 'How long till the interview?'

She glanced at her phone. 'Fifteen minutes.'

'You're early for once! You must really want this job?'

'Yes.'

'Try opening up a bit, Pippa.'

'I don't know how,' she admitted, but then she shook her head. 'I can't do this.'

'Yes,' he said, as if he'd decided that it had to be now. 'You can.'

He steered her out of the main traffic of the corridor and to the side of some vast noticeboard displaying plans for the new wing of the hospital.

And maybe it was because she really wanted the job, or perhaps because Luke Harris was so incredible that he could somehow manage to stop clocks as well as her heart, she decided that he was right, and maybe she could share a little of her fear.

It was more terrifying to be here than in the interview, standing in front of Luke, about to admit a deep and painful truth.

'Everything leads back to Julia...'

'Of course it does.'

She blinked at his matter-of-fact response, but then shook her head. 'I don't want to walk into an interview and get upset, or...'

'Show yourself?'

'I didn't say that.'

'No, *I* did. Pippa, it's not just in interviews. You hold back all the time.'

Luke was wondering if now really was the right time for this conversation. He knew she held herself back. In truth, her reluctance to get emotionally involved with anyone had appealed at first. After all, wasn't that perfect for a temporary relationship?

Only he felt that now he had become emotionally involved, perhaps more than he wanted to be—or more than Pippa wanted him to be. He'd seen her.

He'd seen the Pippa behind the barriers she put up—or perhaps it would be more accurate to say that he'd *glimpsed* her at times. Not just in bed, but sometimes when she looked up and smiled, or when they sat waiting for a puppy to wee… And the real Pippa, when she wasn't hiding, was so direct and so stunning that she really had blown him away.

'I know why they called you back,' he told her.

'Why?' Pippa frowned.

'Because they saw that there was more.' He thought for a moment. 'Of *course* everything goes back to Julia. How could it not? The things that happen to us—'

'Define us?' She almost sneered. 'Shape us?'

'No.' He shook his head. 'But we learn from them. Why do you think I've sworn off relationships and refuse to rely on anyone else?'

'That's not learning, Luke.' She gave an impatient shake of her head. 'Your parents' marriage makes you swear off relationships for life. That's hardly learning…'

'I'm just trying to say…'

He closed his eyes in frustration—not only because she was right, but also because she was wrong! Lately, thanks to Pippa, he *was* learning that things weren't all black and white.

'Okay, I'm not the best example, but you have learnt from your family—'

Pippa cut in with the truth then. 'I'm scared I'll break down.'

'Okay…'

'I haven't cried…not really. Not since…'

'Since…?'

'I honestly can't remember. Since I was four, maybe, or five,' she admitted. 'And I don't want it to be at work, and I certainly don't want it to be in there.'

She pointed to the interview room and Luke looked down the corridor. He'd known she was closed off, but hadn't realised just how serious it was.

She hadn't cried since she was four or five?

'You could postpone the interview,' he suggested. 'I'll even write you a doctor's note!'

'I don't want to postpone it.'

'Okay…' He had a think. 'You did well with Amber and Darcy.'

'Because I was worrying about them—not me.'

'Okay, worst-case scenario, maybe you'll cry a bit if you talk about Julia. Just don't boo-hoo.'

'That's far from my worst-case scenario!' she dismissed. 'Thanks for the sage advice, Luke.'

'Pip, listen to me.' He touched the top of her arm. 'You can talk about your sister if you're up to it, but the moment you've had enough, you stop it right there.'

'How?'

'Oh, what did you say to me?' He smiled. 'That night in The Avery? Something like, *"I don't want to talk about it."* It doesn't matter if it's an interview—you still get to say that.'

She chewed her lip doubtfully, but Luke had enough confidence for them both.

'Look how you've helped Darcy and his parents.' He gave her a soft smile. 'The teddy debate…'

She nodded.

'I had no idea what to say.' He was shepherding her towards the interview room now. 'I doubt many would.'

'There's no right or wrong…'

'Sometimes there is,' Luke said, thinking of his own ineptitude when it came to certain conversations. 'You're good at knowing it.'

It was Pippa who frowned now, but as they reached the bench where she was to wait, he snapped his fingers to get her attention back.

'You could help guide them because you've been there.'

'I haven't lost a child…'

'You were speaking up for Darcy,' he said. 'And you were good at that.'

'What if I—?'

'Worst-case scenario?' he checked.

'What if I lose it?'

'If you're really about to crack, then say one of your contact lenses has fallen out and excuse yourself,' Luke suggested. 'Though I doubt it'll come to that.'

She nodded.

'Okay. Just go in there and show them the real Pippa…'

'Philippa.' She gave him a wry smile. 'They keep calling me Philippa. It's very off-putting!'

'Then tell them you prefer Pippa.' He gave her a squeeze on the arm. 'Best wishes, Pip.'

'Not good luck?' she checked.

'It's not luck you need. Just be yourself.'

'What if they don't want that?'

'Then it's their tough luck.'

'Come through, Philippa.'

It was quite a panel that Pippa found herself facing, but before taking her seat in front of them she took a breath.

'Actually, most people call me Pippa.' She sat down. 'Except my parents when they're cross.'

She was prepared for all their questions, and she also went through her nursing experience and said how keen she was to be part of the start of a new venture.

'Yet I see that you only applied recently,' one of the directors interrupted. 'We've been advertising for some time.'

'I wanted to be very sure,' Pippa admitted. 'There was an Acting Unit Manager role on my ward. However, I realised I didn't want to apply for a caretaking role. If I'm going to be a unit manager, then I'd want to make the role my own.'

'It would be a demanding role,' the director said, and then quizzed her on what she'd achieved in her previous roles relating to standards.

Pippa had practised, so she answered more

smoothly this time. Then came the awful conflict question again.

'How do you deal with it?'

'I try to avoid it,' Pippa admitted wryly, and instead of it being the completely wrong answer she saw that a couple of them smiled. 'It's probably my weakness—personally, that is—but professionally, I know there are times when you can't avoid it.'

'What about angry parents?'

'Most of the time they're more upset than angry,' Pippa said. 'Or frustrated. Or scared…' She spoke from the heart, rather than from the cheat sheet she'd memorised. 'I think moving them away from the child—'

'That can be hard to do.'

'Not usually.' Pippa shook her head. 'I've generally found that if you tell the parent that a conversation might be better had away from their child, most agree, and then you can hopefully address whatever it is really concerning them.'

'Okay.' It was Miss Brett's turn now. 'What would you like to see implemented on the PAC Unit?' she asked, then took off her glasses and stared at Pippa. 'If you were given carte blanche, and could do anything at all?'

Pippa thought of Luke, urging her to be herself, and it made her feel brave enough to answer once again from her heart.

'I'd have a study area,' Pippa said, 'for siblings.' She saw Miss Brett blink. 'And a lounge, perhaps.

Somewhere they can charge their phones, take a break, be apart but not far away....'

'A study area for siblings?' Miss Brett frowned, but it wasn't a dismissive frown, more an interested one. 'Why do you suggest that?'

'I had a very ill sister,' Pippa said. 'She died when I was sixteen.'

'I'm so sorry,' Miss Brett offered, and there was moment of silence, but not a strained one, as Pippa nodded to her offer of water.

'Thank you,' Pippa said.

'Do you mind us asking how old your sister was when she died?'

'Eighteen,' Pippa said. Her voice wavered, but she chose to push on, ready to talk a little about Julia. 'She'd just been accepted into St Andrew's to study History.'

Pippa gave a fond smile, but as she thought back to that time she found it was a double-edged sword. The fond memories of her sister were tinged with her own private heartache that she'd hidden so fiercely until now. She thought again of what Luke had said, about showing her true self, speaking up...

She felt a pinch in her nose that signalled tears. 'Excuse me,' she said, and took out a tissue and blew her nose, then forced herself to speak on. 'I didn't do very well at school—at least not as well as I'd hoped to.' She wanted to explain better...to speak honestly about that time. 'I was always behind with homework and catching up. My sister's illness took precedence—of course it did.'

'How were your parents?'

'Julia was their world,' Pippa said. 'She still is…'

Miss Brett gave her a long, assessing stare. 'They haven't got over it?'

'No. There was bereavement counselling offered, but they never…' She couldn't quite go there, and neither did she want to. 'I really don't want to go into that here,' Pippa said.

Luke was right—she didn't have to.

She turned the conversation back to the interview, though with a personal slant. 'I don't know if there's anything the hospital staff could have done to change the trajectory for my parents, but I do know how the kindness and thoughtfulness shown to me by them meant the world.'

'It's very easy for the well sibling, or siblings, to get lost,' Miss Brett said, nodding. 'Overlooked…' She paused and thought for a long moment. 'A study area for siblings…' She turned to another member of the panel and asked to see the floor plans for the unit, then looked back to Pippa. 'Their own locker, perhaps? Or at least some stationery supplies.'

'And a printer,' Pippa said, and felt her heart start to hammer as she realised her suggestion was being taken seriously.

Then they moved on to speak about their prospective patients, the variety in their ages and conditions. How teenage boys with fragile bones who shouldn't be getting into fights all too often did. How an appendix didn't care if you were already a cancer patient—it just flared up.

It didn't feel like an interview any more, more like an exchange of ideas, and when it concluded Pippa felt that even if she didn't get the position there might still be a study room for siblings incorporated into their plans.

And birthdays would hopefully be remembered.

'How did it go?'

Luke was waiting for her outside.

'It went well, I think.'

'Did you tell them about…?'

'Luke!' She put her hand up to stop him, still attempting to hold herself together.

And then she remembered something she hadn't asked him earlier because she had been so focused on the interview.

'How did things go with your father last night?'

'They didn't.'

'You cancelled?'

'I never asked.'

'But—'

It was Luke's turn to raise a hand, warning her to leave it.

'We should apply for jobs as traffic controllers,' Luke said, and made her laugh. 'Let's go to The Avery.'

They went to the bar this time, rather than the restaurant.

'What do you want?' he asked.

'Champagne,' Pippa said.

'Celebrating?'

'No, I'm just spending your money while you're still here,' she teased.

'Pardon?'

'It was a joke!'

'I didn't hear what you said.'

She went on tiptoe and got an extra dose of his citrussy scent. 'I said…' She cupped her hand and whispered into his ear, 'I'm just spending your money—'

'Enjoy!' Luke said, laughing. 'That dress is making me think unholy thoughts,' he told her, and looking down she saw it was starting to gape. He picked up a strand of previously straightened hair, which was now starting to curl. 'We could take a bottle to yours…'

'I like it here,' Pippa said.

Nice loud music…where you almost had to shout to be heard. So loud that if she blurted out that she loved him, or begged him not to go, he'd put his hand to his ear and ask, *What did you say?*

Safe.

CHAPTER FOURTEEN

'NO WAY THAT'S SANTORINI.'

Luke was ready for work and pulling on his jacket while looking at her attempt from art class the other night.

'It's like a Goya painting,' Luke went on, referring to an artist known for his rather morbid paintings. 'Thank goodness I didn't give you free range on decorating the apartment.'

'I like it,' Pippa admitted.

'I'll see you tonight at work?'

'Yep.'

Luke peered out through her flimsy curtains at the grey sleet and shivered at the dismal sight. 'What a horrible day for a funeral.'

Was there ever a good day to have one? Pippa thought, but didn't say.

When he'd gone, she turned her blanket up to high, set the timer for six hours and deliberately went back to sleep.

It was exhausting being an upbeat, casual lover.

There was pall hanging over the ward when she arrived for her night shift.

The children and babies were oblivious, but Hamish's funeral had been held today and there was an air of sadness amongst the day staff. Pippa could feel it when she stepped into the office for hand-over.

Pippa was in charge of the night shift, and after taking hand-over, even though Darcy wasn't her patient tonight, she popped her head in and saw that he was asleep. In place of Whiskers there was a tatty purple dinosaur. Amber was sitting in the recliner, staring at nothing.

'Hi, Amber.' Pippa went over and sat on a stool by the chair. 'Is there anything I can get for you?'

She shook her head.

'I've made up a bed for you in one of the offices,' Pippa told her. 'If you need a break…'

'I want to be here whenever he wakes up.'

'I know you do, but if you or your husband want to take a short break then at least you'll have somewhere private. Do you want me to show you where it is?'

Amber nodded and hauled herself up from the recliner, and they walked in silence past the nurses' station and down the side corridor.

'It's tucked away,' Pippa said, opening up the door.

'I might lie down for half an hour,' Amber said. 'I've got the worst headache…'

'Of course.'

'Evan's coming in a bit later. He's with family at the moment.'

She was in a daze, and looked so utterly drained that when she sat on the low bed Pippa lifted her legs for her and helped Amber to lie down.

'Hamish has Whiskers and Coco. I think it was the right thing to do.'

'I do too,' Pippa said, and sat on the little bed. 'You listened to Darcy, and that's the most important thing for any child.'

'I'm sorry about your sister.' Amber looked at her. 'I didn't it say before.'

'I know you are.' Pippa gave her hand a little squeeze. 'I'll come and get you if Darcy wakes up.'

She flicked off the light and the door had barely closed before she heard deep sobs coming from the grieving mother—the saddest sound in the world, and one Amber had fought to protect Darcy from.

Pippa wanted to cry too.

She wanted to curl up and cry—for Hamish and his family, for her sister, and also because Luke would very soon be gone. Tonight was his final shift, and Pippa knew that soon she'd have to reset her heart and start all over again.

'Hey…' He came down to the ward about eleven. 'How are they all?'

'Amber's asleep in one of the back offices,' Pippa said. 'I think Evan will be in soon.'

'How's Darcy?'

'Worn out,' Pippa said. 'He had some supper, though.'

Luke checked the labs on a couple of patients, then stopped back at the nurses' station and leant on the desk overlooking her.

'Do you want a puppy?'

'My mother warned me about men like you.' Pippa laughed. 'Seriously…?'

'My neighbour has decided that Sausage is too

much responsibility. She's taking him back to the breeder.' He gave her a smile. 'Maybe we're kindred spirits.'

'Maybe.' Pippa smiled back, but it faded when it dawned on her that he was suggesting that he and his irresponsible neighbour were the kindred spirts, not him and her.

'Come over in the morning?' he proposed, but Pippa shook her head.

'I'll be tired.'

'Later, then? I still owe you a dinner…'

'French champagne to toast your last shift here?' she said, and hoped he missed the slight twist to her words.

'I think I can manage that. Then we can go back to mine for a proper celebration—and no having to get up at the crack of dawn to make the bed!'

'You've sold the flat?'

'Tentative offer.' He smiled, but she didn't quite know how to return it.

All his loose ends were being tied up and he would soon be gone. How could she toast that with champagne? Could she really keep up the pretence of not being emotionally involved until he left?

She needed to stay strong.

'I don't know if I can. I promised my parents I'd go over—'

'Pip,' he interrupted, and at the pursing of her lips checked himself. 'Pippa. If I remember rightly—and I do—you were lying to avoid your parents on the day we first met. Don't do the same to me. What's going on?'

Pippa closed her eyes and took a breath, then opened them. 'Okay, then. I don't like goodbyes.' It was only the tiniest fraction of what she was feeling. 'I don't know if I can sit there, raising a glass…' She tried to keep to the deal they had made. 'We've had a great month…'

Luke saw that she didn't meet his eyes.

He came around the desk and took a seat next to her. 'I'm not on the next plane out of here. In fact, I asked you to take some time off and join me.'

'I know you did.'

'And you still haven't answered.'

'What's the point, Luke?'

'Time away from here?' he suggested. 'A holiday?'

'And then what?'

'Pippa…'

'What if we don't work out?'

'I'm asking you for a holiday, Pippa, not a lifetime commitment!'

'I know that,' she snapped. 'I told you at the start that I'm not brilliant at long-term relationships.'

'It's just a couple of weeks in Scotland,' he pointed out.

'For you, maybe!' Her chair scraped as she pushed it back. 'I'm going to do the meds.'

Luke's mood wasn't great as he headed for the on-call rooms.

He knew he was changing the rules by suggesting a holiday, but he was changing too. He wanted more—and that was new to him. Usually he was more than ready to walk away.

Not now.

But what did he have to complain about? Luke thought, when he saw Evan sitting in the near-empty canteen.

And, yes, he was changing—because rather than walking on by he took a breath and forced himself to walk in.

'Hey.' Luke went over to Evan. 'Taking a break?'

'Yes, I'm just…' Evan stared at his uneaten roll. 'I don't know if we should show Darcy the recording of the funeral service or talk to him about it…'

Where was Pippa when he needed her? Luke thought. He'd been hoping to offer his polite condolences, even answer some medical questions, but this was much harder.

'I don't doubt you'll make the right choices with Darcy,' he said.

Evan nodded wearily, but then a look of agony flashed across his features, so acute that he might just as well have been punched, and as he folded over, Luke was certain he was reliving his choices that fatal morning.

Luke knew he was a good surgeon, but in this department he didn't exactly excel. Then he thought again of Pippa…how her words had brought comfort that night when he'd been berating himself for not transferring Hamish to be with his twin.

'Evan,' he said, placing his hand on the man's shoulder. 'I know you're questioning your decision not to leave the twins at home that morning.' He felt the man's grief beneath his fingers. 'But I've seen the consequences of that far too many times.'

Evan wept.

'I have,' Luke said. 'I've had to sit with parents who *have* made the wrong choices on many occasions. And I am telling you now, you did the right thing.'

'Thank you,' Evan said.

But Luke wasn't finished. 'May I say…?' He took a breath. 'May I say that I'm in awe of the two of you and how you've handled things with Darcy.'

He carried on comforting Evan as best he could. And afterwards, instead of heading to the on-call rooms, he went back up to Paediatrics.

To see Pippa again?

He didn't know why.

To say what?

He wasn't sure of that either.

He just knew that he could not leave things as they were.

He was used to dealing with the usual sulks after a break-up, but he'd asked her to join him in Scotland and he couldn't make sense of her reaction. He was still trying to keep things light—he'd told her he wasn't proposing marriage!

Then he stilled.

There she was, sitting at the desk with the lamp on. She was wearing a cardigan to keep out the chill, and he realised that her contact lenses must have been irritating her eyes because she was wearing glasses.

Suddenly, he was transported back to a day many years ago…

Philippa.

Who'd liked French and Art and…

It was coming back to him now.

Cake.

Philippa—which it turned out she didn't like to be called…

Julia's sister Philippa.

And now he knew her better, he could guess why she hadn't revealed the connection that day.

He watched her reach for a box of tissues and blow her nose. He wasn't vain enough to think it was to do with his leaving.

But he was sure enough in himself to know that it played a part.

A bigger part than he'd ever considered…?

Was Pippa actually…in love with him? And if she was, how the hell did he feel about that?

'Hey,' Luke said, walking over, and she blinked and looked up. 'You do have a super-memory.'

'Do I?'

He nodded. 'It *was* me in the library.'

'Told you.' She smiled.

'You were right—I had been crying that day.'

'So you do remember?'

'I'd just gone home to get my swim kit and caught my father cheating.' He gave a grim smile and then came around and took a seat beside her. 'I insisted that he tell my mother. I thought I was doing the right thing…'

Pippa looked at him.

'She didn't take it well, to say the least.' He exhaled sharply. 'She had a breakdown and ended up in hospital for a few weeks. I thought I'd killed her.'

'I'm so sorry,' Pippa said. 'No wonder you messed up your chemistry exam.'

'Bloody fragmentation.' He rolled his eyes. 'That's why I stay out of people's personal lives,' he said. 'Why I don't do long term…' His eyes never left her face. 'What about you?'

'Oh, I'd love to do long term,' Pippa readily admitted, but then hastily retracted. 'Maybe someday.'

'Yeah…'

'Thanks for remembering,' she said. 'It's silly, really, but it meant a lot to me at the time. I hated it that you'd—' Pippa pressed her lips together.

'Forgotten?'

She nodded. 'It doesn't matter now.'

They stopped talking as Evan came onto the ward and asked about Amber.

'She's asleep,' Pippa told him. 'Do you want me to show you where she is?'

'Let her sleep,' Evan said. 'I might go and lie down with Darcy.'

'So,' Luke said, when they were alone again, 'am I booking the French restaurant? I'll be barred if I cancel on them twice…'

'I don't think so.' She shook her head. 'No.'

Luke checked no one was around and leant in. 'You don't want champagne and a lot of sex?' he asked, feeling the heat from her burning cheeks. 'One more wild night…?'

'I'd rather give it a miss, thanks.'

He was dismayed, but he noticed what it cost her to force out a smile.

Liar!

He didn't say that, though.

As he walked across the ward, he glanced through the glass and saw Evan giving Darcy a drink with a straw and pulling a funny face to make his son laugh.

His own father had done that for him when he'd had his tonsils out. He'd come down from Theatre to check on him in the night, and persuaded him to take some fluids.

Luke didn't care that it was three a.m. He fired his father a quick text before he could change his mind.

Do you want to meet for lunch?

Matthew Harris didn't seem to care about the late hour either. Perhaps he was on a night shift himself.

Does midday work?

It did.

Luke looked back at Pip, who was carrying an angry toddler, bringing him to sit with her at the desk.

Pippa, he amended.

Yet he saw Philippa.

And he actually ached for all she'd been through.

She hadn't just been forgotten by her parents.

She had never really been loved.

Julia wasn't the ghost in that family. Pippa was.

Then, hearing a tap on the window, he turned and saw Darcy in his father's arms, smiling.

For the sake of his son, Evan was too.

As Darcy waved though the glass, so too did Evan, and of course Luke waved back, then gave a little thumbs-up to Evan.

What a brave man, Luke thought, and he realised that the Williams family were going to make it.

Despite all that life had thrown at them, they would get through this.

In their own way…

CHAPTER FIFTEEN

PIPPA WOKE AT two in the afternoon, completely at sixes and sevens.

She wanted to see Luke, of course she did, but she honestly didn't know if she could get through a romantic dinner without falling apart at the seams.

Let alone sex.

And yet she wanted him so badly.

Luke's re-entry into her life had indeed muddied the waters, and there wasn't a soul she could discuss it with.

Well, maybe one soul…

Pippa had never really found any comfort from going to the cemetery.

Julia's was possibly the best-kept grave in the place, given that her mother was here most days.

Today, though, Pippa had it to herself. She took off her coat and placed it on the ground then sat on it. Staring at the grave she looked at all the little things her mother brought and frequently re-arranged.

'I wish I could talk to you,' Pippa said suddenly, her own voice surprising her. 'We always could talk.'

It was true.

She and Julia had tried not to upset her mother, but they had been more honest when it was just the two of them.

'Luke's been working at The Primary,' Pippa said, and realised that on top of everything else she felt guilty. As if she were stepping into her sister's life or her dreams—except that Julia and Luke had never really existed. 'We've been seeing each other. Just a casual thing,' she added hastily. But there was no reason to lie. 'Well, according to Luke… He's asked me to visit him when he moves Scotland, but there's no point.' She voiced another thing that scared her too. 'Can you imagine Mum's face if I told her?'

But in the past trying to protect her mother hadn't solved anything. Pushing down her feelings…even the fact of her existence…

'Pippa!'

She turned at the sound of her mother's voice, and saw that she carried the gardening basket that she always brought to the cemetery.

'I wasn't expecting to see you here!'

'Hi, Mum.' Pippa stood to give her mother a kiss, but it was a haphazard one as she was pulling on her gardening gloves at the same time. Then she put a little mat onto the frosty grass to kneel upon. 'I just thought I'd come… Have a few moments…' Pippa said falteringly.

'That's nice.'

'I was just telling Julia…' she took a breath '… that Luke Harris has been working at The Primary for the past month.'

'Oh!'

That had got her mother's attention.

'We've been seeing each other…'

'Pippa!' Her mother's eyes darted to the grave. 'Not here.'

'Then where?' Pippa said. 'Julia can't hear, Mum, and if she can, well…' She took a deep breath. 'If she can hear then it's nice for me to have someone I can actually talk to about myself…about how *I'm* feeling…'

Her mother stood up and pulled off her gloves. 'The one little relationship Julia had!' she hissed. 'Of all the men in the world, you have to take the one that she cared for the most.'

'Of all the men in the world,' Pippa shouted, 'he was the one *I* cared for the most!'

She took a shuddering breath and felt the sting of tears as she admitted out loud the truth she'd been fighting not to reveal, even to herself.

'He was the one. Even back then.'

She stormed off.

'Pippa!' her mother called out.

'What?' Pippa turned around but did not retrace a single step. 'What do you want?'

'I had no idea about—'

'How could you have? The only thing we ever talk about is Julia! It was my birthday last week. My thirtieth!'

'I know that. There's a card and—'

'I don't *want* a card!' Pippa was too upset to even shout any more. 'Or money. I wanted you to remember…to make a fuss. Just for once not to make me feel guilty for existing.'

'Pippa!'

'You don't have room for me in your heart.'

She felt tears splashing down her cheeks, and she didn't know if she was crying for Julia, for her lost relationship with her mother, or even for Luke, who surely didn't want her desperate love either.

'It's true...'

'Pippa!' Her mother's voice was shocked. 'I did my best...'

'Well, it wasn't enough.'

She practically ran from the cemetery, gulping back sobs as she hurried into the Underground, desperate to make it home...

And there she cried like she never had before.

She had hidden her tears from Julia, and later from her parents, and in the end from herself too. Now Pippa curled up on the bed and cried, and it sounded so much like Amber sobbing her heart out that at the thought of that little family Pippa only wept harder.

It didn't help, though. Because she wanted Luke's arms to be holding her. She wanted the one thing he would never give, and she couldn't put herself through this any longer.

Yes, Julia had been able to laugh and squeeze every ounce out of her life, but she wasn't here any more. Her advice had run out.

Pippa really was alone.

She gulped as she admitted the truth to herself: she was scared.

Scared of being in love.

Scared of being left behind.

Scared of being forgotten.

As Pippa's sobbing slowed, it felt to her as if her sister was in the room. It truly felt as if she could hear Julia's breathless voice…as if Julia was stroking her hair.

'Pip, everybody gets scared at times. I just tell myself I'll let myself be scared tomorrow…'

It had made little sense at the time, but it made every sense now!

Before she could change her mind, Pippa called for a taxi. She had precisely fifteen minutes to transform her red and swollen face into something French-restaurant-worthy.

She slicked on some lipstick and hoped her wild hair would cover the worst as she pulled on the lilac dress he'd stood her up in once already.

Then she pulled on heels and took the Santorini picture from the ledge.

She was ready.

Ready for one final night with Luke.

Then she'd tell him what he could do with his emotionally uninvolved relationships and walk out of his life.

Whatever the day brought—or the night—Pippa vowed to deal with it by telling herself she could be scared tomorrow. Just like Julia.

It only dawned on her as she buzzed his intercom that she'd told him not to book the restaurant.

'Pippa!'

He buzzed her up and stood at the door, wearing

the bottom half of a suit, naked from the hips up and holding a glass of wine. She could hear music in the background.

'I thought you weren't...'

'I'm intruding,' Pippa said, suddenly worried that her replacement was already in situ! 'I should have called first.'

'Of course not.' He held the door open. 'What's this?'

'The Santorini picture you liked.' She gave him a wicked smile. 'It might help clinch the sale.'

'Or have the buyers running for the door. Are you okay?' he checked.

Perhaps he'd noticed that she looked a bit off.

'Contact lenses!' Pippa said. 'Allergies.'

'Goodness,' he replied, and poured her a glass of red. 'You're not allergic to this, I hope?'

'No, that would be lovely.' She took a rather hefty gulp. 'I had a row with my mum,' she admitted.

'Bad?' he asked.

They certainly weren't playing traffic controllers tonight, because she didn't put her hand up to halt him. 'Dreadful. I think I said too much.'

'Well, I can't really imagine you doing that,' Luke admitted, 'but even if you did, there's a lot of hurt and trauma there. Some things have to be said.'

'Yes.'

'If it makes you feel better, I had a row with my dad,' he told her. 'I took your advice and went for lunch with him.' Luke sighed. 'We started arguing in the car park, before we'd even gone in.'

'Oh!'

'But then we actually managed to eat lunch. I don't understand the details, and frankly I don't want to.' He rolled his eyes. 'We've called a truce.'

'That's so good.'

'Thanks to you,' he said. 'Look, I wouldn't want their marriage—but then I don't have to live it, do I?'

'No.'

'Oh, and I told him I'm getting them tickets for that interactive theatre thing for Christmas and that he's to take my mother this time.'

Pippa laughed, and it was a real laugh. Because that was what he did, even on dark days: he made her smile. No, she would never regret this crazy month.

'Is it too late to book the restaurant?'

'Sorry.' He shook his head. 'Not a hope on a Saturday night.'

'Oh, well,' Pippa said. 'Just sex, then…'

'Wow!' he said, blinking.

'Look, I know I've been a bit difficult. But I did warn you I was lousy at relationships.'

'You're hard work for a fling.'

'Yes.'

'But more than worth it.' He placed down his glass and then took hers too and pulled her into his arms. 'How did you leave things with your mum?' he asked.

'I don't know,' Pippa admitted, feeling his naked chest against her cheek and allowing herself the bliss of being held in his arms. 'I can smell baby powder…'

'I like it,' he said. 'I bought a can of my own…'

'You didn't!' she said.

'No, I pinched one of yours for work.' He lifted her face and gave her a soft kiss. 'I'm so glad you came.'

How close she'd come to missing this… Pippa didn't even want to consider it. She could lose herself in his kiss for ever, and she loved the easy way he dealt with her dress, lifting her arms and pulling it over her head.

Taking her hand, he led her to the bedroom.

'Excuse the mess.'

She didn't care if the bed was unmade, especially when he was pushing her down onto it. She let go as he slid her knickers off and delivered the bliss that only he could with his mouth.

'Sorry, Pip,' he said, just as she was about to come. He left her on the edge of heaven as he unzipped and then, patient and tender no more, he was inside her. 'I couldn't wait.'

She wrapped her thighs around him and clung on, because, in truth, neither could she. A rollercoaster called Luke had thundered back into her life, and now he was looking right at her as he took her, and she was looking back at him.

Until she couldn't any more. And then she closed her eyes to the bliss and the noise of them coming together.

'Damn, Pip,' he said as he lay on top of her. 'You've messed up my plans…'

It had been the most rapid, intense sex of her life. She resurfaced, a little bewildered, not just by his words but because all the familiar landmarks were missing.

No cushions.

No rugs.

No ugly pictures on the walls.

'That was unexpected!' he said, as she lay staring at the ceiling. 'I hope the estate agent doesn't bring someone to view—'

'Stop!' She was startled by the horror of that thought. 'I thought it was under offer?'

'Not any more.'

'Did they withdraw?'

'Please don't talk about withdrawing,' he said, and with his hand sliding between her thighs it was indecent with meaning.

'I told you. I'm on the Pill. I take it religiously. I've got the—' She took a breath and then just said it. 'I'm a carrier.'

'Well, thankfully I'm not.'

She frowned. 'How do you know?'

'I got a test. That's what I was trying to discuss.'

'Why would you go and get tested?'

'Because I felt bad for being careless that morning, and I guessed there was a reasonable chance you had the gene. If there were consequences… Well, that would have been one thing we'd have needed to know.'

'You went and had a test?' Her voice was incredulous. 'You did that?'

'I was hardly strapped to monitors and asked to run for an hour with a mask on. It was a cheek swab.'

'But...why?'

'Because I care about you, Pippa. Because we'd have needed to know....'

He said it so calmly, and in such a matter-of-fact voice, when all she'd ever known was panic and fear around the subject.

'Come on—get dressed. We need to eat. Chicken Provençal is waiting.'

'But you couldn't get a reservation.'

'No, but I could get them to deliver. I just need to warm it. We're not eating dinner naked.'

'Why not?'

'I have standards.'

He pulled a shirt out of its plastic bag and retrieved the bottom half of his suit from the floor, then went to select a tie.

'Are we seriously dressing up?'

'Yes,' Luke said. 'We're celebrating.'

Remembering her vow to face anything now and be scared tomorrow, Pippa retrieved the clothes she'd so hurriedly taken off and went into his bathroom.

He'd spun her completely!

But she was going to be brave and fearless...

'Dinner!' he called.

She walked into the living room and found that

he'd set the table. There was even a candle stuck in a wine bottle.

'This looks incredible,' Pippa said as he brought over two plates.

'Never tell Anton that I microwaved it,' Luke said, laughing, and he let her take a gorgeous herby mouthful. 'Or that we had red wine with it...'

'I won't,' Pippa said, and didn't add that she'd never get the chance to now. She was through with sniping and being insecure. Instead, she would enjoy the gorgeous food and wine, and of course the company too.

'Pip...' Luke said, and she looked up at his serious tone. 'I haven't been completely honest...'

'That's okay,' Pippa said.

After all, she hadn't been completely honest with him either. He'd have run a mile, Pippa knew, if he'd known the strength of her feelings for him.

'The thing is,' Luke said, 'I need a break...'

'I get it,' Pippa said. 'This has been great. It really has—'

'Pip!' he interrupted. 'I mean from work.'

'Oh.'

'I'm not going to Scotland for work,' he told her. 'I had a great mentor in Philadelphia, and he was very insistent that it's important to take a break and get away every so often. He goes fishing...'

'You're going fishing?'

'No.'

He was very serious, Pippa realised, and she put down her cutlery.

'I need a month or two away from broken bodies,' he said. 'I scoffed at Carl at the time, but I can see now he was right. I love my job, and I'm going to keep doing it, but I'm going to make sure I take my breaks more seriously.'

'And not take on a month's casual work while you sell your flat?' Pippa said, and raised her glass. 'I'll drink to that!'

'Come with me,' Luke said. 'I know the off-duty's tricky, and that you may have a new job soon, but…'

Pippa was determined to be the bravest she'd ever been. And instead of declining, instead of running from potential hurt, she followed her heart and nodded. 'I'd love to come to Scotland.'

'You're sure?'

'Very.' She gave her bravest smile. 'Can't leave you sex-starved in your little stone cottage.'

'I'll get dessert,' he said, and looked at her. 'What are you smiling at?'

'You,' Pippa admitted. 'How you can just end a conversation—an important one—as if you're calling for the bill!' She even laughed. 'Will you wave me off in the morning?'

'I hope not,' Luke responded, and disappeared into the kitchen.

He came out with a cake, lit with one long, slender candle.

'You didn't have to do that…' She laughed, but there was a lump in her throat that he was trying to make that awful birthday up to her. 'I told you, it was no big deal…'

'It's a very big deal,' Luke said. 'Because as well as asking you to join me in Scotland, I *would* like a lifetime commitment.'

He put down the cake.

And it was not just any cake!

'You deserve cake on your birthday. I'm so sorry I added to the misery of this year's. Now, I was going to make one myself, but in the end I left it to the experts,' Luke explained to his stunned audience. 'Smoked almond praline and chocolate.'

But Pippa wasn't interested in the ingredients, no matter how delicious they sounded. Neither was she interested in the pale white candle, with its twitching flame. She was only interested in the appalling piping that looked so at odds with the exquisite, delicate cake…

Surely they'd delivered the wrong cake. Because instead of *Happy Birthday* it read: *Marry me.*

'I decided not to attempt a question mark,' Luke joked. 'There wasn't room.'

'I thought they'd delivered the wrong cake…'

'It's the right cake. Well, it's certainly the one I piped.'

'*You* piped this?'

'Much to Anton's scorn.'

'Why?'

'It's the little things,' he said, as she had to him one day. 'Though, before you say yes or no, in the interests of full disclosure…'

'You have an ex-wife?' Pippa checked, and he shook his head.

'Children?'

'Close,' Luke said. 'A puppy with bathroom issues.'

'You're taking Sausage?'

He rolled his eyes as he nodded. 'I have to walk him in an hour and then drag all his stuff over here. Oh, and I've taken the flat off the market.'

'Why?'

'I want your dark art on my walls.' He took her hands. 'I don't want to a be a lone wolf. I don't want my parents' messes and mistakes to serve as my lessons in life. I love you, and I think you might have a little more than just a crush on me...'

He knew! Pippa realised.

But he couldn't know just how deeply she loved him.

'I love you too much,' Pippa admitted, and then she looked over to him, wanting to make sure he knew how big her love was. 'I made a heart in art after the library that day. I painted it Kobicha-brown with russet and copper flecks. It was the closest I could get to the colour of your eyes.'

'Gosh...' He pondered that for a moment. 'Have you still got it?'

'Yes...' There was more. 'And I fantasised about you a few times...'

'That's fine.'

'No...' She flushed with guilt. 'I mean, when I was with someone else...'

'Well, I'm glad I could help!' He laughed.

'Luke, I love you, and I think I always have.'

'And I want your love. I want you to hole up with me in Scotland. If you can get time off, that is. And I'll talk to your parents.'

'Let me,' Pippa said. 'Luke, you're still on their mantelpiece. A picture of you and Julia.'

'I understand.' He nodded thoughtfully, then said, 'I don't particularly want our parents at our wedding…'

He held her hands, but it wasn't enough contact so she came around the table and sat on his knee.

'Look, I get that it might not work for you. They've only got one child. So if you think we ought to—'

'Just us,' she said.

'Just us?' Luke repeated. 'Is that a yes?'

'You didn't need the question mark, Luke.'

He'd had her heart since she was sixteen years old.

'It's always been a yes.'

CHAPTER SIXTEEN

IN FEBRUARY SHE would be starting her new role at The Primary, and Luke had landed a plum consultancy job at a famous teaching hospital—one without the shadow of his father hanging over it.

'Six consecutive weeks off each year…'

It was written into his contract, and even though Pippa didn't have quite enough pull to get it written into hers, she had told Miss Brett that she'd be taking the same.

As for Pippa's parents…she'd told them that she was serious about Luke.

At least they were talking…

And the picture on the mantelpiece had thankfully been taken down.

But right now, it was their wedding day.

Pippa wasn't even nervous. How could she be when she felt as if this day had been etched into her lifeline—as if they'd been destined for each other and finally the world had caught up with what had been written in the stars.

As well as that, she was grappling with new underwear, as Luke watched on.

'We're not having sex again until we're legal,' he told her.

'Then hurry up and make me your wife!' Pippa laughed as she pulled on a gorgeous jade dress. 'My favourite colour…'

She looked down at her stunning engagement ring, which sported an emerald with every shade of captivating green—even army-green. She loved it so much.

'Here,' he said, handing her a small box. 'Your flowers.'

Heather and thistles.

Spiky and soft.

A lot like life.

And—also a lot like life—very beautiful too.

Luke picked up Sausage, who was dressed in a tartan bow for the occasion, and they headed off to be wed.

The Wee Neuk was the smallest wedding venue in Edinburgh's City Chambers, and for Pippa and Luke it was the perfect venue for such a special day.

The celebrant greeted them warmly, along with their two witnesses. Their hands were wrapped in silk rope, and they exchanged the traditional hand-fasting vows they had chosen.

'Do you, Luke, take Philippa to be your wife? To be her constant friend, her partner in life, and her true love? To love her without reservation, honour and respect her, protect her from harm, comfort her in times of distress, and to grow with her in mind and spirit?'

'I do,' Luke said in a confident, clear voice.

And those vows, those words, meant everything to Pippa. She took a breath, and the celebrant asked her the same questions.

'Do you, Philippa, take Luke to be your husband? To be his constant friend…?'

Till then, Pippa had done all she could to hold it together. She'd never thought it would be Luke's eyes that would fill with tears.

Of course she knew that he loved her, but it was then, in that moment, that she understood just how much, and what these words meant to him.

'…and to grow with him in mind and spirt?' the celebrant asked.

'I do,' Pippa said, and then she looked at the man her heart loved, and reiterated, 'I really do.'

And with the rope removed, and their promises still hanging in the air, he pulled her into his arms and held her.

Pippa felt a moment of bewilderment and wonder. 'We're family now.'

'We are,' Luke agreed. He looked at the white-gold ring she'd placed on his finger, and then back to her, and said, 'You've got me now.'

And it wasn't said in an arrogant way. He wasn't teasing her for her devotion. He was gently addressing the fact that she'd never really been loved. Well, apart from by one other person…

'Are you ready?' he asked, when the paperwork was all done.

Because there was one more place they needed to be before they headed to a beautiful hotel for the first night of their honeymoon.

And then off to Skye…

Luke held her hand as a driver took them on the hour and a half journey to St Andrew's. There was a light snowfall, and Pippa looked out at the North Sea, which was churning and grey, and then to the gorgeous buildings dusted in white. She gasped at the splendour of the university.

'They won't mind?' she checked.

'I told you—I've made all the arrangements.'

As she stepped out of the car a piper was playing—by chance, Pippa thought at first. But then he walked ahead of them, leading them to the chapel.

'Amazing Grace' had been played at her sister's funeral, but it sounded so much sweeter now, and this time around she was free to cry, even on this, the happiest day of her life.

'I came,' Pippa said, recalling one of her conversations with Julia, when her sister had asked her to visit St Andrew's in her place. 'Thank you,' she said.

And she laid her little posy on the steps, because without her sister's brave spirit spurring her on she might never have had the courage to risk her heart and say yes to Luke's proposition. Even if they had only lasted a month, Pippa knew it would still have been worth it.

'I love you, Julia.'

She always had and always would.

Then she turned to Luke, who was holding Sausage, and took his hand as they walked back to the car. 'I wish she'd been here today.'

'You'd have been fighting like two cats over me...' he teased.

'Stop it!' She nudged him playfully, and then, in the midst of her tears, she started to laugh. And it was so nice to actually laugh as she spoke about her sister. 'You're so sure of yourself!'

'Oh, I am today,' he said.

So sure of their love.

* * * * *

An American Doctor In Ireland

Karin Baine

MILLS & BOON

Karin Baine lives in Northern Ireland with her husband, two sons and her out-of-control notebook collection. Her mother and her grandmother's vast collection of books inspired her love of reading and her dream of becoming a Harlequin author. Now she can tell people she has a *proper* job! You can follow Karin on Twitter @karinbaine1 or visit her website for the latest news, karinbaine.com.

Visit the Author Profile page
at millsandboon.com.au for more titles.

Dear Reader,

When I was asked to write a book around St. Patrick's Day, my mind went immediately to the parade. They're such a spectacle all around the world I knew I could have some fun celebrating all things Irish!

In the manner of those stereotypical romcoms based in Ireland, I thought I'd throw in a wisecracking Irishman and an American seemingly impervious to his charms. Of course that's never the case...

Beneath the surface, Liam is hiding a broken heart and doing his best to raise his daughter alone. Mae, who was jilted at the altar, has moved to Dublin to start a new life—one that doesn't include any significant other with the potential to abandon her. She has locked herself away from the world in order to protect her fragile heart.

So, when she finds herself inextricably linked with Liam through an inebriated St. Patrick, and his enormous Irish wolfhound, her life is turned upside down.

I hope you enjoy every leprechaun and shamrock I've thrown at this book celebrating Ireland, the people and the culture. It's a magical place that deserves to be shared with everyone.

Happy reading!

Love,

Karin x

DEDICATION

For me, because I don't give myself
nearly enough credit! x

CHAPTER ONE

A SEA OF green spread out before Mae Watters. Well, it was a crowd of people dressed for St Patrick's Day. They didn't dye the River Liffey in Dublin green especially for the occasion, the way they did back home in Boston, but it still reminded her of every seventeenth of March she'd spent with her mother at the parade there. And, when she was old enough, they'd graduated to the Irish-themed pubs to celebrate the day.

A year without her had been difficult. Not least because Mae had had no one to turn to when, humiliatingly, her relationship had come to an end. Being jilted at the altar eight months ago, and being left alone in Ireland to pick up the pieces left of her heart, had left her feeling more alone than ever.

It wasn't as though she had any family left in America to go back to—at least, none who wanted to know her. The father who'd left her when she was little could have started a new family and given her half-brothers and sisters, but she'd never know, as he'd disappeared completely out of her life.

'Excuse us.' A family dressed as leprechauns squeezed past her on the footpath, keen to get to the best vantage point for the parade. She envied the young couple pushing the double stroller transporting a baby and toddler, giddy with excitement. Not because she wanted children, or even a husband now, but because of the family unit it represented—something she'd never have. She'd lost too much, too many loved ones, ever to open herself up to anyone again and to have a chance of starting a family of her own.

Perhaps she shouldn't have come here today, when her spirits weren't as high as everyone else's. Music was blasting all along the street and people were singing, clapping and waving Irish flags as the floats came past to celebrate the patron saint of Ireland. All she wanted to do was cry. But it was a rare day off before she started her new job, it was her Mum's home city and she'd thought she'd feel closer to her here. The problem was, she had, until she remembered that the cruelty of illness had separated them for ever. It was a cruel irony to specialise in medicine when you couldn't save your own mother.

'Ye—oh!'

She was jostled off-balance by a man carrying a little girl high on his shoulders as they pushed in beside her, dancing to the music. Usually, common sense would have prevented her from confronting a tattooed male with bright-green hair, but today her emotions were all over the place.

'Do you mind?' She bristled, rubbing her elbow, which had been banged in the melee.

'Not at all, love!' He grinned, the twinkling blue eyes and bright-white smile not intimidating in the slightest.

Perhaps that was why she wouldn't drop the issue.

'Well, I do mind. I was standing minding

my own business until you rudely pushed past me.'

'Sorry, missus. The wee one wanted to see,' he said without a hint of genuine remorse.

'You should pinch her, Dad.'

'Excuse me?'

'It's a tradition. You're supposed to wear green today to remain invisible to the leprechauns, otherwise you get pinched.'

Despite the man's explanation of why his daughter was so keen for him to assault her, Mae wasn't impressed by his behaviour.

'Perhaps you'd be better teaching her something about manners... And it's *Ms*, actually.' She didn't need the reminder that she hadn't actually got to the part where she'd changed her name, or even got a husband.

'Says it all,' he muttered.

Mae could feel her blood starting to boil at the utter gall of the man insulting her when he was the one in the wrong. If not for the presence of the child, she would've had a few choice words to say to him.

'What does?'

'Well, it's that time of the year, isn't it?

When all you Yanks come over thinking you'll bag an Irish husband.'

'How dare you?' she blustered. 'I live here.'

His rude comments made her bypass her usual polite manner when dealing with irascible men, common in her line of work, in which she'd learned to smile and plough on rather than react.

But today she rose to the bait. Probably because she'd finally reached her limit of things she could stand in this wet, miserable country. She had followed her heart here, hoping for the romantic fantasy of living happily ever after with her charming Irish fiancé in the seaside town of Bray, but she'd earned her place with every tear she'd shed since.

Especially when she'd been working to help the inhabitants of this country every day, despite her heartbreak. She'd moved out of the house she'd shared with Diarmuid, of course, but seeing him around the hospital had been too painful a reminder of what he'd done to her. Hopefully her move to the city would help her get over it.

The man took his eyes off the spectacle out

on the street to study her. 'Hmm. Then I'd wager you came back to find your Irish roots.'

Mae could feel the heat rising in her body, surely manifesting itself in those tell-tale red splotches that oft appeared on her neck when she was riled, as though the effort of trying to hold her temper threatened to burst right through her skin.

'My mother came from Dublin.' She tried to keep the hysteria from her voice as she attempted to justify her residence in the city.

'Of course she did.'

Mae was getting used to the dry Irish sense of humour, the gentle teasing that came with a nudge in the ribs and a twinkle in the eye. However, there was something about this know-it-all stranger that was really pushing her buttons today and making her want to scream.

She hated the fact that her life had boiled down to that of stereotypical American in Ireland. It said nothing of the heartache and loss she'd gone through to get here. If she was this touchy over a few teasing comments now, it was probably for the best that she went home, before the crowd really started celebrating the day, leaving her even more of an outsider.

It occurred to her that she wasn't beholden to be polite to this man or stand anywhere near him. Arguing back wasn't going to achieve anything other than upsetting her, when she was thinking about her mum. And, if that smile on his face grew any wider, she'd be tempted to smack it off.

In an attempt to avoid a possible assault charge, or an emotional breakdown in front of the most annoying man on earth, she simply turned and walked away.

'Wait. I'm sorry.' Liam had seen the flash of pain in the redhead's jade-green eyes before she turned away.

He hadn't meant to upset her. His big mouth was always getting him into trouble. Today was supposed to be fun for everyone involved and he didn't want to be responsible for spoiling anyone's day. Sometimes his brand of humour didn't translate well with American visitors, earning him a clip around the ear from his mother even at the age of thirty-two, lest he offended any of her customers at the family pub. Which, today, should be welcoming as many tourists as possible.

Although he was first and foremost an A&E doctor in Dublin City Hospital, he was often roped in to collect empty glasses during busy periods in the pub. He and Shannon, his daughter, spent a lot of time there. Not because he was a drinker, but because his parents lived in the flat above the premises, and babysat when he was at work.

Since his partner of nine years, Clodagh, had left him—for his best friend, no less—he'd had to rely on help with the school run and occasionally in the evenings when he was working. Shifts in A&E weren't compatible with the life of a single dad. It wasn't the happy family life he'd planned, or the life he now wanted, and he was burdened with the guilt he'd let down his daughter, as well as asking too much of his parents for the best part of a year. The last thing he needed on his conscience was knowing he'd caused unnecessary upset to someone else.

Liam watched the blaze of red hair bobbing

through the crowd, a beacon in the green tide that made her easily identifiable.

'Da-ad! I can't see the parade,' Shannon complained as he followed the American away from the prime view he'd gone to so much trouble to secure.

'I know, sweetheart. I just need to speak to the lady again.'

'The pretty lady with the red hair?' Shannon kicked her heels into his chest to indicate she wanted to dismount his shoulders. Liam bent down as far as he could, reached up and lifted her down on to the ground. She took off before he could even ask what she was up to.

'Shannon! Don't run away!' he shouted, to no avail, and was forced to chase after the green tutu disappearing into the crowd. In pursuit of his daughter, he dodged mums with prams and men with cans in their hands, his heart pounding with the fear of losing her in the crowd. Although she knew the city well, she was only seven years old. She was his baby. She was all he had. He caught sight of her as she located the American redhead, though she remained out of his reach.

Shannon tugged on the belt of the woman's white wool coat. 'My dad wants to speak to you. I can't see the parade until you talk to him.'

Unfortunately, his offspring had inherited his lack of tact, leaving him cringing as the woman watched him approach.

'I'm so sorry. Both for my daughter accosting you, and for upsetting you earlier. I was joking about the whole "Irish roots" thing.' He took Shannon's hand and discreetly pulled her to his side.

The redhead arched an eyebrow at him. 'No, you weren't. You were enjoying belittling me. Believe it or not, a high percentage of Americans *are* actually of Irish origin. My mother was a Dublin girl. I moved here last year after she died. So, in future please think before you judge people.'

'I apologise for thinking I was being funny.'

'You're not,' the American and his daughter chorused.

'Apparently...' He tucked that little nugget

away for future reference, something to add to his list of failures.

'Do you often use your daughter to get women to talk to you?' Red asked, clearly enjoying watching him squirm.

It was the price he'd have to pay for sticking his size tens in it in the first place.

'Not often, no. Again, I can only apologise. If you're ever in O'Conner's in Westmoreland Street, I'll even buy you a pint to say sorry.'

'O'Conner's?'

'My parents own it—and you won't pay Temple Bar prices there.'

'I thought you were buying,' she said, quick as a flash.

'Only the first round. The next one's on you.' Were they flirting? He was so long out of the game, he couldn't tell. Though he wasn't interested in any Paddy's Day shenanigans, unlike most of the Irish population, he was enjoying the back and forth between them.

'Dad! Dad! There's Ray!'

Before he could get a definitive answer as to whether or not he'd see his new banter partner again, Shannon was tugging on his shirt and pointing towards the parade. Ray, their next-door neighbour, was walking head and shoulders above the rest of the parade. Easily done when he was wearing stilts, dressed as St Patrick in emerald-green robes, wore a mitre on his head, and carried a staff in his hand, chasing several people dressed as snakes.

'A friend of yours?' the American beauty asked as they watched his antics.

'Ray Jackson. My next-door neighbour.' Despite everyone else's enthusiasm, Liam couldn't quite bring himself to join in on the cheering.

'What's wrong? Did he steal your outfit?'

'No. He has an alcohol problem, and it looks very much to me as though he's been drinking already today.' Not a good idea to be drunk in charge of stilts, he was sure.

Right on cue, there was a collective gasp from the crowd as St Patrick began to topple, almost crushing one of the green leotard-clad snakes in the process.

'Can you keep an eye on Shannon for me?'

He didn't intend letting his daughter out of his sight, even if he had left her with a trustworthy-looking stranger, but being a doctor wasn't a job that finished at five o'clock, or even stopped on a day off.

'But I…'

With a patient and friend to attend to, he didn't wait around to hear the excuse.

'What are you playing at, Raymondo?' he asked, running over to assess the damage. The music and laughter had ceased now, happy faces etched with concern, fingernails being bitten as St Patrick lay in a heap in the middle of the road.

'I think I lost my balance. I'm getting too old for this.' Ray groaned through gritted teeth.

'You don't say. I'm going to have to take these things off you so I can get a proper look at that leg.' The right leg, which was crumpled under the middle-aged saint, looked to be at an odd angle. Liam gingerly began to undo the stilts fastened around his feet.

'Stop! Don't move him,' a now familiar American twang instructed.

'Can you stay back, please? I've got this. And where is my daughter?' Now that the redhead was walking towards him minus her charge, nausea began to swell in his stomach. He should never have taken his eyes off her.

'She's with her grandmother. Now, please move aside so I can take a look.' She knelt down beside him, regardless that her white coat would be covered in green glitter and paint from the road when she got up again.

At least Shannon was okay, and he was glad his mum had found time for a break after all—just in time for another spot of babysitting. He glanced over and gave her a thumbs-up when he spotted her hovering at the edge of the crowd. She gestured that she'd take Shannon back with her to the pub, leaving him to focus on the job at hand.

'Thanks, but I've got this,' he insisted. 'I'm a doctor.'

'So am I,' she countered, bringing them to a stalemate.

'Good for you.' He was surprised that an American doctor should have chosen to move to Ireland to work. This wasn't about egos;

Raymond was hurt and currently holding up the entire St Patrick's Day parade.

He could feel her bristle beside him. 'You don't look much like a doctor.'

'What happened to not being too judgemental? The green hair was "fun dad" showing up for Shannon today. It's my day off.'

'And the tattoos?'

He was tempted to tell her they were the marks of a misspent youth. It wasn't against the medical oath, or any of her business, how he'd chosen to adorn his body. However, it gave him huge satisfaction, seeing her face when he licked his thumb and smudged the Irish flag he'd drawn on his arm this morning to match the shamrocks he'd painted on Shannon's cheeks.

'Listen, I'm glad I have two doctors fighting over me—but no offence, Liam, I'd prefer the redhead.'

'Not appropriate, Ray,' Liam admonished as he rolled up the man's trouser leg to uncover a nasty open fracture. The broken bone was sticking up through the wound, the swelling around the area already apparent. Given the fact Ray wasn't writhing in agony, he suspected the alcohol he'd consumed had gone some way to dulling the pain—small mercies.

'I suppose this will get done quicker if we work together. Dr Mae Watters.' She held out her hand for him to shake, which he duly did.

'Dr Liam O'Conner. First things first, we need to call an ambulance.' He knew there were probably medical staff on hand to cover the parade, but Ray was going to need to be transferred to the hospital for treatment.

'I've done that, and we know he's conscious and responsive, if a tad inebriated.'

'Hey! I—I needed some Irish courage,' Ray hiccupped, the stench of booze and stale cigarettes making Liam and Mae recoil.

'We'll have to stabilise that leg.' It was necessary to immobilise the limb to prevent further injury until he reached hospital. Without a sterile dressing to hand, Liam used the green silk stole around Ray's neck to apply pressure to the wound without covering the bone.

'You can use my belt to fashion something

with the stilt,' Mae suggested, whipping out the tie from the waistband of her coat.

'Just let us know if it hurts or you start to feel nauseous, Ray. The paramedics will be able to give you something for the pain when they get here,' Mae reassured him as Liam worked quickly to bind the leg to the makeshift splint above and below the fracture, careful not to jar the leg any more than necessary.

'Ah, the good stuff…' Ray trailed off and Liam wondered exactly how much he had drunk this morning. He knew he wouldn't be honest with him about his alcohol consumption—he never was—though Liam heard the rattle of bottles going into the recycling bin every morning. It wouldn't be a good idea to mix painkillers with a skinful of alcohol, and he'd be sure to fill the ambulance crew in on his neighbour's history. At least, what he knew of it, from the drunken ramblings and numerous falls Ray had suffered since his partner had died a couple of years ago.

'We're going to be having another talk about your drinking, Ray.'

Ray batted away his concerns with a tut and an eyeroll. They'd both had their personal problems, but Ray had been a visible warning to Liam not to give into the self-pity which had descended upon him too when Clodagh left him just over a year ago. He hadn't wanted to become another shell of a man who could barely function. Shannon needed more from him than ever. She was the reason he got up every morning, and the reason he didn't drown his sorrows in the bottom of a glass every evening. He felt sorry for his neighbour; he saw the pity in Mae's eyes, and he never wanted anyone to look at him the same way.

As much as he might need to blot out the memory of Clodagh cheating on him, ending their relationship and walking out on their family, it would be selfish to do so. Even more than pretending his relationship hadn't been in trouble, because that would've meant admitting his failure as a partner and father. A fact which was public knowledge anyway, now that they were separated.

In hindsight, having a family had always

been his idea of an idyll, not Clodagh's. They had only been dating a few months when she'd fallen pregnant, before they'd even talked about whether or not they wanted marriage and children. It later became apparent that, unlike him, she hadn't wanted either. Whilst he'd been over the moon at the prospect of becoming a parent, she hadn't been as enthusiastic.

Still in her twenties, Clodagh had always given the impression she resented being tied down to the responsibility of having a child. Liam had done his best to carry most of the load, doing most of the childcare, giving her the freedom to still go out with her friends. Perhaps somewhere along the way he'd pushed her out, creating a strong bond with Shannon that mother and daughter had never quite mirrored. Liam had no doubt she loved Shannon, but even now she seemed an afterthought next to Clodagh's work and personal life. He wished he could forget about Clodagh, and her betrayal, just as easily.

When the sirens sounded, the crowd began to part so the ambulance could get through.

'Yeah, yeah. If you tell me you haven't been tempted to lose yourself in a bottle since Clodagh left you, then you're a liar,' Ray rambled.

Though Mae didn't comment, Liam could feel her eyes on him. He refused to look up and see that same pity in her eyes for him.

'I've been tempted, Ray, yes. But it doesn't solve anything, does it? Only makes things worse.' Liam was relieved when the ambulance arrived so they could stop discussing his failed relationship under the watchful gaze of the entire city. There was one pair of green eyes in particular before which he didn't want to appear weak. Not when he'd already made such a sterling impression on his new American friend... Despite her being the first woman he'd felt the urge to engage in conversation since Clodagh had left, now he'd be glad to climb into the ambulance and leave her behind.

He relayed Ray's current condition to the medics and waited as they transferred him into the back of the ambulance.

'Who's coming with him?'

'I am,' both Liam and Mae chorused.

'Which hospital are you taking him to?' he enquired, hoping the geography would give Mae a reason to back off.

'Dublin City.'

'That's where I work.' He played his trump card with a flourish.

'Me too.' Mae killed his sense of triumph dead before he'd even had the chance to blow his horn.

Though she looked surprised by the co-incidence, there was no sign of her backing down. If anything, she looked smug that she had as much right to accompany the patient as he did.

If this feisty American was going to be his new colleague, work was about to get a lot more interesting.

CHAPTER TWO

LIAM WAS ABLE to fast-track Ray through the Accident and Emergency department thanks to his position and a large dose of charm. Mae followed, keen to see the patient through, regardless of her male counterpart seeming to have things under control—or perhaps in spite of. She hated to think of him having the upper hand and getting rid of her so easily. Yes, it was his neighbour, but they'd both been on scene and, since this was her new place of work, she'd just as much right to be here as Dr O'Conner.

It felt weird to call him that. Yes, she'd been unfairly judgemental about his appearance, but his demeanour around her thus far had left a lot to be desired. Even if he had worked well in a medical crisis.

'You can go home, if you want. I'll stay and make sure Ray is comfortable,' Liam told her outside the cubicle.

'I'd rather be here. I don't like his colour, and if you're right about his drinking…. I noticed distention of his abdomen, which could be due to the release of fluid from his liver, and the swelling in his lower legs might be fluid retention.' She was familiar with the yellowing complexion in long-term alcohol abusers and what it meant. All the symptoms she had noticed were indicative of liver disease—not things which would clear up of their own accord, and certainly not if the patient continued to drink heavily.

'I've thought the same thing myself for a long time but it's been next to impossible getting him to go to the doctor. That's why I've ordered a battery of tests while he's here, the full MOT, so I can be fully prepared when I go into battle and try to talk to him about his drinking problem again.'

Okay, so when he wasn't teasing and making rude, stereotypical jokes at her expense, he did sound like a doctor, and a good neighbour. It was one thing to strap up a broken leg and get someone to the hospital, but quite another to order up extra blood tests and wait for the results, on a hunch. Especially when it was his day off and he had a daughter at home.

Mae had heard the snippet of information about his personal life revealed by his inebriated friend and she couldn't help but be curious. Apparently, his partner had left him too—she hoped in less humiliating circumstances than her ex, though she knew that would be scant comfort. She knew what it was like to plan a future, a happy family and a life together with someone. Since he already had a daughter, she supposed he'd been planning a life together too before the bombshell had dropped. Knowing he'd likely suffered the same heartbreak and bewilderment she had gave her a new insight into the man she would no doubt run into again in the future, now they were working in the same building.

'I can have a chat to him too, if that would help? I'm a hepatologist, so this is my area of expertise. I have some contacts who can provide him with counselling, or some rehab options.' Addiction wasn't something cured with a prescription or good will. It took a desire on the patient's behalf to want to change, but it also required some outside help at times. She'd referred many of her patients over the years to various services away from the hospital and, whilst it didn't work for everyone, lots of people had benefitted from different forms of therapy.

'Thanks, but I think I'll try and get through to him first. He's a stubborn so-and-so. I know how to handle him.' When he saw her tense at the merest hint she wasn't up to the battle, he added, 'I wouldn't want you to get offended if he goes off on one.'

That comment didn't do anything to appease her. It only served to remind her of their initial meeting. Then she saw the same twinkle in his eye and realised he was goading her. The growl of frustration which came out of her mouth was as unfamiliar to her as it was amusing to him, as she pushed past him back into the cubicle, ignoring the chuckling behind her.

'Mr Jackson, I think we're going to have to keep you in overnight. Do you have anyone we can contact for you?' She watched Liam walk back into the cubicle, waiting for him to challenge her authority. Although she didn't officially start until tomorrow, and technically this was his jurisdiction, she was very much invested in this patient and his future.

A brief frown marked Liam's forehead before it disappeared again. 'We're running a few blood tests while you're here to see if there's anything else going on inside that body of yours.'

'I thought it was a clean break. Surely all I need is a bit of plaster and some crutches?' Ray was already trying to sit up, probably planning his escape to the nearest pub.

'The leg fracture should be a straightforward matter. However, it's your drinking that's causing us concern.'

Ray rolled his eyes at Liam's assessment.

'I'm a liver specialist, Mr Jackson, and I would like to keep you under observation tonight until we get the results of these tests. We might need to do a few body scans too, just so we can get a clearer picture of what's going on inside. Dr O'Conner has told me that alcohol may have been a factor in your fall today and, combined with the colour of your complexion, it gives me reason to think you might have some liver or kidney problems going on.' The whole time Mae was giving her talk, Ray was glaring daggers at Liam for throwing him under the bus.

'So, it's a crime to have a pint now, is it? It's St Patrick's Day, in case you hadn't noticed. The whole country's enjoying a drink today. Well, apart from you two, obviously.' Arms folded across his chest, Ray looked as belligerent as they came, but Mae was used to dealing with people in denial. They usually only ended up under her care because they'd been ignoring the signs of the toll alcohol was taking on their body, completely in the grip of their addiction, until it was obvious to everyone else around them. By the time they reached her door, they were experiencing severe repercussions of their lifestyle choices.

Of course, not all her patients were in the thrall of addiction; many had illnesses or congenital problems they had no control over. That was why she found people like Ray so challenging and frustrating. They'd had choices. Okay, so life wasn't as simple as saying yes or no to a drink or doing drugs, otherwise the world wouldn't be populated with people lost to their vices—but there was still time to turn their lives around. Too often they had no interest in doing so, content to take the easier path they'd grown accustomed to rather than doing the hard work it took to make the change.

'If it was just one drink we wouldn't be worried, Ray, but we all know it's more than that.' Liam was deep into his 'serious doctor' mode now and Mae could only imagine how often he'd first used the friendly approach to try and get his neighbour to slow down the drinking.

'What else have I got to look forward to if I can't have a beer?' he complained.

Mae might never understand that all-consuming desire for the next fix of alcohol or pills, but she knew how it felt to face that dark abyss, believing nothing good was ever going to happen again. After the wedding that never was, she'd spent some time there, wallowing in the grief for her mother and the loss of her relationship; realising she was destined to be on her own for the rest of her life.

Perhaps it was the strength of character she'd inherited from her mother which had pulled her out of that despair, and for that she gave thanks and counted herself lucky to have had such a badass role model. Not everyone was able to claw their way out of that quagmire, and she was sure her mother had languished there herself once upon a time, as a single parent in a foreign country. After all, she'd left behind her life in Ireland to follow her American tourist love, only to be left with a baby in a foreign country when he'd grown tired of family life. Not unlike Mae's situation, though thankfully she didn't have a child to bring up alone.

But the Watters women had managed to pick themselves up, dust themselves off and build up stronger defences than ever, which hopefully would prevent another emotional collapse. Especially now she'd sworn off serious relationships, negating the risk of ever being blindsided, humiliated and rejected by someone who was supposed to love her.

'There is a life outside of the bottle, Ray. I don't mean to sound patronising, but I think if you have a few days of clarity you'll come to the same conclusion yourself.' Mae knew she was playing with fire, especially when they weren't one hundred percent sure how bad Ray's addiction was. Even Liam had seemed surprised that he'd been drinking so early in the day, so perhaps he wasn't aware of the full extent of the man's difficulties. She didn't want to cross the line, especially when she was only starting her new job, but she wanted to help.

'I can't stay. You know I have to get back for Brodie.' Ray deferred to Liam as threw off the bed covers, clearly not intending to stay put.

'His dog,' Liam clarified.

'He's not just some wee dog that can be left alone. Brodie's an Irish Wolfhound who'll probably be wrecking the house as we speak. He doesn't like being left on his own.' It was clear Ray was using his pet as an excuse to leave, but Mae knew if he left now they'd likely never get him back for another investigation.

'I'm sure someone can look in on him—or, failing that, there are places we could phone to take care of him until you're discharged.' She was desperately trying to come up with answers to pacify him, and failing.

Enraged by the suggestion, he was now pulling himself up into a sitting position on the bed, trying to manoeuvre his injured leg so he could stand up. 'There's no way I'm giving my dog up. He's all I have. He's the only reason I get up in the morning. He has a routine and won't do well without me.'

'Wait, Ray. I can look in on him when I go home. Give me your keys and I can feed him and take him for a walk.' Liam's suggestion at least made Ray pause for thought.

'What about when you're at work? You know he likes company. I can't stay. No way.' Now Ray was on his feet and not even Liam, standing blocking his path, appeared to be enough to prevent him from hobbling away.

'I'll help too. I'm sure me and Liam won't

always be working at the same time, and it's only going to be for tomorrow, right? I can take a book and sit with him for a while after my shift. These tests are important, Ray.'

Mae surprised herself with the offer, but she was desperate, and she could see by the concern etched on his face that Liam was too. Minding a dog for a few hours didn't seem like a high price to pay if it meant improving the quality of a patient's life. Not that she'd be volunteering to pet-sit for every lonely patient that crossed her path or else she'd end up be-friending every cat lady in the city.

Both men were looking at her as though she were mad.

'You would do that?' Ray asked quietly, and it broke her heart to think that giving a few hours of her time to help him out was such a big deal to him.

'Yes.'

'That's settled. Ray, get back onto the bed, and Mae and I will see to Brodie. Happy St Patrick's Day.' Liam grinned and she couldn't help but think he'd somehow got the better of her.

* * *

This had been a bad idea all around. At first Liam had found some satisfaction in the idea of the haughty American trying to wrangle his next-door neighbour's giant mutt. It didn't seem so funny now that she was encroaching into his personal space. With both of them heading the same direction, and having volunteered to look after Ray's beast of a dog, he hadn't had much choice but to travel back with her to pick up Shannon and head home.

'After you.' He held the pub door open for Mae, half-expecting a lecture about how she didn't need anyone holding doors open for her. Instead, she tipped her head to him and walked in as though it was her local, without a hint of trepidation.

'It's not what I expected,' she said, glancing around before taking a seat in one of the booths.

'No? Not enough diddly-dee music or leprechauns leaping about for you?' he teased.

On cue, the traditional Irish penny-whistle music his mother liked to put on for visitors suddenly filled the bar. Mae chuckled, her shoulders heaving with every laugh at his expense.

'It's for the tourists, you know,' he tried to explain, fighting to be heard above the piercing tunes and Mae's deep, warm laugh.

In other circumstances, he might have been embarrassed at being shown up like that. He'd had enough of being made to look foolish when his partner and his best friend had been carrying on an affair right under his nose. It had been difficult to face people in public after that, wondering who'd known, and if people had been laughing at him behind his back.

With Mae, it was different. This game of trying to get the better of one another was a private joke between them—one that he was in on, not the butt of—and so far, this one-upmanship was the basis of their newly formed relationship. For work purposes only, of course. He wasn't interested in anything else so soon after his recent heartbreak.

Apart from anything else, bristly Mae didn't seem the motherly type, and that was something he would definitely be looking for in a potential partner—a sign that he'd found a soul mate who wanted to settle down and emulate his parents' happy marriage, which he envied. He'd thought when Clodagh had fallen pregnant that that would be the beginning of his dream coming true. He'd not realised that, instead of finding someone who wanted to settle down, his partner was someone whose head would be turned by a flash surgeon who only cared about his own wants, with no guilty conscience about splitting up a family.

'Well, you can tell them I'm not a tourist. Not any more.' She fixed him with an intense stare, but beneath it he could see the hint of a smile. This was how they'd butted heads earlier, but thankfully she appeared to have forgiven him for being a clumsy big oaf. Still, it wouldn't hurt to butter her up, in case he needed her help in the future at the hospital, or during their spell of dog-sitting.

'What can I get you to eat and drink? I'm not sure we've got any of the green stout left but I'm sure we've still got some boiled bacon and cabbage.' He couldn't seem to help bait-ing her, although he knew to stay away from the matter of her own heritage. It was clearly a touchy subject, and no wonder, if she'd recently lost her mother. Liam's family were so supportive of him and Shannon, he'd feel as though he'd lost a limb if anything ever happened to either of his parents.

'I'm fine, thanks. If you just want to take me to Ray's house to meet the famous Brodie…' She clearly couldn't wait to get out of the place but he knew his mother would never forgive him if he didn't make an introduction. She'd be offended if he brought someone into the family business and she didn't have the opportunity to show off her hospitality skills.

'All in good time. There's no way my ma is going to let me go without a feed in me. Besides, I'll have to wait until Shannon has had her tea as well, before I can go. Now, what can I get you to drink?' He wouldn't dare to presume.

'White wine would be great, thank you,' she said, apparently resigned to the fact they were staying for dinner.

'Good choice.' Liam made his way over to

the bar, keen to put their order in before the crowds of hungry tourists descended in earnest after a day in the sunshine.

He also wanted to chat to his mother to explain the circumstances. As someone who was always pushing for him to meet someone else, it would be easy for her to get carried away with the idea Mae was someone more than a new work colleague, and he wanted to nip that notion in the bud.

'How's Shannon been?' he asked, helping himself to a chip out of the basket his father was just plating up with some tasty-looking steaks.

'She's upstairs with your mum having something to eat. I'm glad you're here; I need her down here to help me serve up the food.'

'Shannon?'

'Your mum, you eejit.' His father gave him a good-natured clout around the ear for winding him up. He was never too old to tease them, or for a slap when he deserved it.

'Can I get two plates of pie and champ?' His stomach was rumbling. Usually by now he'd have had sampled most things on the menu, but events had overtaken his appetite, and he hadn't eaten since breakfast.

'Two plates?'

'Yeah, I've got a new work colleague with me. We had to miss most of the parade to go to the hospital.'

'The girls said there'd been an accident. Everything all right?' His father stopped stirring and slicing long enough to show his concern.

'Ray had one too many before he decided to head up the parade dressed as St Patrick, wearing stilts.'

The busy chef resumed his duties, shaking his head. 'I won't serve him in here any more. He's only hurting himself.'

'I know. I've had a chat with him and we're keeping him in overnight. Meanwhile, I'm helping to look after Brodie.'

His good deed earned a hearty laugh. 'Good luck with that.'

Liam helped himself to another chip. 'I know. Shannon will enjoy it, though. I'm just going to pop upstairs to see her and mum. We're sitting over at table two by the door— the redhead in the white coat.'

As Liam opened the swing door to go upstairs, his father leaned his head round to gawp at his companion, and gave an appreciative whistle and nod.

'She's a colleague, Da,' he reiterated before disappearing upstairs to repeat it all over again.

Mae sat people-watching whilst waiting for Liam to return to the table. It wasn't quite the quiet, reflective day she'd expected to have, but perhaps that wasn't a bad thing, when she'd started to spiral into grief, thinking about her mum before Liam and his daughter had rudely crashed into her self-pity.

She envied the jovial atmosphere the customers exuded, standing at the bar, waiting impatiently for their drinks. Every now and then the general hubbub was interrupted with raucous laughter or cheering as those dressed head-to-toe in green, or sporting fake ginger beards, egged each other on in stupid drinking games. They were clearly here for 'the craic', as they said around these parts, whereas she'd come to the parade to reminisce about those fun days she'd had with her mother. At least battling with Liam and Ray had taken her mind off more depressing matters.

She watched a man dressed in chef whites walk over, older than the other members of staff behind the bar, carrying a glass of wine and a glass of something dark.

'Thank you.' She accepted the wine as he pushed it across the table but nearly choked on it when he sat down in the seat opposite.

'My boy tells me you work at the hospital.' Ah, so this was Mr O'Conner senior.

Although the realisation that this wasn't an ageing stranger hitting on her helped ease her anxiety a bit, it was clear he'd come to check her out on his son's behalf. She didn't want to be rude, or make a bad impression, but she certainly wasn't in the market for commitment with a man with a small child.

'Yes, I'm a liver specialist. I went with him to make sure Ray, his neighbour, was okay.'

'That's bad business, that,' he said, shaking his head. 'He hasn't been the same since his wife died. A bit like our Liam. Since Clodagh ran off with his best mate, he's focused all his attention on Shannon and work. I mean, he's always been a good dad, but he doesn't make any time for himself, you know. He's still young and, if the women swooning over him in here are anything to go by, he's still a catch, wouldn't you say so?'

It was easy to see where Liam got his charm from, as his father gave her his best crinkly-eyed smile and put her on the spot.

'I, er, yes, I suppose he is attractive.' There was no reason to deny it. She had eyes—the dark hair, blue eyes and hint of scruff around the jaw was certainly an arresting sight. It was when he opened his mouth she found herself spluttering to find words.

'That's nice to know. You're not too bad yourself.' Liam chose the optimum moment to embarrass her, in earshot of the compliment she'd been duped into giving. In that moment, she was too mortified to process the one he'd paid her in return.

He set a plate of food in front of her, and another on the other side of the table. 'Da, you're in my seat.'

His father got up, not a bit put out by the discourtesy of his offspring. 'Sorry, what's your name again?'

'Mae.'

'Nice to meet you, Mae. I'm Paddy.' He held out his hand and waited until she shook it.

'Hello, Paddy.'

'Are you married?'

'Okay, Dad, that's enough of the inquisition. We're just here to get a bite of dinner then go and see to the dog. Don't you have a dinner rush to see to? There's a queue of people waiting to be served over there.' Thankfully, Liam's distraction seemed to work as he drifted back over across the bar floor.

'Nice to meet you, Mae. Hope to see you again.'

She raised her glass to him but he'd already disappeared into the throng.

'My dad,' Liam explained a little too late as he dug heartily into his dinner.

'I figured. I didn't order any food, though.' She looked down at the mound of mashed potatoes and spring onions paired with a huge slice of juicy meat pie.

'I did. We haven't eaten all day, and my parents would never let you leave without a meal anyway. It's champ with steak and ale pie. Eat up.'

Mae poked at the chunks of beef in meaty gravy encased in flaky pastry and cautiously took her first forkful.

'It's delicious.' Though she didn't think she could finish the huge portion, there was no denying the rich, dark steak pieces and creamy mash were tasty.

'See. How long since you've had a home-cooked meal?' he asked once he'd swallowed down his mouthful.

'I cook,' she protested. 'But you know the hours are hectic. I suppose it's been a while since I made anything substantial.'

She had to admit she was more prone to batch cooking once in a wonder, then freezing the results. So, more often than not, dinner was zapped in the microwave after a long shift at the hospital.

'Now you know where to come. Especially if you're going to be in the neighbourhood seeing to Brodie.'

'Sure.' She had no intention of running the risk of seeing Liam or his family again. As nice as his father seemed to be, and his mother probably was, she didn't want to be involved in their happy family set-up. She'd been doing just fine on her own this past year.

They both tucked into their meals and Mae realised she was hungrier than she'd thought.

'Sorry about my dad, by the way. Mum will likely be the same. They're not used to me bringing anyone in here. Though I did tell them both we're merely work acquaintances.' He stopped eating long enough to press home the point, fixing her with those piercing eyes.

'It's fine. My mum used to be the same, always trying to marry me off to any eligible bachelor.' Perhaps that was why she'd jumped into an engagement so soon after her mother had passed, trying to fulfil her wishes that she'd find a man and settle down. Thank goodness she hadn't been alive to witness the debacle that had been her wedding day.

'I suppose he told you the whole sorry saga about me and Clodagh?' Although he asked the question casually, Mae wasn't sure if he'd be hurt to know his father had indeed been telling a complete stranger about his failed relationship. She certainly wouldn't have wanted hers to be common knowledge. That was part of the reason she'd moved here, so she could be anonymous again, and not the poor, jilted fiancée who'd been left standing at the altar.

In the end she decided to be honest. It wasn't as though Paddy had gone into great detail about his son's personal life. He had no reason to. 'He just mentioned that she'd gone off with your best friend. Sorry.'

She was surprised when he smiled.

'It's not your fault Dad's a blabbermouth, or my partner and best friend were lying cheats. Most people at the hospital know anyway, so I'm sure you would've found out at some point. It's been a year—well, eleven months, two weeks and a day, to be precise. You'd think I'd be over it by now. Although, since we met in here during a karaoke night, it's hard not to think about her every time I set foot in this place.' He was trying to brush it off but Mae could hear the bitterness behind his words.

She recognised it. Although her ex hadn't cheated on her, as far as she was concerned he'd still betrayed her. He could have saved her the humiliation she'd felt in a church full of people they knew if he'd only had the courage to call things off before then. He'd taken some leave since, and actively avoided her, though she'd spotted him once or twice at work. He'd never offered a face-to-face apology, or a full explanation, other than a brief note to say sorry and that he simply wasn't ready for marriage. The actions of a coward she was glad she hadn't married in the end.

Once she'd got over the heartache of their relationship ending so abruptly, their future together being over without her having a say, she'd been left with a seething rage inside her. To this day she would find it hard not to punch him in the face, should she ever set eyes on him again. She wondered how Liam had restrained himself from doing the same to his so-called friend, or if indeed he had.

'It must have been very difficult. Especially when you had a daughter to think about.' Mae considered confiding about her own relationship disaster, so he didn't feel so bad about sharing, but it wasn't something she was ready to talk about yet when it was still so raw.

'At least one of us did,' he muttered under his breath.

'Does she see her mother?' It was none of her business, yet Mae found herself drawn to this little family. Probably because this was the most conversation she'd had outside of work in months.

'Not as often as she should, but it's a little awkward, I guess. She's still with Colm.'

'Ouch.'

'Yeah. Mum and Dad do the handovers every second weekend, so we don't have to see each other, but I know Colm, and he isn't a family man. I can't see him wanting to give up his Saturday nights out to watch cartoons and eat pizza with my daughter.'

'Sounds like my idea of a good time,' Mae joked, when she could see how difficult the whole situation was for Liam to talk about.

She was rewarded with that dazzling smile. 'Mine too. I suppose we'll get into a routine at some point and we'll find our "new normal". It's just taking a while to get used to.'

'When's the last time she saw Shannon?'

Liam screwed up his face, deep in thought, so she knew it hadn't been recently. 'About two months ago, I think. She took her to the cinema. Had her back by lunchtime.'

'At least Shannon still has her mother in her life. I know it must be difficult for you, but it's the best thing for her. I may not have children of my own, but I know what it's like to only have one parent in your life. My dad disappeared out of mine when I was little, so I never knew him. I don't even know what he looks like. I think that's what made losing mum harder—knowing I still have a parent out there, but one who doesn't want to be in my life. Shannon will appreciate you putting your own feelings to one side to accommodate the relationship she still has with her mother when she's older.'

Over the years, she'd sometimes blamed her mum for her father's absence, thinking she could have done more to keep him in their lives, or tried harder to find him. Deep down, Mae had to accept her father simply had no interest in having a daughter, and that was no one's fault but his.

At least Liam was trying to find a solution to his change of circumstances. All she'd done about her problems was run away from them.

'I hope so. I need a reason for maintaining contact with Clodagh other than some ember of hope that we can still make things work and be that happy family I convinced myself we were.'

Her heart broke for him. That sudden thump of realisation that a relationship was over hurt badly, left a person dazed, confused and struggling to figure out what had happened. She couldn't imagine still having to see her ex twice a month and pretend as though he hadn't ripped her heart out and stomped on it. It was the reason she'd moved to the city in the first place. Liam was stronger and more courageous than she could ever hope to be. Or else he was simply just a good father.

The woman who'd identified herself as Shannon's grandmother when Mae had handed her over earlier appeared in the bar with the little girl. Both had Liam's amazing eyes and dark hair, though he'd obviously inherited his height from his father's side of the family.

'You must be Mae. I'm Moira, Liam's mum. I think you already met Shannon.'

'Yes. Hi again, Shannon. It's good to see you both in nicer circumstances.' The last time she'd seen them, she'd been desperate to get away to treat the injured Ray lying in the middle of the parade. It had been a hasty explanation about how she'd been entrusted with Moira's granddaughter before she'd handed her over and disappeared into the melee.

'I hope he hasn't been making a nuisance of himself and showing us up.'

'Not at all. Liam has been very accommodating.' At least, he had since the hospital.

'You got something to eat and drink, then?'

'I did, thank you. It was delicious.' Mae's compliment drew a flush of pleasure to the woman's cheeks.

'You're welcome to stay for a few drinks. I don't mind Shannon staying overnight if you two want to hit the town.' Moira's gaze flicked between Mae and Liam and his sigh was audible.

'I've told both you and dad, we're just colleagues. Mae's only here to help out with Ray's dog. Now, have you got all of your stuff ready to go, Shannon?' Liam was on his feet, ready to go.

'Everything's in the bag and she's had her dinner.'

'Thanks, Mum.' Liam kissed his mother on the cheek and took the rucksack from her.

'Are we really going to see Brodie?' Shannon asked, her eyes wide with excitement.

'Yes, we need to feed him for Ray. Mae's coming with us, if that's okay? She's going to be looking after him for a while too.'

Mae just knew, if his daughter had had any objection to her being there, Liam wouldn't have hesitated to rule her out of the equation, quite rightly putting Shannon's feelings above all else. She admired that about him, even if there were other aspects of his personality which managed to irritate at times.

'Yay!' Shannon clapped her hands but Mae imagined that was more to do with her excitement over seeing the dog than her accompanying them.

Liam lifted his car keys. 'We're just a few minutes away. My car's parked around the corner.'

'You're driving?' Mae knew the fondness for alcohol on today of all days, and was surprised he'd take the chance of driving his daughter, even if he'd only had a couple of beers.

A puzzled frown marked his forehead. 'Yes. Why wouldn't I?'

'You've been drinking,' she spat out of the side of her mouth, so no one else would hear.

The frown deepened. 'Soft drinks only. Do you really think I would put my daughter in a car with me if I was drunk?'

Liam was almost shaking with the effort it was taking not to explode with rage. She could see it in the tension of his body, the set of his jaw and the flash of anger in his eyes.

She'd messed up.

'Sorry, I just thought with you spending so much time in the pub…' She trailed off, knowing there was no way of justifying the fact she'd jumped to conclusions.

'My Liam's not a big drinker, and I certainly wouldn't let him drive Shannon around if he was.' It appeared she'd managed to upset his mother too with her quick, inaccurate judgement. The last thing she wanted to do was offend the family when they'd been so warm and welcoming to her.

'I know; I'm sorry.'

'It doesn't matter. Come on, Shannon.' Despite his assurance it wasn't a matter worth dwelling on, Liam walked out of the pub without another word, pulling his daughter along by the hand.

'It was lovely to meet you. Thank you for your hospitality.' She gave Moira a weak, apologetic smile before following the pair out of the door.

As Liam buckled Shannon into her car seat in the back of the car, Mae waited patiently on the pavement to attempt another apology. Liam closed the door and turned to her.

'Okay, so now I can see why the stereotype thing was annoying. You're not just a Yank claiming she's Irish because her great-granny once ate some colcannon, and I'm not a drunken Irish lout. Can we start over?'

She was so relieved his anger had been short-lived, and that he'd owned up to being irritating to her this morning. It showed a strength of character she didn't usually come across. She doubted Liam was the sort of man who would have stood her up at the altar and let her find out their relationship was over at the same time as the rest of the congregation. He was the type to be upfront and honest, someone who wore his heart on his sleeve. If she ever thought about dating again, those were the first and foremost qualities she would look for in a potential partner.

But she wasn't, so it didn't matter. And why was she thinking about Liam and dating in the same context? He was a new work colleague, he had a daughter and he clearly got his kicks from pushing her buttons. Everything she should avoid at all costs.

She couldn't work out how she'd ended up in his car, with his daughter in the back seat, on her way to dog-sit for his neighbour, but she did know it was asking for trouble.

CHAPTER THREE

LIAM HESITATED BEFORE turning the key in the lock and took a deep breath, not sure what might be behind the door, or what he and Mae had got themselves in to.

'I have to admit, I haven't been inside Ray's house since his wife died. I have no idea what we might be walking into.'

'How bad can it be, right?' Mae shrugged but she was hanging back on the front step next to Shannon, waiting for him to take the first step inside.

They found out as soon as he opened the door. The stale smell of dog, beer and cigarettes hit them all at the same time.

'Wow.' Liam took a step back.

'Goodness.' Mae held her hand over her nose.

'It stinks in there,' Shannon declared very undiplomatically as she screwed up her nose.

'Let me go in and open a few windows.' The gloomy hall suggested Ray hadn't even opened the curtains, never mind the windows. He meant for Mae and Shannon to wait outside, but they followed him in, so he didn't have time to clear a path through the empty bottles, cans and post all lying in their path.

'He can't come back to this.' Mae began picking up the litter. 'Is there a recycling bin?'

'There should be one out the back. I'll go and get it.' Liam walked through the debris field in the kitchen to retrieve the recycling bin from the yard. The yard hadn't been looked after any better than the inside of the house, three-foot-high weeds sprouting from the cracks in the paving.

'Where's Brodie?' Shannon asked when he returned.

'I don't know. Maybe he's in the lounge. I'll check.' He left them filling the bin with the empties and braced himself for whatever else was in store.

The door was barely open before he found

himself flat on his back with a hound licking his face enthusiastically.

'Brodie, I presume?' Mae was standing above him, not trying very hard to keep the smile off her face, whilst his daughter was laughing hysterically beside her.

'Uh-huh. Get off me, you stupid mutt.' It took some effort to prise the beast off him so he could stand, only to have Brodie jump up on him again, his huge paws landing on Liam's shoulders.

'He's not a mutt, he's gorgeous.' Mae ruffled Brodie's scruffy grey fur, earning her a new fan.

'I suppose we should feed him. I'll show you where everything is then you can go. Shannon and I will walk him.'

Mae's frown stopped him from planning the rest of the rota.

'I'm not going to go now and leave you to tidy this place on your own. We can hardly let Ray come back to this. It's certainly not going to do anything to improve his mood.'

'I can't ask you to clean up this mess.'

'You didn't. I volunteered.'

He was surprised someone as well turned out as Mae would even offer to dirty her hands in a stranger's house. If he'd known it was this bad, he would never have brought her here. In future, he was going to have to keep a closer eye on his neighbour, who obviously wasn't coping well on his own.

'Okay. Shannon, can you play with him while we're in the kitchen?' He didn't have to ask twice. She was already digging into the pile of dog toys in the corner and throwing them for Brodie, who was quick to switch his loyalty.

'Will she be all right with him?' Mae hovered in the doorway, apparently reluctant to leave the scene.

'He's a big softy, honestly. She plays with him all the time. I wouldn't leave her in there otherwise.' Liam was doing his best not to take offence, as it seemed his parenting was being questioned once more, and chose instead to believe Mae was simply concerned.

'I know. Sorry.'

As far as he could tell, she worried a lot about other people. Why else would she be here now, helping to clean a patient's house? Ray wasn't her friend or neighbour, just someone she knew was having some trouble at home. They'd all been complete strangers to her until this morning and there weren't many people who would have got involved outside of their work commitments. It showed she had a big heart, and was possibly as lonely as he was, if she had nothing better to do with her evening.

She hadn't mentioned having to get home to anyone, not even a pet—something most people would've used as an excuse to get out of cleaning, and he wouldn't have blamed her if she had. It was different for him: he knew Ray. He should have realised there was more going on other than him drinking one too many and too frequently. As a doctor, he should have seen the signs of depression, which had obviously set in after his partner had walked out, and the potential signs of liver disease. Perhaps he had been too wrapped up in his own problems and self-pity to notice. Now Mae had helped him to peel back the layers to see what was going on behind the scenes, he felt as though he had a duty to be a better friend and neighbour to Ray.

'So, Brodie's food is in this cupboard, his food bowl stays in the kitchen and his water bowl in the living room.' Liam set about filling the bowl before starting in on the kitchen clean-up.

Mae was brushing up the dog hairs littering the floor whilst he began the mammoth task of washing the dishes. It looked as though Ray had used every plate and glass in the cupboard without ever thinking to clean one. He shuddered at the thought of whatever germs lingered on the cluttered, dirty surfaces.

'You're quite the domestic god, aren't you?' Mae teased as he scrubbed the pots clean.

'I've had to be, since it's just me and Shannon at home. It wouldn't be fair to have her growing up in this sort of mess. Doing the dishes was always my department, anyway. Clodagh was afraid of breaking a nail. Although, I will admit to buying a dishwasher since she left; I'm not super-human.'

With only him doing the household chores and taking care of Shannon, he'd had to make better use of his time, as well as asking for help from his parents when he'd needed it. Despite trying to do everything on his own at first, it had soon become apparent that he couldn't juggle parenting and work all on his own.

'I have a dishwasher and I live on my own. Time's too precious in between shifts to waste it washing dirty plates,' replied Mae. That answered one question, at least, though Liam couldn't help but push for more. After all, she'd learned more about his family circumstances over the course of one day than most people who knew him. He only thought it fair he should know a little more about her too.

'So, what are you doing, wasting it here? It's your day off; you should be out celebrating somewhere.' He wasn't blind, or stupid. Mae was an attractive, successful, caring woman. There had to be men, and women, desperate to spend time with her. Liam was sure it wasn't a lack of interest that was keeping her in the singles market and wondered what had happened to make her think it was a better choice than being with someone. It was certainly to do with heartache: he knew the symptoms.

'I've not long moved to the city. I don't know many people yet, and to be honest I'm after a quiet life these days. The past months have been a little fraught, to say the least.' That sad look in her eyes, the sigh of resignation and her apparent need to hide away from the world suggested a recent break-up. He'd gone through the same stages after Clodagh and he wondered if she'd reached the rage part of the process yet.

'Oh? New start in the big smoke?' That was one thing they didn't have in common. Born in Dublin, Liam had lived there his entire life, and had never wanted to live anywhere else—except when Clodagh had left, when the moon wouldn't have been far enough away for him to be from she and Colm, his so-called best friend.

Mae, on the other hand, seemed a more adventurous soul, having travelled from America in the first place. He couldn't imagine

moving to a different country and not knowing anyone, not having that support system
which had got him through some of the dark-
est days of his existence. Whatever had happened, it must have been serious enough for
her to leave what was familiar to her to start
all over again in another country.

'Yeah, but not in the exciting "Boston girl
moves to Dublin" way you probably think it
is. I didn't get sick of the country life, it got
sick of me.' She gave a half-hearted attempt at
a smile and Liam could almost feel the pain it
caused her even to fake it. Kind of like when
he'd promised Shannon everything was going
to be all right, and desperately tried to hold
things together at the same time.

'You want to talk about it?' It had taken
him a couple of days before he'd admitted to
himself, never mind anyone else, that Clodagh had walked out on him. But, when he
had finally confided in his parents, it had
been a relief to share the burden—to spill all
the hurt and betrayal he'd felt, his fears for
the future and worries about Shannon. They'd
helped to quell the panic in him, promising

to help where they could, and that was when the tide had begun to turn. He'd been able to see a future, albeit different from the one he'd planned with Clodagh. Eventually he'd managed to get some semblance of a life back together, even though the scars would always remain.

Although he couldn't promise to do as much for Mae as his parents had done for him, he hoped a listening ear might go some way to easing the pain. She deserved some help after everything she was doing for Ray.

'No. Yes.' This time he knew the smile was for him.

'I think it's only fair, when you've had all the gory details of my relationship laid bare in the space of a few hours. It puts me on something of a back foot when we're going to be working at the same hospital...'

'I would never say anything!' She had such a look of horror on her face at the mere suggestion she would use any personal information against him that he had to confess, it was simply another attempt to get a rise out of her. He couldn't seem to help himself.

'I'm joking. It's my defence mechanism when I think things are getting too serious. Probably part of the reason Clodagh had enough of me. She always said I needed to grow up. How ironic is that, when she left the father of her daughter to run off with the hospital playboy?' His thoughts began to drift back to the shadows of the past and he was grateful when Mae scooped some suds from the sink and flicked them at him. A distraction from his relationship woes was always welcome.

'I must remember that. It'll save me from losing my temper with you so often.' She nudged his elbow with hers so he could see she hadn't taken offence—this time.

'I am serious about offering a shoulder to lean on. Here, have this one; I'm not using it at the minute.' He slouched one shoulder down and she leaned her head on it for a split second before they both burst out laughing.

It felt good to do that again—to have a brief moment of happiness when he wasn't worrying, or over-thinking. And it was nice to have someone to do it with, even if Mae was only here because of Ray. If it hadn't been for the accident and her insistence on being involved, he doubted she would even have spoken to him again unless forced into it.

Mae's laughter soon turned back into another sigh. 'It's hard, isn't it, to just pick up and move on? How do they do it? Where do they get the audacity to ruin someone's life and walk away without a care in the world?' Now she really was beginning to get riled, and he was glad this time it wasn't because of something he'd done. That fiery red hair certainly matched her temper, that feisty nature revealing more about her Irish heritage than her DNA.

'I guess some people just don't have a conscience.' He could never have lived with the guilt of cheating on Clodagh, never mind walking away and leaving her to raise their daughter alone. From what he could tell in the short time he'd known Mae, she would never have acted that way either, when she couldn't even imagine letting Ray walk back into a dirty house.

She was quiet for a moment, as if debating

internally whether or not to share something. Gazing out of the window, not meeting his eye, she spoke so softly he nearly missed it. 'I was jilted at the altar. Literally.'

Liam didn't know what to say; it was such a shockingly cruel thing to have suffered. He supposed this was how she'd felt when she'd heard about Clodagh's betrayal. No words seemed adequate to convey just how sorry he was that this had happened to her.

'That's awful. I thought that only happened in films. You know, the ones where the heroine gets her revenge in the final act and her deadbeat ex gets his comeuppance?' He didn't know how else to make things right for someone who clearly deserved to be treated better, other than to try and make her smile.

Liam had hoped the image of her ex losing everything, or being humiliated in a similar fashion, would ease the pain a little, but it didn't.

'I wish. Unfortunately, I'm still in the "licking my wounds" phase.'

Sometimes, in his low moments, he fantasised about his ex-best friend being dumped for someone more exciting and carefree to see how he liked it. Not that it achieved anything other than to put Liam in a bad mood. He hadn't reached the stage where he wished any harm to the mother of his daughter, and he wasn't sure he ever would. He was probably still in love with the idea of the little family they'd been, rather than Clodagh. He also had to accept some of the blame for their relationship breaking down, he supposed. The fact he'd remained oblivious to her seeing his friend right under his nose said how little they'd communicated, or had even been involved in each other's lives.

In hindsight, they'd been ships that passed in the night at times, his shifts often clashing with Clodagh's work at the local hotel, though he'd never know if that was intentional or not. He'd been under the mistaken impression they were still working as a team and hadn't realised she was unhappy after eight years together. Perhaps he simply hadn't wanted to believe it, if it would have meant admitting his family wasn't as perfect as he'd imagined. Clodagh had had a point about him never growing up when he'd still believed in the fairy tale and the happy-ever-after, thinking it happened by magic. Not that it took work and communication to maintain a healthy, happy relationship. He was only realising that now, too late.

'It passes—eventually. I'm so sorry he put you through that. Assuming he wasn't a cruel man who intended to embarrass you, I can only assume he simply didn't have the balls to tell you he didn't want to get married. I'm sure it wasn't anything you'd done, or deserved. He must just have left it too late to fix things and you suffered as a result. I think I'm guilty of doing the same thing with Clodagh—ignoring the strains in our relationship until it finally snapped and there was no way of fixing things. By the time I had to face reality, she'd already moved on.'

'Were you married?'

He shook his head. 'I proposed several times, but she said she didn't need a bit of paper to verify our relationship; that having Shannon was proof enough, even though we hadn't planned her. I suppose not wanting to get hitched to me was a blessing in disguise, or a sign she never intended to stick around—I'll never be sure. But I wanted the wedding, and thought we'd even add to our family some day. I guess we were both on different wavelengths. I wanted to settle down and commit, Clodagh was looking for a way out. I just didn't want to see it.'

Mae was listening intently, and he realised giving her a shoulder to lean on had also made him take a closer look at what had happened to Clodagh and him. Yes, she'd broken his heart along with his trust, but there had been signs. On occasion she'd tried to arrange date nights for them to 'talk' on the rare evenings they'd both been at home, but more often than not he'd spent that time at his parents' place. Talking about his feelings hadn't been his strong point—at least up until they'd been ground into the dust. When Clodagh had given up asking him, he'd assumed she was okay with the close relationship he had with his family. That was probably when she'd given up on them, and had moved on to his so-called best friend.

Mae shrugged. 'Perhaps we're both just romantics at heart. Both oblivious to any problems because it would ruin the fantasy. I think the reason I got so upset when you called me out about moving here to find myself a husband was because it was true. I was lost without my mum and, when I met Diarmuid at a medical conference, he represented everything I was missing in my life. I followed him back to Ireland looking for something to fill that void. It was asking too much, apparently, putting pressure on him that he couldn't handle. I learned my lesson about relying on anyone but myself for my own happiness.'

There was a resignation in Mae's voice that he knew was a defence mechanism because he'd just built one himself, determined not to let another person close enough to inflict that level of damage to his heart ever again. He wasn't sure how long he could sustain it, when his tragic heart still held out hope for that happy family he'd always longed for.

'You deserve more, you know.' He stopped washing the dishes to turn and look at her properly, trying to instil his sincerity and that belief into her psyche, willing it to go beyond the insecurities her ex had left behind.

She gave him a wobbly smile. 'We both do.'

Perhaps it was the proximity to one another, or that recognition of one wounded soul finding another, but something seemed to happen between them—as if a switch had been flicked, awareness suddenly crackling between them. Liam knew she was beautiful but in that moment he saw her frailty, her vulnerability, and he found himself inexplicably drawn to her. Especially those sweet lips she'd just parted with the tip of her tongue, as if waiting for him to show her the tenderness she did deserve.

For a moment it seemed to him that the only sound in the room was of their breathing, rapid and ragged. Anticipation and expectation filled the air between them. He was going to kiss her, he wanted to kiss her... and her eyes and lips said she wanted him to kiss her.

Then he heard Brodie bark, Shannon laugh and he came back down to earth with a bump. He'd only met this woman this morning; he had a daughter to think about, and he couldn't go around kissing random women in front of her. She'd been through enough turmoil, for him to start confusing her like that. It wasn't as though he even wanted to start a new relationship with anyone, so kissing Mae was a really bad idea—as tempting as it was.

He stepped back without saying a word and saw Mae compose herself again, the moment over.

They continued with their chores in silence, the unburdening of their souls, and their almost kiss, clearly taking its toll. If he was honest, he was a little embarrassed to have revealed so much personal information to someone he'd only met, and he suspected Mae felt the same way, even if they'd both clearly needed to vent. It was also probably the reason they'd nearly kissed, finding a solace in one another that they hadn't had with anyone else since having their hearts broken.

It was a relief when Shannon and Brodie came charging through the door, breaking the awkward atmosphere that had settled in the kitchen.

'When can we go home, Dad? I'm tired.'

'Very soon. I've just got to feed Brodie.'

'Why don't I do that and let you get Shannon to bed? I can take Brodie for a walk before I go home.' Mae was giving him an excuse to leave, and Liam would take it. He needed some time to regroup, to think about what he had told Mae and, more importantly, why. It was clear they had a lot in common, despite initial impressions, but he didn't want to get into some kind of dysfunctional therapy-based relationship where, every time they saw one another, they'd lapse into introspection about their break-ups, bemoaning their exes…or thinking they'd found the solution with their lips. It wasn't going to help either of them move on.

'You can leave the key under the mat for me when we're done. I'll see to him in the morning.' Then, hopefully they'd only see each other in passing at the hospital.

For someone who'd sworn never to let anyone into his heart again, he'd opened the door wide enough for her to have a peek inside after just one day of getting to know one another. He couldn't afford any more slip-ups.

CHAPTER FOUR

MAE HAD AN emotional hangover. She hadn't slept well and, quite frankly, felt ill thinking about how much she'd shared with Liam yesterday. And what she'd almost shared. It would be easy to put her effusive diatribe about her marital humiliation down to it having been an emotional day for her personally. She'd been upset about having the first St Patrick's Day without her mum, and in her home town.

However, deep down, she knew the reason she'd told Liam all the gory details was because he was another jilted unfortunate. The circumstances might have been different, but they'd both been left hurt, scarred by the betrayal of their trust. In her defence, he had spilled the gossip on his doomed relationship first, and she'd known he wouldn't judge her for having been rejected so publicly. Her greatest fear was that other people would side with her ex, believing he'd had a lucky escape, and that there must have been something wrong with her for him to have walked out on their wedding day.

If anything, Liam had made her see the fault had been on both sides. He'd accepted some of the guilt for not having seen the signs his relationship had been in trouble and, when she looked back, she could say the same. She'd been the one making all the wedding preparations; Diarmuid had never really got involved. Talk about their future had been a one-sided affair at times, and she'd put that down to cultural differences—Irish men weren't really known for being great at expressing their feelings. Well, she'd been partly right—he simply hadn't been able to tell her he wasn't ready for marriage.

Yesterday had been a revelation. Once they'd got over their first meeting, talking to Liam had felt like talking to a friend. It had been therapeutic, in a way. Being able to confide in him was akin to the valve in a pressure cooker being released. It was as though all the hurt, rage and confusion she'd been left with these past months finally had somewhere to go and it had all come pouring out—unfortunately for Liam. She'd clearly mistaken his empathy for something more and thought he was going to kiss her at one point, embarrassing them both. In the end, she could sense he'd been glad of the excuse to get away from her when she'd offered to walk the dog.

So she didn't understand why he was at Ray's bedside now, knowing she'd be here.

'I know visiting time's over but I sweet-talked the nurses into letting me see Ray. Please don't chuck me out.' He batted long, dark eyelashes at her, which were almost as mesmerising as the bright blue eyes they framed.

She held up her hands. 'I'm just here to give Ray an update.'

'You can say whatever it is that has put that frown on your face in front of Liam. He's the only visitor I've had.' Despite the circumstances, Ray didn't appear to be feeling too sorry for himself. Rather, he seemed resigned to the bad news she'd come to deliver. It was the part of Mae's job she detested, but all too familiar in her line of work. Liver problems weren't often fixed with a prescription and a bandage.

She pulled the curtain around the bed to afford him some privacy and took a seat at his bedside. 'As you know, Mr Jackson—'

'Ray,' he corrected.

'As you know, Ray, we had some concerns about your liver function so we ran some blood tests. Unfortunately, the results of those tests suggest there's something serious, called alcoholic hepatitis, going on. We would like to do an ultrasound to get a better idea of what we're dealing with before we proceed in case there are any complications with the condition, and to rule out things like gallstones. You're also suffering from malnutrition. Alcohol suppresses the appetite, so you're not getting a well-balanced diet. We want to keep you here a little longer for investigation and to make sure you're well enough to go home.'

Ray nodded his head sagely. 'Am I dying?'

'We're nowhere near that conclusion. For now, we just need to see what's happening inside, then we can put a treatment plan in place. At this moment in time, there is no cause for alarm. If you're able to stop drinking completely, the liver can regenerate itself and undo a lot of the damage. We will refer you to a dietitian and a counsellor to help with that.' Although there was clearly an issue, it wasn't going to help having Ray worrying about it. They needed to keep him calm in the meantime.

'What about Brodie? I can't lie about here knowing he's at home alone.'

'He's grand, Ray. Dr Watters and I have been checking in on him. I'm sure another couple of days won't make much difference.' Liam looked to Mae for confirmation that they could make it work, given they both knew how serious Ray's situation could become if left to continue untreated—perhaps even fatal. It was something neither of them would want on their conscience, even if it meant the two of them coming into proximity outside of work for a while longer.

When she realised she'd hesitated too long, she spat out a quick, 'Of course. We'll look after him. I'll go around once my shift is done. He's no trouble at all.'

A little white lie she felt was needed in this situation.

'You rest up, Ray, and don't worry.' Liam rose at the same time as Mae.

'Easier said than done,' Ray grumbled.

'We'll do our best to take care of you, and Brodie,' Mae promised as she left him to rest.

Liam waited for her in the corridor. 'I didn't know it was so serious, otherwise we could have at least provided him with some proper meals.'

It was clear he was feeling guilty, but Mae knew he'd been too busy going through his own personal problems to keep track of his neighbour's health too.

'Does he have any family? I don't see any listed in his file but perhaps you know of someone who could be with him? It might not be a bad idea to have someone close by.

He'll need support to give up drinking altogether.'

'None that I know of. He never had any children, and he's never mentioned family. That's probably why he fell apart after his wife died. She was all he had.'

Mae could see how he'd fallen into despair so easily. At least she'd had work to distract her after losing her mum and Diarmuid in the space of a year. If she'd been stuck in the house alone day after day, she might very well have succumbed to the melancholy in some form or another. Losing a loved one affected so many aspects of a person's life, even their personality; she considered grief an illness in itself.

'I guess it's up to us, then.' She didn't see any way to disentangle herself from the situation now. She and Liam were inextricably linked, at least for the duration of Ray's hospital admission. Perhaps even after, depending on whatever ongoing treatment he needed.

Ray might find he was too exhausted after all his appointments to give Brodie the exercise he needed. Liam had admitted he needed extra help to manage Shannon and work, so it would be asking too much to expect him to do everything on his own, especially when Mae had no other commitments. After yesterday's heart to heart, he was aware she had no life outside of work, so she couldn't very well cry off helping now without it seeming as though she was avoiding him. Which was what she would prefer, given all that she'd shared with him last night. It would have been nice to have some breathing room, a little time and space for him to forget the most humiliating details of her personal life, and nearly kissing him, before they'd been thrown together again.

'Sorry. I know I should have asked before volunteering us both for Brodie duty again, but if I hadn't he'd have tried to discharge himself.'

'Not a problem. It's not as though I have anything else to do with my time off than keep an Irish Wolfhound company.' It was absurd, really, that a dog had a better social life than a city doctor but she supposed that had been her decision.

Since moving here only a couple of weeks ago, she'd cocooned herself in her apartment to protect herself from any other men with the capacity to break her heart. Like all her recent decisions, it probably hadn't been the best idea. She hadn't taken that time to meet new acquaintances and now she had no one to call for a chat, or with whom to go for a coffee. Perhaps she'd have to rethink her hermit lifestyle and try to make a few friends in her new job. Otherwise, she was going to have a very small social circle to call on when she needed company, which only included a single father and a needy hound.

'Thanks. Listen, about last night…'

Mae's insides bunched together at the mere mention of their time together, the thought of everything they'd shared in that kitchen coming back to haunt her. 'Let's not talk about it ever again.'

Liam gave a hearty laugh. 'Yeah, it was a bit full-on. I just wanted to say that I'm not usually so…open. I don't want things to be awkward between us when we'll probably see each other here at the hospital from time to time, and now that we're Brodie's full-time carers for the foreseeable future. Rest assured, I won't bend your ear every time I see you about my tragic personal life. That's not me.'

He omitted all mention of the almost-kiss and she was grateful. Hopefully they could put it behind them and pretend it had never happened.

'No, you're more likely to tease me until I lose my temper.' She couldn't resist putting him in his place about their first interaction which seemed much longer than only yesterday—though she was relieved to find Liam was also obviously having regrets over sharing so much yesterday. They'd clearly both needed to talk and had simply found themselves in a moment of weakness. She didn't think either of them would make the same mistake again.

Liam grimaced. 'You're never going to let me live that one down, are you?'

'No.' Not when she enjoyed seeing him squirm.

'Ouch. I guess I deserve it. Anyway, I guess I'll see you tonight.'

'Tonight? I thought it was my turn with Brodie. Aren't you working?'

'Not tonight. My, er, mother has invited you over for dinner. I know, I know, I told her we're just friends, barely even colleagues. I also made the mistake of telling her you're new to the area, and don't know many people here yet, so having a meal with the family is mandatory. Sorry.'

Mae could see from his eyes and the furrowed brow he wasn't any happier than she was about the situation but they were both committed to the event now. If he hadn't issued the invitation, his parents would have been upset, and if she declined they'd be offended. It seemed they were destined to spend another evening in one another's company.

'Hmm. Well, I'll agree on the basis that any talk about exes is off the table. I've done enough soul searching to last a lifetime, so I'd like to just enjoy a nice meal with your family without even thinking about Diarmuid.'

'Done.' Liam held out his hand for her to shake. 'Although, I can't speak for my mother…'

Her washing-machine stomach churned at the prospect of her having been jilted on her wedding day becoming dinner conversation for Liam's whole family. If they were anything like him, they had absolutely no tact or boundaries. Not a good match for a sensitive, self-confessed hermit.

'Thanks for inviting me over, Mr and Mrs O'Conner.' Mae handed over a lovely bouquet of pastel-coloured flowers to his mother, instantly earning her mega brownie points from his already over-keen parents.

Liam had been fielding questions since last night about where she lived, who her parents were and, most importantly to them, if she was single, and if so why. Not that he told them any of the personal information Mae had entrusted him with. He certainly wouldn't have appreciated her sharing anything he'd told her in confidence with anyone else, even if his parents had no such qualms.

'It's lovely of you to come. Doesn't Mae look beautiful, Paddy?' Whilst his mother brought a blush to their guest's cheeks, his father was battling the embarrassment of having to pay someone a compliment.

'Aye. Grand,' he muttered, before shuffling away into the kitchen in the flat above the bar.

Dressed casually in jeans and an off-the-shoulder white fluffy sweater, red wavy hair tumbling loose and wearing a pair of cowboy boots, Mae was beautiful. She also couldn't have looked more American if she'd tried.

Liam could understand why his parents were not so subtly pushing to get them together. On paper she was everything a man could want—beautiful, smart, successful; the list went on and on. It was just a shame neither of them was interested in a relationship after having been so badly burned by their last ones. Not that he was probably even her type, when she found him so irritating. Given what he'd heard about her ex, he imagined Mae's type was all talk no action, cowed by a successful, confident woman and clearly afraid of commitment—about as far removed from Liam's personality as possible.

None of which would dissuade his parents from believing that they should at least try—for his sake and Shannon's. Their belief that all he needed to move on from Clodagh's betrayal was another woman was jarring to say the least. As childhood sweethearts who'd been together for decades, they would never understand what it was like to have their heart ripped out the way he'd had. He was playing along tonight to keep them happy, but had made another attempt to convince them they were merely acquaintances before Mae's arrival.

It hadn't been a fun task, asking her over after last night, and he'd been afraid things would be awkward. Apart from their deep and meaningful conversation, he didn't want her to think he was pushing for more, either romantically or in terms of reaping added personal information. Thankfully Ray had given him an excuse to be in her department, at least, giving them more reason to spend time together. Liam was glad he and Mae had managed to get over any embarrassment and had made an agreement to veto any further talk about exes to make this evening bearable.

'You sit there beside Liam, Mae. Shannon, you sit beside me and Paddy can go at the end of the table.' His mother issued orders for the seating plan at the table in the small living room, leaving Mae and him exchanging a knowing look that said they'd go along with this to keep the peace.

'You really didn't need to go to all this trouble for me!' Mae exclaimed as his father loaded the table with dishes of chips, mash and veg, along with a selection of roast meats. A typical Sunday dinner, especially made midweek for their visitor.

'Liam said you've just moved to the city. This is our way of welcoming you,' his mother insisted as she took Mae's plate and filled it for her.

'But you fed me last night!' Mae laughed.

'Now you're a regular.'

Liam didn't even bother to hide the smirk on his face. His mother had an answer for everything when it came to getting her own way. Now Mae would see how they'd both ended up here tonight again.

She didn't argue any more, simply digging in to the mountain of food which was handed to her. She was learning fast. 'Well, thank you, Mrs O'Conner. You've certainly made me feel welcome.'

'Moira, please.'

'You need some veg, Shannon.' When he spied his daughter's plate consisted mostly of chips, Liam piled on some broccoli, much to Shannon's disgust.

'Don't you just love these?' Mae speared a floret on her fork and studied it intently. 'It's like eating mini trees.' She popped the whole thing in her mouth and chomped down.

Liam observed his daughter watching the whole thing, then she very slowly lifted a piece of broccoli to her lips and bit down. A couple of mouthfuls later, and the whole thing was gone. It was the first time in weeks she hadn't had a temper tantrum at the table when he'd tried to get her to eat anything remotely healthy.

He blamed himself for his daughter's predilection for junk food. When Clodagh had first left, he couldn't face cooking or eating, and it had been easier to order a takeaway for Shannon. Then he'd been trying to over-compensate for all the turmoil she'd gone through in the separation, letting her make her own meal choices for a sense of control and comfort. He'd wanted her to be happy, and he hadn't wanted to be the bad guy, forcing her to eat something she didn't like. However, as a doctor, he knew all too well that that would lead to consequences later on and meal times had become something of a battleground lately. Something not aided by his mother, who liked to spoil her only grandchild too.

Apparently, all he'd needed was an attractive stranger to make her think there was fun to be had in eating broccoli and she would be converted. He wouldn't complain, but he did wonder if he now needed to have Mae in attendance for all meal times. A good female role model wasn't to be underestimated and, though his mother spent a lot of time with Shannon, he wondered if he would have to rethink his current bachelor status if he was going to avoid further clashes with his daughter. She had yet to hit puberty, when there'd be those turbulent teenage years to come…

Mae gave him a wink across the table and he offered a smile in return, until he noticed his mother watching their interaction. Not wishing to give her any more false hope, he instead focused on clearing his plate.

'How's Ray? Liam said you'll be looking after that dog of his for another few days.'

Liam was relieved his mother's line of questioning wasn't focused on Mae's relationship status, at least.

Mae finished swallowing her food before she answered. 'Yes. We're going to be keeping him in to run a few more tests.'

He knew Mae, as Ray's doctor, wouldn't be comfortable sharing details of her patient's condition without his consent, so he did it for her. 'Ray's in a bad way, Ma. The drinking has caught up with him and he has liver damage. We'll know better once he's had an ultrasound to see how bad he is, and what treatment he'll need.'

He could see the news had shocked his parents, his mother crossing herself and promising to pray for him. His father remained silent but he knew he was simply processing the news. Sometimes it was difficult for his dad to reconcile how he and his mum made their living with the serious drinking culture that seemed to dominate the area. Although Liam knew they didn't serve those who had an obvious problem, some people, like Ray, hid it better, and his family shouldn't feel responsible for grown adults making the wrong decisions.

'Is he going to die, Daddy? What will happen to Brodie?' Shannon, who had been sitting quietly absorbing the conversation around her, now voiced her worries.

'We're going to give Ray the best treatment we can, that's why he has to stay in the hospital for a while longer. So we can make him better.' Mae chose her words carefully, trying to reassure Shannon things would be okay.

Neither of them could promise that Ray wouldn't die if he didn't stop drinking and, as much as Liam wanted to stop Shannon from worrying, it wasn't fair to give her false hope. It could make things more difficult in the long wrong if something did go wrong, and losing his daughter's trust would kill him.

'Mae's his doctor, so you know she'll take good care of him, and we'll look after Brodie for as long as we're needed. We won't leave either of them alone, okay?'

'Thanks, Daddy.' Shannon leaned across to give him a hug, so he knew just how much that meant to her.

He found himself welling up, not only at his daughter's compassion for their neighbour, but also at her display of affection towards him. Sometimes he really just needed a hug—another reminder that being on his own for the rest of his life wasn't something he wanted. One day he'd have to take that chance and risk his heart in the hope the gamble paid off. That he'd get that happy family he'd always dreamed about.

'Don't you worry your head, sweetheart. Mae and your dad will look after Ray, and Brodie,' his mother promised.

Shannon finished her meal, then asked to

play games on his phone, and he was pleased that their combined efforts to reassure her everything would be okay appeared to have had the desired effect. He supposed it was better that she'd asked rather than keeping her concerns to herself, but he realised he'd have to be more careful about what he said around her. She'd seen and heard more than she should at her age. Liam was ashamed to admit he hadn't reacted well when he'd discovered Clodagh's cheating, and there had been rows before she'd left. He was trying to make up for it, to be a better father to Shannon, and that meant protecting her from other people's problems where he could. She didn't need to worry about things that were beyond her control.

He could also do with taking a leaf out of his own book. Clodagh had made her decision, and what he'd done, or hadn't done, to contribute to that decision no longer mattered. There was nothing to be gained from continually castigating himself about the past. It was more important to think about the future and the life he and Shannon could still have. Just because things hadn't worked out between her mother and him, it didn't translate they could never have a happy family again with someone else.

What it did mean was that he had to be open to another relationship, had to be brave enough to open his heart again and make sure it was someone who wouldn't hurt his daughter or him again. It was a lot to ask, and a lot of that responsibility to make another relationship work would weigh heavily on his shoulders when he knew he'd been part of the problem in the failure of his relationship with Clodagh.

His talk last night with Mae had at least opened his eyes to the things he could've done differently, so hopefully he would learn for the future. If he'd only been able to talk to Clodagh the way he had with Mae—with honesty and by digging deep into those emotions he'd been afraid to voice out loud for so long—they might have been able to salvage their relationship. Now he could only hope he'd use what he'd learned about himself to improve a relationship he was yet to have.

The next step was to put himself out there again, show willing when it came to dating again—though he was worried that he might end up unravelling about his ex, the way he had with Mae, and put off any potential partners. He was lucky she'd even agreed to come here tonight, but he supposed that was only because they'd both made it clear that it was out of a sense of duty rather than a wish to be with each other. He was safe with Mae.

At least with her he didn't have to pretend he was holding it all together; he wasn't under pressure to impress or perform. Mae had seen him at his most raw, wallowing in self-pity and recriminations. Far from scaring her off, she'd been able to empathise with his situation. And she'd still agreed to come tonight. She must be as lonely as he was.

Despite her initial reservations about accepting Moira's and Paddy's invitation to dinner, Mae had enjoyed it. It was nice to be part of a warm, loving family, even for a little while, and they had made her feel as though she belonged there. It didn't seem to matter that she was an American stranger to them, with no romantic links or otherwise to their family. As an acquaintance of Liam, she'd been accepted regardless, and had been regaled with stories, jokes and an evening of excellent company. She was almost sad to leave, knowing she was going back to a house where she left the TV on constantly simply so there was some noise other than the sound of her own thoughts.

It was this need to replace the comfort of the little family she'd had with her mum that had most likely led her into her relationship with Diarmuid. A rebound of sorts, trying to replace one love in her life with another. It probably would never have worked long term, because Diarmuid could never have adequately filled the void her mother's death had left inside her. He hadn't been right for her, and eventually she would have seen it too. It just happened that Diarmuid had realised it first, even if he had gone the wrong way about breaking up with her.

Diarmuid had represented an escape from her grief, planning their marriage and future together at a time when she'd been afraid she'd never have one, fearful that she'd be on her own for ever. Now she had to accept once more that that was the more likely scenario than that she'd ever trust enough to share her life, and her heart, with anyone again.

After her father and Diarmuid walking out on her, she didn't trust another man not to do the same. No one could guarantee she wouldn't end up alone and heartbroken again. She'd seen it with her mother time and time again: her dating, falling in love then being left when the man had grown tired of the relationship, until she'd been left alone to deal with her illness. Mae had been there for her, of course, juggling her medical career with her mother's needs, but she'd seen how upset her mum had been because she'd been let down again. Her latest beau had bailed out on her once he'd known she would need a lot of care.

If she did ever date again, it would be a casual thing, in which she wouldn't hand over her heart and trust someone not to stomp it into the ground when they tired of her. She needed to protect herself.

Still, that didn't mean she didn't miss the cosy atmosphere of a family dinner. She'd only known the O'Conners for a couple of days but they were becoming a familiar part of her new life in Dublin. It wouldn't be easy just to walk away and pretend they'd never crossed paths. She would always be drawn here any time she was in this part of the city. Whilst there was no problem in dropping in every now and then to say hi, she had to make sure she didn't confuse her relationship with Liam with her longing to belong…again.

However, Shannon was yawning, and she couldn't very well stay on after Liam went home just to feel part of something again.

'I think I need to go home and lie down after that. I'm full! But thank you for a lovely dinner.' Mae said her goodbyes, sure her waist had expanded a good two inches since she'd arrived.

'Any time, love.' Moira saw her to the door and kissed her on the cheek.

'Nice to see you again,' Paddy added.

'Shannon and I will see you down to the door. Night, Mum and Dad.' Liam hugged his parents and waited until they'd both kissed Shannon goodnight before he opened the door.

The moment they stepped out of the bubble, the noise of the outside world came rushing up the stairs to meet them: screaming, shouting, glasses smashing; it sounded as though war had broken out down below.

'I'll go and see what's happened,' Liam said, trying to usher Mae and Shannon back inside.

Moira took her granddaughter by the shoulders but Mae wasn't going to be so easily restrained. Both she and Paddy followed Liam downstairs.

'What's going on?' he asked the bar staff, who were standing staring at the open door.

'I think a fight has broken out from the pub across the way. Do you want me to close the doors before it spills over into here?' The hipster-looking barman, with a ginger ponytail and beard, clearly wasn't looking to get involved.

'No. There might be people hurt out there.'

'It's not our problem, son.' Paddy tried to dissuade him from getting involved but Liam was already holding open the door, ready to go out into the fray.

'I'm a doctor, Da. Of course it's my problem,' he said, before stepping out.

Mae followed him out, eager not only to help if she was needed, but also to make sure Liam didn't get into any trouble himself. It was clear that this was an ongoing issue between father and son: Paddy ran a self-contained family business he wasn't willing to put at risk for any reason; Liam, on the other hand, couldn't help himself from offering help, as she had seen yesterday at the parade—and probably even when it wasn't wanted or appreciated.

She admired his dedication to his profession, but also his bravery in wading in. If she'd been on her own when a drunken brawl had broken out, she couldn't be certain she'd be heading in the direction they were now. It was only knowing she had Liam as back-up that gave her enough strength to follow him out there.

'Somebody help. He's bleeding!' A clearly distressed and inebriated young woman was standing over a man sitting on the ground, blood pouring from his head turning his once white T-shirt a startling scarlet.

'Yeah? He deserved it. There's more where that came from.' A great, big oaf of a man, his belly drooping from underneath his too-tight football shirt, was staggering about in the middle of the street, waving a broken bottle.

'The Garda are on their way,' someone shouted from the crowd, which had backed away from the man with the makeshift weapon.

'Phone an ambulance too,' Liam commanded, advancing on the feuding pair.

'Liam, be careful.' Mae had no idea what he was planning, but her heart was in her mouth at the thought he was about to get in the middle of this nasty fight. He waved a hand behind him, and she wasn't sure if it was to tell her to be quiet or to stay back. It didn't matter because she didn't intend to do either.

'I just need to check your friend's head

wound. I'm a doctor.' Like a zoo keeper trying to wrangle a wild animal, Liam slowly edged forward on his toes, a hand out in front to demonstrate he meant no harm.

'This is none of your business.' The angry man waved the bottle in Liam's direction but the threat did nothing to deter him.

'I'm a doctor. It kind of is.'

'He'll live. That's what he gets for spilling my beer.'

'I'm sure he didn't mean it.' Liam nodded over to the injured victim, presumably trying to get him to make an apology in order to calm the situation.

No such luck.

'It's hard not to bump into him when he's the size of a flaming house.'

'Say that again!' The man lunged forward at the insult, and Liam jumped in between the pair.

Mae didn't want to watch; she couldn't even breathe, thinking that he was going to get himself into real trouble. But she wouldn't leave in case he needed her.

'Just give me the bottle, mate, so no one

else gets hurt.' Liam tried again to reason with him.

'I'm not your "mate". I'm nobody's "mate".' The big slug of a man jabbed the bottle at Liam.

Mae let out a scream, but Liam had jumped back at the last minute, so all the man managed to stab was air.

'Hey, you, you big bully, he's only trying to help.' Mae couldn't help herself. It wasn't in her nature to simply stand back and watch as someone got hurt, any more than it was in Liam's. Plus, he wasn't just someone. He was a colleague, and someone she'd begrudgingly become used to having around these past couple of days.

'Mae, what are you doing? Get back.' Liam was staring at her, madder than she'd ever seen him, brow knitted into a serious scowl and jaw clenched so tight, it looked as though he might actually break something.

'He can't just threaten people and get away with it. This man has a daughter, you know. He's a single parent, yet he's waded in here, trying to help. What does he get in return, someone trying to stab him with a broken bottle and take him away from her? What kind of country is this? What kind of man are you?'

Her rant at least distracted the attacker. He was probably wondering if he should make a charge at her to shut her up, but he did take his eyes off Liam and drop his guard for a moment.

It gave Liam the opportunity to make a grab for the bottle, catching him unawares. Although, once the thug realised what Super Doc was trying to do, he fought back, causing a tug of war between the two over the bottle. Seeing the situation was still precarious, and with no one else appearing to want to intervene, Mae launched herself at him. She jumped onto the man's back, digging her boots into his sides, covering his eyes with her hands, and generally trying to disorientate him. The burly guy did his best to shrug her off, but she clung on as though she was riding a bucking bronco, slapping him, kneeing him in the back and desperately trying to get him to drop the weapon. In the end, he had no choice, deciding it was more important to deal with her now.

That was when she realised she could be in trouble. Liam pulled the bottle out of his hand and threw it away, but not before he got a punch to the nose. The sight of the blood streaming down his face was enough to distract Mae and she let up on her assault for a moment, worried that he'd been seriously hurt. Her bronco took the opportunity to fling her off his back as though he was swatting a fly, sending her flying onto the cobbled street below. She landed with a hard thud, her backside taking the brunt of the fall.

Their burly attacker took one look at the chaotic, bloodied scene he'd created and took off, lumbering down the street, pushing people out of the way, but at least he was gone. The immediate threat had passed and, judging by the sound of the police sirens coming closer, it wouldn't be long before the Garda would pick him up.

'I don't know whether to hug you or shout at you for being so stupid.' Liam came over and held out a hand to help her up from the ground, the other pinching the bridge of his nose in an attempt to stem the bleeding.

Whether it was the shock of what had just happened setting in, the genuine concern she saw on his face for her or the sheer relief that he was okay, she didn't know, but she burst into tears all the same.

Liam helped her to her feet and pulled her into a hug.

'I'm going to get blood all over your lovely sweater,' he whispered into her ear, as the crowd gave them a round of applause for their efforts, before filtering back into the various pubs they'd exited to watch the show.

'I don't care. I need a hug.' She buried her head in the crook of his shoulder, luxuriating in the warm, manly feel of him around her. The security of his embrace was everything she needed after the drama and upset.

When the hug lasted a probably inappropriate amount of time for two people who professed to be work colleagues only, Liam let go.

'Er…if you're okay, we should probably go and check on the patient.'

'Yeah. Just a bruised…ego,' she said, patting her backside to make him laugh.

'It's fine, there's no need to fuss,' the man with the very obvious head wound insisted as they approached him.

'Let me clean it up and take a look for myself. We did just take on that maniac with a broken bottle for you,' Liam reminded him.

'Didn't ask you to, did I?'

'Don't be so ungrateful, Mikey. You could have brain damage or anything.' A woman who must have been his girlfriend gave him a slap on the arm, showing the most sense out of the two of them.

'This is all we've got inside, Liam. What the hell happened to you?' Paddy arrived carrying a first aid kit, apparently having missed his son's heroics. It was probably just as well or else he'd likely have joined in.

'It kicked off a bit. You should have seen Annie Oakley here, taking on the big guy wielding the broken bottle.' Liam took the first aid kit and began cleaning the head wound, ignoring his own injuries.

Paddy looked at her with a mixture of surprise and bewilderment. 'You tackled a man brandishing a weapon?' He turned to Liam. 'And you let her?'

'She wouldn't listen.'

'The guy was distracted at the time.' Mae tried to downplay her part in the melee, and the seriousness of it, neglecting to mention he'd been trying to stab Liam when she'd jumped aboard.

'Anyway, it looks as though the Garda have caught up with him.' Liam pointed down the street where the police were chasing down their assailant, tackling him to the ground and forcing handcuffs on him.

Mae was relieved they wouldn't have to worry about him coming back. She'd had enough excitement for one night.

'Let's get you sorted, then.' She moved over to where Liam was tending the patient.

'That's going to need stitches.'

'I'm not going to hospital. Sod that.'

'If you don't, that's going to keep opening up. We can only patch it up for now.' Liam dabbed around the wound with an antibacterial wipe, drawing a sharp intake of breath from his reluctant patient.

'It's a deep wound. Dr O'Conner is right, it needs stitches. An open wound could get easily infected and lead to more problems. Best to get it treated now.' Mae retrieved a sterile dressing from the first aid box and taped it over the large gash in his skull.

All they received in response for their efforts was a grunt, although his girlfriend did offer to buy them both a beer. By the time the paramedics arrived on scene, Mae was glad they were relieved of their responsibility.

'What about you, sir? You look as though you've been in the wars too. You might need a check over too.' One of the ambulance crew tried to persuade Liam to have some treatment, which she could have told him was a waste of breath.

'It's just a bloody nose. We're both doctors, so I'm sure we can sort it ourselves, can't we, Mae?' He looked at her to confirm he didn't warrant an ambulance ride and a wait in Accident and Emergency, despite the blow he'd taken.

Though she was tempted to throw him under the bus, both to tick him off and make sure he was all right, she knew he didn't want the hassle.

'Sure,' she said, with more enthusiasm than was believable, earning her a glare from Liam.

'Well, you don't want to go back in there. You'll scare Shannon.' Paddy used typical Irish humour to disguise any concerns he would have had over his son's involvement in the brawl.

'I know. Best not tell my ma, either,' Liam made him promise. 'I've got the keys for Ray's house and we have to sort the dog out anyway. I'll get myself cleaned up then come back for Shannon.'

'I'll pass on your details to the guards if you're sure you're both okay?' Paddy looked at Mae for reassurance before he was content to go back into the pub without them.

'We're grand,' she said, attempting her best Irish accent.

Paddy gave her a thumbs-up, leaving the scene at the same time as the paramedics with their uncooperative passenger. Now that the two of them were alone in the middle of the street, it seemed as if the whole thing had been a figment of their imagination. Except for the blood covering Liam's face and shirt and the bruises she could feel forming on her butt cheeks.

'So… Ray's house?' Mae packed up the rest of the first aid kit to take with them, hoping they wouldn't need to use anything other than some antibacterial wipes to clean Liam's face. The blood appeared to have stopped streaming at least since she'd plugged his nose with some cotton.

'Ray's house,' Liam confirmed, pulling the key from his pocket and waving it so close to her face she had to slap his hand away.

'You can be so annoying, you know.'

'Yeah, but you love it. Why else do you keep coming back for more?' Liam grinned.

Why indeed? Though she was grateful no longer to be so concerned about his wellbeing she felt physically sick, Mae knew there was a reason she was drawn to Liam. She did like him, regardless that he could push her buttons. He was that elusive combination of being fun and a friend—both of which had been missing in her life for some time. Liam and his family were refilling the well of good times and company that had been empty for too long, bar fight notwithstanding. It did mean they were going to be spending more time together alone, when the feelings she'd been having during the tussle tonight had been definitely more than a passing concern.

As long as he kept up this annoying man-child version of himself, she'd survive. Hopefully.

CHAPTER FIVE

'HELLO, BOY.' LIAM scratched Brodie behind the ears as he came to meet them at the door. 'I think we'll bring him in next door for a change of scenery while I get changed. I don't want to drip blood all over Ray's house. Can you grab Brodie's lead and food bowls?'

Mae located the dog's belongings, leaving Liam to wrangle on the lead and pour some food from the giant bag into the bowl, which she carried next door. Liam led them all to his house. As he turned the key in the lock, Mae experienced a little flutter in her belly as she was allowed over the threshold into Liam's inner sanctum. There was a certain intimacy in entering someone's home for the first time—a trust that she had yet to place in anyone sufficiently to let them breach the sanctuary of her new place. Despite Liam having shared so much with her yesterday, she got the impression he valued his privacy. This was a privilege, even if she'd only been invited in because of the events tonight.

She followed him down the hall, where he flicked on the light, illuminating the homely kitchen. It was tidy except for the childish drawings and pots of paint littering the farm-house-style table: the mark of a man who took pride in his home, yet wasn't afraid to let his daughter have fun expressing herself.

He took the lead off Brodie, which resulted in the dog doing a mad dash around the small kitchen, knocking over one of the dining chairs, before returning to jump up and lick Liam's face.

'Who's such a good dog?' Mae muscled in on the action, fighting for the wolfhound's attention. He was another one she was getting used to having in her life.

Brodie left Liam's attentions to enjoy Mae's cuddles. Ray hadn't mentioned any house rules so, after Liam and Shannon had gone home last night, she'd spent her first dog-sitting shift cuddled up on the sofa with Brodie, watching TV. He wasn't a fan of wildlife programmes, it turned out, restlessly looking for the animals who'd had the audacity to come into his house. However, he'd settled down when she'd put on her soap operas. Clearly he found it as comforting as she did that the people in the kitchen sink dramas had more problems than her.

Neither she nor Brodie would have expected to see each other again so soon.

'You're so fickle,' Liam chastised Brodie, who was standing on his hind legs, feet on her shoulders, nuzzling his head into her neck, not caring a jot what Liam thought about his swapping allegiance so quickly and easily.

'Ah, he loves me.'

'Huh,' Liam grunted. 'He loves anyone who'll feed him and pay him attention.'

'Me too.' Mae grinned.

'Then you must be head over heels for me.' Liam tossed the comment over his shoulder as he made his way past the love-in going on between Mae and Brodie.

It brought Mae up short. Whilst she wasn't

head over her heels for Liam, she knew she liked him. She just didn't want him to know that.

'For your family, maybe. Your dad can cook, your mum is *very* attentive and your daughter is super-cute. I'm afraid you're none of those things. Just…irritating.' She wanted to get the message across that she was *not* falling for him, then she set down Brodie's dinner so he'd love her a little bit more.

'Irritating, huh?'

'Also frustrating, and reckless when it comes to getting involved in fights that have nothing to do with you.' She added that one on behalf of his parents and daughter, who would've given him grief over his actions if they'd known what he was up to at the time.

'Ah, but never boring.' Without warning, he stripped off his shirt and ran it under the cold-water tap in a vain attempt to rinse the blood out of it.

She didn't know where to look. Well, she knew where she wanted to look. Her eyes were drawn to his broad back and the smooth muscles of his arms and, if she tipped her head forward a little bit, she could see the pert pectoral muscles.

'Do you want me to give you the full show?' He'd caught her red-handed. Her embarrassment was only topped by the provocative dance he proceeded to do, hands behind his head, thrusting his hips towards her.

Despite the heat infusing her face, she was enjoying the full, uninterrupted view of his lean torso. Then Brodie nudged her arm with his wet nose to remind her what she was supposed to be doing here, and it wasn't ogling a new work colleague.

'Get over yourself. I simply hadn't expected you to be getting naked. Some warning would have been nice or, you know, you could have stripped off in another room.' She huffed.

'I would still be half-naked, so...'

'Maybe I should just strip off my top half and expect you not to be surprised.' It was so unfair men got to whip off their shirts at the drop of a hat and everyone was supposed to be cool with it. What if she hadn't wanted to know what body was beneath the tight shirts?

It wouldn't have kept her up all night wondering. Now she knew exactly what he looked like naked from the waist up, sleep definitely wasn't going to come easily. For someone who apparently ate very hearty, carb-laden meals, he had no business looking that good.

'Feel free. I'm not about to stop you.' He leaned back against the sink, arms folded, with that smug look on his face that almost made her want to call his bluff, to make him blush and bluster and think about nothing else but her being naked too. Except she couldn't promise that would happen. Whether he'd be turned off by her curves, wrinkling his nose in disgust, or they got into a game of one-upmanship that led to them both ending up stripping off completely, she couldn't take the risk.

'Pig.' It was the only comeback she could come up with in the moment. Not particularly witty or relevant, but hopefully it would end any expectation that she might whip off her sweater just to prove a point.

'Spoilsport.'

Grr. She just knew he was grinning behind her back.

* * *

Liam always used humour to deflect when he was uncomfortable and this was no exception. It had given him a thrill to catch her watching him like that, with undisguised interest in his body, and boosted his ego. That was something he needed after having been unceremoniously dumped, apparently found lacking in personality and physicality. Okay, so Mae had called him irritating, but he knew she enjoyed their banter as much as he did, otherwise she wouldn't have accepted the dinner invitation tonight.

Of course he hadn't anticipated them being caught up in a bar fight, and having to bring her home to patch him up—another step further into his private life and a big deal for him, when the only other woman who'd been in this house, except his mum, was Clodagh.

It was the threat, or promise, of her stripping off which had nearly been his undoing. His imagination had run away with him in that moment, thinking about where that could lead, until his head had been full of kissing, of hands caressing each other's bodies then ripping the rest of one another's clothes off… That was when he deployed the humour missile, knowing that teasing her would defuse any heat before it even had a chance to catch light.

He gave them both some time to cool down and washed up the couple of dishes he'd left in the sink before he fetched the first-aid kit, along with a clean shirt, and started to clean himself up. The first splash of cold water over his face stung his nostrils and filled the sink with swirls of raspberry-coloured streams of water. The intake of air through his gritted teeth drew Mae's attention back to him from Brodie's dinner.

'Let me tend to that. You can't even see what you're doing,' Mae tsked, clearly still irked by him, but her nurturing instinct was too strong to ignore his plight. He'd take it. It wouldn't do to tick her off so much she wouldn't help him with the dog any more. Plus, she made his evenings much more interesting.

Liam hadn't realised how staid his life had become of late until Mae had appeared, shaken things up, and given him a reason to leave his house other than to feed the next-door neighbour's dog or go to his parents' pub, which was only a few minutes' drive away.

He and Shannon had been hurting so hard, trying to find a new normal, get into a different routine from the one they'd been used to, that they'd locked themselves away from the world. Perhaps it was a defence mechanism—keeping out all the bad stuff, staying where they felt safe. It had taken an uptight, smart-mouthed American to show him the error of his ways. He still had a life to live, and so did Shannon, and he couldn't take away her freedom, even if he was trying to protect her in the process.

Taking her to the parade yesterday had been the first time they'd done anything fun and spontaneous since her mother had left. Although Ray's antics had ended their day out prematurely, there had been snatches of the old them, just Daddy and daughter enjoying their time together, instead of being bogged down in worry about their future without Clodagh. He knew Shannon missed her mother, but she mentioned her less now as she got used to it being the two of them.

Mae had helped to extend their socialising, even if it had just been going to his parents and next door. At least that meant they still felt comfortable, being in familiar surroundings, regardless that Mae was brand new to them. He was surprised how easily his mum, dad and Shannon had taken to her. It made it so much easier to be around her, knowing they felt comfortable around her too. Even if he was feeling distinctly uncomfortable now.

He silently thanked them for providing him with another opportunity to see and talk to her again outside of the workplace. She was becoming the brightest parts of his days, which had been pretty damn miserable until recently.

They sat down at the kitchen table, which they'd cleared of all Shannon's art work. Mae took some cotton and was now dabbing away the rest of the blood around his nose. It was the tender look in her eyes, her gentle touch, that he was struggling with most.

He had his parents' love, of course, but that physical and emotional connection as she tended to him was something he'd been missing, probably long before his relationship had collapsed.

The intimacy between Clodagh and him had virtually disappeared. They'd barely been in the same room even to accidentally touch one another, never mind do anything else. He'd put it down to over work and stress on both parts. Long shifts and looking after a child was all-consuming, even harder when there was only one parent in the household. He'd spent so much time these last months being a doctor, father and jilted partner, he'd forgotten what it was like simply to be a man. To have feelings that weren't negative, or wrapped up in someone else's, was new, exhilarating.

What was more, Mae was no longer looking at him as though he was merely an irritant, or a patient, but a man. She was studying him the same way he was watching her— with interest. He offered a smile and received one in return, albeit slightly hesitant.

'Thank you, Mae. For Ray, for yesterday and for this.' For making him feel like a normal man, attractive and wanted, with desires of his own.

She held his gaze for a while, and with every second the air between them grew thicker with anticipation and tension. That same urge to kiss her as he'd had last night came rushing forward and it was all he could do not to act on it. Then she turned away on the pretence that she had to pack away the first-aid things right there and then and saved him from making a fool of himself.

'You should probably put on a shirt. You don't want to add pneumonia to your list of ailments. I doubt you can afford to get sick when you have so much on your plate.' She flitted around the kitchen like a nervy butterfly, putting the used cotton ball in the rubbish and cleaning the sink.

This skittish version of her was new to him. She'd been so self-assured, both in combat with him and in a medical setting. It was clear she felt unsettled and he was sure he was the cause. They'd both been left hurting after their last relationships had spectacularly imploded, but he didn't think they should suffer for their partners' decisions for ever. They hadn't deserved the way they'd been treated in the past, and they didn't deserve to be punished now, afraid to open themselves up to anyone else in the fear they'd be hurt all over again.

A little flirtation, acknowledging an attraction, shouldn't be something to fear. It wasn't going to help them open up emotionally in the future if they saw it as something destructive. Not communicating had been his downfall in the past and he didn't want that to continue for ever. Not when he still had hopes that some day he'd be in a happy, healthy relationship, raising the family he'd always wanted.

'I thought you liked this look.' He'd neglected to put on the clean shirt under the pretence that he didn't want to get blood on it until he was all cleaned up. Now he knew it was because he liked to see that look in her eyes, that appreciation of his body, and the ego boost it gave him. He moved over to where she stood, knowing he was invading her personal space, waiting for her to push him away or draw him closer.

'Stop it. Please.'

To Liam's horror, there were tears in Mae's eyes as she quietly pleaded with him.

'I'm sorry. I didn't mean to upset you.' He always took things too far and now he'd crossed the line, mistaking her kindness for something more. Immediately stepping away, he tugged the shirt on over his head and covered himself up. As much as he wanted to comfort her, hold her and apologise profusely, he knew she probably just wanted to leave.

'You didn't. I mean…it's not you.' She angrily wiped away the tears before they dared to fall. 'I just can't handle anyone else playing with my emotions.'

'I wasn't… I didn't mean to…' He threaded his fingers through his hair and tugged, deserving every second of the self-inflicted pain and more. Guilty of only thinking about himself as usual, he'd neglected to realise she hadn't been having as much fun as he had during the exchange.

'I know you were only teasing but I'm still

a bit raw after Diarmuid. Having these…feelings isn't something I'd planned. I know I'm just the silly American but please don't make fun of me.' She was shredding the wrapper from the antiseptic wipe she'd used to clean him up, obviously fretting about what had nearly happened. But he'd been right about her feeling the attraction between them too. Her tears and the flight response was the manifestation of her fear at admitting it.

'I wasn't making fun of you. I promise.' Suddenly, the anger over their situation welled up inside him until he wanted to smash things, though it wouldn't have done anything only upset her more. It seemed so unfair. Clodagh and Diarmuid weren't likely to beat themselves up over their failures. Especially when Clodagh had moved on to the next relationship before she'd had the courtesy to tell him theirs was over.

He had to make do with pacing the floor like a captive animal as he raged about the unfairness of it all. 'Why should we feel guilty or ashamed that we might actually fancy one another? We're not kids, nor are we the ones in the wrong.'

Now he knew that Mae wanted the same thing as he did, but was too afraid of making a fool of herself, he knew it was down to him to make the move. He crossed the distance between them in one step. Mae tilted up her chin to meet him as though she'd been waiting for him to come and claim her, and he did.

He captured her face in his hands, her mouth with his, and kissed her as though they were free from all the worry that seemed to dictate their every move, every thought. For those few seconds, free from consequences and future regret, he kissed her with every ounce of passion he felt for her, channelling every one of those hopes and dreams that his future wouldn't be marred by the failure of one relationship into one kiss.

Mae latched her lips onto his, tentatively dipping her tongue into his mouth to meet him, letting her hands slide under his shirt and around his waist, mirroring every one of his movements, until their bodies were entwined like jungle vines, stronger together than in isolation.

A need for more of this freedom from the usual intrusive thoughts in his head, more of Mae and this rush of passion she'd awakened inside him, spurred Liam's libido. This wasn't the time for over-analysing and worrying about the future; he wanted to stay in the moment. And the moment was telling him to be with Mae.

'Should we be doing this?' she asked breathlessly as he kissed his way along the curve of her neck, brushing her hair away so he could continue his pursuit across her shoulder.

She gasped when he dipped his head lower and pulled her jumper down to expose the swell of her breasts in her lacy white bra, but he knew she didn't want him to stop. Not when she peeled off his jacket and just this moment unbuckled his belt. That jolt of awareness slammed into him as her fingers traced the buttons of his fly and he had to take a moment to remember to breathe, to try and clear his head a little, before he embarrassed himself.

'Probably not.' His laugh was a little shaky, much like his legs and his breathing.

This had been unexpected, exciting, and he was going back for more.

With extra urgency their mouths clashed together and their hands tugged at one another's clothes, their breathing ragged, their want evident. Mae couldn't even think straight, and she didn't want to if it meant putting an end to this. She was enjoying it too much.

It was nice to feel wanted, to know she hadn't got carried away again imagining something that wasn't there. Okay, so this was never going to be her romantic fantasy come true. They'd spent half their time winding each other up, plus he was a single dad, both of which were not keys to a successful relationship. No, kissing Liam was simply a chemical reaction and nothing else. He was right: she shouldn't beat herself up because she found someone attractive; she hadn't taken a vow of chastity, or broken any laws. They were two adults enjoying each other's company.

It helped that he was an amazing kisser. She didn't know from one second to the next whether to expect him to be soft and tender, or hard and demanding, but she was enjoying both aspects of his attentions to her lips. It made her think of what he was capable of in other areas, and she found herself keen to find out first-hand, caution be damned. Neither of them wanted anything serious; both were likely on the rebound and in need of a serious ego boost, not to mention a physical release. She was sure it had been some time for both of them since they'd last had anything resembling a sex life.

The loud ring of Liam's phone had him break off the kiss as though he'd been scorched, spinning round to discreetly adjust his clothes as he answered the call, as though they'd been busted by someone walking in unannounced. Mae busied herself wringing the last of the water out of his T-shirt on the draining board, hoping she didn't look as dishevelled with lust as she felt. She was dizzy from the sudden cold turkey she was now undergoing after the withdrawal of Liam's lips from hers. It was surprising how quickly she'd got used to kissing him. It had been intoxicating.

'Yes, Dad, I'm fine. I'm, er, just cleaning myself up. Yes, you can bring her over. No, I'm not going to scare her. Okay, I'll see you soon.'

Mae scrubbed at the blood on Liam's shirt rather than try and make eye contact.

'Dad's on his way over with Shannon,' he said.

'I should probably leave before they get here.' Before she did anything else likely to get her into trouble.

'Are you really still going to pretend that this isn't happening?' He was so close she could feel his warm breath on her skin. Enough contact, apparently, for her body to go into meltdown.

He opened his mouth and she assumed it was because he was about to make another wise crack. She hadn't expected him to kiss her again. Her eyes fluttered shut, her heart picked up an extra beat and her lips parted to accept him, as though her body was already pre-programmed to welcome him at the drop of a hat—or a T-shirt. This time the kiss was fleeting, barely there, and possibly the most frustrating moment of her life. Give or take coming to terms with her ex's behaviour, and inability to have spoken to her at any point in time before she'd made it down the aisle.

He took a step back and smiled. 'See? You want this. You want me.'

Still worked up by the kiss, and waiting for the next instalment, her body was inclined to agree.

'You're so full of yourself.' She dipped into her bag of self-protecting aides and pulled out a handful of sarcasm to chuck back at him.

'I'm only stating the truth.' He reached out and brushed a lock of hair away from her face.

Mae's eyes fluttered shut and she revelled in the brief contact. 'But what would it achieve?'

So they had chemistry, but falling into bed after knowing one another only a couple of days would be asking for trouble. Especially when they had to work at the same hospital.

'Er…how about fun? Remember that?'

'Remind me. It's been a while.'

Now that she thought about it, it was something that hadn't been in abundance even before the ultimate rejection. The weeks and months leading up to the wedding had been spent agonising over every detail, worrying that everything would go to plan. There hadn't been much room to do anything fun in between work and organising the big day.

Perhaps that had been a large part of the problem between Diarmuid and her. Even if he had complained they weren't spending enough quality time together, she probably wouldn't have done anything about it, because her attention had been completely consumed with the wedding, on having the best day of her life and proving the romantic fantasy had come true. She'd neglected the reality of their situation too long and their relationship had flatlined as a result.

A good time hadn't been high on her list of priorities since then. That spot had gone to simply surviving.

'No commitment other than to make each other feel good.' He dotted tiny, ghost-like kisses down her neck, sending goose bumps popping up all over her skin.

'That does feel…sound nice.' He was scrambling her brain with every touch of his lips on her body.

'Mmm-hmm. Doesn't it?'

'But Shannon… Your dad…' As nice as this was, the pair were going to be here soon, and there was no way there would be time to fit in everything she wanted to do with Liam in that small window. If anything, it would leave her frustrated to start something they couldn't finish properly.

'I know. Tonight's out of the question. So, I have a proposition.' He stopped kissing her and retreated back into his own personal space, leaving her dazed and confused.

She needed the breathing room because she was so disorientated and under his spell right now, she would agree to anything.

'What?' Even to her ears she sounded breathless, as though she'd just run a marathon. Her heart was racing too, the exhilaration of the moment doing more to fuel the adrenaline in her body than any form of exercise. Well, almost any… Her thoughts drifted to whatever indecent proposal he had in mind and whether or not her heart could take it.

'Neither of us are in the market for a serious, long-term relationship. Let's face it, we'd probably drive each other up the wall. But, it's also clear there's an attraction here. One we would be acting on right now if my dad hadn't interrupted.' The devilish glint in his eyes only upped the level of Mae's frustration, unaided by the fact he'd yet to get to the point.

'Yes, and he's going to be here soon with your daughter.' *So get on with it!*

'I know we haven't known each other that long, that we're going to be working at the same hospital and have Ray as a mutual connection. Sleeping together could make things complicated. If we let it.'

'What are you suggesting?' She had been trying not to think beyond tonight, or let herself feel anything that wasn't in the moment. Now Liam was ruining the mood by talking about the future consequences.

Liam cleared his throat. 'A fling.'

'Excuse me?' For a moment Mae thought she'd misheard him.

'I don't see why we should deny ourselves some fun. We haven't done anything wrong and we deserve some happiness. But I also know we're both still hurting from our last relationships. I thought perhaps, if you agree, we could keep things casual. You know? See each other in private.'

'You want to be my booty call?' The idea had its appeal.

'We would be each other's booty call. No strings, or expectations, other than having a good time.'

'That's a big promise.'

Liam ducked his head with a grin, almost bashfully. It was nice to see that perhaps he wasn't as confident as he often portrayed. She liked seeing that softer side of him. It represented him opening up, letting that brash exterior slip so she could see a more vulnerable Liam. The one who didn't want to risk getting hurt again either.

'I just know we would have a really good time together.' He pulled her close, capturing the gasp of surprise on her lips with his. The kissing alone was sufficient to prove his point.

Except she wasn't usually that kind of girl. At least, not one who got involved with fathers of young children. He was showing her a way round that, so the level of commitment that would normally have required wasn't an issue. But she was already so involved with his family, it seemed impossible to separate, or juggle, those relationships. After Diarmuid, she'd made a promise to herself not to get involved with someone she could lose her heart to so easily. She didn't want to lose herself in that commitment to a relationship and, seeing how close he was to his daughter, Liam seemed the worst person to rebound with. Even if he was suggesting something a lot more intriguing than potential heartbreak. Although the thought of exploring all kinds of possibilities with Liam was tempting, she just wasn't sure it would be worth taking the risk.

'I don't know, Liam. It's one thing getting carried away in the heat of the moment, but this is a crazy idea you're asking me to make a logical decision about.' Now she'd been given time to think, all the red flags were waving in her face. She certainly didn't want to agree to something now, when she was wound so tightly with arousal for him, only to regret it when her brain wasn't so fried by lust.

There was a rap on the back door as Paddy appeared with Shannon.

'Sleep on it. We can talk about it tomorrow,' Liam whispered, before going to greet his daughter and reassure her everything was okay.

There were so many things wrong with that last comment, but they wouldn't have the privacy to go over her fears now the rest of Liam's family was here.

Namely that there was no way she'd sleep tonight with erotic images of Liam in various stages of undress roaming unbidden in her head, and the prospect of more if she chose. Plus, she didn't think she could face talking about it again tomorrow without being affected by what had happened here tonight. Common sense told her she should put a stop to any romantic notions now and rule this as an error of judgement, a moment of madness which definitely should not be extended indefinitely. However, deep down she knew she wasn't strong enough to say no to this once-in-a-lifetime opportunity.

CHAPTER SIX

MAE HAD BEEN ignoring his texts. Liam had briefly considered calling and leaving a voice message when she invariably didn't answer his call, then decided it would seem too needy—the opposite of the arrangement he'd proposed. He still couldn't quite believe that he'd suggested a fling, or that she'd even agreed to consider it. Clearly his libido had been doing the talking last night, afraid that he wouldn't get to finish what they'd started.

He wasn't sure how this would work on a practical level when they would have to co-ordinate work and his responsibility as a father. It wasn't as if he could parade Mae through the house in the mornings and not expect Shannon to notice. The logistics would be difficult, though he couldn't bring himself to regret anything when she'd said she'd contemplate the idea of a fling.

It had been a last grasp to maintain the momentum which had sprung between them in the kitchen—not the most romantic place on earth, but it hadn't stopped them from engaging in one of the most passionate encounters he'd ever experienced. It was all he'd been able to think about, along with the possibility of having something more with Mae.

He knew a relationship was off the cards. Neither of them was emotionally ready to jump into anything serious, but it was clear they still had needs. A fling seemed the easy solution to fulfil their want for one another, and the ego boost might even help them when they were ready to move onto another relationship. They could avoid all the complications of family getting involved in their personal business by keeping it quiet, and it would give him something more than dinner with his parents to look forward to.

The only problem with his sexual master plan was the growing suspicion that, in the cold light of day, Mae had changed her mind and decided she didn't even want a casual fling with him. If she was agreeable to the idea in theory, he was willing to find a solution to ensure they could spend time together. Whether that meant meeting at her place, or booking rooms by the hour when Shannon was in school, he wanted to make this work.

From the second he'd made the suggestion, he hadn't been able to think about anything else other than being with Mae. Although a rejection from her wouldn't be the same as Clodagh leaving him for his best mate, it would still hurt. It would also make things awkward when he had to consult her on a patient and he still hadn't had her answer. That wasn't the sign of someone who couldn't wait to embark on a racy, passionate fling.

'Is there any update on Dr Watters?' he asked the head nurse, who'd been the one to put in the call requesting Mae's expertise. Whilst Liam knew Mae wouldn't have blown him off when it came to a patient— she was too professional—his behaviour last night had been anything but, and he could only hope that wasn't the reason she'd been avoiding him.

'Why don't you ask her yourself?' Liam's A&E colleague nodded to the space behind him.

He took a split second to compose himself, to brace for the look of contempt that was likely there on her face, before he turned around. But she was too hard to read when she was in doctor mode. Hair tied back, not a strand out of place, wearing a smart skirt and blouse, she looked immaculate. A far cry from the flushed, dishevelled version of Mae from last night. He knew which one he preferred: the Mae who couldn't keep her hands off him, not the one standing here with an indifferent expression on her face.

'I'm here. What do you need me for?'

It wasn't a loaded question for anyone but him. He needed her for company, for kissing, for feeding his ego, and hopefully for more. Although, judging by this cool reception and her refusal to reply to his messages, he'd be lucky if she even let on she knew him.

'We have a patient coming in who's taken

an overdose of Paracetamol. I can handle it, but I thought it would be good to get your input to try and limit the liver damage.' He'd known Mae was in today. They'd cross-checked their schedules to work out the times for looking after Brodie and he remembered there was a brief cross-over period this afternoon when they would both be in attendance.

Though he didn't take any joy in the fact someone had felt so desperate they'd thought to end their life, it gave him a chance to see Mae. She was also the best person to have on hand in this instance. An overdose of Paracetamol could result in potentially fatal liver damage. They only had a very small window of time to help and they were all lucky to be able to utilise Mae's expertise.

He'd seen more than his fair share of drug overdoses due to prescription and illegal drugs in the emergency department, accidental or otherwise. Some had been too late for medical intervention no matter how hard the staff had tried to provide assistance. Those were the cases he took home with him, the names and faces he couldn't forget because he felt as though he'd failed them. Even if Mae didn't want to speak to him personally, he'd willingly set aside his pride to have her here if it meant saving someone's life.

That invisible hum of tension before an emergency admission hung in the air. Everyone waited to launch into action the moment the doors swung open, powerless until they did. When the familiar fluorescent jackets of the ambulance crew blazed brightly as they crashed into the department with their patient on a stretcher, the hospital staff circled, ready to take over. They quickly transferred the patient onto a hospital bed, accepting the responsibility for the young woman's life, and relieving the ambulance crew so they could move on to their next job.

'Twenty-six-year-old female: Anne Marie Hagen. History of depression. Found unconscious by her best friend after breaking up with her boyfriend. Apparently surrounded by empty Paracetamol packets. She's breathing but hasn't retained consciousness.'

As always, the initial transfer was noisy

and busy, getting all the details of the case, and doing a preliminary assessment.

'Do we know how long ago this happened?' Mae asked.

'Her friend saw her about two hours ago, so it can't be that long.'

'Okay, thanks. We're lucky we got to her so quickly. Anything past eight hours would have limited what we can do.' She went on to order the usual bloods and urine sample, with the most important results being the liver function.

'Are you happy to go ahead with administering activated charcoal?' Liam asked, monitoring Anne Marie's blood pressure and pulse to make sure she didn't suddenly deteriorate.

He hadn't asked Mae to attend just so he could take over. He trusted her judgement, an expert in this field, but he wanted to be useful.

'Yes, and can we get an IV of acetylcysteine set up, please? Given that we're still within that time frame, we should be able to prevent serious hepatotoxicity.'

It didn't matter that this girl had tried to

take her own life; they would work together to save her as best they could. She was a patient, someone who'd clearly been so distressed she hadn't seen any point in continuing. It was always difficult when such young people were involved: they should have had their whole lives ahead of them. Now, thanks to Mae and everyone else involved, she still did. Of course, Anne Marie would have to be referred to the mental health team, but that was for her own benefit. Hopefully they would help her move past whatever issues had led her to make this choice, so she wouldn't ever try this again.

Although they couldn't know for certain if a break-up had been the catalyst for this, Liam understood how totally devastated she must have been to have attempted to end her life. When he'd discovered Clodagh and Colm in bed, he'd thought his life was over too. He hadn't seen a way past it and it was only having to look after Shannon which had forced him to get up out of the doldrums every morning and go through the motions of a functioning adult. Inside, though, he might as well have died. Suddenly his whole life had been taken away from him. He didn't know who he was any more, or what to do without Clodagh there. There had been a grieving period; it was only natural after the loss of a relationship.

He was still in the angry phase, and he just knew Anne Marie would get there too once she'd had a little time to think things through. The overdose had probably been an impulse reaction, a way to shut down the pain. Perhaps, as in some cases, it had been a cry for help—a signal to those around her that she wasn't doing okay and needed more support. With Mae's assistance, and a follow-up treatment plan, he hoped Anne Marie would eventually be able to put the whole thing behind her and start over, the way he had.

Yes, he still had some kinks to work out when it came to his love life—namely that he needed to find the courage to invest in another relationship. He imagined that would happen faster if Mae agreed to this crazy arrangement where they could have all the benefits of a relationship without having to commit their hearts to it, playing it safe.

'Okay, that should keep her stabilised for now. I'll want to see the results of the liver function test to see what we're dealing with, and she'll need a referral to psych.' Mae was winding down her part in procedures and Liam knew she wasn't going to stick around longer than necessary, to avoid talking to him. He didn't want to let that happen without a chance at least to clear the air in case he never got to speak to her again.

Mae was ready to leave, to get away from the sad circumstances of the patient that had hit too close to home, and the man she hadn't been able to get out of her head since he'd kissed her.

Suddenly, alarms were going off and medical staff swarming back around the bed again.

'She's gone into cardiac arrest!' one of the nurses shouted, forcing Mae immediately to turn back.

'We need a defibrillator over here!' Liam

yelled, waiting as the patient's clothes were cut open to give access to her chest.

He started chest compressions, keeping the blood pumping around her body until they could apply electric shocks. After a while he stopped to check for a response, but it was soon clear they would have to use the defibrillator to try and restart the woman's heart. Once pads had been attached, Mae took up the paddles. 'Stand clear.'

Making sure no one was touching the patient or her bed, liable to get a shock themselves, Mae delivered the first shock. She waited to check the heart rhythm but, with no improvement, responsibility transferred back to Liam.

Again, hands locked, arms straight, he began more chest compressions. He flicked a glance at Mae, which she didn't want to acknowledge. It was concern that they weren't going to bring this patient back after all. Mae had to retain a certain professional detachment at work, but in circumstances like these it was impossible not to be affected.

This was a young woman who'd had her

whole world in front of her. Yet, she had come to think, for whatever reason, that her life was no longer worth living. Mae knew that feeling. Running from the church, after realising Diarmuid wasn't going to turn up, it had crossed her mind to throw herself in front of the nearest bus. Then she wouldn't have had to deal with the loss, the humiliation and the heartbreak her fiancé's actions had caused. If she hadn't had her mother's strength, the outcome of those first few days after their breakup could've been very different.

These painful personal dramas, which seemed so all encompassing at the time, did eventually become easier to live with. She only hoped Anne Marie got the opportunity to realise that, to see she could still lead a very full life.

Liam stopped CPR to check the patient's heart rhythm, then it was Mae's turn again.

'Stand clear.' She delivered another shock with the paddles, watching Anne Marie's body jerk as she did so.

It seemed like such a violent act, but she'd seen time and time again how it often gave people a second chance at life, and she only hoped this woman would be one of them. Life was short. Certainly too short to give up on it at such a young age.

She thought of Diarmuid and herself. In a way, she'd been guilty of giving up her life for him, even though she was still functioning on an outward level. Moving away had been a start, as had getting herself a new job, but in terms of her personal life she might as well have died. It was only natural she'd wanted to protect herself, but she'd basically let Diarmuid win. She'd decided that he was the only man who could ever mean anything to her. She really didn't want to live with that for ever. He'd gone on to have another life. They both deserved the same—to move on from the heartbreak and start living again.

Suddenly, the expectant air around the cubicle was filled with the steady beep of Anne Marie's heart, and Mae had to fight back tears. They'd done it. Now this woman had been given another chance at life, it would be down to her to move on from the past and look to her future. Mae knew she had to do the same.

'Let's get her stabilised.' The medical team swung into action, getting her settled again, though she would probably be transferred to the intensive care unit once she was stabilised so they could keep a close eye on her. Hopefully, once they got all the toxins out of her body, she would be well on her way to recovery.

'Thanks for your assistance, Mae... Dr Watters,' Liam said to her once their job was done and the nurses took over the responsibility for the rest of their patient's care. Mae found some satisfaction in him stumbling over her name, and suspected that he'd found the circumstances more difficult than usual too.

'Just doing my job.' Her slightly quivering voice and bottom lip weren't in keeping with the self-assured comment. At times it was much more than a job, it was a reminder of her own vulnerabilities, and today especially had been something of a wake-up call. However, she didn't intend to make a show of herself by crying in front of the team. Apart from Liam, they wouldn't understand why she'd get so emotional over a random patient. It wouldn't look good or do anything for her reputation at her new place of work if they thought she couldn't cope with any vulnerable cases. So she turned on her heel and walked away, not looking back, hoping she'd at least managed to portray someone in charge of her emotions.

Liam could see Mae was upset even if she'd acted professionally and efficiently with him to get their patient back. He checked with the rest of the team that they had everything in place for Anne Marie before he ducked out for a few minutes.

'Mae,' he called down the corridor, jogging towards her. She could have pretended not to hear him, so he appreciated that she waited for him, though he supposed it was only out of propriety rather than a favour to him. She couldn't very well refuse his company for a few moments without people sensing there was something going on and jumping to conclusions.

They walked in silence out of the department and down the dimly lit corridor in the old part of the hospital which afforded them a little privacy. Liam pulled her aside under a staircase, away from prying eyes and listening ears.

'Are you okay?' The question which had been hovering on his lips since she'd left A&E finally burst from his mouth.

Mae nodded, her wide, glistening eyes and chewed bottom lip saying otherwise.

'You can talk to me. I'm not going to make any judgement because you got upset over a vulnerable, young patient. You're only human, Mae.' He wanted to reach out to her, to give her a hug and offer some comfort, but he didn't want to overstep the mark...again.

She swallowed hard and he could see the effort it was taking her not to cry. As much as he wanted to tell her it was okay to show emotion, Liam knew Mae was too proud to be seen so vulnerable at work.

'Knowing Anne Marie was in so much

pain that she thought ending her life was the only option available triggered a lot for me. I'll be okay...don't worry.'

Liam dismissed her attempt to fob him off. It was obvious she was in pain too. 'I've been there too, after Clodagh. We all have our dark days. What's important is that we pick ourselves up again, eventually, and move on. Hopefully Anne Marie will be able to do the same once she realises nothing is worth ending a life for.'

'But have we moved on, Liam? Yes, we're getting up, going to work and acting like normal human beings, but we're still holding back from being with anyone else. Instead of protecting our hearts, aren't we punishing ourselves by holding back?'

Liam smiled. 'Isn't that what I've been saying? I don't want to be alone for ever, and yes, we run the risk of getting hurt again. But if we don't even try...'

'I know. I'm beginning to realise that I still deserve a love life. I don't want to end up sad and lonely, thinking that's all there is for me.'

'Having someone who thinks you're beautiful and amazing does not necessarily mean he's going to hurt you. I kissed you because I like you, because I think we could have something special together.'

He was about to apologise for getting things so very wrong when Mae got there first.

'I'm sorry I didn't answer your messages. I just… Last night was very confusing for me.'

'I get that. It sort of crept up on us both then completely consumed us.' Even now, the passion which had swept them away was bubbling back up to the surface now that he was so close to her again.

'When I had time to mull things over, consider your proposal, I thought perhaps it was short-changing us both. That we were worth more than a purely physical relationship and we'd only be doing it because our exes had battered our confidence.'

'And now?' The hesitation he saw in her eyes, and the fact she hadn't tried to move away from him, led him to believe she might just have had a change of heart.

'Seeing Anne Marie, what she was prepared to do, to give up… We all deserve better. I don't need any more heartache, or another man to throw my life away on, but I'm not dead yet.'

'And I don't have room in my life for anything serious that will take my attention from my daughter. But we both have needs.' At least they were on that page together.

Mae inched closer and danced her fingertips along the buttons on his shirt, making his skin burn without even touching him. 'But I think you were right about what you said last night—we deserve to have a little fun. Neither Diarmuid or Clodagh are going to rule the rest of our lives. Choosing how we do this is our route to freedom.'

Liam liked this decisive Mae, and not just because she was giving him what he wanted. She was taking control of the situation, of her life. He didn't mind, when the whole thing had been his idea in the first place and he'd certainly be reaping the benefits if she agreed to be with him for any amount of time.

'So, really, sleeping together is our first step to independence.' Liam nuzzled into her neck, luxuriating in the scent of vanilla and summer berries clinging to her skin. The pulse in her throat beat hard against his lips and he knew she was as turned on as he was already.

'Uh-huh. Really, we're doing each other a favour...' She gasped as he slid his hand beneath her shirt to touch the bare skin of her back.

'And I do like to be helpful.'

'I have noticed this about you. One good turn deserves another and all that.' She took him by surprise then, kissing him hard on the lips, tangling her fingers in his hair and bringing every nerve end to attention.

The buzz of her pager which eventually broke through their erotic haze to remind them where they were.

'Sorry. I have an appointment to get to,' she said with a grimace.

Liam reached out to trace the smudged lipstick around her lips. 'You might want to redo your make-up beforehand.'

There was that rosy glow in her cheeks again. 'I might just do that.'

She went to walk away, then stopped and turned back. 'So, how are we going to do this?'

They needed a plan about how they would actually get the time alone needed for this secret fling. Even a casual arrangement required some planning when he had to juggle his job, his daughter and dog-sitting an Irish wolfhound.

At least he had tonight covered.

'Mum and Dad promised Shannon she could sleep over later.'

The smile on Mae's face at that news gave him a warm glow inside, knowing he'd been the one to put it there. He hoped by the end of the night she'd be grinning from ear to ear.

'You are sexy. You are wanted. You are fierce. You are an independent woman who does not need a man in her life for anything other than sex. You do not need to see him as anything other than a sex object. You are not, under any circumstances, to fall for him,' Mae told the woman in the mirror with a wag of her finger, but she doubted even the stern look was enough to convince her of any of that.

Well, maybe the being wanted part. Liam had made it pretty clear he was physically attracted to her even if he didn't want any emotional entanglements—which, she reminded herself, was something she needed to avoid too.

She'd spent all last night and most of today vacillating about whether or not she should take this leap into sexual freedom with Liam. That was what it would be for her. An affair free from the emotional restraints of a relationship. She wasn't even sure she was ready for that. But after the way Liam had kissed her, the way she'd felt today when they'd been alone, she was willing to try.

Even now she shivered with the anticipation of what the night had in store. She was standing in her underwear, still deciding what to wear. She lifted the body-skimming polka-dot wiggle dress and held it against her body, then dismissed it. It was sexy, but she worried it would look like she was trying too hard when this was supposed to be a casual hook-up. Now she re-thought the red lacy lingerie in case it looked too obvious, too desperate— too 'my fiancé jilted me and I need someone to find me attractive so I can feel good about myself'. But she remembered this was just about sex, so there was no need for subtlety.

The doorbell rang and she grabbed her second-choice outfit from the bed—a white boho dress with flowers, which she couldn't have worn out in the Irish March weather, but which hopefully showed enough leg to capture Liam's interest.

One last swipe of lip gloss, a quick tidy of the bedroom and she padded downstairs barefoot to answer the door. A deep breath, shaky release and she came face to face with the man who'd been stalking her every thought recently.

'Hi.' That grin was enough to make her believe she'd done the right thing by taking the risk with this crazy scheme.

'Hey, you. Come in.' Mae peered outside to see if anyone had witnessed his arrival. Although she barely knew anyone in the street, she had a feeling that everyone was watching, knowing she was about to embark on a scandalous sex fest…hopefully.

He side-stepped into the hall, one hand behind his back, seemingly feeling as awkward about this as she was. She took comfort in the fact he obviously didn't make a habit of this sort of thing. It was apparent he hadn't been with anyone since Clodagh, but that didn't mean he hadn't been a playboy in his youth.

'Is everything okay, Liam?'

'Yeah, sure.'

'It's just, you're acting kind of weird. If you've changed your mind…' The thought that he might be trying to find a way to let her down gently hit her hard, deflating her ego immediately. It told her just how much she'd been looking forward to being with him when the disappointment settled into her very bones.

He suddenly thrust forward a bunch of flowers. 'I bought these on the way over, then I thought it might seem a bit much, since this isn't really a date. I didn't want you to read too much into it and think I was trying to turn this into something more already. I just thought I should bring you a gift.'

'Thank you. They're beautiful.' Sheer relief made her want to laugh but she bit her lip, not wishing to offend him. It was a sweet gesture—yes, totally unnecessary, but it proved that he wasn't used to this any more than she was.

'So are you.'

Her heart melted at the whole first-date vibe that was going on, expectation thrumming between them as they skirted around the reason he was here.

'I'll just go and put them in some water.' She needed some too, her mouth suddenly dry, the tension becoming too intense to bear in the cramped entrance hall.

'You've got a nice place here. Not too far from the hospital,' he said, following her to the kitchen.

'Yes, I like it.' The conversation was weirdly formal and stilted, so unlike their usual verbal encounters. Discussing their commute to work wasn't in keeping with the idea that this was going to be fun and exciting. A passionate fling, to her mind, shouldn't involve small talk and gifts: it was supposed to be ripping one another's clothes off, too busy kissing to waste time speaking.

She stood at the sink to fill the vase, wondering if this had been a good idea. If it turned into a disaster it would only make things worse. It was supposed to be an ego boost to make them feel better about themselves after being dumped. An awkward, unsatisfactory fumble wasn't going to help her move on. If anything, it would put her off getting involved in any capacity with another man.

She poured herself a glass of water and sighed as she took a sip. The fantasy had been nice while it had lasted. Before Mae had a chance to voice her second thoughts, Liam came to stand behind her, slipping his arms around her waist.

'I've been waiting all day for this,' he whispered into her ear, melting any concerns that this wasn't going to live up to her expectations. His breath against her neck brought her body back to full attention, as though it had been waiting just for him.

As her heart kicked into overdrive, her nipples tightened and arousal burst through the dam walls, she knew she needed Liam.

'Me too.' She could hardly speak, her body entirely focused on Liam's touch—including her brain.

He kissed her neck where the hairs were already standing to attention, her body hyper-aware of him being so close. A soft sigh escaped her lips, which she soon caught again with an intake of breath when he slid his hands under her dress. Skin on skin, he travelled up her thighs, slowly, carefully and confidently. He paused when he reached her panties and she held her breath, waiting to see what he would do next. Much to her dismay he didn't rip them off and toss them aside, but kept skimming the sides of her body until he reached her chest. He pressed himself closer so she could feel how turned on he was, his hardness nestled against her backside. She didn't think she'd ever been so aroused when still fully clothed.

Then he yanked down her bra and the front of her dress, exposing her breasts to the cool air and his strong hands. Her entire being was straining now for his attention, that aching need taking her over completely. When he cupped her breasts and tugged her nipples, she almost orgasmed right there and then.

Unable to remain passive, Mae spun around to kiss him. She began to pull at his T-shirt, desperate to expose his body too, but she had to give up on her quest when he refused to relinquish his quest to drive her insane. He lowered his head and caught her nipple in his mouth, sucking as he kneaded her breasts with both hands. Mae braced herself against the kitchen work top because her legs had apparently stopped working.

He licked, sucked and played with her until she was begging him to give her some release. 'Liam, please…'

She didn't have to ask again. Without hesitation, he put his hands up her dress and whipped her underwear down her legs. Mae was so wet by then, his fingers slid easily inside her. She had to cling on to him for support now that he was totally in control of what was happening to her body. He literally had her at his fingertips. Slow strokes, quick circles and his steady persistence brought her hurtling to release. Liam maintained eye contact as she climaxed, making it all the more intense.

It surprised her, overwhelmed her, as she came again and again. Only when every tremor had finished rippling through her body did he finally release her.

'Are you okay?' he asked softly.

'Uh-huh.' She didn't even know what words were any more.

Liam grinned. 'I'll take that as a yes. You want to take this upstairs?'

She nodded, though even that took effort. Her body no longer felt like hers, more like a marionette manipulated by Liam, and without him she didn't know how to move any more. He took her hand, but they'd only taken a couple of steps when her knees buckled and she had to grab hold of him to remain upright.

'Although I'm not sure if I can.' She was no virgin and, though it had been a while, she still remembered every lover she'd ever had. None had had this effect on her, making her orgasm so hard, so quickly, it left her incapacitated. Especially when they hadn't even slept together. If this was just a taste of the power he could have over, how they could be together, Mae already knew she wouldn't want this to end between them.

That definitely wasn't in keeping with their casual agreement.

Liam caught her before she fell and swept her up in his arms, ignoring her protests that she was too heavy. 'Sure, there's nothing of you.'

To prove his point, he carried her straight upstairs with a swagger to his step, which might have been caused by the pride of bringing Mae to climax so easily, or by the erection pressing against his fly as she nuzzled into his chest. Either way, the encounter had bolstered him mentally and physically and he couldn't wait for more. As long as Mae was up to it.

She seemed wiped out. He supposed it was a lot to process after being on her own for such a long time. He could only imagine how he was going to feel after the same, not that it was making his jeans any more comfortable. The last people they'd slept with were people they'd been in relationships with, partners they'd loved and who'd ultimately found them lacking in some way. This might only be a sexual release for both of them now, but that didn't mean there wouldn't be some emotional involvement. If not with each other, at least for themselves. They needed it—to know they were normal, they were wanted and that they were able to move on from their pasts.

'That one.' Mae pointed towards the door at the end of the landing.

He nudged it open, taking her into a room filled with photos and trinkets of her life in Boston, a little nest of comfort she'd built for herself in this new country. The fact that she was giving him permission to enter into this sanctuary showed how much trust she was putting in him not to hurt her—another reason this couldn't go beyond a non-meaningful fling. Mae deserved someone who would put her feelings above everyone else's, and he couldn't prioritise her over Shannon. All he could do was make her feel good, make her feel appreciated and wanted, for as long as they had together.

He set her down on the mattress, nestled in the bank of cushions adorning the bed. With an impatient swipe of her hands, Mae nudged them onto the floor, then proceeded to strip her dress over her head. She tossed it on the floor with her bra, so she was lying there beautifully naked waiting for him, the red hair spread around her making her look like Venus come to life.

Liam had a sudden moment of imposter syndrome, believing he wasn't worthy of being here with her. That he was as bad as her ex, using her to satiate his needs without considering her feelings enough. Those negative thoughts only lasted until she hooked her fingers into the belt loops on his jeans and pulled him closer.

'Aren't you going to join me?' Despite her bravado, he could see her nervously worrying her bottom lip with her teeth and realised she needed this as much as he did.

'If you insist.' As eager as he was to get naked with her, he took his time undressing, watching the appreciation and desire turn her eyes to glittering jade. The T-shirt went first, joining the pile of clothes and cushions on the floor. He reached for her hand and moved it over his chest, down his stomach and briefly over his crotch.

'I like it when you touch me.' His honesty manifested itself almost as a growl, his voice so thick with arousal and lust for her.

Mae sat up, alert once more, the weariness dissipating as she took her cue. Kneeling on the bed, she unbuckled his belt, every deliberate movement extending the foreplay. When she popped open the buttons on his fly, it was all he could do to restrain himself, but he wasn't going to rush the best thing to happen to him in months. Instead, he stood tall, clinging on to his resolve as she pushed his jeans away and teased his erection through his boxers. She gripped him through the cotton fabric and he gritted his teeth together, fighting every natural urge that came rushing forward at her touch.

When she pulled his underwear down and exclaimed, 'Well, hello, soldier!', all bets were off. He loved this playful, flirtatious side to Mae. Along with her touch, it helped him forget about everything his ex had done to him and simply enjoy the moment with her.

In a hurry to kick off the rest of his clothes, he almost stumbled onto the bed with her, spurred on by her little giggle. Lying face to face, Liam kissed her, luxuriating in the soft, welcoming feel of her lips against his. She'd become his sanctuary.

Something between them seemed to have shifted in those few seconds. The frenzied passion was now a sensual exploration as they caressed each other's naked bodies, the kisses tender and softer than before, as if they were drawing comfort from one another rather than embarking on what was supposed to be a wild, reckless shag-a-thon.

Mae must have thought the same, as her gentle strokes along his shaft now became insistent and demanding, until he couldn't think straight, forcing all his energy into not embarrassing himself, and also wanting her with a hunger that was eating him from the inside out.

He moved so she was underneath him, her soft breasts pushed so temptingly against him he couldn't resist, especially when she was so responsive every time he touched her there. With one breast cupped in his palm, he grazed his teeth over the sensitive bud atop, tugging on it until she was groaning and writhing with a mixture of frustration and pleasure. He knew, because he felt it too. He was enjoying all the sensations, wanting instant gratification but also wanting to make this last for ever. The horny excitement, the restlessness and stimulation of being together and not yet consummating their relationship, were all preferable to feeling miserable, analysing where he'd gone wrong and worrying about the future.

Mae liked him, and clearly wanted him, and that was enough for now. She grabbed his backside and pulled him flush against her—a woman who knew her own mind and wasn't afraid to show him what was on it.

'I need to get some protection.' He'd bought a packet of condoms in preparation and, though he was loath to move from his current position, they were lying in the heap of clothes on the floor.

'In my night stand. Hold on.' Mae rummaged one-handed in the drawer beside the bed and produced a foil packet.

He raised an eyebrow. 'I don't mean to be judgemental, but I was under the impression you hadn't been with anyone since... you know.'

He hated himself for even thinking it, never mind saying it. It was none of his business if she'd been in bed with half the country, but he found himself irrationally hating anyone who'd been here with her before him. Part of the reason he'd bonded with Mae was that they'd been in similar circumstances relationship-wise and, to him, that included post-break-up celibacy, so they'd experience this breakthrough in their emotional and physical development together.

Ugh. So much for 'no strings' if he was jealous of anyone she potentially could have slept with before they'd even met.

'Sorry. Sorry. I have no right to say anything about your love life.'

Mae held his face in her hands and locked her eyes on to his. 'I haven't been with anyone since my non-wedding day. I haven't wanted to be with anyone until you. And I haven't any intention of sleeping with anyone but you for the near future, okay? I bought them especially. I mean, if we're embarking on some sort of sex-fest until we're both rendered incapable of walking and talking, we don't want to run out, right?'

'Right. I'm sorry...'

Mae placed a finger on his lips. 'No apologies. Just fun.'

'Just fun,' he muttered against her finger before drawing it into his mouth and sucking it hard.

Mae continued the battle of one-upmanship by putting the condom on him herself, Liam breaking out in a sweat as he fought so hard to maintain his composure.

'You do not play fair at all, Dr Watters.' Pinning her hands to the bed, he kissed the smug smile of satisfaction from her lips.

He nudged her knees apart and positioned himself between her legs, entering her in one swift move that seemed to stun them both. It certainly took him a long, hot minute to recompose himself, once the fireworks had stopped going off in his head. Mae's little gasp when he entered her soon turned to a sigh of satisfaction as he moved inside her. Every time they joined together was a test of his restraint when he just wanted to give himself over to the euphoria he was experiencing. Dipping in and out of her felt like a new reward every time.

Greedy for more, he hooked her legs over his shoulders and pushed deeper, harder, faster. Mae's gasps became louder, quicker, more ragged. Then he realised his breathing was rapid too, that pressure to give in to his release becoming so intense, he thought he'd explode.

He watched where their bodies were joined as he slid in and out of this beautiful woman, realising how privileged he was to be in this position. To be with Mae. He kissed her, long and passionately, showing her how grateful he was with every thrust of his hips. He waited until she tightened around him, clutching at his back as her orgasm hit, until he found complete satisfaction too. Mae's cry was drowned out by his roar of triumph, their bodies rocking together until they had nothing left to give and his throat was raw.

Yet he found himself reluctant to move away when it was all over, only doing so when his knees were too weak to hold him up any longer.

'This might just kill me,' he said, rolling over beside her.

'Yeah, but you'll die happy.' Mae turned on her side and kissed him.

'Amen.' He lay on his back, fighting to get his breath back and praying this wouldn't be the last time they had this. That it was only the beginning. He needed this feeling, needed Mae, to help him forget all the bad stuff and, yes, make him happy. It was a long time since he'd had anything in his life to smile about and now it would be hard to wipe the grin off his face.

'What are you smiling about?'

'This. You, and how you make me feel like a king,' he said honestly. There was no point in hiding it, not when communication had been his downfall in the past and he wanted this to last with Mae for as long as possible.

'I think you did all the hard work…this time.' Mae stood up and walked towards the bathroom, giving him an envious view of her pert backside. Though he was sorry she was leaving him in bed without her, he kept hold of her words, the twinkle in her eye and the promise that they would do this all over again.

CHAPTER SEVEN

MAE STARED AT the reflection in the bathroom mirror. She didn't recognise the flushed face staring back or the twinkle back in her eyes, and her hair made her look as though she'd been thoroughly ravished in bed. Which she had. The wanton woman smiled back at her. This was exactly what she needed: fun; an ego boost… Liam.

And it felt safe, knowing he couldn't break her heart, because she wasn't going to give it to him. He could have her body; she'd give it willingly after he'd showed her exactly what he could do with it. The rest she intended to keep under lock and key, knowing she couldn't trust anyone not to damage it—including herself.

That said, she wasn't in a rush for their

tryst to end just yet. She splashed some water over her face and freshened up before going back into the room. The sight of Liam stretched out naked on her bed convinced her that, just because this was supposed to be casual, it didn't mean he shouldn't stay a little while longer. Since Shannon was staying at his parents' place, and he didn't seem to be in a hurry to leave either, Mae slid back into bed next to him.

'No taxi waiting for you?'

'No…sorry, do you want me to leave?' He sat up immediately and reached down for his clothes, clearly mistaking her teasing for a hint he should leave.

'No. Not at all. I just thought that might be how these things work—you know?—wham, bam.'

'There was no "wham bam" involved, but I do thank you, ma'am—very, very much.' Liam punctuated the words with kisses dotted along her collarbone, making her feel she never wanted him to leave.

'I just… I don't do this. I guess I'm just trying to figure out what the rules are.' She didn't want to misstep and have it end when she was already enjoying the benefits.

'We make our own rules. If we want to cuddle after, hey, that's normal—I think. As long as we're both comfortable with what's happening, I don't see any reason to bolt the second the deed is done.'

'The deed?' She chuckled.

'You know what I mean. We're only here for one thing.' He let his hand drift along the curve of her waist, barely touching her, but her body responded all the same, ready to accept him all over again.

'Yeah, but there's no rush, is there? Shannon's with your mum and dad, and it seems foolish for us both to spend the night alone in separate houses. Not that I'm expecting you to stay over, or anything. But, you know, we can hang out, order takeaway and watch trash TV. If that doesn't seem too much like breaking the rules?' She didn't want to frighten him off but it would be nice to have some company. Since moving in, she'd spent every night on her own, and it seemed a little churlish to send him home simply because it breached the 'hook-up and done' code.

'Look.' He turned onto his side, giving her a serious look. 'We both know the score. Neither of us is going to read more into what's happening than what we've agreed to. I'd actually enjoy doing something normal, like ordering some food and vegging out in front of the telly. In company, for once. No, this probably isn't like any other casual relationship because we already know each other, and we work together. As long as we are both happy, I don't see the problem. If that changes, then we'll reconsider our arrangement. Deal?'

'Deal.' Mae shook his outstretched hand. It didn't seem odd at all to make a deal whilst lying naked with a co-worker, the way her life had been going lately. Infinitely preferable to moving halfway across the world and being dumped on her wedding day.

'Okay, so… Chinese, Indian, burgers…?' Liam lifted his phone and began scrolling.

'Chinese,' she said without hesitation, her stomach rumbling, having been too nervous to eat anything before their date.

He held the screen so she could see the menu and pick what she wanted to eat, then he added his order, along with extra portions of rice and noodles. 'Done.'

When Mae saw the size of the order he'd just put in, she began to get concerned. 'The way you've been feeding me recently, I'm going to end up the size of a house.'

She'd already put on a little weight on after the wedding, during her comfort eating stage.

'I like your curves,' he said, grabbing hold of her backside and pulling her flush against him. 'Besides, we can always work off a few calories.'

'Yeah?' With his eyes darkening with desire, it was clear how he planned to work out. His idea of exercise sure beat those dreaded early-morning gym trips. She might just cancel her membership and employ him as her personal trainer instead.

'Well, the app says delivery is going to take at least an hour. I think we could squeeze in a good workout, you know? Build up an appetite.' He was moving over her again, covering her with his body and rolling her onto her back. Mae submitted completely and willingly.

'We wouldn't want to get lazy. It's important to balance diet and exercise for your well-being,' she muttered as he dipped his head to capture her mouth once more.

Mae sighed into the kiss, reaching up to wind her fingers in Liam's hair and claim him as hers for a little while longer. This was all temporary—a fantasy she was allowed to indulge in to make her feel better about herself. It was working. When she was with Liam, he treated her like a goddess. She was no longer the rejected bride not worthy of love but a sexy, confident single woman embarking on a passionate fling. Liam O'Conner was just the tonic she needed.

'You want another beer?' Mae shouted from the kitchen.

'Why not? I can always walk home.' Whilst he had no intention of going to work with a hangover tomorrow, he was enjoying the evening.

Eating a takeaway while watching soap

operas was a normal night. Liam did it all the time. So why did it feel so special just because he was doing it with Mae? Probably because it felt comfortable, knowing she was happy to do it. Even on the nights he and Clodagh had been at home together, she hadn't wanted to sit in with him, preferring to go out with 'the girls'. He'd been too boring, too staid, because he'd simply wanted family time together. Secrecy was a big part of his arrangement with Mae, for everyone's sake. It also meant there wasn't any pressure to go out clubbing, or try to be someone he wasn't. This was enough for her, and so was he.

'There's enough food left to feed the street.' She tossed him a beer and curled up beside him on the sofa.

'We can box it up and put it in the fridge once it's cooled down. I'll have it for breakfast.'

'Yuk.' She screwed up her nose and took a slug of beer from her bottle. 'I don't know how you can eat so much and still look so good.'

'I do have to work at it. I've got a home

gym, and eat salads in between parent visits usually. I've made an exception for you this week, but it's nice to know you think I'm hot.' He was teasing her but she was definitely giving him an ego boost. Not only with her comments, but the way she'd responded to him in bed, where he knew he was most definitely doing something right.

Liam supposed sex had kind of taken a back seat between Clodagh and him due to shift clashes and, if he was honest, a lack of interest. They hadn't made enough time, or effort. Yet he seemed to be able to find both for Mae. Perhaps he'd known deep down that he and Clodagh were over and had checked out long before she had.

In which case, he couldn't blame her for having gone elsewhere. It was being with Mae that showed him all that had been missing in the relationship—passion, fun and enjoying one another. He'd settled for less because he wanted to save his family, provide some stability in Shannon's life and be the good parent he'd had growing up, but family life had been far from perfect. Some day he hoped he could have it all: a romantic, fun relationship that also nurtured a loving environment for his daughter to grow up in.

'You know you are. Confidence is not something you seem to have a problem with.'

'A common misconception about me. Yes, I'm an extrovert, but that doesn't mean I don't have hang-ups like everyone else. You know how it feels when you've been rejected—it hurts.'

He saw her wince and mentally kicked himself for bringing up her past relationship woes and spoiling the evening. 'Sorry. I just mean we're here together tonight because we're too afraid to commit to a proper relationship again. This is safe until we're ready to trust someone with our hearts some day.'

Mae scrambled to sit upright, her legs tucked under her to bring her up to the same height as Liam. 'So you think you'll want to do the whole serious relationship again? That's not for me.'

'No? Never, ever?' He let out a long breath. 'I don't think I could do that. I need to be with someone.'

'Why is it so important? You're doing okay, just you and Shannon. Why do you need to bring a third party in to make you happy, knowing they could do the opposite?'

He had to think on that one for a bit, knowing her fears were justified. It wasn't that he hadn't considered it: it was why they were keeping this secret, after all. He didn't want Shannon to get hurt, and by keeping things casual with Mae he was protecting his own heart. Especially knowing she didn't want another serious relationship. Ultimately, though, he thought the risk would be worth taking if he could still find that special someone to share his life with.

'I know a lot of people resent their parents, or choose partners that are the complete opposite to who they were, but you've met my mum and dad. They're great, right?'

She nodded with a smile. 'Yes, they are.'

'Growing up in that place was the happiest time of my life. I know it's unconventional, and it was noisy, and they were always working, but they always made time for me and each other. Family was the most important thing, and I still believe that. I just want that sort of security for Shannon, as well as for me. I know she has me and her grandparents, even her mother on occasion, but it's not the same. I want someone to share the parenting with, to cook dinner with after work, to go on holiday and make plans for the future with. Maybe even have more kids some day. I don't want one failed relationship to take all of that away for ever.'

Mae watched him with something he was sure was a mixture of surprise and sadness. As though she didn't believe he could still want all of that, and sure she was too afraid to.

'I can sort of see where you're coming from, even if my childhood has given me a different perspective on that. I never knew my father: he split when I was little, leaving Mum to raise me. I loved her so much. She was like my best friend, you know? So strong and independent and caring. Losing her… Well, it was devastating.' Her voice faltered. 'I tried the serious relationship thing with Diarmuid, but in hindsight I think I was just looking for a replacement—something to fill the void the loss of my mother had created. I realise now I'm not going to find that with anyone. She's simply irreplaceable.'

Liam saw through her smile to the heart-break and loneliness inside her. At least he had Shannon and his parents to keep him buoyed, and remind him he was loved. Mae had no one and it was a shame she wanted to keep it that way.

'By your own admission, your marriage was probably a mistake. Something you rushed into. That doesn't mean there isn't someone out there who's perfect for you, that you could be happy with. Didn't you ever want a family of your own?'

It was a simple enough question, but it packed a powerful punch straight through Mae's defences and straight to her heart. Liam *saw* her.

'I did, at one point. I mean, when you grow up in a one-parent family always struggling for money, it's the dream to have the whole family package, including a dad to love and support you. When I met Diarmuid, I thought we would have that too. I guess it was better he left me when he did, rather than walk away later on an entire family. It's made me think about what a lucky escape I've had and how careful I need to be in future. I don't want to inflict a difficult childhood on an innocent child because I got carried away in a romantic fantasy.

'The reality of life is that relationships don't work out. I've accepted that. I mean, if you'd known Clodagh was going to leave, would you have started a family?' Mae threw the question back at him even though she knew she was treading on dangerous ground, because Shannon was everything to Liam. She just wanted him to realise the gravity behind her making that kind of decision—choosing to protect potential offspring before they even came into existence.

The uncharacteristic scowl suggested perhaps she had strayed too far beyond those blurred lines between a fling and something more personal. She doubted a no-strings arrangement included deep and meaningful conversations about their life choices and motivations.

'We can't live our lives on "ifs" and "buts", Mae, or we'd never accomplish anything. Okay, so it didn't work out between Clodagh and I, but I wouldn't be without Shannon. Would I have done things differently given a chance? Yes. Perhaps I was more invested in the idea of family than putting in the work to make sure we stayed together, but I don't regret becoming a father. I regret letting her and Clodagh down by not doing enough to make the relationship work, but I'm not going to let it steal my future from me. I've learned some lessons, and hope it will help me if I do ever get into another long-term relationship, but there's no point in looking back any more. Being with you has shown me that.' He grabbed hold of her feet and pulled her, so she slid down the couch towards him, and kissed her.

Mae's eyes fluttered shut and she let the feel of his lips dictate her mood instead of the noise currently buzzing in her head. She wanted to focus on Liam kissing her, on being together right now, instead of worrying about the future.

Except she couldn't put his words to the back of her mind just yet. He still wanted marriage, a family and everything she'd thought was possible once upon a time. She wished she had his optimism, or even that she could be 'the one' for him and that they'd all live happily ever after. Life had cruelly illustrated to her that it wasn't a realistic expectation, even if Liam did make a good argument.

Fear held her back from being with someone. From being with Liam. She was scared of being rejected again, of her heart taking another beating, of planning a future together and having it whipped away from her again. The only thing worse than having to go through that again, of losing someone else she loved, would be having a child live through it too. She wouldn't be able to live with the guilt of that. Yet the way Liam talked about his daughter, the love he obviously had for her, made her heart ache a little more. It was as though she'd lost an entire family because of Diarmuid, because she could never let anyone get close to her again after the way he'd treated her.

In moments like this, being with Liam, she was beginning to have second thoughts about remaining alone. 'For ever' seemed like a long time, especially if it meant not having company like this, with someone who knew her. What she had with Liam wasn't something she'd be able to replicate in the future. A casual fling with some random guy she met in a bar or club was never going to have the same depth as this thing with Liam. She knew that after only one day. This wasn't just sex, it was amazing sex, and she wondered if that was because they knew more about each other than two strangers who'd simply hooked up one night.

The passion and desire had likely built up from seeing each other at work and not being able to touch one another. She wondered if that was sustainable. It certainly felt like it, when they were already pulling at each other's clothes again, impatient to experience that ecstasy together all over again.

More frighteningly, perhaps she was beginning to ask herself if this could be more than stealing a few hours together. Liam had been open about wanting a partner willing to settle down and raise a family with him and, whilst Mae didn't know if she was open to that possibility, she had definitely grown close to Liam and his daughter.

The question now was whether or not she was willing to risk her peace of mind for more time with Liam.

Liam was wrapped around Mae's naked body, trying to get his breath back—again. This time they hadn't made it to the bedroom and, despite the uncomfortable confines of the sofa, his body was finally getting weary. He was in danger of falling into a food and sex coma, having over-indulged in both. Not that he was complaining. He just needed a little time before he was ready for action again.

'I should probably go,' he muttered into the back of her neck as they lay spooning on the couch.

Mae groaned and wriggled against him,

not doing anything to persuade him he should leave.

'We both need some sleep.' He half-heartedly tried again to convince them both to move, but he was pleasantly exhausted, and quite happy to remain in situ with Mae in his arms.

'You could stay. I mean, it's too late to walk home, if you could even manage to stand right now, and it seems pointless paying for a taxi when your car's outside…'

'I don't know…'

'I just thought, you know, if you wanted to stay on the couch for the night. Sorry… I didn't mean to over-step any boundaries.' Mae sat up, extracting herself from his arms and grabbing the clothes she'd discarded earlier.

'Hey. I know you were only thinking of me. Don't worry. It's just that I don't have a toothbrush and I don't want to spoil the illusion of this erotic fantasy with my very real morning breath.'

Liam didn't want her to feel bad because he hadn't immediately jumped at her invitation. He'd hesitated because it had crossed his mind that staying the night wasn't in keeping with the idea of 'just sex', but he supposed they'd crossed that line some time ago. Having dinner and discussing their past relationships over drinks probably wasn't the norm for this kind of set-up.

It wasn't that he didn't want to stay the night: it would be easier, and it would mean he didn't have to go home to an empty house. He was merely worried that staying over with Mae might become too comfortable. This felt more like the beginning of a relationship than something that wasn't supposed to have any emotional attachment for them. He already knew he had feelings for Mae that went beyond the physical—a bad move when she'd told him in no uncertain terms she didn't want a commitment.

Yet, they were electric together, and that wasn't something he could easily walk away from. Especially when his legs were like jelly after all his exertions tonight.

'I'm sure I have a spare in the bathroom.

If you want to stay…if it's not breaking the rules…'

'I'm not going to stay on the sofa, Mae.'

'Oh. Okay. Do you need me to order a cab?' She looked a little crestfallen and Liam almost felt bad about teasing her.

'If I'm sleeping here tonight, I want to do it in your bed. These bones of mine are getting too old to spend the night anywhere but in a nice, comfy bed.' That definitely wasn't in keeping with the idea of just sex, but they'd already crossed so many boundaries that others might consider casual that it hardly mattered now. Not if it meant waking up in Mae's arms. Who knew when they'd next get to spend time together, never mind an entire night? Liam intended to make the most of his child-free time.

Although Mae was smiling, seemingly pleased by his decision, he did sense some hesitation before she took it when he held out his hand to her.

'I only meant to sleep. I don't believe you can have too much of a good thing, but I do think some recovery time is necessary before you indulge again.' Liam grinned, fully intending to indulge again before he finally had to leave. He knew they were both exhausted, with jobs and lives of their own to go back to tomorrow, but they could let the fantasy go on a little bit longer.

'A sleep, a shower and some breakfast in the morning should set us both to rights again.' Mae led the way back upstairs, with Liam keen to follow.

'That sounds like a plan.' And an excellent way to start a new day. It was a shame this was probably only a one-off when the thought of waking up in Mae's bed, with her naked beside him, was likely something he could easily get used to.

The sound of his phone buzzing roused Liam from a deep sleep. It took him a few seconds to come to in the dark and realise where he was. Then Mae stirred beside him and he was tempted to ignore the call and snuggle back under the sheets with her. Instead, one glance at the screen and he was straight out of bed, phone in hand.

'Dad? What's wrong?' It was three o'clock in the morning and he knew his parents wouldn't have called him unless something was seriously amiss.

'Sorry to wake you, son, but it's Shannon.'

Liam's stomach plummeted through the floor. 'What's happened?'

He bounded down the stairs and grabbed his clothes from the floor, dressing one-handed while waiting to hear whatever bad news his father was about to impart.

'Now, don't panic…'

The very words were guaranteed to make him panic.

'Is she all right?'

'She's had a fall. I'm not sure if she was disoriented in the dark, or if she was sleep walking, but she fell down the stairs. The poor lamb knocked herself out for a bit and I think she might have broken her arm. I've phoned for an ambulance but I thought maybe you could get here quicker to take a look and reassure her.'

He could have, if he hadn't been drinking

at Mae's house, but he didn't want to tell them that and complicate the situation any further.

'I'll be there as quick as I can.' Liam hung up so he could order a taxi, cursing himself for taking his eyes off the ball. In paying more heed to his libido than his daughter, he'd failed her and left her to get hurt whilst he'd been out pretending he was a single man with no responsibilities.

Liam lifted one of his shoes and fired it across the room, watching it ricochet off the kitchen door. A pointless exercise, since he had to go and pick it up again or he couldn't leave the house, and it did nothing to alleviate the guilt and frustration he was experiencing. He was angry at himself for going against everything he'd promised himself and Shannon after Clodagh had left. Spending the night with Mae hadn't been putting his daughter's needs first, and it certainly hadn't been the action of a man trying to be a better father. It had been selfish and foolish, and now his daughter was going to pay the price for his mistakes, again.

'Is there something wrong?' Mae appeared

in the doorway, hair in disarray, eyes half-closed with sleep, tying the belt of her dressing gown around her waist.

Liam clenched his teeth together, trying to ignore the fact that her bare legs seemed to go on for ever and that he knew exactly what was under that robe. 'Shannon fell down the stairs and hurt herself. I have to get to the pub.'

'I'm so sorry. Let me come with you.'

'The taxi's on its way. I'm not waiting for you. My daughter needs me and I've already let her down tonight.'

'I swear I'll be two minutes. Let me help. If I'm not down when the cab comes, you can go without me.' She hovered in the doorway, waiting for him to give her the nod, to let her know things were okay between them.

Although he was regretting leaving Shannon tonight, it wasn't Mae's fault. She'd done everything right. That was the problem. He hadn't wanted to leave, and he knew that was bad news for the future. A fling between them was always going to be complicated and he simply couldn't afford this level of distraction taking him away from his daughter.

He also knew turning up together would cause problems. His parents weren't stupid; they'd know they'd spent the night together. Since he was already having second thoughts about continuing whatever this was with Mae, explaining the circumstances was not going to put him in a good light with anyone. He would need to come up with a pretty good excuse as to why she was with him at this time of the morning if he was to avoid embarrassing everyone involved.

However, if the ambulance was too far away and Shannon had been seriously hurt, he might need an extra pair of medical hands. His daughter's welfare had to come before his personal problems—something he should have remembered before he let her get hurt. Now he would simply have to swallow his pride and get to his daughter as fast as possible. Any difficult conversations to be had with his parents and Mae would have to wait until he knew Shannon was all right.

'Two minutes,' he said gruffly, hoping it expressed both his impatience and a hint that this was already over between them.

Mae raced back upstairs and he opened the door, waiting for the glare of the taxi headlights to turn into the street, part of him hoping it would appear before Mae did, so he didn't have to face the problem of her being there. Mae would understand if he went without her. After all, a single dad called away to deal with his daughter in the middle of the night wasn't the fun he'd promised. It represented the sort of commitment she'd told him she didn't want in her life.

When she did bounce back downstairs ready to go, clad in jeans, sweater and pulling on a pair of running shoes, it prompted him to ask himself why. If Mae was prepared to involve herself in his domestic dramas, it had to be because she was more invested in Shannon and him than she'd even realised. Whilst ultimately that was what he wanted, someone who'd be there for Shannon and him, he knew that wasn't the future Mae saw for herself.

There was no point in fooling themselves that this was going to work. It wouldn't be fair to anyone when it inevitably ended, no one satisfied with what they'd settled for.

They would have to put this down to what it was—a one-night stand with added complications—and go back to their own separate lives. It had been nice while it lasted, a brief respite from beating himself up over his personal failures. Once he was assured Shannon was okay, it would be back to business as usual.

The cab ride over to the pub was excruciating. Liam hadn't spoken to her since they'd left the house and she knew it was because he regretted everything that had happened between them. If they hadn't been so caught up in one another, Liam would have been at home with Shannon and she wouldn't have hurt herself. For someone who'd been so careful to protect his daughter until now, he'd be devastated by these events.

Mae could have let him go to deal with the situation himself, but she'd feared if she did she might never see him again, at least outside of a professional capacity. She still wasn't ready for their time to end just yet and hoped by showing him she cared about Shannon too they might be able to salvage something between them.

Although she'd sworn not to commit to anything or anyone capable of breaking her heart somewhere down the line, she was already in too deep with Liam to walk away now. If they couldn't manage to keep things casual, she hoped they could at least take things slowly if she was to venture back into a relationship.

Talking tonight, enjoying each other's company, making love and going to bed together at the end of the day were all things she'd been missing in her life. Liam had shown her what she could still have if she was brave enough to open up her life, and her heart, to the possibility of being with someone again.

Yes, it was scary embarking on something with a man who had such a great responsibility as a father but, if being a part of his family was what it took for him to continue seeing one another, Mae was willing to try. As long as they went into it with their eyes open, aware of how they'd both been scarred in the past, and promising never to reopen those old wounds with actions of their own, they might stand a chance.

'Thanks.'

Liam threw some money at the driver outside the pub before getting out of the car without even looking back to see if Mae was following. Obviously his primary concern was for Shannon, but it still hurt she didn't warrant a smidge of his attention.

'She's inside. We thought we'd keep her downstairs so the paramedics could get to her easier.' Paddy met them at the entrance of the dark pub, which seemed so eerie at this time of the morning with no one else around, the noise of customers seemingly a distant memory.

They crossed the rain-soaked cobbles and rushed inside, both praying Shannon wasn't too badly injured.

'The ambulance is on the way. We loaned the car to Sean tonight so he could go to the cash and carry for us in the morning, otherwise we would have driven her ourselves.' They found his mother cradling Shannon in one of the booths in which only a few hours ago people would've been sitting, drinking and having fun.

'It's fine. We're here now. Daddy's here, sweetie.' Liam moved so Shannon was resting her head on his lap instead of his mother's.

Mae saw the look Moira gave Liam and her, but she made no comment and received no explanation, though it must've been obvious what had gone on. She must look a mess with mega bedhead, not to mention her make-up sweated off after her sex session with Liam, wearing the first clothes that came to hand. That alone would've signalled what they'd been up to, even if arriving together in the early hours of the morning hadn't.

She felt herself heat up under Moira's scrutiny and ducked into the other side of the booth from Liam, out of harm's way. 'How is she?'

'There's quite a bad gash at her temple. Is your head hurting, sweetie?' Liam brushed her blood-matted hair away from her face, the look of love in his eyes for his daughter so intense, it made Mae want to weep.

It was a promise to love and protect her at

all costs. Mae had never had any man look at her that way, parent or partner. Nor was she likely to if she didn't open up her life, and her heart, to let someone close enough to love her like that. At this moment in time, she was tempted to go against everything she'd promised herself and take a risk on love again if it meant Liam might look at her like that some day.

'Where were you, Daddy? I had a bad dream and I couldn't find you.'

Mae didn't know which was worse to witness—the little girl's distress, or the cloud of guilt that moved over her father's face. She wanted to reach out and hug both of them, but knew that would be over-stepping so many boundaries in front of Liam's family and he wouldn't appreciate it.

'I know, Shannon. I'm sorry. I'll never leave you on your own again, okay? Now, can you be a big, brave girl and let me see where you're hurt?'

Shannon nodded slowly, naturally wary but trusting her father not to do anything to cause her any unnecessary pain. Liam would blame himself for Shannon getting hurt, of course—that was the nature of a good parent—but it was an accident that no one could have prevented. Mae wasn't ashamed to admit she envied their relationship when it had been missing in her life for too long. She'd never had it with her father and, now that her mother was gone, there was no one in her life she could trust implicitly always to look out for her like that. If she didn't take a few risks, she never would.

'Could you put some more lights on, Paddy, please? And Moira, could you pass me the first-aid kit?' If she was going to be seen here tonight as someone other than the harlot who'd tempted a good dad away from his daughter, then Mae needed to earn her place.

Immediately, Paddy and Moira sprang into action, and she was sure they were simply glad to have a part to play too. Now that they could better see what they were dealing with, Liam helped Shannon on to the table.

Mae began cleaning the wound on the little girl's temple. 'This might sting a little bit,

Shannon, but we have to clean the area to see how deep the cut is.'

'I need to see this arm too, love.' Liam tried to persuade her to let him assess what damage had been done there, but Shannon cradled the limp limb closer to her body, refusing his request.

Once Mae had finished dressing the head wound, she moved around to join Liam at the end of the table to face Shannon. 'You're lucky. You have two doctors who want to help you feel better. Won't you let us take a look? It won't heal unless we do, and you don't want to go about with one wing for ever, do you?'

That made Shannon smile, especially when Liam quacked at her. 'You're my little lame duck, aren't you, Shannon?'

'Quack, quack,' she responded, and tentatively held out her arm for Liam to look at it.

'Good girl.'

Carefully, Liam felt along the bruised arm, Shannon flinching when he reached her elbow. 'Okay, I think there's a fracture there. We need to stabilise that until the paramedics get here. Is there any update on that?'

'I'll phone again.' Paddy disappeared back behind the bar.

'Moira, do you have anything we could use as a splint? Like a piece of wood, or even a rolled-up newspaper would do for now. We could tie that around her arm temporarily to immobilise it.'

Mae wanted to do something other than sit waiting for someone else to help Shannon. She hated to see her in pain, as much as she disliked watching her father's anguish. It was important to her that she could be there for them and Mae realised that she'd already made that commitment she was so afraid of. Once Shannon was treated at the hospital and they knew she was all right, Mae would discuss the matter with Liam. If he was on board, she'd like to take that first step back into the relationship world with him.

'Here you go. I brought a couple of towels too.' Moira returned with some makeshift medical supplies for Mae to use whilst Liam reassured his daughter they were working in her best interests.

'Shannon, if you can hold your arm out,

Mae is going to tie some things around it to keep it straight. We need you to stay still until she's all done.' Liam had one arm around Shannon's waist, holding her close, with the other presenting the broken limb for Mae to work on.

She was grateful he was allowing her to be of some assistance when she knew he was quite capable of doing all this on his own. Hopefully it was a sign that he was ready for her to be part of their lives too.

'When you get to the hospital they'll put a proper cast on it for you, but we're just going to tie this on now so it doesn't hurt any more when you move it.' Mae used the bandages in the first-aid kit to hold the temporary fix in place, but she was relieved when she heard the sirens outside.

'I'll go and direct them in.' Paddy, still in his pyjamas, rushed out into the street so they didn't waste any time trying to locate their patient. A short time later, he returned with two paramedics, carrying their first-aid gear.

'Over here.' Liam waved them over and

Mae moved out of the way so they had full access to examine Shannon.

'It looks as though someone has beat us to it,' one of the men commented on seeing Shannon's home-made splint.

'We're both doctors, but unfortunately we didn't have the means to get her to hospital ourselves tonight. Shannon had a fall down the stairs while she was staying with my parents. She had a bad knock to the head, and was briefly unconscious, but she's responsive and seems fine at the moment.'

'No sickness or dizzy spells?'

'No. She was out cold for a few moments, the longest time of my life. We just didn't want to do anything that might do her more harm than good.' Moira was hovering by the table, understandably concerned with her granddaughter's welfare, and no doubt blaming herself as much as Liam for the accident.

'That's fine. We'll do an X-ray on that arm at the hospital, Shannon, and try and make you more comfortable, but there's nothing to worry about. Is Mum or Dad coming with us in the ambulance?'

'I'm her dad. Mae's just a friend.' Liam asserted his position, and Mae's at the same time, as he scooped Shannon up into his arms, ready to leave.

'I guess I'll phone a cab to take me home.' Despite her role in the drama, Mae was left feeling like a spare part with no real reason to be here, with Liam willing to leave her with his parents in an awkward post-hook-up situation.

'That's probably for the best. I'll call you later.'

The promise to get back in touch was the only thing saving her from total humiliation. It wouldn't do to get too needy; Liam was always going to put his daughter first. He was that kind of man, and if he hadn't been she probably wouldn't even be thinking of venturing into something beyond casual with him. It was precisely because he was loyal and loving that made her want to take that risk.

'I have the number of a local firm,' Moira

informed her with a pat on the arm Mae hoped was more out of friendship than pity.

'Okay, sweetheart, I'll just be downstairs if you need me.' Liam tucked Shannon under the covers and edged towards the door. She'd wanted to sleep in his bed, and after the night they'd had and the guilt he was still carrying he couldn't say no.

'I just have to make a phone call then I promise I'll be right up again.' He didn't want to leave her, even though he knew she was safe and would likely be asleep before he reached the bottom of the stairs. It had been a long night for everyone. But he had also promised to call Mae.

Although it was late—technically speaking, it was early morning, but since no one had slept he still counted it as night—he suspected Mae would be up. She'd been great tonight, helping with Shannon, and he was sure she'd want to be kept up to date with her progress. He'd already called his parents to let them know Shannon was fine, with no sign of concussion and a cast on her arm to show off in school that day. Their profuse apologies hadn't been necessary when it was his fault he'd left Shannon there, his only thoughts having been of the time he'd get to spend with Mae. He hoped his reassurances would help them get some sleep.

This call was going to be a little more difficult and painful. He'd waited until he'd come home to give him some space to think things over first, and to afford some privacy. Mae had been upfront about not wanting anything serious, so she deserved the same respect when it came to ending things.

She answered the call the second it rang. 'How is she?'

The concern in her voice made Liam ache all the more for the life he really wanted with Mae and Shannon. If only he could be sure that it would work between them, that she could commit to his family, he wouldn't have to choose between his daughter and her. It was a contest she could never win.

'They put a cast on her arm, but other than that she's fine. Currently asleep in my bed.

She's understandably clingy and didn't even want me to come down and phone you.'

'In that case, I won't keep you. I just wanted to know she was okay.' Mae was about to end the call but that wasn't what Liam wanted—none of this was. But, if he didn't have this conversation now, he'd have to do it at work and it wouldn't be fair to ambush her like that.

'Listen, Mae, tonight has really opened my eyes. I just don't think a casual fling is going to work for me...'

'I was thinking the same thing.'

Good, at least they were on the same page. It should make things easier if, as he thought, she'd realised the responsibility of looking after his daughter would be more commitment than she was ready to give.

'So, we'll just put this down to a lapse of judgement? A very, very nice one while it lasted, but I can't justify the time away from my daughter. I should have been with her tonight. She was looking for me when she fell, and I just can't let her down like that again. It's probably best we just go back to being work colleagues. I hope you understand.' It wouldn't do to beg her to consider something long term and more serious when he wasn't sure either of them could commit to that. He'd already messed up, and it had only been one day, so the damage he could manage to inflict on his relationship with his daughter was unimaginable and not worth the risk.

'Of course,' she said eventually, letting him breathe a sigh of relief.

'Okay, then… I guess I'll see you around.'

'I guess so.'

'Bye, Mae. I'm sorry things didn't work out.'

'Me too, Liam.' Her voice was quiet but she was the first to hang up.

Liam didn't have much practice at ending relationships; his last experience had been him on the other end of that conversation. It hadn't been his intention to cause Mae any pain, though she seemed to sympathise with the position he was in. He hadn't wanted her to get upset or feel rejected.

But, if he was honest, her stoic response stung. It was as if what they'd had together tonight didn't really matter. In other circumstances, he knew they could have had something really special, mostly because they already had. To find she was able to simply forget it so easily was not only a knock to his ego, but confirmation that she wasn't the one for him after all. If he was ever going to let someone back into his life permanently, it would have to be someone who would fight for them, who would show a commitment to Shannon and him that Mae obviously didn't want.

CHAPTER EIGHT

'AT LEAST YOU love me, Brodie, eh?' Mae cuddled her furry friend closely and shared her bag of crisps with him. Though he didn't seem interested in the soppy movie she'd selected for the evening's entertainment, he was enjoying the hugs and attention. It didn't even matter about the slobber and crumbs he'd got all over her leisure wear, as long as she had him to hug tonight instead of being completely on her own.

She'd substituted an Irish wolfhound for Liam: that was how great a hole had been left in her life in just a matter of days. It was her fault for breaking her own rules. No matter how short the fling, she apparently couldn't separate her emotions from a physical relationship. Although, sleeping with someone she would see on a regular basis had always been asking for trouble. Having dinner with his family and getting to know his daughter were extra red flags she'd chosen to ignore. Little wonder then that, when he prioritised Shannon's welfare over some fun with her, Mae had been bereft.

She had hoped they'd have a chance to explore their relationship a little more, but he'd made it clear he wasn't interested beyond the one night. At least she'd been able to walk away with her dignity intact, if not her heart. She'd known the score; it wasn't Liam's fault she couldn't control her emotions because she'd only gone and fallen for him.

In the short space of time she'd got to know him, she'd opened her heart and had been preparing to share a little bit more with him. He and Shannon had showed her what she was missing out on by shutting herself off from the possibility of love and family. She didn't feel any better now after a brief, albeit passionate, tryst with Liam than she had after a serious relationship with Diarmuid.

'Perhaps I should just give up on men altogether and become a dog lady,' she said to Brodie, who licked away her tears then snatched the last crisp out of her hand. Betrayed by another male.

For a little while she'd been able to believe that a future with someone was possible—a relationship, maybe even a family some day. Being dropped like a hot potato the second his daughter had needed him, though understandable, had been nonetheless crushing. It simply reiterated the notion that everyone left her eventually. Although, in this case it had happened pretty darn quick. Maybe this time she would learn her lesson and not give her heart to anyone again. She couldn't trust anyone with it, not even herself.

All the lies she'd told herself about not getting emotionally involved with Liam, knowing she liked him, had just been to cover the fact she wanted to be with him. Now here she was, crying and pouring her heart out to a dog, when her fling with Liam was supposed to have been just a bit of fun. Apparently, she wasn't capable of that without losing her heart and her mind over a man. Over Liam.

The tears started again and she buried her face in Brodie's fur, drawing some comfort from his warmth. It said a lot about her life that she was spending her evening with a dog because she was so lonely, a feeling that had only been exacerbated by having spent time with Liam and his family. She hadn't just lost him but Paddy, Moira and Shannon too. Once Ray was out of hospital, she wouldn't even have Brodie.

It would be easy to pack up and move on somewhere else where she wouldn't run the risk of seeing Liam again and endure the pain of knowing they couldn't be together. But she couldn't keep doing that after every failed romance. She wanted to settle down and be happy, even if that meant being on her own.

'You're very grumpy tonight, Daddy.' Shannon pouted at him.

'Am I? Sorry, sweetheart, I just have a lot on my mind.' Mostly a certain woman he couldn't stop thinking about.

It had been a couple of days since he'd ended things and, though it had ultimately been his decision, he missed Mae. It was funny how close they'd become in such a short space of time and how much impact she'd had on his family. His parents and Shannon had been asking after her ever since. He'd excused her absence as a clash of shifts but he couldn't use that line for ever. It was awkward when his mum and dad knew they'd slept together; that'd been obvious when they'd both arrived in the early hours after Shannon's accident. It was more difficult still when they knew he didn't just hook up with anyone.

No one since Clodagh, in fact. Mae was special, they all knew that, but they respected him enough to make his own mistakes and not throw it back in his face. He'd done enough self-flagellation about losing her to suffice. Although, he had noticed his mum phoning to check in with him more often, sending home-made comfort food with Shannon every day. As much as he was indulging heavily in the baked goods and carbs, none of it could replace the feel-good endorphins he'd only had when he'd been with Mae.

He was beginning to wonder if he'd jumped

the gun. If they might have been able to work something out that suited them both so he hadn't had to lose her altogether. She'd been quick to accept the end of their arrangement without quibble, so he supposed there was no compromise to be had. In hindsight, telling someone who'd been burned so badly in a relationship that he'd only accept a partner who'd be there for him and his daughter might have been overkill. Those high expectations were never going to be attainable after only one night together but it was too late now to go back.

Yes, he had regrets and, given some time to think things through more clearly, he would've done things differently. Right now, he'd do anything to have Mae back in his life in whatever capacity he could. She'd helped with Ray and Shannon, not to mention the fracas outside the pub. They'd worked as a team.

More than that, she'd been there for him when he'd needed it. Liam had found a peace with Mae that he hadn't had in a long time, and their short-lived fling had been the explosive candle on the cake. It was no wonder Shannon thought he was grumpy when he'd been mad at himself these past days for throwing all that away. They were both missing her, and ending things hadn't achieved anything in the long run when they were hurting anyway.

'I miss Mae too.' His daughter was more astute than he gave her credit for, though he didn't want to get into a conversation about why Mae was no longer in the picture. Shannon was too young to fully understand the intricacies of adult relationships. Apparently, so was he. He was still trying to understand his own actions and could only think that his knee-jerk reaction in ending things with Mae had been his defences kicking in. When Shannon had been hurt, that was all he'd been able to think of, and how he was to blame. It was something he was too used to doing since Clodagh had left him doing the sole parenting, but he realised now, too late, that he was entitled to live a life of his own, just like Shannon's mother.

'We're both busy people. You're my main

girl, Shannon, and don't you forget it.' He put an arm around her shoulders and gave her a squeeze before opening the back door. It was then he realised he must have left it unlocked after their last visit. Thankfully, Brodie made an excellent burglar deterrent, and he would have heard him bark if a stranger had attempted to get in.

Shannon shrugged him off. 'Da-ad. I'm not going to be a kid for ever, you know. You really do need to get yourself a life.'

She flounced off into Ray's house, giving him a glimpse of the teenage years yet to come, and he knew she was right. Some day she wasn't going to want him anywhere near her and then where would he be? Likely sitting drowning his sorrows in his parents' place, lamenting a lost love that he let get away.

'You're such an eejit,' he chastised himself, only for his daughter's squeal coming from the living room to make him forget all his recent bad decisions for a moment.

'Shannon? What's wrong?' He burst through

the door, half-expecting to see her lying hurt somewhere.

Instead, he was met with the sight of her hugging Mae, with Brodie jumping on both of them, trying to be a part of the happy reunion.

'Hey,' Mae said quietly when she spotted him, furtively glancing around the living room, as if he'd caught her doing something she shouldn't. There was an empty family-sized bag of crisps lying on the sofa in between the pile of cushions, her shoes had been kicked off onto the floor and the credits of a movie were playing on the TV. She'd obviously been here for a while. If he'd known that, he might have come over earlier.

'Hey. Sorry. I didn't think you'd still be coming over to see to Brodie.' He had assumed she would have ditched the dog-sitting, in an attempt to avoid him, when it was as much a favour to him as to Ray.

'Of course I would. I promised Ray. I wouldn't leave Brodie on his own simply because we'd agreed not to see each other.' She frowned at him and he realised immediately what an injustice he'd done even to think that of her. Mae would never have purposely left anyone in the lurch. She was too good a person. Perhaps deep down he'd known that and had come over tonight because there was a chance of running into her like this.

'Did you and Daddy fall out? Is that why you've been crying, Mae?' Shannon asked, eyeballing the two of them before Liam had a chance to apologise to Mae for underestimating her.

'I haven't—'

'That's adult business.' He managed to talk over Mae in his lame attempt to distract his daughter. 'Sorry, I didn't mean to interrupt.'

'I was just saying I haven't been crying. It, er, must be my allergies.'

'What did you do, Daddy?' Shannon, not fooled by either of them, was fairly and correctly putting the blame on his shoulders for any upset Mae had suffered.

Now that Shannon had pointed it out, he could see the red rings around Mae's usually bright and clear green eyes, and she didn't look at all like her normal glam self. She was wearing pale-pink sweatpants and a matching baggy sweater, without a trace of make-up on her face. Whilst he still thought her beautiful, it was apparent that she hadn't put in her usual effort with her appearance.

He was guilty of the same tonight, dressing for comfort rather than style because it didn't seem important. Nothing did against the ache in his heart, which had been growing stronger since the last time he'd seen Mae. He almost hoped that her casual attire was an outward reflection of her heartache too, so that he knew he'd meant more to her than a one-night stand.

'He didn't do anything, Shannon. Your daddy just wants to spend all the time he can with you.' Mae stepped in to save his blushes, as his daughter was probably gearing up to give him a stern telling off.

'I see him every day,' Shannon said, rolling her eyes to make them both laugh. There he was, trying to be present in her life, when it seemed as though he was nothing but a nuisance. Perhaps he should let Shannon make all the important decisions in their lives from now on. She certainly wouldn't have let Mae walk away so easily.

'That's because he's a very good dad. I haven't seen my father since I was a little girl. You're very lucky you have someone so lovely taking care of you.' Mae was fixing Shannon's braid over her shoulder and Liam knew she was feeling the loss of her mother all over again. She was someone who should never have been on her own when she had so much love to give. It was clear in the way she was with Shannon, so loving and tender, that she would have made a great mum. If only men like him had treated her better, she might have believed it too.

'Did your daddy go away, like my mummy?'

'Yes, he did, but aren't you lucky you still get to see your mummy?'

The hitch in Mae's voice hinted at the pain she was still going through at the loss of her own mother, something he thankfully had no experience of, but sympathised with. After all, he'd fallen apart when a loved one had simply moved out of the house and the relationship; he could only imagine losing someone for ever. He had spent these past days thinking of nothing else and he knew he couldn't waste the second chance he'd been given. Opportunities to reconnect didn't come around often and he didn't want to spend the rest of his life hating himself for not grabbing it with both hands.

'Not every day, but I see daddy all the time when he's not at work.' Blissfully oblivious to Mae's distress, Shannon was very philosophical about her circumstances, showing just how much she'd adapted to the new dynamic already. Better than her father, it seemed.

'That's what makes him such a good daddy. He wants to be there for you all the time so you never, ever get hurt again.' Mae gently touched the cast on Shannon's arm, and Liam got the impression she felt as guilty that it had happened as he did.

It occurred to him that accepting responsibility for an accident that had been beyond her control was ridiculous, yet that was exactly what he'd done. He'd blamed himself for something he could never have prevented, to the extent he'd thought he had to stay glued to his daughter's side—a notion she clearly wasn't a fan of and, now he could see the situation from a different point of view, something completely unnecessary.

'That's just silly. He's not with me when I'm at school, or asleep.' She had a point. There was nothing to say she wouldn't fall or have an accident when he was at work or in a different room. He couldn't be in two different places at once and it was stupid to think otherwise. It was time he stopped using his daughter as an excuse to keep Mae at a distance and make that leap of faith.

'Shannon, could you go into the kitchen and give Brodie some water? I'd like to talk to Mae.' He wanted a little privacy so he didn't embarrass Mae, or himself, if she wasn't interested in anything more between them, and if he'd imagined the lingering embers of their passion still glowing, waiting to be stoked once more.

Shannon skipped off with Brodie galloping behind her. Mae faced him, her arms wrapped around her body, hugging herself in an expression of self-defence and anxiety.

She wasn't the same spiky American he'd sparred with during their first meeting. Although she'd let down those protective barriers and let him in, he'd wounded her with his actions, and he was sorry for that.

'Sorry. I wasn't expecting anyone over. Ray will probably be home tomorrow, so I was just saying my goodbyes to Brodie. I'll tidy up before I leave.' She glanced around at the evidence of her pity party. Liam recognised the signs, since he'd left a similar scene behind at home—his wallowing illustrated by chocolate wrappers and empty coffee cups.

He shook his head. 'That's not what I wanted to talk to you about. I, er, I missed you.'

She gave him a half-smile which he wasn't sure came from pity or something else. 'I missed you too.'

He wanted to say more, but instead he gathered her into his arms and held her tight. He felt huge relief when she wrapped her arms around him in response, instead of recoiling or pushing him away, which she would have had every right to do.

Eventually Mae let go. 'How's Shannon? She seems okay. No permanent psychological damage?'

He could tell by the way she was biting her lip that she was teasing him.

'Okay, so I was being a little bit over-protective and a tad over the top.'

'Just a tad. But I understand why. She's your daughter. You feel responsible, and you're afraid that she'll get hurt because of your actions.'

'Exactly.' And Mae's grasp of his situation, her empathy, was why he wanted to fight for her.

'I would never want her to get hurt either. You have to do what's best.'

'Yes…yes, I do. For once, I want to do whatever's best for me, and I think that's to have you back in my life. I know you don't want anything serious, Mae, but do you think we could still see each other? You know, maybe go out every now and then?' It wouldn't be the instant happy family he'd dreamed of, but he was willing to take things slowly if it meant he would still have Mae around.

'With Shannon?'

'Not if you don't want that…' He didn't want to frighten her off if she was even considering forgiving him and wanting to try again.

'I think maybe it's time we both stopped being afraid of being with each other. We can't hide away for ever, living in fear that we'll get hurt again, and letting the good things slip away from us. We're good together.' She slid her arms back around his waist, that connection making him remember their night together, and promising the thrill of more.

'That we are. So… I can stop pretending to Shannon and my parents that we're only colleagues?' If Mae was willing to try again, it seemed plausible that they should be open about it this time.

She cocked her head to one side. 'You really think we ever had them fooled?'

He thought about it for a split second. 'Nah. I think they knew before we even did.'

'We better prepare ourselves for the "we told you so" conversation.'

'It's fine. I can handle it. It's better than the, "you eejit, why did you let her go?" one I've been having with myself.'

'You are an eejit, but you're my eejit.' Mae tilted her face up to his and sealed their new beginning with a tender kiss.

'Always,' he replied, knowing he'd found the woman he'd been missing in his life long before they'd even known each other. It had taken them some time to work out that they were meant to be together but, now they had, Liam would do everything it took to make the relationship work.

He and Mae had finally found in one another the family they'd both been searching for.

EPILOGUE

'SHANNON, DON'T GO too far. Stay where we can see you!' Mae shouted after the little girl as she ran ahead into the woods.

'As if we could miss that dog, and since it's glued to her side there isn't much chance of losing either of them. It gives us a few minutes' peace, at least. Maybe even time to make out.' Liam nuzzled into her neck, his warm breath on her skin already making her wish they hadn't got out of bed this morning.

They'd only been together six months, but it was enough time for both of them to know it was what they both wanted and needed. She'd moved in with Liam and Shannon after a few weeks of dating, neither of them having wanted to waste any time that could've been spent together. It made practical sense too, making sure there was usually someone at home for Shannon, and saving on the travelling. On the odd occasion they were both working, Paddy and Moira were only too happy to babysit. Mae felt as though she was part of a real family now. Especially on those Sunday afternoons when Liam's parents cooked them a roast dinner that couldn't be beaten.

They'd even got the dog to complete the family picture. Technically he was still Ray's but it had made sense for them to take Brodie on a more permanent basis while Ray was working to overcome his alcohol issue. Ray was attending support meetings, and stopping drinking had definitely improved his health. Although his condition was irreversible, abstaining from alcohol would give him a longer life expectancy than if he'd continued to drink. He'd even put on a little weight since he'd started eating better, aided by the home-cooked meals Liam's parents sent round for him. Mae and Liam had him round for dinner every now and then to check in with him and give him some company.

Ray kept Brodie with him during the day, but mostly it was down to Liam and Mae to feed and walk the wolfhound. Shannon was absolutely besotted with the mutt, and Mae was sure he had helped her adjust to the upheaval when she'd moved in. She still saw her mother on occasion, which gave Mae and Liam some alone time.

They were very much still in the honeymoon stage, but the way he made her melt every time he touched her convinced her it would always be the same for them. In and out of the bedroom they made a good team, and she was thankful that both she and Liam had taken that leap of faith in one another to try and make things work.

'Not the kissing *again*.' Shannon voiced her disgust at the kissing they'd progressed to, so engrossed in one another, they hadn't heard her come back.

In typical Liam style, he responded by planting a smacker on his daughter's cheek. 'I wouldn't want you to feel left out. You're still my number one girl.'

'Ew!' Shannon wiped away all trace of him

with the back of her hand. 'Can we go and have dinner now, Daddy? You said we could go out to celebrate.'

'Oh? That's the first I've heard.' Mae turned to Liam, wondering what they were celebrating, other than having an afternoon off together.

Out of the corner of her eye she saw him gesturing to Shannon to zip her lips. He was always surprising her with romantic meals or movie nights, working hard to ensure they weren't just parenting Shannon together but constantly investing in their relationship. She appreciated that, along with the daily conversations that kept them a part of each other's lives even during those busier times. He was doing everything to make sure this relationship worked and keep her happy, though he only had to be in her orbit to do that. She'd never felt so safe and loved.

'I have something for you. Or, rather, Brodie does. Come here, boy!' He called the dog, which bounded over, and on Liam's direction jumped up on Mae, his front paws resting on her shoulders.

'What is it?' She was too busy fending off Brodie's kisses and trying to keep her balance to understand what was going on.

'On his collar.'

There, attached to Brodie's name tag, was a beautiful diamond ring. She looked at Liam, her mouth open, eyes wide, afraid to believe what was happening. When he knelt down in the pile of leaves on the ground and took her hand, she just about stopped breathing.

'Mae Watters, I know we haven't been to-gether long, but this feels too right not to act on it. Will you please be my wife and make our little family complete?'

It was all too much, and she felt the tears pricking the back of her eyes at the pure love for her this man emanated. Even Shannon was clapping beside him, apparently in on this plot and accepting it, which was much more important. They hadn't discussed mar-riage. After Diarmuid and her last doomed wedding day, she hadn't thought she'd ever want to make that level of commitment again. But these past months with Liam and Shan-non had been the happiest of her life, and she was ready for more. Ready to commit herself to this family.

'Yes! Yes, I will, Liam O'Conner.' She held out her hand whilst he wrestled the ring off the dog to place it on her finger. 'I guess you were pretty confident I was going to say yes if you already planned a celebratory dinner?'

'If that didn't work, I was hoping I could kiss you into submission.'

This time Shannon cheered when they kissed, and they didn't care who was watching.

Mae couldn't help but think her mum would be proud she'd discovered her Irish roots after all.

* * * * *

MEDICAL

Life and love in the world of modern medicine.

Available Next Month

All titles available in Larger Print

Forbidden Nights With The Paramedic Alison Roberts
Rebel Doctor's Baby Surprise Alison Roberts

....

Rescued By The Australian GP Emily Forbes
An ER Nurse To Redeem Him Traci Douglass

....

Marriage Reunion With The Island Doc Sue MacKay
Single Mum's Alaskan Adventure Louisa Heaton

Keep reading for an excerpt of a new title
from the Special Edition series,
THE COWBOY'S ROAD TRIP by Stella Bagwell

Chapter One

"Dad, are you serious? You want me to make the trip to Idaho?"

Beatrice Hollister stared in astonishment at her father. Hadley was the family patriarch and owner of Stone Creek Ranch, the only home she'd known for the entire twenty-six years of her life. Now as he sat behind the wide cherrywood desk, eyeing her with an indulgent look, she had to wonder, what had come over him? Out of his eight children, he'd never chosen Beatrice to deal with a family matter, especially one that would require her to travel hundreds of miles away from home!

"I don't understand why you're so surprised, Bea," he said. "Ever since your brother Jack made the trip down to Arizona to meet our distant relatives, you've been complaining how you never get to go anywhere or help tend to family business. I thought you'd be jumping for joy over the idea of traveling up to Coeur d'Alene. Do you not want to go?"

His eyes narrowed as he asked the question and Beatrice fought the urge to squirm in her seat. Hadley had always been a loving father, but no one in the family would deny that the tall, burly man could be intimidating at times. Especially if his patience was tested. This was one time Beatrice didn't want to test it.

"Of course I want to go, Dad! You've taken me by surprise, that's all. I never expected you to trust me with this important meeting with Scarlett. After all, she might be the key to finding the missing branches of the Hollister family tree."

Even as she said the words, her mind was whirling. If everything went as planned, she was going to see her grandmother. A woman she'd never met and had only seen in one grainy black-and-white photo taken sixty years ago. Beatrice hadn't yet had time to consider how she felt about coming face-to-face with a relative who'd been estranged from the family for more than fifty years. She'd worry about that detail later. At the moment, all that mattered was the trip itself and the fact that her father had chosen her for the important task. Usually, he turned this sort of assignment over to her older brothers.

His expression wry, he said, "Just because you're not a bookworm like your twin sister hardly means your mother and I think of you as an airhead."

Her father's description caused her to chuckle. "I'm relieved to hear my parents don't think I'm empty-headed. But in the smarts department, Bonnie is a hard act to follow. Between the two of us, she got most of the brains. But I hardly feel bad about that. She has the most brains than any of your eight kids."

He shook his head. "You got plenty of brains, too, Bea. Your problem is that you don't use them to their full extent."

Beatrice didn't have to wonder what her father's remark meant. Both her parents believed she was wasting her college degree in fashion design by working as a clerk in a women's boutique in Beaver, Utah, a town with a population of less than four thousand and only a thirty-minute drive from the family ranch. Neither her mother nor her father really understood that she wasn't ready to take on a more demanding job. She made a decent salary at Canyon Corral and she loved her job. For now, she was perfectly content.

His broad shoulders settled back against the leather executive chair. "I imagine you've been wondering why I'm not going to make the trip to Idaho myself. After all, Scarlett is the woman who gave birth to me and my two brothers."

The notion had crossed Beatrice's mind. But considering the circumstances, she wasn't surprised her father had declined to face the mother who'd chosen to desert him and his siblings when they were very small boys.

"To be honest, Dad, I'm glad you're not making the trip to Coeur d'Alene."

He made a sound that was somewhere between a snort and a laugh. "Why? So you can make it for me?"

She gave him a sheepish smile. "Okay, I am excited about going. But I'd hate for you to be—well, hurt. Seeing Scarlett wouldn't be easy for you."

His expression solemn, he absently tapped his fingers on the desktop. "That's kind of you, sweetheart, to consider my feelings. But I think you and your siblings understand that I've never thought of Scarlett as my mother. To me, she's only a shadowy image of a woman who clearly made my father miserable. Or maybe he made her life unbearable—none of us really know why their marriage imploded. I'd be lying, though, if I said I haven't wondered about her and why she left Lionel. After all, they made three sons together. There had to have been something between them."

Obviously. Something like lust, Beatrice thought. The physical attraction between her grandparents must have run mighty hot for a while.

Curious at her father's choice of words, she said, "You just implied that she's the one who left Grandfather. I've never heard you say that before. Is that the way things actually happened? Scarlett divorced Lionel? Or was it the other way around?"

Shaking his head, Hadley shrugged. "I don't really know the truth about who initiated their divorce. You know how your grandfather was about his past. What little he ever mentioned about Scarlett was always bitter. But he never explained why the split between them occurred or why she basically disappeared afterward."

And since Lionel had passed away several years ago, they'd never get the truth of the matter from him, Beatrice thought sadly. "Well, let's just hope Scarlett is willing to talk about her late ex-husband. Otherwise, you're going to be wasting your money sending me all the way to northern Idaho."

He swatted the air with one big hand. "No matter what Scarlett agrees to say, the trip will be worth it, Bea. Learning that she's still living and locating her is bound to lead us closer to information we need about my father—your grandfather."

For nearly two years, the family had been trying to uncover background information about Lionel Hollister. Particularly, evidence of his birth taking place in Utah. But so far they'd had no luck. Reaching out to Lionel's ex-wife seemed like a long shot to Beatrice. But if her father was willing to take the chance, she wasn't about to be the one to dampen his hopes.

She shot him an optimistic smile. "I hope you're right, Dad."

"You couldn't hope it any more than I do, honey," he said, then added, "Now, I imagine you're wondering about the details. How you're going to get there and that sort of thing."

Nodding eagerly, she said, "I am. Will I be driving? I hope so. It'll give me a chance to see the countryside."

He chuckled. "And do some shopping along the way? Well, don't worry. You're going to be driving. That is, if I can persuade someone to be your traveling companion."

Beatrice instantly scooted to the edge of her chair. "Traveling companion? Dad, I don't want—"

Her words broke off as a knock sounded on the closed door of her father's small office.

"Hopefully that's him right now. So try to be on your best behavior, Bea," Hadley said to her. Then, in a louder voice, he called to the person at the door. "Come in."

Beatrice looked over her shoulder and her mouth promptly fell open as she recognized the rugged cowboy walking into the room.

Kipp Starr!

Her father wanted *him* to be her traveling companion? Surely not! She'd only met the man a few days ago!

He took a few steps into the room, then pushed back the cuff of his denim shirt to glance at his watch. "Oh. You have company. Am I early? You did say one?"

Smiling, Hadley was quick to assure him. "You're right on time, Kipp. Come in and have a seat, and I'll explain what I wanted to speak with you about."

Beatrice watched the Idaho rancher lift off his black Stetson and, holding it in one hand, ease his lanky frame into the wooden chair sitting at an angle to her right. From the first moment she laid eyes on the man, she'd dubbed him as one hot stud. Tall, with long legs and broad shoulders, he was every inch a man. And when you added the muscular body to his chiseled features that were dominated by a pair of warm brown eyes and a layer of three-day-old whiskers, he made the perfect image of a saddle tramp riding straight out of the 1880s. Tough, rough and oh, so sexy.

Kipp had come to Stone Creek Ranch a few days ago to visit his sister, Clementine, who'd just gotten engaged to Beatrice's brother Quint. And because he'd arrived so near to Christmas and had no family or parents of his own, her parents had convinced him to stay on through the holiday. Beatrice couldn't deny she was drawn to Kipp. But this was one time in her life she'd not openly expressed her attraction for a man. Mainly because she had the horrible suspicion that if Kipp knew she was darn close to developing a crush on him, he'd laugh right in her face.

Hadley said to Kipp, "I know you and Quint are going out to look at some of the pregnant ewes this afternoon, so I'll get right to the point and not keep you long. When were you planning on going back home to Idaho?"

Beatrice felt her cheeks grow warm as Kipp glanced uncertainly at her, then back to Hadley.

"Monday morning," he answered. "That is, if the weather is permitting flights out of Cedar City. I'm hearing a winter storm might be bringing snow. Hopefully I'll be back at the ranch before it hits."

Hadley thoughtfully stroked his chin. "Have you purchased your plane ticket yet?"

He shook his head. "Bonnie offered to do it for me, but I haven't yet told her what day to make the flight for."

"Good. That will save her having to cancel the ticket."

"Cancel?" Kipp repeated the word with a blank look. "I don't understand, Hadley. I—uh, I've enjoyed my time here on Stone Creek, but I promised the foreman I'd be back to the Rising Starr this coming week."

"I realize you have obligations," Hadley told him. "And as much as we'd love for you to stay, we understand that you need to get back. But I'm suggesting a different mode of transportation. That is, if you'd be willing to put up with Beatrice for two days or so."

Kipp slowly turned his head to look directly at her and Beatrice was shocked to feel her cheeks growing hot. What was wrong with her, anyway? She'd always felt comfortable around men. Even sexy hunks like Kipp Starr. In fact, her family often called her man crazy. So why was she suddenly feeling tongue-tied in front of this cowboy?

"Are you going to Idaho?" Kipp asked her.

She forced herself to breathe. "Dad is sending me up to Coeur d'Alene."

A faint frown pulled his dark brows together. "Oh. That's in the northern part of the state. I live in the southern area."

"Yes, Clementine has told us that the Rising Starr Ranch is located near Burley," Hadley said quickly. "So I do understand Coeur d'Alene is a good distance out of your way. But I don't want Beatrice traveling alone. And since you're headed back to Idaho, I thought you might be willing to accompany her up to Coeur d'Alene. She could drop you back by your ranch when she heads back home. That way she'd only have to make the drive from Burley back here to Stone Creek Ranch by herself."

"Which I can certainly do." Beatrice spoke up firmly. "In fact, Dad, I honestly don't know why you think I need anyone with me on this trip. I'm perfectly capable of handling the drive by myself."

Hadley leveled a look at her that said if she didn't quiet down, he'd gently usher her out of the room.

"You have two choices, Bea," Hadley said flatly. "Travel with Kipp or stay here."

Beatrice argued, "But Kipp might not want to make such a huge, unnecessary loop of driving around the state."

Hadley turned his attention to Kipp. "Don't hesitate to tell me if you're not up to this, Kipp. I won't hold it against you. Nor will Bea's mother, Claire. But just so

you know, we don't expect you to do this out of the goodness of your heart. I intend to pay you a nice sum for your
time and effort."

Beatrice wished she could slink off and never have to
face Kipp Starr again. If it took money to persuade the
man to join her on a three-day trip, then she'd rather not
go at all, she thought.

*Liar. Liar. Just the thought of spending three whole
days in Kipp's company has you feeling like you could fly
over the moon. No matter if your dad has to coerce him
into making the trip.*

The taunting voice going off in her head very nearly
drowned out Kipp's reply.

"I'd never accept your money, Hadley. You and Claire
have been such gracious hosts while I've been staying
here. If accompanying Beatrice will help you out, then I'm
more than glad to make the trip with her." He shrugged
one shoulder. "Besides, I have to get back to Idaho one
way or the other. And I've never been fond of plane rides."

Hadley gave him a grateful smile, while a strange mixture of joy and relief washed through Beatrice. Kipp would
be making the trip with her! She wanted to jump to her
feet and do a joyous jig. But she'd reserve that happy reaction for when she raced upstairs to give her twin sister
the fabulous news.

Glad to make the trip with her.

Hell, when did he get so good at lying? The last thing
Kipp wanted was to be cooped up in a vehicle with a chatty
blonde ten years his junior.

Not that he didn't like Beatrice. He did like her. What
little time he'd spent around her, he'd found her friendly
and sweet and oftentimes funny. But a man could take just
so much sweetness. And so much temptation, he thought

grimly. Whether he wanted to admit it or not, there was something very provocative about Beatrice Hollister. Something that pulled at him every time he was near her.

"You've made me one happy father," Hadley said to him. "I won't worry knowing that Beatrice is in your capable hands."

The man's trust in him made Kipp feel like a heel. If Hadley were to guess some of the carnal thoughts that ran through Kipp's head whenever he looked at Beatrice, he would've already sent him packing. He certainly wouldn't ask him to chaperone her on a long driving trip.

He cleared his throat and refrained from glancing in Beatrice's direction. Not that he needed a second glance to remind him just how fresh and pretty she looked sitting in the wooden chair. With her long hair flowing down her back in a cascade of golden waves, her blue eyes smudged with just enough smoky color to give them a smoldering look, and her full lips the color of pink cotton candy, even the briefest look at her was more than enough to play on a man's senses. Not to mention his libido.

"I'll do my best to see that she gets to Coeur d'Alene safely, Hadley," Kipp said to the rancher, then asked, "When did you plan for Beatrice to be leaving? Does she have to be in Coeur d'Alene on a certain day or time?"

"That's the easy part of the situation, Kipp. Doesn't matter exactly when Bea gets there. She has a two-week vacation coming that she hasn't yet started. So she can follow any timetable that suits you. If you're aiming to be back on your ranch on Monday, then you might need to leave a day or two earlier to make up for more traveling time."

"Right." He glanced over at Beatrice to see she was looking directly at him. A faint smile curved the corners of her lips and he found himself focusing on the soft, plump curves and wondering how it might feel to kiss them. Damn it.

"Can you be ready to leave in the morning? Or is that too soon?" Kipp asked her.

Her eyes widened a fraction. "Certainly. I'll pack tonight."

"Then it's all set," Hadley said with approval. "I'll have one of the hands make sure Bea's truck is ready to travel. And I'll leave it up to you, Kipp, to route the drive. I'm sure Bea will do her best to persuade you to stop at every fashion boutique you pass. But don't pay her any mind. Just remind her that the two of you aren't on a shopping trip."

Beatrice groaned. "Oh, Dad, you're going to have Kipp thinking all I do is spend money on frivolous things."

Hadley chuckled. "Don't you?"

"No! For your information, my savings account is growing!"

"How can that be? Only a few weeks ago you were asking to have your bedroom closet enlarged."

Her father was clearly teasing her, but Kipp could hear a flash of annoyance in the tone of her voice. Apparently she didn't appreciate Hadley painting her as superficial.

"Dad, you know very well that Bonnie and I share a bedroom, a closet and most of our clothes."

"Yes, and just about everything else," he said with an impish grin at his daughter. "Except boyfriends."

"Thank goodness. I'd be bored out of my mind if I went out with a man of Bonnie's choosing!" she exclaimed, then suddenly seeming to remember Kipp was present, she looked over at him. "Sorry, Kipp. All of this nonsense has to be boring you. Just rest assured that I won't be asking you to stop for any shopping sprees. I'll do all my shopping after I leave you at Rising Starr Ranch."

Since Kipp had arrived on Stone Creek Ranch, he'd

spent most of the time out with the men doing ranching chores with the Hollister brothers and the ranch hands. But even in the little time he'd passed in the house with the family, he'd quickly learned that Beatrice and her twin sister, Bonnie, were practically identical in looks, but far different in personalities. Bonnie, the elder of the two, was quiet and reserved in manner and dress, while Beatrice was outgoing and a bit flamboyant. Yet even with their differences, it was easy to see the two sisters were extremely close.

"I'm not worried, Bea." At least, Kipp's worries weren't about her wanting to stop and spend her daddy's money. No, he was more concerned about keeping his hands off her.

Hell, Kipp, what's the matter with you? You're not in the market for romance. Especially with a woman like Beatrice. Her head is filled with visions of love and happy-ever-after. She's not old enough to know how ugly things can get between a man and a woman. And you don't want to be the one to show her.

She gave him a cheery smile. "Thank you, Kipp. I promise to be on my best behavior."

Hadley let out a grunt of amusement. "When she says that, Kipp, you better watch her."

Kipp was wondering how to reply to Hadley's comment when the landline on the rancher's desk rang.

While he excused himself to answer the call, Kipp looked at Beatrice. "Considering how close you and Bonnie are, I would've thought she'd be joining you on this journey."

She shook her head. "Dad could never manage all the ranch's paperwork and phone calls without Bonnie handling things. And anyway, she's not keen on meeting new people. It makes her uncomfortable."

"I'm new and she doesn't appear uncomfortable around me," he reasoned.

"Yes. But you're—our kind. Dad is sending me up to Coeur d'Alene to meet Scarlett Hollister Wilson—and she is considered a dragon lady by our family," she said with a frown.

Her explanation only planted more questions in his mind but he didn't voice them out loud. He figured the less he knew about the Hollisters' personal family matters, the better off he'd be. He had his own family dragon lady to worry about.

The click of the telephone receiver landing back in its cradle had Kipp glancing around to see Hadley had ended the call and was rising from his chair.

"You two will have to excuse me. Jack needs me over at the cattle barn," he explained. "If you have any more questions about the trip, Kipp, we can go over them tonight."

Kipp quickly rose to his feet. "At the moment, I can't think of anything. But if I do, I'll let you know," he told Hadley. "Uh, can I be of help over at the barn?" he offered.

"Thanks, Kipp. Nice of you to offer, but this isn't a manual job. Jack is dealing with a cattle buyer. The man wants the best for the least. You know how it is. I've got to go over there and be the ringmaster."

Yes, at one time Kipp had helped his father deal with cattle and sheep buyers. But those days were long gone. His father was dead and Kipp had no authority over any of the sales or purchases of livestock on the Rising Starr. It was a fact he tried not to dwell on, but most days the situation pushed itself into his thoughts anyway.

"Sure, Hadley. I'll catch you later."

He watched Hadley leave the room before he glanced over at Beatrice. "Well, I need to head on over to the ranch yard. Quint's probably waiting for me."

Smiling, she rose from the chair, and as she walked over to him, he couldn't help but notice how her brown suede skirt outlined the shape of her hips, while the hem swirled at the top of her black knee-high boots. He figured if the weather was warm, she'd be bare legged with her feet encased in a pair of strappy sandals. But with it being the middle of winter, he doubted he'd get a glimpse of her legs, or for that matter, any bare skin.

She said, "Before you go, Kipp, I want to thank you. I'm sure traveling hundreds of miles out of your way is not necessarily what you want to do. But if you hadn't agreed to make the trip, Dad would've made other plans. And they wouldn't have included me."

"I wouldn't say that. I'm sure he could have found someone to make the drive with you."

Strangely, the idea of Beatrice traveling with some other guy didn't appeal to him, at all.

She shook her head. "Not likely. Maybe it's because Bonnie and I are his youngest, but Dad is very protective of us. Even though we're twenty-six, there are times he still seems to think of us as teenagers. I think if you'd refused to go, he would've probably gotten one of my brothers to make the journey."

She smelled like wind and a rain-soaked flower garden, and he found the scent as tempting as the upturned corners of her lips.

"All your brothers are very busy men. I can't imagine him sending any of them away," Kipp told her. "Unless this trip to Idaho is super important to him."

One of her slender shoulders made a negligible shrug. "Well, it's not a make-or-break thing for the ranch or the family, but it is important to him. He's searching for back history about his father and there's a woman in Coeur d'Alene who might be able to provide it. I'm going to meet with her."

Frowning, he asked, "Can't he speak with her on the phone and save you all this traveling?"

She turned her gaze away from him to focus on a window at the opposite end of the room. The view exposed a portion of the backyard where a low rock wall was bordered with some sort of shrubs. Presently the plants were covered with gray tarps to protect them against the winter weather. Kipp figured the yard would look splendid in the warm summer months, but for now everything was dormant.

"Dad was told that for some reason, she won't take phone calls. She's elderly, you see, so maybe her hearing isn't good. Anyway, she does receive visitors. So here I am, headed to Idaho." She flashed him a smile. "With you."

With him. The two of them together. For miles and miles. He couldn't think of anything more torturous or tempting. "Sorry. I shouldn't have questioned the reason for the trip. It's really none of my business. Besides, I've been around Hadley long enough to see he doesn't do things on a whim. He has to have a reason."

She let out a soft little laugh and Kipp wished he could feel just a fraction of the humor and joy that Beatrice radiated. She was basically a happy person. He could see it in her eyes and the flash of her smile. If she'd ever experienced a broken heart or a huge disappointment, she'd obviously made a complete recovery.

"Dad thinks everything through," she told him. "Which tells me he feels comfortable with you being my—companion."

Resisting the urge to clear his throat, he said, "I'll do my best to get you up to Coeur d'Alene safely."

She stepped closer and surprised him by placing a

hand on his forearm. The contact reminded him of a time he'd accidentally burned his arm on a branding iron. The scorching heat had shot all the way up to his shoulder. Beatrice's touch was equally fiery.

"Thank you, Kipp. And I'll do my best not to be a pest."

He could think of plenty of things she might be, but a pest wasn't one of them. "I'm sure you'll be a model traveler, Beatrice."

She said, "You've been here on the ranch for a few days now. Don't you think it's time you started calling me Bea?"

Her gaze met his, and as Kipp found himself looking into the blue depths of her eyes, he realized it was high time he made a quick exit from Hadley's office.

"Okay. Bea it is." Turning, he walked to the door. Then, with his hand on the knob, he glanced back at her. "See you later."

Smiling, she gave him a little wave, and Kipp hurried off with his mind spinning. He didn't know what he'd just gotten himself into. But he had a feeling nothing about the next two or three days was going to be easy.

NEW RELEASE!

Rancher's Snowed-In Reunion
The Carsons Of Lone Rock
Book 4

**She turned their break-up into her breakout song.
And now they're snowed in…**

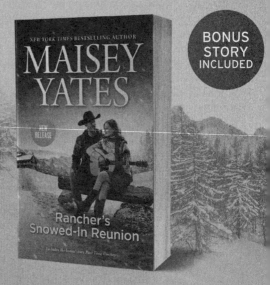

Don't miss this snowed-in second-chance romance between closed-off bull rider Flint Carson and Tansey Sands, the rodeo queen turned country music darling.

In-store and online March 2024.

MILLS & BOON

millsandboon.com.au